THE

FROZEN

CROWN

HARPER Voyager

An Imprint of HarperCollins*Publishers*

THE FROZEN CROWN

A NOVEL

GRETA KELLY

THE FROZEN CROWN. Copyright © 2021 by Greta Kelly. All rights reserved. Printed in the United States of America. No part of this book may be used or reproduced in any manner whatsoever without written permission except in the case of brief quotations embodied in critical articles and reviews. For information, address HarperCollins Publishers, 195 Broadway, New York, NY 10007.

HarperCollins books may be purchased for educational, business, or sales promotional use. For information, please email the Special Markets Department at SPsales@harpercollins.com.

Harper Voyager and design are trademarks of HarperCollins Publishers LLC.

FIRST EDITION

Designed by Paula Russell Szafranski
Map design by Nick Springer / Springer Cartographics LLC
Frontispiece © Kris Wiktor / Shutterstock

Library of Congress Cataloging-in-Publication Data has been applied for.

ISBN 978-0-06-295695-8

21 22 23 24 25   LSC   10 9 8 7 6 5 4 3 2 1

To my husband, EJ.
For believing even when I didn't.

The Lands of Kinvara

SWITZKIA

SERAVESH

KIZUOKA
PROVINCE

The Kinnet Sea

Khan-e-Fet

SHAZIR
PROVINCE

ASHBRAH
ROVINCE

AVSHIR
PROVINCE

NUKUSHBET
PROVINCE

TAMETT
PROVINCE

CALORMANA PROVINCE

V I S H I R

MINOSSOS
PROVINCE

THE
FROZEN
CROWN

1

I pulled the cloak closer about my shoulders, ignoring the bead of sweat dripping down my spine. From my hilltop perch, the walled city of Eshkaroth wasn't much to look at. The smallest holding in the Free State of Idun, it had only a few hundred inhabitants crowded about a crumbling seaside castle. The legion at my back could take it in an afternoon, but I hadn't come to start a war.

I'd come to end one.

General Arkady edged his horse closer to mine, and an expression I couldn't quite name creased the maplike wrinkles of his face.

"What do you see?" I murmured, my voice too low for the soldiers behind us to hear.

His silence was like a great intake of breath. "A city," he replied. "Whole and alive."

Tears prickled my eyes and I blinked them away, telling myself it was the bite of the winter wind making them water. Not because of the fact that a city like this, gray and humble though it looked from here, no longer existed in Seravesh.

Our homeland, pillaged and burning and crawling with invaders, lay less than a mile north of here. But with the jagged peaks of the Peshkalor Mountains shading my back, I might as well have been a hundred miles away. The strangled screams of everyone I'd left behind echoed through the passes, reverberating through my skull. Though my mind knew our last hope lay in the city below, my heart begged me to return to Seravesh. As if even standing on these southern slopes, a few days and a world away from home, was a betrayal.

"Raise the banner," General Arkady growled at the soldiers around us. "Hood up, Princess," he added, softer this time.

I glanced over my shoulder in time to see an all-too-familiar form separate from the line of cavalrymen. Vitaly twitched his reins and his mount leapt forward, cantering past me in a streak of dark hair. A stretch of fabric blew behind him: a black wolf on a field of blue. The banner of the Kingdom of Seravesh snapped in the cold breeze—the same banner from which my Black Wolf Legion took their name. A raucous cheer erupted from my waiting soldiers as Vitaly rode down the ridgeline.

A low rumble began in the general's chest, like he couldn't contain his displeasure at this undisciplined display. I hid my smile by drawing up the black wolf head of my cloak. The scene Vitaly had caused wasn't something the city below could ignore. Their lookouts were surely scouring the line for a leader, and my cloak was distinct. They would see it and report my presence.

Vitaly circled back to us, pulling up his horse with a grin.

"Are you done?" Arkady asked, casting a baleful look at the younger man.

Vitaly winced, but his smile didn't quite fade. "Just trying to keep spirits up, sir." He glanced over his shoulder, no doubt taking in the men's haggard faces. Crossing the mountains always exacted a toll, but a cadre of enemy soldiers had stalked us over the range this time, only turning back when it was clear we were headed for Eshkaroth.

Arkady's eyes narrowed. "And what good will high spirits

do? They must think we mean to attack now. The envoy's probably making a run for it as we speak. If he came at all."

"No." The word bubbled out of me before I could stop it. The envoy had to be here. If he wasn't—

"Look." Vitaly stabbed a finger toward the castle, his face bright with triumph, as two flags were raised from the battlements: the blazing shield of Idun, and the lion of Vishir.

Relief washed over me. My call for aid hadn't gone unanswered. If the Vishiri emperor had sent an envoy, my cause was not lost. I could make my case, beg for help, and with it, claim my throne. We were *so* close.

With my men behind me, I urged my horse toward the city, thundering through Eshkaroth's muddy streets. People watched us from the narrow windows of slanting, decrepit buildings. Their dim eyes were leeched of curiosity, of wonder. Not even a dozen giant men of the north could rouse their awe.

I let their indifference slide off me. I wasn't in Eshkaroth for them. I was there for the Vishiri envoy. My father once told me the Vishiri emperor had a weakness for the exotic and the strange. So I would do my barbarian best to catch his interest from a thousand miles away. His interest and, if the Two-Faced God was merciful, his help. Someone had to stand up to the Empire of Roven.

A chubby man wearing a gold torc threw his arms open when I rode into the castle courtyard. "Many welcomes, my lady," he called with a well-oiled smile. "I am the maester of Eshkaroth."

A north wind blew across my face, carrying my own unvoiced scream. I hadn't ridden through my lost kingdom, through the frigid wastes of the Peshkalor Mountains, to meet with a maester. I'd come for the Vishiri envoy. Was he even here?

"There is a Vishiri flag on your battlement."

"Ah." The maester's smile faded with his understanding.

"Governor Erol would have greeted you personally, but since Prince Iskander finds our climate rather unforgiving, the governor sent me in his stead."

I closed my eyes. Iskander. Of course the emperor sent Iskander. I slid off my horse, passing the reins to a stableboy before making my way up the steps. My guard closed in around me as I swept into the castle, pushing the fat little maester so far off to the side he had to run to keep up.

The Great Hall was packed with nobles, all crowding to get a glimpse of the Vishiri prince. The prince himself was at the other end of the hall, swaddled in blankets despite the overwhelming heat of six blazing hearths. A man I recognized as Governor Erol leaned in close to speak with Iskander, but the prince wasn't paying attention. His eyes were on a flock of girls who preened idiotically under his regard.

I suppressed a sneer, focusing instead on the activity around him. From across the hall, I could see the diaphanous forms of curious ghosts gathered about the oblivious prince. I imagined what would happen if he could see the wraiths straining to get a glimpse of him, and I swallowed a laugh.

Beside me, a servant banged his staff against the dusty stone floor. "Her Royal Highness, Princess Askia Poritskaya e-Nimri of Seravesh."

Iskander turned. I smiled.

Untying the cloak and handing it off to the servant, I stalked down the length of the hall. A ripple of gasps followed me. I didn't care. All that mattered now was the prince.

He rose as I approached, taking in my leather britches and tight-fitting shirt with wide eyes. A sword swayed at my side and two daggers were strapped to my thighs. Another two poked out from the tops of my boots and two more were tucked into my wrist guards. He drank me in like I was a fairy tale come to life. I didn't even mind how his eyes lingered on my breasts. All the more to tell his father, the emperor, about the savage princess who needed his help.

Governor Erol rose, too, a wide smile flashing beneath his curly white beard. "Many welcomes, my lady. Idun is honored by your presence."

"Thank you for your hospitality, Governor." I motioned and Vitaly came forward with a dark jar. "A gift for you. El-Shimat tea. My father's recipe."

My father, Sevilen e-Nimri, had been the greatest healer of the age. And while I might not have his healing magic, I kept his grimoire; the governor's rheumatism was well known.

He pressed his left hand to his chest and bowed. "I am humbled by your generosity, my lady—"

"I can't believe it. It really is you," the prince said, rushing forward.

Iskander had been a pretty boy and had become a handsome man. He was only a few years older than me, twenty-three or twenty-four, with a lean, well-formed body and a smooth, angular face. His ebony hair fell into dark, guileless eyes, and he smiled at me with real pleasure. It annoyed me for a reason I couldn't name.

"Indeed. Hello, Iskander."

"I didn't recognize you at first. You've grown."

I cocked an eyebrow. "Yes. Well, time will do that. We were quite young when we last saw each other."

His smiled flickered, and something dangerously close to pity rose in his eyes. He glanced at my neck, at the puckered scar across my throat, and swallowed. No doubt he was remembering the last time we met.

"Well, it suits you," he said, somewhat lamely, like he sensed how much I hated the feeling of his sympathy. "In fact, I think I'll have to give you a new nickname. Do you remember what I used to call you?"

My mind flashed back to my eighth summer, when my family lived at the Vishiri court. Iskander and his little friends had taken one look at my pale skin and red hair and decided I looked like a maggot.

"Do you remember what I did when you used it?" I snapped my jaw shut, but it was too late to recall the words. Arkady stiffened beside me. Prince Iskander's eyes bulged, clearly and suddenly remembering how I had tackled him to the ground. I held my breath, praying he wouldn't leave.

A hint of pink colored his dusky skin, but he smiled and began to laugh. "Very good, my lady. No more nicknames. Though that would be a sight to see, eh?"

I nodded, too relieved to smile.

"You must be tired after your journey," Governor Erol said with an amused glint in his eye. "The maester has prepared rooms for you and your men. Tomorrow night, we shall hold a ball in your honor—but in the morning, I've organized a hunt for Prince Iskander."

"Yes, I'm quite excited for it. Though I'll have to beg warmer clothes off you, Governor," Prince Iskander said, rubbing his hands together as if he'd caught a chill. "I don't know how you survive this cold."

"You call this cold?" I laughed. "Wait a week, then you might see real snow."

Iskander's smiled faltered. "Alas, we do not have a week. We leave at the full moon."

I jerked back, his words striking me like a blow. They *were* a blow. "That's only three days from now." My godfather wasn't sending aid, I thought. This wasn't a negotiation. He was sending his regrets.

"Yes. It's . . . unfortunate we can't stay longer," Iskander said, shifting from one foot to the other. "We must sail before the winter storms come."

"Well, then," I started, my mind scrambling for purchase. "We'll have to use our time wisely. I would hate for it to be another six years before we see each other again."

Prince Iskander beamed. "That we must."

The governor leaned forward with a clever gleam in his eye. "I've heard you're quite the horsewoman. Would you care to join us on the hunt?"

I could have kissed him. We both knew my window of opportunity was already half closed. He was giving me a chance—perhaps my only chance. An opportunity to snatch a moment alone with Prince Iskander and convince him to take me to Vishir. "I'd love to." I cocked my eyebrows, smirking at the men around me. "If you think you can keep up."

Hope seared through me at the warmth in Iskander's voice. This wasn't the end. Iskander could be swayed, I knew he could. All I had to do was convince him to take me to Vishir. After that, well, there was nothing I wouldn't do—nothing I wouldn't give, to convince the emperor to save my people.

2

My first night in Eshkaroth was a sleepless one. Arkady and I had stayed up late trying to figure out how to convince Prince Iskander to take up my cause in only three days. *Make that two*, I thought. My gaze flickered to the morning sun shining weakly in the clouded sky above the courtyard.

"Change his mind." That's what Arkady had said when he left my room last night. I loved Arkady—he was my dear friend and mentor—but that was, perhaps, the most useless piece of advice I'd ever received. I wasn't going to my neighbor asking for sugar. I was begging an emperor for an army.

And time was short, I thought, worrying at the scar on my neck. I had this morning to convince Iskander, or today would be lost. The whole cause would be lost. My horse whickered, nudging my shoulder with his nose as if urging me to hurry.

While servants bustled across the courtyard, readying mounts and loading supplies, Arkady and Vitaly stood beside me. Arkady wore his usual scowl while an unperturbed Vitaly held the reins of their horses. A young lord in his own right, Vitaly had been among nobility all his life. The fact that he wouldn't be intimidated by the prince was the only reason the general had allowed Vitaly to come after the stunt he pulled yesterday on the ridge.

I'd have insisted upon it anyway. Vitaly was so personable, I had no doubt he'd charm Iskander. The Day Lord knew Vitaly had been friendly enough to charm even me when I first returned to my grandfather's court, broken and alone. Vitaly had been my only friend for a good long time.

"Don't worry, my lady," Vitaly said, as if he could sense my anxiety from the way I was shifting my weight. "You have time to convince the prince to help."

"Do I?" I asked, patting the smooth fall of my gelding's red coat. "He'll be surrounded by retainers who certainly won't want him to be convinced."

"Ah," he said with a shrug. "We can get him away easily enough." His gaze darted from me to the general and back again, a sly smile curving his lips. "I'm reminded of the midsummer hunt two years ago when you helped me separate a certain lady from her husband."

I laughed quietly, both from the memory and from the prudish look of shock rippling across Arkady's face. "The difference is that that young woman *wanted* to get away from her husband. I'm not so sure Prince Iskander will want to be alone with me, but . . ." The idea sparked in my mind and I considered everything I knew about Iskander. He seemed like the kind of man who was ruled by his passions, the kind who liked a good game. All I had to do was draw him in.

"Look lively, my lady," Arkady murmured, as Prince Iskander exited the keep, flanked by two of his own men.

My plan exactly.

"Good morning, Princess Askia," Iskander said, hurrying down the steps.

"Good morning. I hope you're ready for some sport."

"I was born ready," he proclaimed, laughing at his own bravado. Over his shoulder, I saw one of his companions—a small weasel-faced man—sneer.

I smiled. "Do you know what we'll be hunting today?"

"I'm told there are deer and wild turkey in the foothills, but the governor says the real prize is something called a *domuzjov*. Whatever that is."

"It's a kind of wild boar," I said. "They have more hair than the type you have in the south. Bigger, too, and faster. Their hair turns white in the winter, so it should be a challenge with the snowfall last night."

Iskander bounced on his toes with boyish excitement. "You know, it's been an age since I've been on a proper hunt. It gets the blood up like nothing else."

Except war, I thought, looking down as I shoved the thought away. It wasn't Iskander's fault his people thrived while mine suffered.

"I'm surprised Your Highness is willing to risk the foothills," the sour-looking man said, brushing imaginary dust off his sleeve. "Are the mountains not part of Seravesh?"

I drew my shoulders back, sensing a trap waiting to be sprung. While the mountains did belong to my kingdom, here in the southern slopes, the fact was more of a technicality. The people who actually lived there were Idunese in everything but name. "The mountains are on Seraveshi lands, but I'm not worried for our safety. The range provides an excellent shield against the worst of the fighting."

The man smirked. "So good a shield that Seravesh looks peaceful from here."

I glanced at Iskander who was glaring a hole in the lord's face. "Looks can be deceiving."

"And words can't? I read the letters you sent the emperor begging for aid against the so-called Roven invasion. Perhaps your words were overblown. Why, even the Seraveshi ambassador to Vishir endorsed the regime change."

"Before he conveniently disappeared," I shot back through

clenched teeth. The ambassador was a good man—there wasn't a chance in hell his endorsement wasn't a product of torture.

The nobleman's dark eyes met mine, a challenge glimmering in their depths. "Conveniently for whom?"

"Ishaq, please," Iskander said, putting a quelling hand on the older lord's arm. "This is meant to be a fun outing. There will be time to discuss more serious things later." He nodded to me, his expression filled with promise.

But there wouldn't be, I thought as Governor Erol and a party of nobles entered the courtyard from a small side gate with a dozen servants leading in the horses. Iskander's men would make sure I wouldn't have a chance. If I wanted to talk to him, I'd have to make an opportunity, and sooner rather than later. Erol walked up and said his hellos, but I wasn't listening. I caught Vitaly's eye and gave him a conspiratorial smile.

The hunting party rode northeast out of Eshkaroth, and in a matter of minutes we were in the forested lowlands of the Peshkalor Mountains. Our path veered past the encampment where my men were waiting.

The Black Wolves appeared out of the fog, their gleaming armor resplendent in the morning light. Three thousand men of the north greeted us with howls and cheers. I grinned at the sight of them; at Iskander's delighted laugh and Ishaq's glower. My countrymen. My people.

We continued northeast, and the hills became steeper, the forest denser.

The hunt began.

In that difficult terrain, the true horsemen soon separated themselves from the rest. With Vitaly's help we divided the groups further by scaring up a flock of wild turkey, pushing them south with the remaining riders. I took the lead north with Vitaly and Iskander's second man, a chubby lord called Marr. Thankfully, Prince Iskander kept up with us, handling his hot-blooded stallion with expert precision. General Arkady was content to stay behind, no doubt doing his best to keep everyone else out of the way.

As one of the bloodhounds let out a long, baying howl, I flashed Iskander a challenging grin. Vishiri stallions might be fast, but they were made for flatlands. In the mountains, with the ground wet with snow, my destrier was an even match for speed. We raced after the dogs, weaving through the trees so fast it felt like I was flying, and for one precious moment I was home. My hair whipped back and the cold stung my eyes, but it was the best feeling in the world. Beside me, Iskander whooped a wild laugh.

The dogs were going mad. They had the boar surrounded on three sides, but the animal wouldn't give up without a fight. It sprinted through the forest, bucking its tusked head at any of the hounds that ventured too close.

I leaned lower over my horse, letting the animal have its head. From the corner of my eye, I saw Iskander loosen his spear and heft it in his right hand. I smiled, urging my horse onward. With a mighty groan, the prince heaved the spear. It hurtled thirty feet before tearing into the boar's back. The hog squealed. Injured, enraged, but not yet defeated.

I veered right, up an embankment, flanking the beast before dropping the reins, using my legs to steer. I lifted my bow and fired two shots in quick succession. The first pierced the boar's flank. The second found its mark. The arrow's broad head shot straight through the boar's side, burrowing through the right lung and into the heart. The boar took a handful of stuttering steps, then fell, skidding into the snow.

"Well done, my lady," Vitaly cried as I rode back to the men.

"Great shot," Iskander said earnestly.

I grinned and a childish corner of my mind hoped that proving myself would be enough to convince Iskander to help me.

"Thanks," I replied, dismounting beside the others while servants rode in to tend to the boar. "You learn a few things, traveling with an army for six months." The reality of why I'd been traveling with an army for so long made me falter. This was as alone as Iskander and I were going to get, I realized. Now or never.

"Don't let her fool you," Vitaly said, grinning. "She's been training with the Black Wolves ever since she returned to Seravesh."

"Truly?" Surprise was obvious in Iskander's voice. "That's not a hobby I've ever heard of for a noblewoman, let alone a future queen."

I shrugged, straining for nonchalance. "I wasn't the heir when I returned to Seravesh. I . . . well, you know my parents' story." It was high drama, the kind of salacious tale that court gossip thrived on. A Seraveshi princess running off with a Vishiri healer, turning her back on family and a crown for love. Somehow the fact that my mother, and me by extension, were exiled for disobeying my grandfather's wishes was usually omitted from the doe-eyed love tale. "My father's healing abilities took us all over the world. While we spent some time in various courts, including your father's," I said, nodding to Iskander, "we spent most of our time on battlefields."

I paused as memories of my parents' last battle rose unbidden in my mind. I closed my eyes for a moment, forcing the dark thoughts away. "After my parents died, I returned to Seravesh, but it was a long time before I proved my worth to my grandfather and his court." Although I tried to smile, my face didn't seem up to the task. "But I've been around soldiers all my life. So I haunted the training yard. Eventually, General Arkady took pity on me and trained me. Helped me gain acceptance at court."

"You don't give yourself enough credit, my lady," Vitaly said quietly. "The general trained you because he saw your potential. You were accepted at court because others saw it too. I should know. My father held a feast at our castle when the king named you his heir." Vitaly's smile was edged in sadness.

"Your father will feast again when I get you home, Vitaly." Blood rushed out of Vitaly's face. He nodded once and looked away. I frowned. Vitaly often looked sad when he spoke of home, but this was different.

"Your Black Wolves," Lord Marr said in broken Idunese. "Very big. Big men." He puffed out his chest, miming a much larger man.

Iskander laughed. "Truly, the men of the Black Wolves are enormous, not to mention devoted to you. I've no doubt you'll have your country back by this time next year. What army could stand against you?"

Impatience flashed through me. The prince traveled all this way, but he still didn't understand. "It's not that—"

"Heeellp meeee."

The sound seemed to come down from the trees almost below my level of hearing. I froze. Ice tiptoed across my skin, but it wasn't the ice of a cold winter day. It was a deeper cold, the kind that lingers at the edges of all things.

Iskander looked at me with open confusion, but I couldn't respond. Death magic spilled out of my chest, pooling beneath my skin, and silently, I called out to the void—to the source of the scream that only I could hear.

She appeared at the top of the hill like a pocket of fog the sun couldn't reach. She was small, but something in the way her ghostly shoulders drooped made me think she wasn't a child. The spirit flickered, like maintaining even this diaphanous form was an act of will.

"My lady?" Vitaly's voice was tight, face pinched. His hand was on his sword.

Iskander's fingers brushed my arm. "What's wrong?"

Wind gusted down the hill, making dried leaves skitter

across the frost-hard ground. A sickly smell, both sweet and meaty, crawled up my nose. It was the iron tang of spilled blood, the rancid scent of spoiled meat.

"Do you smell that?" I asked, my voice low as the horses whickered and stomped a nervous dance.

Vitaly's sword scraped against its scabbard as he drew the blade. "Go get the general," he barked at the servants tending the boar. "You should go, too, my lady."

I nocked an arrow in response and started up the hill, leaving my horse with a white-lipped servant. The ghost waited for me as I trudged up the hard winter earth, Vitaly and Iskander at my sides, Lord Marr at my back. The ghost was younger than I'd thought, late teens perhaps, but her face was aged with horror.

Up ahead the hill dropped away into a deep valley that made the small gully we'd come from look like nothing more than a boot print in a muddy street. At the bottom, nestled between the black pine forests and the ever-rising peaks of the mountain range, was a village.

Was a village.

The freshly fallen snow should have blanketed the roofs of the few dozen homes. Smoke should have been billowing merrily from each little chimney, promising warmth and comfort in the face of a chilly winter day. Children in bright-colored clothes should have been running though the fields rolling up snowballs and making angels in the hillside.

My whole kingdom was filled with what should have been. Bile rose in my throat. I forced it back, willing myself not to scream.

"Lady Night, have mercy," Iskander breathed. His dark skin had gone gray in the face of what lay before us.

"Roven shows no mercy," I said quietly.

Houses charred to ash stained the snow. Smoke, like the

ghost of the fires that destroyed this place, rose in lazy coils before disappearing in the breeze. Bodies lay scattered in the streets and on the hillside, so small it was almost possible to pretend they weren't corpses but for the carrion birds pecking away at soft skin.

"We need to get out of here," Vitaly said, his voice low and urgent. "The Voyniks could still be in the woods."

My eyes darted to the ghost at the thought of the elite Roven soldiers surrounding us. *"Are the soldiers still here?"* I asked silently, ice blooming in my limbs, making my muscles seize. I cursed my magic and the tether that came with it. I was barely brushing the edges of my power and yet the tether was there, yanking me back. Stomach churning, I focused everything I had into making the ghost-girl speak.

"No." Her eyes slid past my face. She turned, not looking at the ruined village, but at a spot some yards away—at a dark shape lying too still on the ground. *"It's been days."*

I tried to swallow, but my mouth was too dry to pull it off. "If the Voyniks planned to stay here, they wouldn't have burned the village."

"How do you know it was burned on purpose?" Iskander asked, a slight tremor in his voice. "Anything could have happened."

"Anything?" I stalked forward, dragging Iskander with me by the force of my pent-up anger. "Did anything happen to her?"

I pointed at the ghost-girl's body with the tip of my arrow. She lay facedown, arms and legs splayed like she'd been running when struck. She'd probably died before she hit the ground, given the fissure of severed cloth and flesh that made up her ripped-open back. The wound was so deep, the alabaster column of her spine shone in the light like the mountains around us writ small.

Iskander sucked in a breath, stumbling back a few feet, his

flight taking him straight through the dead girl's ghost. His eyes met mine and his legs seemed to lock, like he was forcing himself to stay still. "Roven Voyniks did this?"

I nodded. "There was a cadre of soldiers tracking us south. They turned back once it became clear we were heading for Eshkaroth. They must have stopped to have fun on their way."

It was a real struggle not to look at the ghost-girl as I spoke, to not see the silver tears running down her face or the accusation in her eyes. *You brought them here?*

Iskander licked his lips. "How do you know it was Roven? Your cousin could have—"

"Goran is a puppet." Even speaking his name made me want to scream, my cousin who betrayed his blood and his people all for the pretense of a crown. "He hasn't the strength to lead an army or a kingdom. That's why he went north to Roven in the first place. Emperor Radovan gave Goran an army, let him kill our grandfather and take the throne. But the Roven army never left.

"That the throne is mine by right is beside the point. While Goran wears the Frozen Crown and pretends to be king, our countrymen are conscripted into the Roven army. And the young women?" The ghost-girl fell to her knees, her sobs stabbing through my gut. I shook my head, unable to continue.

Not even the witches were safe. Perhaps especially not the witches. Magic was a rare gift all over the world, and no one coveted it more than Radovan. His spies were everywhere, sniffing out the faintest whiff of power, abducting witches from their homes and pressing them into Radovan's army or killing them outright if they refused to obey.

Lady Night save me if Radovan ever found out I was a witch. Nothing would stop him from coming for me.

"This," I began, pointing at the girl's body and the smoking ruins beyond, "was Roven's doing. And make no mistake, it's

Roven we're up against. My cousin might call himself king, but he bought the Frozen Crown with Radovan's army and his own people's blood. That army ensures his obedience to Radovan. By this time next year, Seravesh will be nothing but another province in the Roven Empire."

"My lady, please." Vitaly's voice was brimming with fear. He held his sword with a white-knuckled grip, eyes scouring the tree line for enemies. "We must turn back."

"I agree," Lord Marr added, with an expression that couldn't be argued with.

"But the bodies . . ." Iskander's protest died midsentence.

"Will be attended to." My voice sounded too brittle to my own ears as I signed the symbol of the Two-Faced God in the air over the girl. *"I will avenge you,"* I promised.

"I don't want vengeance. I want to live."

"Is Emperor Radovan really so invested in holding Seravesh?" Iskander asked as we rode south and back into the relative safety of Idun. "Surely if you cause enough trouble, he'll cut his losses and withdraw support."

"That's what we hoped too," I said, pulling my mind away from the memory of the ghost-girl's tears. "In the beginning, we raised hell: cutting supply lines, ambushing their holdings, harrying them in every way possible. Yet for every soldier we killed, Roven sent two more. It didn't stop us. It was war. Battle after battle, we won and lost in turn, but we didn't give up. Until the emperor sent his vengeance."

The words clung to my lips, but I had to go on. Iskander had to understand. "There was a city in the foothills of the mountains, on the western edge of Lake Litramov. It was called Nadym, the Little Sister. On clear nights, you could see its light from the capital, Solenskaya.

"On the night of the harvest moon, an army came down from the mountains, surrounded the city, locked its gates, and burned it. Branko, Radovan's fire witch, obliterated every timber. They say you could hear the screams all the way from the capital.

"That you could smell it even farther."

A choked sound clawed out of Vitaly's throat, a jagged broken thing. He gulped and pushed ahead alone.

Silence lay over us like a shroud. I didn't break it. Let Prince Iskander think about what he'd heard. Let him remember that girl's broken body and imagine the blood-soaked chorus of screams that haunted my dreams—the people left to die for Roven's greed. Let him tally that against all the reasons not to help me.

"How many?" he finally asked.

"Eight thousand."

"Lady Night . . . and then you came south?"

I nodded, affirming all the things that had not been said: the desperation of my plea, the help that was in his hands to offer.

"And then I came south."

3

T hank you for the dance, my lady," Governor Erol
said, bowing over my hand.

"The pleasure was all mine," I replied before
sliding into the crowd.

The Great Hall of Eshkaroth couldn't quite live up to its
name. It was so overpacked with Idunese and Vishiri nobles,
the room was fit to burst. The maester, bowing to the crush of
people, opened the six doors on either side of the hall so guests
could mill about on the veranda outside. It was a cold night, but
the press of bodies and the six roaring hearths compensated for
the chill.

Nervous energy crackled through the room as news of the
sacked village passed quicker than plague. I smiled and nodded
to those I passed but didn't stop to speak with anyone. Folding
my hands together, I hoped no one noticed the way my nails dug
into my skin, hoped my smile disguised the way my teeth bit at
the edge of my tongue.

I glanced toward Prince Iskander, trying to plan my next
approach. His retainers had him penned in by one of the fires
and there was a steady stream of nobles lined up around him,
no doubt pestering him with prospective trading contracts and
unmarried daughters—or both. He handled it with equanimity,

which was impressive but intensely irritating since every time *I* approached, Lord Ishaq or one of his potpourri-scented companions headed me off and shunted me to the side.

Why? Was it Iskander's doing? Hadn't my words moved him at all? How could Iskander stand there having the greatest time in the world after seeing that poor girl and her butchered village?

Perhaps I'd have Vitaly create another diversion, I thought, finding him watching me in the crowd. My grim-faced shadow was glaring daggers at anyone who neared me. No doubt he was filled with the same helpless rage as I was. Attending a party? After what we saw in the mountains? After what had happened to our country? But that's exactly why I was here. I had a job to do. One that was hard enough without an overzealous and despair-filled guard stalking me across the hall, I thought, looking away. Perhaps Arkady should have assigned someone else to guard me tonight.

I peered through the peacock-colored crowd but couldn't spot Arkady's solemn face amid all the laughing guests. The nobles of Idun seemed determined to enjoy themselves despite the bloodbath that had sent Idunese and Seraveshi soldiers into the mountains to scout out danger and lay the people of that poor village to rest. Still, there was a brittle edge to the merriment. It was like this was the first time these pampered people had to stop and consider the Roven threat.

Which probably wasn't far from the truth.

Idun was clamped between two great empires: Roven to the north, Vishir to the south. It controlled the only major throughway from the eastern sea to the western sea. Servants passed trays of caviar from the farthest reaches of Roven, chocolate and fruits from southern Vishir, and all manner of sweets from the eastern Vishiri province of Kizuoka.

Nothing from Seravesh, though. Nothing from the six kingdoms already claimed by the greed of Roven. Would these flippant people even remember me in a year? Would they remember Seravesh had once been free? Or would they, too, be crushed?

The thought pulled at the edges of my carefully composed expression. Abandoning my search for Arkady, I angled left toward one of the doors. Perhaps fresh air would renew my spirits.

The veranda was empty and I walked up to the railing thanking the Two-Faced God for that blessing. This side of the hall faced north, and in the moonlight, I could see the jagged peaks of the Peshkalor Mountains reaching into the sky. I could almost imagine I was back in my own castle. Almost. Except the mountains were too close. There was no Lake Litramov spreading out before me like a second sky. I couldn't see Nadym in the distance.

I never would again.

"Would you care for some company, my lady?"

I turned. Prince Iskander stood in the doorway, framed by firelight. Lord Marr was beside him. The sour-faced Lord Ishaq was nowhere to be seen.

An invisible fist clenched my heart. "Please."

Please.

Iskander approached, but Lord Marr remained in the door. "If you will excuse me, my lord. I have forgotten to tell Lord Ishaq . . . the governor was seeking him." He gave me a conspiratorial smile. "My lady."

Lady Night bless him, I thought, as Lord Marr bowed back inside. But when I turned to Iskander, my smile faded. His expression was grim, and there was an unmistakable sadness in his eyes.

"Lord Marr was quite moved by your story . . . by the plight of your people."

"Oh?"

Iskander nodded. "He is originally from Tamett Province."

Vishir's Tamett Province rebelled against the empire some fifty years ago. Lord Marr would have been a boy, but a person could never forget something like that. "I see." I swallowed. "And you?"

Prince Iskander took a deep breath and looked at his feet. "It would take a hard man to see what we saw today and not be moved. What's happening to Seravesh is awful."

"Awful is just a word, Iskander," I bit back. "The reality is indescribable."

"I understand, but—"

"You understand?" I asked, unable to keep the derision from my voice. How could this cosseted boy ever understand? "You saw one burned village. I've seen a hundred. What is your understanding, if you won't help?"

"I would help you, Askia." His voice was so gentle I almost screamed. "If it were up to me, I would give you the men today. But my father—"

"Your father sent you here. I'm not asking you to champion my cause. All I'm asking you to do is take me to Bet Naqar so I can petition your father myself."

"There's no point in taking you if my father's going to say no."

Something inside me cracked. "You know this? He said this to you?"

Iskander shifted. "No, but Lord Ishaq says so."

"Lord Ishaq is not the emperor."

"But Ishaq is one of my father's chief advisers and a vizier on the council. What he says matters a great deal." Iskander took a deep breath. "Ishaq says there's a simple way for you to make peace with Roven."

"Oh?" I clenched the railing to keep myself from hitting him.

"Marry Radovan."

"What?"

"The emperor has made you an offer of marriage—the Roven emissary in Bet Naqar said as much before we left. If you accept the offer on the condition of Seravesh's freedom, the war will be over. Your cousin will be ousted."

My mouth snapped shut. Could anyone really be this naïve? A prince of Vishir too. Is this why his brother hadn't bothered killing him yet—was it not worth the effort?

"I understand it may be distasteful to you to marry in this way, but it's the reality for people in our position," he said in a maddeningly superior tone. "If it means the end of your people's suffering, then—"

"The Roven emissary says it, so it must be true? Iskander," I exclaimed, looking away from his poor, gullible face.

"What do you mean? He lied?" Iskander clasped my shoulder. "Help me understand, Askia."

I looked up, searching the stars for a way to make him see why marriage wasn't an option. At length, I asked, "How many wives does your father have?"

"Seventeen." He shrugged at my delicately raised eyebrow. "He likes to collect." There was something darkly amused in Iskander's voice, like he knew all about the lusty ballads northerners sang about his father's wives and was laughing at our ignorance.

"Emperor Radovan of Roven has had only six wives. He takes them from the lands he conquers. I guess he likes to collect too."

I turned back to the mountains, speaking to the sky. "They say the Tower of Roshkot in the capital of Roven is the highest building in the world. They say it's beautiful, a wonder of creation. He keeps his wives there, but it's nothing like your father's menagerie. Radovan doesn't lavish his wives with gold and gifts. No. He takes them to the deepest, darkest places of Roshkot, places of forgetting, and tortures them. After a month, he brings them to the top of the tower. He brands them with his prayers and throws them off. The Two-Faced God, he says, always answers his prayers."

I turned to Iskander, pinning him with my eyes. "If I thought for one second marrying Radovan would free my people, I'd do it. I'd gladly step to the very edge of Roshkot and carry Radovan's prayers into the abyss."

I grabbed his forearm. "It doesn't stop him, Iskander. Six women married him to ensure the transfer of power was peaceful, and it was. Until they died. Who now remembers the people of Polzi or Khezhar or Nivlaand? No one. Because they don't exist. Everything that made them different and unique is gone. Radovan won't spare Seravesh. Not for me. The only thing he responds to is might, and I intend to match his. If only you give me a chance."

Iskander didn't reply, but that was all right. I could see his mind working. He wanted to help me, I knew he did. But would he? Bringing me to Vishir would be a declaration Iskander was on my side, that he would stand for me. Was he strong enough to stand alone?

He licked his lips, and I was suddenly aware of how very close he was standing. He reached out to touch me, but brought himself up short. Flushed.

I gave him a tired smile, "Good night, Iskander."

I walked to the door with heavy steps, but I could feel his eyes on my back.

"Askia?"

A smile curved my lips. I turned. Iskander opened his mouth . . . and froze. His expression flashed from hopeful to shocked to something I couldn't identify. He lunged.

The world slowed. I tensed a second before his body flattened mine, crushing the air from my lungs. My head smacked the floor. The world went black.

Sight returned after a few seconds. Iskander was still on top of me, but he was looking over his shoulder. I felt movement around me, saw a hundred panicked faces, but I couldn't make sense of it. Iskander had called my name and then tackled me. Why?

I remembered the look on his face. The shock and fear. Then I saw it. Embedded into the oak door, right where I had been standing.

A dagger.

Sound returned in a cacophony of shouts and bellowed yells. I turned my head and groaned as pain lanced through my skull.

"Easy. Not too fast." Iskander helped me sit up. His body was still angled against the crowd. "Are you all right?"

I probed my scalp with ginger fingers. There was no blood, just the beginning of a giant knot. I tried to nod, but pain made me wince. "I'm all right. Help me up?"

Iskander half lifted me to my feet, bracing me while the world righted itself. General Arkady pushed his way through the crowd, silence rippling around him. My hands tightened on Iskander's arms. I knew that expression. That awful combination of rage and sorrow. It was the same expression Arkady wore when he told me I had to flee my home.

"Who?" I asked.

Arkady stepped aside. Behind him, four of my guards dragged up a limp form. Limp not because he was injured or dead, but because he wasn't fighting. My would-be assassin had never intended to survive. His face was laden with guilt, with grief.

For the second time in as many minutes, my breath hitched. My legs threatened to buckle. The world faded at the edges of my vision.

"Vitaly."

4

Stone-faced soldiers from Vishir and Idun closed ranks and whisked Iskander and me out of the Great Hall. They deposited us in a dimly lit sitting room, leaving guards posted at the door and windows. I took a seat by the fire, back erect, hands folded. Watching. Waiting as rage slowly devoured me.

Iskander paced the length of the rectangular room. His footsteps echoed through me, rapping out an uneven beat that demanded answers. Why? Why did Vitaly do this? He was my friend.

A queen has subjects. Not friends. A few weeks before his death, my grandfather had called me to his office and issued that warning. About Vitaly, specifically. Friendships were liabilities. Weaknesses.

I hadn't believed him. But here I sat, frigid beside the fire, counting down the hours of Vitaly's wasted life.

The door creaked open, and Governor Erol slid into the room. His boots were wet and crusted over with mud. There was blood on his right sleeve. "My lady," he whispered. "General Arkady requests your presence below."

"What news is there?" Prince Iskander pressed.

"Nothing."

"Nothing? But it's been hours. If we were in Vishir—"

"We are not in Vishir," Erol said. "One of the princess's men, a man called Illya, has been running the interrogation. Believe me when I say he knows his business."

Iskander paused. "And still there's nothing?"

I rose, gathering strength about me like a cloak, and spoke with supreme indifference. "The Black Wolves are trained to resist interrogation. If Vitaly was persuaded to rebel, pain is unlikely to motivate a confession."

Iskander's eyes went wide. "Then why let him be tortured?"

"What else is to be done with a traitor?" I asked, my voice sounding hollow to my own ears. "Lead the way, Governor."

I had seen many castles in my life. They were as different and varied as flakes of snow. But without fail, enemies were kept below. I followed Governor Erol down one staircase and the next, into the earth, into the cold, the dark and the damp.

The silence told me we were close: leaden and brittle all at once. The dead were gathering, filling the cells closest to the center chamber. I felt their eyes on me, but their faces didn't bear looking at. They weren't there for me anyway. They were there for Vitaly.

We reached the last closed door, and Iskander paused. "Are you sure you want to do this?"

I wanted to say no, to scream and run. "This isn't the first traitor's death I've witnessed. Open the door."

There was nothing like the smell of a place to mark its true nature. Blood and filth could be washed away, but agony and fear? The smell of true misery always lingered.

Vitaly hung naked in the center of the room. His whole body shook, his shackles rattling with the sound of approaching death. Strips of fair skin had been ripped from his rib cage. Rivulets of blood flowed down his torso from punctures to his liver and kidneys. His toenails littered the floor. Impossibly, he was still alive. Illya knew his job.

I looked away, locking away my horror and heartbreak before anyone could read them on my face. Wasted effort, for everyone was looking at Vitaly. Or, almost everyone.

Illya watched me from the edges of the room, the weight of his attention pushing me perilously close to the edge. It was his eyes, I thought, trying to distract myself. They were so gray they were almost silver. Mirrorlike. Always reflecting things better left unseen.

Things like pity—not for Vitaly. For me. Like Illya could peer through the frail armor of duty and see what ordering Vitaly's torment was doing to me.

It was too much, that understanding which tested the bounds of my control. I couldn't let these men see how much Vitaly's betrayal cost me.

"Leave us." The demand fell from my lips like the flat of a blade against flesh. Iskander made an incoherent noise of protest before someone shushed him. Only when the door shut on their backs did Vitaly's eyes meet mine.

He watched me like I was life itself, like I was water in the desert. Like I had the power to save him, this traitor, this friend.

"Why, Vitaly?"

Hope drained out of his face. As the silence stretched between us, my thin cord of control cracked. I lunged, grabbing his chin, forcing him to look at me. "Why did you do this? Why do I deserve to die?"

Tears fell from his eyes, rolling through dirt and blood as they fell, staining my hands.

"Please," I rasped, a sob rising in my throat. "Just tell me why."

He closed his eyes. Pulled his face away.

I fell back and found that we were not alone after all. The

dead had come, broken men and women, who, even in death, could not escape the torment of this room. They surrounded us, their night-filled eyes latched on Vitaly. Claiming him.

I spun on my heel and shoved through the door, as my unvoiced sob hardened into something sharper. "Bring him."

THE BLACK WOLVES WAITED IN THE FOOTHILLS. THREE THOUSAND men stood in perfect rows and perfect silence, each of them but two breaths from violence. I sensed their rage, for it was within me too. Betrayal bubbled under my skin. The Wolves watched Vitaly. Vitaly watched me.

He knelt on the frozen ground, shackles clamped around useless arms. A filthy robe covered the worst of his wounds, but his face was so ashen it was clear he wasn't long for this world. There was no more hope in his eyes, just acceptance.

"My lady?" Prince Iskander stood by my side. His lips were set into a frown, but I felt his sympathy in his every worried glance.

Sympathy I didn't deserve. Vitaly might have thrown the dagger, but it was my weakness that had driven him to it. I hadn't been smart enough to foresee the invasion. I hadn't been fast enough to stop the burning of Nadym. Did Vitaly think I wouldn't be strong enough to turn back the Roven tide? That I wasn't ready to give anything, everything to free our people?

"Lord Vitaly Kavondy, Lieutenant of the Black Wolves of Seravesh, you have been found guilty of treason, espionage, and the attempted murder of Her Royal Highness, Askia Poritskaya e-Nimri." Arkady's words echoed off the surrounding hills sharp enough to cut skin. "The penalty for your crimes is death. I strip you of office and name. May my fallen brothers hunt you across the Marchlands. May the Two-Faced God turn you away from Its light."

I stepped into the echo of Arkady's words, clenching my

sword's hilt to hide the tremor running through my hand. "Confess now, and one last request shall be granted." The acceptance in Vitaly's face turned to pity. Though my words rang across the mountains, colder than winter snow, he obviously heard the lie in my tone, this man I had loved as a brother. A dull depthless pain throbbed through my body. "Why?" I asked in a voice meant solely for him. "I can stop him. I promise you there isn't anything—"

"No, Askia, it's not—" A long breath gushed out of him and he sagged toward the ground. "Radovan is going to do it again, like he did to Nadym, but this time to Kavondy. My family." His words came out in a gurgled rasp, like he didn't have enough air behind them. Blood bubbled on his lips. "A man came to me. He put his finger to my forehead and drew me into the burning ruins of Nadym." Vitaly gulped, like he was trying to swallow back dread. "He said Radovan would unleash Branko. He said Kavondy would burn unless I killed you. But I had to do it here. With the world watching, he said. I don't think he ever intended for me to succeed. But if it saves my family . . ."

His words echoed into the hollow place where my heart used to be. This wouldn't save his family. They were probably killed the moment Vitaly left for Idun. My rage guttered. I didn't have the strength to tell him.

I bowed my head. "Request?"

"Sing the dirge for me, my lady. Please."

It wasn't allowed, not for traitors. General Arkady would have killed him for the presumption. But that was Vitaly, bold and bright to the core. To the end.

I circled Vitaly's still kneeling body and tilted his head until it rested on my stomach like some horrid mockery of an embrace. I smoothed his black hair out of his eyes with one hand and drew my sword in the other. My heart stilled, frozen between one beat and the next.

He looked up at me, tears falling from his clear green eyes. "I will serve you better when I see you again."

I closed my eyes against the oath, but not before seeing Arkady stiffen and Iskander frown. I pushed them out of my mind. Now was for Vitaly, and the rest he was forsaking. I swallowed back tears, refusing to let the grief surface, but Vitaly knew. He always knew.

Vitaly smiled.

I raised my blade to his throat and, in one smooth motion, cut. The sword dropped to the blood-spattered ground, and I clutched his body to my chest. Vitaly's eyes were locked on mine. His mouth worked in silent gasps. I refused to look away, even when his blood rushed over my hands. His body convulsed. His skin went gray. I held him as he died. Till his last drop of blood fell. To his last breath. Until he was gone.

I forced myself to breathe past the pain rending my heart, as Arkady laid Vitaly down on the frozen earth. Hands shaking, I pulled off the black mourning shawl that encircled my neck and covered my hair with the gossamer veil.

Cupping my bloody hands in front of my eyes, I sang. My voice rang into the cold air and bounced off the mountains. It was not strong, not clear or beautiful, but it was filled with all the things I could not say.

The last note faded, and the wind kicked up in answer to my sorrow, howling across the ridge. I grabbed the edges of my veil to keep it from flying off. When I looked up, Vitaly stood at the head of his corpse. The calm on his earthly form was utterly absent from his ghostly one. His eyes froze me, willing me to act.

I had to do it here. With the whole world watching.

Governor Erol cleared his throat. "My lady, I must express my deepest sympathy to you. This attack on you—"

"This wasn't an attack on me," I said, my voice as frigid as glacial ice. "This was an attack on you."

Erol opened his mouth, but I wouldn't be interrupted. I would make them understand.

"Use your brain. Vitaly was a member of my close guard for years. If it was simply a matter of getting me out of the way, he had ample opportunity. This wasn't an assassination. It was a message. To *you*."

I stepped closer, taking in the unsure faces of the men around me. "Emperor Radovan may have ordered my death, but he was putting my blood on your hands. A foreign royal killed in your court? Not only the rightful queen of Seravesh, but the Vishiri emperor's goddaughter, murdered with the whole world watching . . ." I let my words trail off, but the implication was clear. "Roven is coming, Governor. Be ready."

I turned to Prince Iskander. "Your father will need to be ready too. Tell him."

Iskander's jaw clenched. Something unknowable shone in his eyes. "Tell him yourself. We leave at dawn."

5

I sat alone at the stern as the *Lord's Vengeance* cut west through the sea, sending ripples of hot air across my face. The ship's night crew went about their business with silent efficiency, leaving me to my solitude. Funny how quickly solitude becomes isolation. I glanced across the deck and frowned at the closed door of the captain's cabin. Iskander and his men had been closeted there for days, recovering from seasickness.

Movement flashed in the corner of my eye. I peered into the darkness waiting for the clouds to shift. In the light of the crescent moon, Illya's towering form appeared beside the mainmast. Watching. Always watching.

I dipped my chin in a shallow nod and turned away, looking east toward Idun, toward the men I'd left behind. The Black Wolves had stayed in Eshkaroth to help Idun prepare for the invasion that would surely happen come spring. There'd been no choice, of course. General Arkady had to stay with the army. It was where he belonged, or at least that's what he claimed.

Arkady hadn't met my eye when I said good-bye. Something vital had changed between us, broken when Vitaly turned. Like Arkady didn't trust himself with me anymore. So he stayed behind and sent Illya in his stead as captain of the guard.

I had to admit there was no one better to ensure my safety,

but I needed more than a bodyguard. I needed an adviser, some-one who understood court politics, who knew how to maneuver among nobles. Someone like Vitaly.

I shied away from the thought even as the ghost appeared beside me, his body humming with the need for retribution. Vitaly had made his choice, and with Arkady in Idun, it was Illya who remained, questionable though his help was.

I was close with all my personal guards, but despite my over-tures of friendship and almost a year of service, I knew next to nothing about Illya. One of the hundreds of refugees from the Seravesh-Raskis border, he was perhaps ten years older than me, exceptionally tall, powerfully built, and the deadliest sword-master in the Seraveshi army. This fact alone was enough to grant him fame and friends, fortune even, but Illya wasn't that kind of man. Something about him put people on edge. Put *me* on edge, I realized, thinking back to that moment in the dungeon when Illya had looked at me and seen . . . everything.

What was I supposed to do with that exposure? Run from it? Or embrace it? I couldn't decide, not with the nudge of Illya's gaze still on my back.

I heard a door open and close behind me, but it was the re-lieved sigh blowing across the ship that made me turn. Iskander stood outside his cabin door. He smiled and made his way over, looking pretty good for someone who had spent the past five days with his stomach in his throat.

"May I join you?"

"Of course." I studied him as he eased down beside me. "Are you feeling better?"

He shrugged noncommittally. "I'd hoped I'd outgrown sea-sickness on our first voyage, but apparently not."

"At least you're better now."

"Just in time too. We arrive tomorrow."

I nodded but couldn't think of anything to say.

"You should get some rest."

"Can't."

"Well, you should try. You'll want to look your best for my father."

I resisted the urge to push the heat-dampened hair out of my face and shot him a sidelong glance. "Why? It's not like I'm courting him."

"Really?" he asked, a sly glint in his eyes. "You might have better luck if you did. Women sure seem to love him."

He shrugged, the gesture doing nothing to dispel the undercurrent of jealousy in his voice. I frowned, both at his tone and his suggestion. My journey to Vishir was meant to free Seravesh, not chain it to yet another empire. "I don't think you'd like me for a stepmother."

"What? You're not the doting type?"

"What do you think?"

Iskander laughed. "Well, that will disappoint my brother. Enver said the first thing you'd do, if we let you come to court, was seduce my father."

I made a face. I didn't remember anything about the emperor's eldest son, but this one sentence was enough to put me off. "What's Enver like?"

"He's a prat," Iskander said, mouth twisting. "An unfortunately influential prat."

"Oh? A court darling, is he?"

I spoke in jest, but Iskander's expression darkened.

"Enver sits on the Council of Viziers."

"Truly?" The council was responsible for the day-to-day running of the empire. That Enver sat on it was a huge sign of favor. "He's quite young for such responsibility. Is he really qualified?"

"No. My father appointed him out of pity. Everyone knows it."

"Why?"

"Because Enver was never supposed to happen," Iskander

said, an edge to his voice. He took a deep breath, eyes trained on the darkness. "My father has many wives, but he married my mother with the understanding she would bear his only children. He loved her." He looked self-consciously at me and away again. "She understood that his . . . affections would not belong only to her. But she refused to be just one more queen. My father agreed.

"It wasn't easy for my mother to conceive," he said, squirming in his seat. "My father's reign was tenuous in those early years, and an empire without an heir cannot be stable. He was under a lot of strain. Eventually, my mother allowed him to try and conceive with one of the other wives. She chose Enver's mother, Na'him."

"Wait, it was your mother's choice? Not your father's?"

Iskander shook his head quickly. "No, of course it wasn't up to him. Look, I know what people think about the menagerie, but it's not . . . What I mean to say is that my father has only one real wife: my mother. The role of principal wife is highly sought after and coveted throughout the empire."

Coveted? Right. What woman wouldn't want to handpick her husband's lovers? "What about the other wives?"

Iskander's throat bobbed. "In an empire as large as Vishir it would be easy for any one province to think they might be able to break away. The wives are our assurance that they won't. Each time an emperor assumes the throne, one noblewoman from each province is sent as tribute to ensure their loyalty to the crown."

"So the other wives are political prisoners?"

"Yes. It's not like my father has a relationship with them. It's not . . ."

"Sexual? Well, that makes it all right, then," I said, my voice so dry the deck between us should have burst into flames.

"It helps the provinces too," Iskander said, a note of defensiveness creeping into his voice. "Their families receive a handsome dowry, and any wrongdoing by the emperor could very easily cause a war. That's why it was my mother who made the choice, so her family couldn't object. My mother approached Na'him and negotiated the arrangement with her and her family."

Iskander's expression faded from embarrassment to bitterness with a sour smile. "The kingdom needed a male heir. At the time, Na'him was the youngest of my father's wives, the most likely to be able to conceive. Na'him's family wasn't terribly powerful. And Na'him had no aspirations for power, so she wouldn't threaten my mother's position." An angry huff of air chuffed out his nose. He shook his head. "That choice made Enver what he is. My mother has never forgiven herself."

"Because eventually she did have a son?"

"Three months later. In less than a year, the empire went from having no heirs to two."

I nodded in understanding. Unlike most kingdoms, the oldest Vishiri prince wasn't guaranteed the throne. The *surviving* prince was.

"After I was born, my mother insisted Enver be sent away. She couldn't stand seeing her great error pushed in her face every day."

"Your father didn't allow it?"

He snorted. "He did, actually. Na'him cared nothing for motherhood. Enver's birth didn't change her. And my father is what he is. We bear his blood, but an emperor must always be wary of sons. He allowed Enver to be sent to live with Na'him's family. He gave Na'him leave to go with Enver, but she didn't want to. Her life in the menagerie was more luxurious than anything her family could give her."

He shook his head at the water, and I wondered if he realized how sad this all sounded. A child born out of necessity, then shunted to the side when he became inconvenient.

"Sometimes, I think that was my mother's second great mistake. Maybe if Enver and I had been raised together, we could be brothers. Not rivals." He shrugged, like he was trying to shed the weighty mantle of *what if.* "The few summers we spent together in our youth weren't enough to create any kind of affection. He never liked me and absolutely loathed my younger brother, Tarek," he said, referring to the brother my father helped birth, and who died only a year after my parents. "There's nothing of love between us now. He wasn't raised to feel it."

"Are you sure?" I asked, still feeling strangely sorry for boy-Enver.

He exhaled a mirthless ha. "Do you know who his uncle is? Ishaq. He raised Enver. Made Enver the heartless creature he is today."

I recalled the haughty way Ishaq had treated me in Eshkaroth and frowned. "How did Enver get onto the council?"

"When the old lord vizier died, Ishaq nominated Enver for the empty seat. Ishaq argued that Na'him's neglect of Enver was a disservice to Vishir. Her indifference was keeping a possible future emperor from learning anything about rule."

"Na'him's indifference?" I asked. "What about your father's indifference?"

Iskander's lips twitched a smile. "Well, Ishaq couldn't very well call my father an unfit parent, could he? My father gave Enver the council seat like it could make up for his loveless childhood." Iskander shook his head at his hands, brows drawn together. "As if a council seat can make Enver a leader."

Pity-laced uncertainty wormed through me. A council seat might not make Enver heir, but it could certainly get him the favor of court. I wondered who favored Iskander for the throne. Or did he only have an influential mother on his side?

We sat in silence for a while longer, looking at the same night, but surely seeing different things.

"Why did you do it yourself?" Iskander asked at length, his voice so small it was nearly lost to the waves. "Execute Vitaly."

I sighed. He'd never killed anyone. If he had, he wouldn't have had to ask. "He was my subject. No matter what he was in the end, Vitaly lived by my word. If his death was to fall from my lips, then it should come by my hand. That's the price we pay to rule."

He nodded. "I understand."

"No. You don't. But you will. Someday." I let him chew on that for a while and hoped I hadn't wounded his pride.

"What did Vitaly mean," Iskander whispered, "when he said, 'I will serve you better when I see you again'?"

Vitaly appeared on the far side of the prince, looking at me. His cold eyes filled with longing. Not for life or revenge, but redemption.

I turned away from Vitaly, willing myself into a stillness I couldn't quite feel. "In Seravesh we believe an oath doesn't just bind you in this life but in the next. Vitaly swore to be loyal to me. He failed in life. Perhaps he'll do better when we meet again on the other side."

It wasn't a lie, but it wasn't the truth, either. Some of my men knew there was something more to me, something that tasted of magic. They never asked, and I never told, but they must suspect. How else would Vitaly have known to swear that oath to me?

Even in its lightest form, magic was dangerous. My father was a healer. He wielded the purest form of magic, and it got him killed. It got my mother killed. It almost got me killed. So how could I possibly tell Iskander I could still see Vitaly? That he was watching us right now?

I tried not to see the suspicion in Iskander's eyes, or the knowing lilt to his smile as he stood. "Get some sleep, Askia."

Iskander walked away, but I hadn't the strength to move. My eyes were on the ink-black horizon, on the shores of a northern continent that had long since vanished from sight. Somewhere out there in the darkness was a land of endless forests and crystalline lakes, a land of rolling farm fields and snow-tipped mountains. My home was crying out to me like a child begging for aid. And I could not fail her.

THE SALTY STING OF SWEAT ROLLING INTO MY EYE ROUSED ME FROM a fitful night's sleep. I swore and peeled myself off the bed, glaring at the sun through my cabin's tiny porthole. I stood for a few bleary-eyed seconds, heat and lethargy making me long for a cold bath.

There was nowhere on board for me to bathe, though, so I did my best to clean myself with the meager water from the washstand. My hair was far too long to wash, so I wetted the crown of my head, washing out as much of the oil as I could. Lady Night, I hoped I didn't stink.

I lay naked on the cabin floor, hair splayed out above me, and tried not to sweat. It was a vain effort. The ship was stifling; not even a whisper of wind reached me. I may as well have been lying in an oven.

When my hair finally dried, I sat at the cabin's sole chair and carefully pinned the strands up at the base of my neck. I dressed with exaggerated slowness, but each layer added a fresh hell of burning heat. The gown was beautiful; its emerald fabric exactly matched my eyes. The sleeves and skirt were embroidered in gold-threaded whorls sewn in intricate waves. But it was wool. Perfect for winter in Seravesh. Absolute murder for Vishir at any time of year. I shook my head. Longing for a better gown was a waste of time. This was the nicest one I owned. It would have to do.

I left my cabin the moment I was dressed, and I climbed the steps to the main deck, praying for a breeze. The sun was up in full blazing glory, blinding me momentarily as I passed from darkness to light.

No breeze. Great.

"Good morning."

I smiled vaguely in the direction of Prince Iskander's voice and blinked the sun spots out of my eyes. When my sight returned, I went to the railing where he stood with Lord Marr and took in the sprawling city of Bet Naqar.

Northwestern Vishir was all desert. That it could support any city was incredible, but Bet Naqar was inconceivable. The city emanated a steady hum of industry, like the pulse of a living thing. Beyond the massive harbor, I could make out homes and shops, temples and mansions. And the palace . . .

"Is Bet Naqar like you remember?" Lord Marr asked.

I shook my head. "It's so much bigger."

"And it gets bigger every year."

Energy snapped and sizzled over my skin. It had been six years since I'd last set foot on these shores, and then I was just a child. My past experience meant nothing now that there was a kingdom depending on me to wrest aid from an empire that spanned half the world. Why should they help me when every one of their provinces must be constantly fighting for money and influence?

I squared my shoulders, refusing to bow beneath the pressure. "Tell me what to do."

Iskander flashed a solemn smile. "We'll ride directly to the palace once we make landfall. My father is holding an audience, like he does every three days, and we will try to attend." Iskander took a deep breath. "He may, or may not, choose to see you."

My mind immediately rejected the possibility. I couldn't fathom it, refused to. We were family . . . after a fashion. When my father had saved Iskander's mother and Prince Tarek, the emperor had named me his goddaughter.

"Your status as goddaughter will weigh in your favor," Iskander said, reading my thoughts.

"But the emperor has over two hundred godchildren," Lord

Marr added. "All of them eventually come for handouts. Better you treat him as one ruler to another."

I nodded, wrapping my hands around the railing. "What else?"

"Should he see you, greet him formally, thank him for his hospitality, and excuse yourself," Iskander said.

I looked between the men. "Are you sure?"

"Yes."

"It's the Vishiri way," Lord Marr explained. "We like to get acquainted with a person before discussing business."

"It could be a few days before my mother officially welcomes you to court, and you won't be able to attend any court events until she does," Iskander warned. "Give them a taste, but leave them wanting more."

There wasn't time to wait. How could I squander my first meeting on niceties? But Arkady wasn't here to advise me. Iskander and Marr were all I had. I nodded reluctantly.

Iskander bit his lip. "The emissary from Roven will be present."

My vision flashed red.

"Count Dobor is extremely influential," Marr warned. "He will want to see you. Acknowledge him, but do not get drawn into conversation."

"All right," I said through clenched teeth. Avoiding the Roven emissary wouldn't be hard; not killing him on sight would be.

"Good." Iskander sighed. "Now, you can't go looking like that. What else do you have to wear?"

"Nothing." Amazing how much bitterness I could pack into one word, but it wasn't like Roven had given me time to pack when they took my castle.

"Oh." Iskander winced, clearly realizing how his words sounded. "Not that it's not pretty, but we won't arrive at the palace until midday. You'll melt."

"Don't worry, my lady. Your necessities will be provided,"

Marr said, kindly. "In the meantime, you will be more comfortable if you wear what you wore when we first met."

"Are you sure?" Vishiri fashions were just as modest as in the north. A woman in breeches would no doubt cause a stir.

Iskander smiled. "Oh yes. Father will love it."

"You only get one chance at a first impression," Marr said when I still looked unsure. "Make it count."

I forced a smile and retreated to my cabin. The second the door slammed shut, I ripped off my dress and shoved it into my trunk. Pressing my palms against the wall, I closed my eyes.

Count Dobor.

The name hissed through my mind. The logical part of my brain reasoned that, of course, the Roven emissary would be at court. Of course, I would have to meet him. It didn't stop me from wondering if I could kill him and get away with it.

You don't have time for this, I thought, shoving the anger away. I might not get to slit Dobor's throat today, but stand out? That I could do.

I laced myself into my leathers and yanked the pins out of my hair. With only my fingers to guide me, I braided the left third of my hair. It took a few false starts, but when I was finished, a tight plait ran all the way down my scalp. I brushed out the rest of my hair and layered in tiny braids here and there, fastening little bells to the ends the way my distant shieldmaiden ancestors had once done.

The ship groaned and shuddered to a stop. It was time. Shoving my weapons into place, I wrenched open the door and walked straight into Illya.

I stiffened with surprise at the sight of him emerging from the gloom. He'd shaved both sides of his head, leaving a long strip of ash-blond hair braided down his back. Dark green tattoos—evidence of his Raskisi heritage—etched his scalp, weaving across half his bare chest and down most of his right arm.

He really was unfairly attractive, I thought, prying my eyes away from his chest.

"Are you ready?"

"Yes, of course," I replied quickly. Too quickly. The false optimism in my voice writhed between us. "Shall we go up?"

Rather than wait for his reply, I made to move past him, only to feel the brush of his fingers at my wrist. "You can do this, my lady," he murmured, in a voice filled with certainty.

"Do I have a choice?" My voice was so dry it drew a faint smile from Illya's lips.

The ship swayed, knocking me back into the wall. Illya would have fallen onto me were it not for the giant hand he braced on the wood beside my face. The heat of his body, somehow different from the stifling warmth of the ship's underbelly, slid electric across my skin. His throat bobbed, muscles rigid, like he felt it, too, and was struggling to pull away.

Somewhere above us, a bell rang, breaking the spell. I nodded, darting for the stairs—for the relative safety of duty—as I tried to ignore the feeling of his eyes on my back.

Thankfully Iskander and Marr were waiting on the deck. Their conversation dropped dead to the sea when they spotted me. I shrugged. "You said to make an impression."

Iskander looked me up and down, a wicked glint in his eyes. "Mission accomplished."

THE DOCKS AND SLUMS OF BET NAQAR WERE FILLED WITH CROWDS of pinched-faced men and women. They reached out, straining against our escort, begging for money, for food, for water. I took in the desperate faces of the women, the helpless white-knuckled rage of the men, and the hollow eyes of children whose stomachs were distended with hunger. "Who are all these people?"

Iskander swallowed, his eyes snagging on an impossibly thin

child standing near the edge of the road. "Refugees from the northern edges of the Mashra Desert. The monsoon rains have been light for the past few years, and drought is pushing people into the city."

My stomach twisted. I'd been so preoccupied by the needs of my people, I never considered that things might be less than ideal in Vishir. I wished I had something to give these people, but my pockets were as empty as theirs.

The fetid stench of the lower quarters eventually gave way to the homey smells of the middle-class neighborhoods. Butchers and blacksmiths, souks and teahouses peppered the winding streets of Bet Naqar. Our route twisted and turned around unexpected corners, up and back again with no rhyme or reason. The streets grew ever wider. The homes became grander, and the fine-looking people in this part of the city showed no signs of hunger or strain.

We rounded a curve to find Palace Hill looming over us. The palace walls were so high, I could only see the needle-sharp tops of the many guarded minarets peeking over the top. Soldiers crawled over the battlements like ants, sounding horns and pulling open the gates.

We rode two by two through the narrow, thirty-foot gates into the courtyard. I dismounted, and my gaze rose past the vaulted arcades lining the forecourt, past the six tiers of half domes ringing the circular palace, to the massive dome that scraped the clouds. The Vishiri called it the Palace of the Sun and Moon, and for good reason. Every inch of the roof was tiled in gold and silver. In the full light of day, it burned my eyes to look at, that second-sun palace of Bet Naqar, but at night it would glow like a twin moon.

Six minarets marked the border of the palace: two of them behind me at the gates, two more in the middle. The final two were so far away, they looked small.

I willed my face to stillness, aware many of my guards were gaping with wide-eyed wonder. I wished they didn't look so dumbstruck. It was only a courtyard, but I couldn't bring myself to scold them. Such architecture, such massive opulence, simply didn't exist in Seravesh. I was keenly aware that my castle could fit easily inside the walls of the palace complex ten times over.

"Eyes front," Illya growled, jolting my guard to attention.

A silver-haired man emerged from one of the arched openings in the arcade. He stopped a perfect yard from Iskander and made his obeisance with a flourish of his red silk robes. "My Lord Prince. If you wish, I will show your guests inside for rest and refreshment."

Iskander smiled. "Please have rooms prepared for Princess Askia, Lord Chamberlain. In the meantime, we must attend to the emperor."

"It is an audience day today, my lord," Ishaq said tightly. "Surely your father will be too busy."

"I am aware what day it is, Ishaq," Iskander replied with an airy wave. "Lead us in, Chamberlain."

The chamberlain bowed and, as he led us inside, I was struck with the dizzying feeling of déjà vu. I'd expected to find the palace smaller than it was in my memory, diminished by time and my childhood imagination. Not so.

My first impression of the Great Hall was one of sound and space. Over seven hundred feet long and five hundred wide, the cavernous hall soared into the air. Row after row of massive stone pillars supported the domed roof a dizzying four hundred feet above. Gilt and covered in a myriad of stone and jeweled mosaics, it was hard not to feel humbled by such grandeur.

The rough-spun robes of Vishiri peasants clashed against the silks worn by the nobles, as they all waited to plead their case before the judges holding court in the outer fringes of the hall. It was probably the only time the classes came together, though they still self-divided despite the egalitarian nature of the court. Only the sight of me drew them together.

A ripple of whispers started at my back and crested into a wave that outpaced me, crashing at the other end of the hall. Curious eyes raked across my face and down my body. I stalked forward back straight, chin high, feigning a confidence I didn't feel.

Armaan ibn Vishri the Tenth, Emperor of Vishir, sat on a massive golden throne raised on a dais high above the crowd. He was younger than I remembered, only in his forties, with smooth olive skin. The sun glinted off his perfectly shaven head. His expression was mild, but his sharp cheekbones and chiseled jaw reminded me strongly of Iskander.

The entire hall seemed to collectively hold its breath and lean in as we reached the edge of the dais. I caught a flash of pale skin and spotted an older man with night-colored hair and a wispy beard slide to the front of the crowd.

Count Dobor. Seeing him here, so close to the emperor, made fire lance through my skull. I tore my attention away before he could catch my eye. He was nothing. Not now.

The emperor stared at me with an amused glimmer in his gaze. A hint of a smile played about his full lips. He turned away and whispered something to the woman sitting at his right. She was perched on a small chair, her dark skin luminous against the bright turquoise fabric of her gown. Her black hair was gathered into a golden net, though one stray ringlet had wriggled free, falling elegantly into her wide almond-shaped eyes—Iskander's eyes. Clearly, this was Queen Ozura, Armaan's principal wife and Iskander's mother.

On the emperor's other side stood a young man of Iskander's age. Though the brothers looked very much alike, I probably would have known Enver from the eloquent look of distaste he gave Iskander. No doubt, Enver had hoped his rival had drowned at sea.

"Welcome home, son," Armaan said. "Your mother is over-joyed to see you safely in our halls once more." He paused, that smile still hinting at his lips. "And with friends, I see."

"Thank you, Father. I can't tell you how good it is to feel the heat of a Vishiri winter after the cold of the north," Iskander said smoothly, smiling almost ruefully at the crowd. "As for my friends, allow me to reintroduce you to Her Royal Highness Princess Askia Poritskaya e-Nimri of Seravesh."

The emperor gave me a sweeping look and opened his arms. "My lady, welcome back to Bet Naqar. It is truly a bright day when one of our daughters returns to Vishir."

"Thank you, my lord. It's truly a joy to return to the land of my father."

"The joy is mine," he said, pressing one hand to his heart. "Go. Take your rest. We will renew our acquaintance in the coming days."

I let myself smile at the genuine warmth in the emperor's voice. Not trusting myself to words, I bowed my head to the emperor and his queen.

"Go with the chamberlain," Iskander murmured. His hand grazed my arm, setting the hall buzzing once more.

I shot a glance at his hand and arched my eyebrow. Iskander gave the barest of shrugs, a devilish twinkle in his eye. "Trust me. I'll see you soon."

Giving Iskander the slightest of nods, I followed the chamberlain through the crowd of curious and calculating faces pray-ing that no one sensed the dread humming at the edges of my mind. I had been so focused on getting to Vishir, but now that I was there?

Lady Night, give me strength. I knew I'd need all of it to succeed.

6

My spine gave a satisfying pop as I stretched in the heavy wooden chair. The small book-lined study in my enormous Vishiri apartments was bathed in late-afternoon sunlight. The trill of birdcalls echoed in from the arched windows, and I longed to go exploring. *Work first*, I thought, turning back to the desk.

I shook my head at the way my childlike handwriting butchered the normally fluid Vishiri script and folded up the letter. My spoken Vishiri had always been better than my written, but there was no improving it now. The letters were done. Seventeen in all, one to each of the lord viziers who oversaw the day-to-day running of Vishir.

Maybe looking like a novice would help. From what I remembered, gender roles at court could be strict. I suspected it was probably unorthodox for a woman to write to any man, much less those on the Council of Viziers, but as a foreign royal, I hoped for some leeway.

Hoped. Though I was half-Vishiri, and had spent time in this very court, my memory of court etiquette was limited to the six months I'd lived here as an eight-year-old while my father helped Queen Ozura through the final months of her pregnancy. The year I spent here when I was fourteen would have been more helpful, but that was the year after the Shazir put us all on trial—the year after my parents' murder. I had only hazy, almost nonexistent memories of that time. My lost year.

My first, and last, lost year, I vowed. I wouldn't let my cousin Goran or Radovan turn me into a victim. Not again.

I looked up at the sound of footsteps and saw Illya walking toward me through the open doorway. He stepped into the study and jerked a shallow bow. "This lady and her servant are here to see you," he said in toneless Seraveshi before stepping aside to reveal two short women standing behind him.

The younger woman stepped forward hesitantly. She looked to be in her early twenties, with long, gleaming ebony hair. Behind her, an older woman wearing white servant's robes watched me boldly from beneath wiry eyebrows. Several large satchels hung from her wide shoulders, and she clutched their straps in meaty fists.

I looked back at the young woman and cocked my head. "Who are you?"

"Lady Nariko," she said, making her curtsy with almost liquid grace. "Pleased to meet you, Your Highness."

I blinked, wondering if the name was supposed to mean something to me. "How can I help you, Lady Nariko?"

"I've come to wait on you, my lady," Nariko said, like this should be abundantly clear. She smiled at my obvious confusion. "Prince Iskander said you lost the ladies who served you in Seravesh."

"Oh. So Prince Iskander sent you?"

Nariko blushed, like the thought of Iskander speaking to her was too exciting to bear. "No, of course not. The prince told his mother. Queen Ozura sent me. She said I must help make your transition to life at court as smooth as possible. Starting with your wardrobe," she said with a bright smile, before turning to the hard-eyed maid. "You can go get set up."

The maid nodded to Nariko and crossed the study to the open doorway on the right of the desk, ignoring both Illya's glare and my confusion.

Lady Nariko gave me a rueful smile and motioned toward the door. "Shall we?"

We found the maid waiting for us in the dressing room. For a glorified closet, it was a massive space. One end of the rectangular room was occupied by a floor-to-ceiling mirror that reflected the light coming in from the veranda on the opposite wall. There were couches and poufs and chairs, as well as a large vanity table and two walls' worth of open-faced closets, only a fraction of which I'd used to hang the handful of gowns I currently owned.

"If you would step onto the pedestal," Nariko said, nodding to the low box beside the maid. "We'll have you undress so Soma can take your measurements. The royal clothier will start on your wardrobe immediately."

I strode over to the pedestal and let the maid untie the laces of my rather drab gown without comment.

Nariko gasped as the fabric fell from my shoulders. I felt her eyes rake across my back, across the myriad of scars that puckered my flesh and the brand at the base of my spine. I looked over my shoulder, skin prickling, and watched Nariko take in the mark: the blazing sun of the Day Lord burned in outline on my lower back. It was the sign of the Shazir, the priesthood of zealots who killed my parents. The urge to turn away, to cover myself at the horrified expression on her face, was almost unbearable.

I closed my eyes for a moment, fumbling with the stick in my hair until my tresses fell like a curtain over my back. "It's all right," I said, summoning a tired smile and forcing myself to meet Nariko's shocked gaze. "They don't hurt."

Lady Nariko composed her lips in a smile of her own, her cheeks pink. "I'll just start making a list of things you might need."

"If you would please raise your arms, my lady," Soma said in a toneless voice.

She took my measurements, studying my body with a dispassionate gaze. Her thin mouth turned down at what she saw. No doubt I wasn't what she expected for a princess.

I glanced at the mirror and looked quickly away. What beauty I'd possessed had been worn away from war, malnourishment, and months living in the frozen wild. My body was all edges, from knobby knees to sharp elbows.

My hands curled and I felt the calluses on my palms. *I might not be beautiful*, I thought. *But I am strong.*

I followed Nariko's path into the bedroom with my eyes. That space was another large affair, perfectly appointed with an overstuffed canopy bed and a set of bedside tables. It was covered in blue tile, though I couldn't quite make out its geometric pattern from my vantage point.

On the far wall of the bedroom, I could just see a set of double doors leading out to one of the palace's many gardens. Pale chiffon curtains were drawn over the open doors—identical to the set covering the doors behind me. The fabric danced in a gentle breeze.

With parchment and quill in hand, Nariko took careful note of everything in the room. She even opened one of the bedside tables, scribbling down a list of what she saw. *Odd*, I thought, and then it hit me. I was being searched.

I almost laughed. It was being done so casually, so openly, that I could have kicked myself for not realizing it sooner. Queen Ozura hadn't sent Nariko to serve me. She'd been sent to spy. I knew I should be angry, but it was all so ridiculous, I couldn't muster the emotion. Anyway, making a fuss wouldn't change anything. They'd simply come back when I was away, only then they'd think I had something to hide.

So I played along with the fiction that Lady Nariko was

organizing a list of things I might need. I was sure I really would end up with all kinds of frivolous necessities, so it wasn't a complete waste. I suppressed a smile, wondering what the prim-looking Lady Nariko thought about all the weapons littering the room.

As I thought it, Nariko slid her hand under my pillow and jerked back with a hiss. Clutching one hand to her chest, she flipped the pillow off the bed. The small dagger I'd stashed there had slipped partway out of its sheath.

"Are you all right?" I asked dryly.

Nariko started and spun, not quite meeting my eyes. "Oh, yes. Just a cut." She blew on her palm like she was cooling a sting.

"I'm finished, my lady," Soma said, rolling up her measuring tape and stepping away. "I will take your measurements to the clothier so he can begin making your new garments." Her eyes flicked to the scar on my throat. "Shall I tell him you prefer a high neckline?"

"No." My voice came out harsher than I'd intended and one of Soma's dark eyebrows rose. My hand went immediately to my neck, where a ridge of puckered flesh hooked around the nub of my right collarbone. I traced the familiar outline as it disappeared over my shoulder, and blew out a long breath, forcing my hand down. "No," I repeated, softer this time.

Soma nodded once, something almost like respect in her eyes. She turned and, without a backward glance, walked out of the room.

I cocked an incredulous look at Nariko, who laughed softly and came to my side. "It's not personal," Nariko whispered. "Soma treats everyone that way."

"It's a wonder she's still employed."

Nariko shrugged. "She's an old friend of Queen Ozura," she said, handing me a robe.

I took it, but my eyes did a double take on the pristine white silk. Momentary confusion clouded my mind as my brain struggled to process what my eyes had seen. Or hadn't seen. *Something is off...*

I blinked the thought away and refocused on what Nariko was saying.

"Your clothes should be ready in a few days," she said, sitting on one of the room's many couches. "If you have any color or fabric preferences, simply let Soma know."

I nodded, sinking onto the seat beside Nariko.

"You're lucky," she continued. "The royal clothier has the best designs. I would love to be dressed by him, even just—" Nariko pressed her palm to her chest in apparent longing.

Her injured palm.

Alarm bells went off in my head, because as I watched her tuck a lock of hair behind her ear, I saw no blood on her dress. Not even a drop.

"You're a healer," I said, cutting Nariko off midsentence.

Nariko's dark eyes darted to mine. "I am," she replied. "It's one of the reasons Queen Ozura sent me to wait on you. After all your months in the wild, she thought you might want a polish."

"What am I, a set of silver?"

Nariko gave an unladylike snort. "It was meant as a kindness."

"All right. Well . . . thanks," I said, struggling to find a reason for the queen's benevolence.

Nariko bit her lip, her gaze dropping to my neck. "I could take away your scars. If you want."

I clenched my hands together to keep from slapping them protectively over my neck. "No."

Nariko flushed. "I'm sorry, Your Highness. I didn't mean to overstep. I was just—"

"No, it's all right," I said, stemming the hurried flow of Nariko's panicked apology. "I'm not offended. I know most women would feel self-conscious, but the scars . . . they're not flaws. They're reminders of what the Shazir took from me, from the world, when they killed my parents."

"I understand."

Nariko's tone was so heartfelt I frowned. "Did you know my parents?"

"Only by reputation, but . . . the Shazir are a threat we all fear."

Something leaden fell into my gut. "What do you mean? Shazir Province is on the other side of the continent."

A grimace marred Nariko's doll-like face. "They *were* on the other side of the continent."

"What do you mean?"

Nariko licked her lips. "When your family was in Shazir Province and the earthquake hit Mount Khan-e-Fet—"

"It was a natural disaster," I said in a low voice. "My family had nothing to do with it."

"I know, but the earthquake destroyed the Shrine of the Day Lord—the god's own home. To the Shazir, it was an attack."

I waved a hand, dismissing the Shazir and their madness, their hate. They rejected the truth of the Two-Faced God, that the Day Lord was but one-half of the deity, the bright face to Lady Night's darkness. "My mother wasn't a witch, and my father wasn't an earth witch. He was a healer. The greatest healer this empire has ever seen. It was his power that saved Queen Ozura's life when she was pregnant with her youngest son, and everyone knew it. How could they have possibly caused the earthquake?"

"I know. Believe me, I know . . . but your father was one of the leaders of the Shadow Guild. Witches were blamed."

And your parents were murdered. Nariko didn't say the words. She didn't need to. They hung unspoken in the air between us.

"Afterward, the Shazir began leaving their province in droves, some to the army, others to the temples," Nariko said. "Most priests of the Day Lord in Bet Naqar are Shazir now. Or they sympathize with them. Now everything bad that happens, from wildfires to illness, they blame on Lady Night, the witches who carry her blood, and the Shadow Guild that protects us."

"And people believe them? They honestly think witches are causing a drought?"

Nariko's shoulders lifted in a helpless shrug. "Didn't used to. But the monsoon rains are failing, and the Mashra Desert is expanding. Refugees are pouring into the city, desperate and destitute."

I scowled. "But it's impossible. No one has that kind of power."

"No. But it's easier to blame a person than it is to blame a god."

Nariko's words rang in the hollow space in my chest. "So the Shazir are here."

"Yes."

"Is the Shadow Guild doing anything?" The guild was made not only to facilitate the trade of magical services, but also to protect the witches of Vishir.

"There isn't really anything they can do," Nariko replied, shaking her head. "The Shazir haven't done anything but talk."

"They killed my parents." I clamped my jaw shut, pressing my lips together to contain my bottomless, unquenchable anger.

"Even so. They are here, and things are . . . tense. Tense enough that anyone who isn't known to be a witch, like myself, might be better off keeping their powers secret."

Nariko gave me such a serious look; I felt a bitter smile rise to my lips. The Shazir spent five days torturing me to make me confess my powers. If they couldn't beat the truth out of me when I was a teenager, they were unlikely to do so now.

The ghost of a little boy appeared at the edge of my vision. He sprinted full tilt across the dressing room, arms wide like he was pretending to fly. Something in me eased to see him, and for a wild second, I considered dipping into my magic if only to hear his voice. I looked back at Nariko. "Then I suppose it's a blessing that I'm not a witch."

Nariko nodded and stood, smoothing her hands over her dress. "I'll ring for dinner."

I watched Nariko stride into the adjoining parlor, where a discreet bellpull hung from the ceiling. She tugged on the rope, no doubt letting the kitchen staff know food was desired. My stomach growled, and I suddenly realized I hadn't eaten all day. I'd been too busy.

I hadn't even had time to arrange for the letters to be sent. "Nariko. I wrote some letters this morning, for the Council of Viziers. Could you make sure they're delivered? I've left them in the study."

Nariko stiffened. She turned back to me, wide-eyed. "I'm not sure that would be wise, Your Highness."

I smiled at her discomfort. "Please, Nariko. You've seen me naked. I think you can call me Askia."

A slight laugh wormed out of Nariko's lips before she schooled her features and came back into the dressing room. "My lady . . . Askia, I don't think it's wise for you to send letters directly to the council. You are an unmarried woman."

"I'm also the rightful queen of Seravesh. I need these men on my side if I have any chance of getting the army I need to take back the Frozen Crown."

Nariko's brow furrowed with thought. "It would be better if one of your men wrote on your behalf."

"Only Captain Illya speaks Vishiri, and he can't write it. Please, Nariko."

Nariko blew out a deep breath. "I'll see what I can do."

"Thank you."

Soma shuffled through the parlor door, and for a moment I thought she was bringing food. Instead, she carried an armful of gowns. Behind her, Illya and two of my guards came in, arms laden with more clothing and several trunks filled with Lady-Night-knew-what.

"Oh, perfect," Nariko said, lifting the garments from Soma's arms and hanging them up in the empty closets.

I took in the array of jewel-colored fabric, struck dumb momentarily. "What is all this?"

"Queen Ozura asked the royal clothier to send you a selection of suitable gowns to wear while your wardrobe is being made." Nariko petted the train of a cerulean dress with a loving glint in her eye. She turned back to me and beamed. "Your other necessities are in those trunks," she said, pointing to the four trunks my guards had deposited on the far wall of the dressing room. The ghost-boy ran back into the room, bouncing on his toes as he inspected the boxes. Why did he look so familiar? The urge to tap into my powers was overwhelming, but I mastered it. I couldn't risk the tether turning my skin to ice.

Still the boy smiled like he was ready for an adventure, but his smile—it was Iskander's smile. Recognition finally tore through me. Lady Night have mercy. This little ghost-boy was Prince Tarek, Iskander's brother. Vitaly appeared beside the boy. He gave me a mournful look and bent, whispering something in Tarek's ear. His smile faded. He glanced regretfully at me and shrugged before disappearing.

The small hairs on my neck rose, and I turned to find Illya's gaze hard on my face, watching me watch the ghosts. I let one of my eyebrows rise in question, and in challenge, wondering all over again how much my men knew. And with Vitaly's betrayal still fresh on my mind, I wondered how much was safe for them to know?

7

Illya was waiting for me in the door of the small yellow-tiled parlor after I dressed. He kept his face carefully blank as I sat at the little table. Without words, he posted himself behind my seat. His shadow stretched across the table, so long and still I could've told time by it.

He'd seen something, I knew, but what he thought, I wasn't sure. It should have worried me—the fear of exposure—but having him at my back brought unexpected comfort.

Nariko sat beside me, just as three white-robed women entered from a service door across the room. Each carried a tray filled with food and plates, which they arranged carefully and silently on the table before leaving again.

My eyes clapped onto the food laid out before me: namely, the red-glazed tagine that took up the center of the table. The clay cooking pot was lidded by what looked like an upside-down ceramic funnel. Wafting out of the top of the conical lid was the heavenly smell of *mesouf*.

The traditional Vishiri dish instantly reminded me of my father. My family traveled so much, we never really had a home to call our own. My father, unusual in every way, was more than capable in the kitchen. Whenever Sevilen was feeling nostalgic for home, he would unpack his tagine and make mesouf.

Nariko removed the tagine's top, revealing a glistening mound of couscous. Boiled in broth and butter until tender, the grain was tossed with garlic-seasoned chicken and chopped carrots, tomatoes, chickpeas, and sliced zucchini. Garlic and turmeric, paprika and cumin commingled in the air until I was sure I was salivating.

With almost agonizing slowness, Nariko served first me and then herself. My hand itched to grab the fork, but she was still holding the serving spoon. Nariko looked nervously from me to the empty plate on the other side of the table, the serving spoon hovering in midair.

I rolled my eyes in understanding and glanced over my shoulder at Illya. "Would you care to join us, Captain?"

"No." He said the word with such distaste, I might have been offering him beetles.

I shrugged. His loss. I picked up my fork as one of my guards marched through the door.

"Your Highness, Prince Iskander is here. He's waiting in the sitting room."

Though my guard spoke Seraveshi, Nariko perked at the sound of the prince's name. "What is it?"

"Apparently, Prince Iskander is in the sitting room." I set down my fork with regret. "I should go meet him."

A pained, almost panicked look crossed Nariko's face. "But you can't, my lady," Nariko gasped. "It's not appropriate. Unmarried men and women are not to socialize in private."

"How can it be private if you're there?"

Nariko tsked at the mocking laughter in my voice. "Only a blood relative can chaperone, preferably your mother."

"Well, that's not likely," I muttered, my annoyance easing when Nariko winced. "Look. Nariko, I know you're trying to help, but I'm going to see Prince Iskander. He's the only reason I'm here, and the only ally I have in Vishir."

"But it's almost dark," Nariko protested.

"Because the sun can prevent something untoward from happening?" Rising, I tossed down my napkin. "You may remain here if you like, Lady Nariko, but I'm going to say hello."

Nariko opened her mouth, but Illya and I were already walking past. I pushed open the sitting room door and looked across the gold-tiled space to where couches and armchairs were arranged around an enormous wooden coffee table. Iskander was sprawled in one of the armchairs, staring absently at the teal-tiled ceiling. He started when I entered, pulling up with a grin.

I smiled, surprised at how happy I was to see him. "Hello, Prince Iskander. I hope you haven't been waiting long."

"No, not at all. I only wanted to see how you were getting on."

"I'm fine, thank you," I said, taking the chair next to his. "Your mother sent a couple of her women to tend to me, and I'm afraid I've had no choice but to relax."

"I'm glad you're enjoying yourself," he said with a note of dry humor in his voice. "I must say, the rest seems to be agreeing with you."

I was saved the trouble of having to respond to the backhanded compliment by Nariko entering, with an overladen tea tray. Whatever unease Nariko felt about Prince Iskander's presence was disguised perfectly. She crossed the room and curtsied gracefully to Iskander, who mostly ignored her.

"Please, join us, Lady Nariko," I said. I almost invited Illya, too, but he was eyeing Iskander with such a loaded expression the invitation died on my lips.

"Thank you, my lady," Nariko said. "How nice of you to visit, my lord." There was a hint of coolness in Nariko's tone that voiced her disapproval.

Iskander's lips twitched with a slight smile. "I came to deliver good news. My mother says the menagerie will be sending you an invitation tomorrow. If all goes well, she will formally introduce you at court this week."

"Excellent," I said, relief filling me. "Did she say when we're meeting?"

"No, but most of my father's wives don't wake before noon, so it won't be early."

I couldn't care less what time it was. I would meet them at midnight if they asked it. Anything to help my cause. "What are they like, your father's wives? I remember almost nothing about them."

"Probably because they don't matter," Iskander replied with a careless shrug. "They are, by and large, silly, spoiled women who think of nothing but themselves and their clothing allowance."

The condescension in Iskander's voice made my eyebrows rise. I looked to Nariko for confirmation, but she ducked her head and poured the tea. "They can't all be frivolous."

"They really are," he replied. "Only my mother matters."

I frowned, then remembered what Iskander told me about the menagerie's politics on our journey to Bet Naqar. Queen Ozura was unlikely to allow rivals in her own domain. I wondered how long her reach was, from behind the locked doors of the menagerie. "What is she like? Queen Ozura, I mean."

Iskander's expression softened. "She's . . . different. Strong. Kind of like you."

"Stay for dinner," I said on impulse. "Tell me about her."

Beside me Nariko squeaked, fumbling her cup and dribbling tea all over the tile. I shot her a look only to find her vigorously shaking her head.

"It wouldn't be appropriate, my lady."

I flashed Iskander a humorless smile. "Lady Nariko has been trying to remind me of the finer points of Vishiri etiquette."

"How's that going?" he asked.

"Truthfully? It's a complete waste of my time and her effort."

Iskander chuckled and threw Nariko a wicked smile. "All you can do is try, Lady Nariko. My mother will forgive you for failing. Eventually." Nariko's face went crimson and he turned to me with a shrug. "She's not wrong, you know. The court will talk."

"I'm here for an army, not to play court politics," I said, tossing the warning aside. "Are you staying, or what?"

"Oh, I'm definitely staying."

8

I ran my fingers across the water-smooth texture of my silk
sleeves. The indigo fabric wrapped around my thin frame,
magically softening it into feminine curves. White petals
were embroidered on the full skirt. They seemed to fall
from the fabric, trailing down to the hem as if caught in a breeze.
It was, bar none, the finest piece of clothing I'd ever worn.

Between the dress and the hour it had taken to wrestle my
burgundy hair into submission, I had never looked so pretty.
Perhaps even beautiful. But beauty had always seemed like a
frail sort of weapon. Still, any weapon was better than none, I
thought as my eyes flicked to the scar at my neck.

I'd told Nariko it was a reminder, but not just for me. It would
also remind the emperor of what happened the last time he stood
by and did nothing. I sent a silent prayer to the Two-Faced God
that the emperor wouldn't make the same mistake twice.

"It's time, my lady."

I turned away from the cold, unforgiving woman in the
mirror and left the dressing room, tugging Nariko along in my
wake. Illya waited for me in the study, bent over the desk where
I'd written my letters.

He froze when he saw me. His gray eyes searched me, like

for a moment he wasn't sure who I was. "Are you ready?" he asked, and I felt the weight behind those simple words.

Today was the start. If all went well, Queen Ozura would formally invite me to court. I would be free to find allies and gather support, but free also to fail.

Vitaly's ghostly form stepped out of the shadows at the edge of the room. His colorless eyes burned with determination. I knew because that determination was in me, too, right down to my bones. Forbidding me from failing. I nodded. "Yes. I'm ready."

Nariko led me, Illya, and a pair of guards through the airy halls of the palace. The long, lofty corridors were tiled in bright geometric patterns, and everywhere there was light. Tall windows studded the walls beside wide open doorways, which let in the slight breeze coming off the coast.

The palace of Bet Naqar was built almost like a beehive, with corridors and rooms offset against pockets of open space for fountains and footpaths and gardens. It was another way Seravesh differed from Vishir. In Seravesh, you had to guard against the elements, hide behind thick stone and narrow windows, lest the cold find you. Here, there was no need to fight the weather. It was welcomed into your home like a cherished friend.

Two guards came to attention when we approached the closed doors of the menagerie, barring our way with a dramatic crossing of their spears. I shot a glance at Illya. He knew no men were allowed within, but he still looked mutinous. Only when he and my men stepped aside were Nariko and I allowed to enter.

The doors opened into a sitting room that was as big as the Great Hall in my castle. A wall of crenellated doorways overlooked a lush garden whose flowers filled the air with the scent of jasmine. Beyond the flowers, I could make out a tall hedge wall that marked the edge of a maze.

On the opposite wall, another line of doorways led to a pool of crystal clear water deep enough to swim in. As I thought it, a woman appeared, surfacing from beneath the water. She swam lazy laps about the pool, her dark skin glistening in the sun.

Before I could ask Nariko who the swimmer was, three women entered from a door across the room. Two were unfamiliar, but I'd recognize the leonine face of Queen Ozura anywhere.

My mind blanked as surprise mixed with outrage. Three queens. Only three out of seventeen had bothered to come. After everything my father had done for Vishir, they couldn't even deign to see me.

Nariko dipped into a low curtsy, her movement jolting me out of my momentary shock. I schooled my features, hoping no one saw. The other queens seemed oblivious, but a slow smile spread across Ozura's face.

"Askia, thank you for visiting. You honor us with your presence," Ozura said.

"The honor is entirely mine, Queen Ozura," I lied in a colorless voice.

"Please. In this place, you are among equals. You must call me Ozura. Will you sit?"

When I nodded, Ozura led us to a circle of chairs and couches in the center of the room. There was a low table in the middle, overflowing with tea and fruit and pastries. Ozura sat in a high-backed chair upholstered in gold brocade and motioned for me to sit beside her. The chair indicated was so low I might as well have been sitting on the floor. I had to angle my long legs off to the side, or else my knees would have scraped my chin. Nariko, who stood behind Ozura's chair, caught my eye and gestured subtly to my skirt. I tugged the fabric down to cover my ankles.

"Allow me to reintroduce you to the other queens," Ozura said, gesturing to the woman sitting on my left. "This is Marya."

Easily in her seventies, she was by far the oldest of the emperor's wives. Marya smiled warmly at me and took out some knitting from a basket beside the couch. On the divan opposite

Marya was Hiriku. She had thick black hair and a beautiful oval face, though her expression was marred by her bottom lip protruding like a child's pout.

"We have met before," Hiriku said, her voice hot with outrage. "It was after you came back from Shazir Province—"

"Hiriku," Marya scolded.

"What? It wasn't so long ago. And she stayed with us for ages. I thought she would be a new wife. I brushed her hair for hours and hours," Hiriku said, oblivious to the glares of the other queens, to the stiffening of my spine, to the scream that was trying to claw out of my throat.

"Enough," Ozura said, her voice sharp enough to silence Hiriku.

"There's no reason to discuss such dark times," Marya said, squeezing my hand.

Dark times indeed. After the Shazir killed my parents, after they . . . did what they did to me, they sent me back to Bet Naqar with a horse trader selling stallions to the emperor's Khazan Guard. Broken beyond words, they bundled me up and shunted me away to heal in the menagerie. I supposed it had been a kindness, but I remembered so little of that time I couldn't say for sure. Lady Night have mercy. Why were we discussing this?

"The other wives were detained," Ozura said, stepping smoothly into the awkward silence that followed. "They do send their regards, but I hope you're not offended by their absence."

I was offended, and I let that little anger draw me back to the present, away from the internal chasm that yawned open whenever the Shazir were mentioned. Vitaly flickered into existence behind Hiriku. His presence was all the reminder I needed of why I was here.

"The world outside the menagerie holds little interest for them," Ozura continued, looking out the doors to where the woman still swam in the pool. I got the impression Ozura was trying to give me time to recover, and I was grateful in spite of myself.

Yet there was no softness in Ozura's eyes when she looked back at me. No pity either. I liked her better for it. "You look very well, but my, have you grown up fast. It seems like yesterday you were a child, running around the palace, playing with the boys."

Since this was a rather charitable description of my interaction with the palace children, I said nothing but managed a smile.

"How old are you?" Ozura asked.

"Twenty-one."

"Time to be married," Hiriku said, helping herself to a pastry.

"Past time." Marya arched an eyebrow at me over her knitting. "It's a tragedy, a pretty creature like you. How did your grandfather keep the suitors away?"

"Was it because of the Shazir?" Hiriku asked, looking at me with thoughtless puppy eyes until Marya poked her with a knitting needle. "Ow," she hissed. "I was only asking."

"No," I said, cutting Hiriku off before she could say anything else about the Shazir. "My grandfather was picky about such arrangements, but I was engaged once."

"Oh?" Ozura said. She leaned back into her chair, transforming it into a throne by the force of her presence. "Do tell."

"I was promised to a prince from the Kingdom of Raskis." I shifted, impatience racing down my spine.

"Oh? What was he like?" Marya asked.

"I don't know," I confessed. "I never met him. Roven invaded Raskis just after the engagement was announced."

"Does your prince serve Emperor Radovan now?" Marya asked.

I bit down hard on my tongue. How could they not know what Radovan was doing? Couldn't these silly, sheltered women see Radovan wouldn't stop with Seravesh, or Idun? Vishir was the ultimate prize.

"No. After Roven invaded, the king's daughter Princess Eliska gave herself to Radovan and became his wife in exchange for Raskis's freedom. There was peace for a while, but Radovan eventually killed her. Raskis revolted. They held Roven at bay for a time but not long. The entire royal family was killed."

Marya frowned. "What terrible luck you have."

I frowned right back. Luck had nothing to do with it. Besides, what did a failed engagement matter when Roven was systematically wiping kingdom after kingdom off the map?

"Is it true Emperor Radovan has made you an offer?" Hiriku asked.

"Yes, but I rejected it."

Hiriku's jaw dropped. "Why?"

"Why?" My eyebrows rose. "You mean aside from the fact he helped my cousin kill our grandfather and seize control of my kingdom? Perhaps because his armies are crawling through my country, raping and burning as they go. Perhaps because he's already killed six wives."

"Are you a witch, Askia?" Ozura asked.

I jerked back in surprise. And suspicion. Why did she want to know? And why did it matter now, in the context of Radovan and his many dead wives?

Ozura leaned back in her chair, her amber eyes sharp and appraising. I knew she was weighing my every word, my every expression.

I almost said yes, but the confession died on my lips. For all Vishir pretended to cherish their witches, this was the land that birthed the Shazir. And my parents died to protect my secret. "No."

"Oh?" Ozura tilted her head to the side, her eyes narrowing ever so slightly in disbelief. Tarek poked out his head from behind Ozura's chair. He smiled at me in childish gloating like he knew something I didn't.

"Many people assume because my father was a witch, I must be one too."

"Hmm." Ozura drew herself up, sitting straight-backed and aloof. I looked away, feeling like I had failed some kind of test.

"Well, now you're here, we can help you find a suitable match," Marya said, seeming oblivious to Ozura's cool demeanor.

"Though I must tell you, my son will not be on that list," Ozura said with a little smile.

"What?" My mind went blank. "No. Ozura, please. I have no desire to marry Prince Iskander."

"Really? Then why did you dine with him privately last night?"

"He's an ally—"

"Didn't Lady Nariko tell you how it would look?" Ozura pinned me to the spot with the strength of her barely suppressed anger.

"No." I hurried to say when Nariko blanched. "She did say it would be considered inappropriate by Vishiri standards, but—"

"But you invited him anyway. And now the families of the women who will marry him are looking to me, wondering why he is publicly shaming them by going to bed with you."

"We didn't go to bed," I sputtered, feeling like the floor had dropped out beneath me and whatever control I'd come here with fell with it. "Lady Nariko was there the whole time, as was the captain of my guard."

"Well, I know that, dear, but why should anyone else believe it?" The anger in Ozura's voice banked into exasperated curiosity so quick, my mind stumbled.

"It'll be all right," Marya said, smiling as though I hadn't just been shamed by the most powerful woman in Vishir. "We were all young once."

"Indeed," Ozura said dryly. "There are things you're going to have to learn if you're to live here, Askia. Chief among them is the proper place of women in regard to men. Unmarried men and women cannot be friends. It invites gossip, and gossip has ended more powerful women than you before." She half turned in her chair and gestured carelessly to Nariko.

Nariko reached into her pocket and, without looking at me, removed a sheaf of letters. *My* letters. The letters that could save my kingdom if only they reached the right people. Ozura snatched them out of Nariko's hands and dropped them on the table with an audible flop. A low ringing sound began in my ears.

"It's highly inappropriate for you to write to a married man. You must be properly introduced first, and even then, I wouldn't recommend it."

My embarrassment cooled into something far worse: cold and uncontrollable anger. I curled my hands into fists, digging my nails into my palms.

"We will help you, of course," Marya said. "With your mother gone, someone has to. Oh, and I was so fond of her." Her eyes went to the scar across my neck and flicked away again dismissively.

"And what did your fondness do?" My voice came out in a dry shaking rasp. "What did your regard mean when her life hung in the balance?" I met Ozura's cold eyes and hurled the next word like a slap. "Nothing. Because that's all your precious Vishiri manners allow you to be. I'm not here for a husband. I'm not here hoping to call this cage my home. I am here because my people are dying. So don't waste my time telling me you're ashamed of my behavior." I stood, my eyes trained on Ozura, on the only woman in Vishir who supposedly mattered. "I'm ashamed of you, sitting here while half the world burns. Who will help you when Radovan comes?"

I spun on my heel and walked away from the queens, from the outrage on Ozura's face and the shock on Nariko's. I stalked past the fear in Tarek's eyes and the despair in Vitaly's, and fled.

9

I felt my men exchange uneasy glances with one another as I stormed past them, but I was too far gone to care. The walk back to my rooms wasn't long enough to take the edge off my anger. I tossed open the doors and stalked through the rooms until finally reaching the parlor.

On the table, sitting beside the remains of my breakfast, was one of the letters I'd planned to send. Nariko had helped me craft it, given me the proper form of address for the leaders of the Khazan Guard. The sight of it brought me up short. My mouth twisted with the bitter feeling of betrayal.

"What happened, my lady?" Illya stood beside me, his gray eyes flat and hard.

The question and the stare almost broke something in me. Disappointment and embarrassment pushed against my anger, but I couldn't give into it yet. Not in front of Illya. I was perversely pleased when Nariko appeared in the doorway. It gave me a reason to cling to anger.

"Why are you here?" My voice was cold enough to shatter steel, and Nariko had the good sense to blanch.

"Queen Ozura said I am to serve you."

"You mean she sent you to spy on me. To spread lies about me."

Illya rounded on Nariko. "What have you done?" he asked in a voice that rumbled like the movement of mountains.

"She kept the letters I was sending. Rather than giving them to people who could help us, she gave them all to Queen Ozura."

"I was trying to help," Nariko said in a tremulous voice. "It isn't appropriate for an unmarried woman to write to a man. It would ruin your chances at court. They'd all be laughing at you right now if I'd done as you asked."

"So you thought it would be better to have the queens laugh at me?"

"Trust me, they weren't laughing. Queen Ozura said—"

"I don't give a damn what Queen Ozura said. It's what *you* said that concerns me. It's because of your words she called me a whore."

Illya took a half step forward, a growl reverberating in his chest. Nariko jumped back and knocked into the wall. She gulped but didn't run. Instead, she stood her ground, balling up her tiny fists. If I had been in a better mood I would have applauded her; it took backbone to stand up to Illya when he looked at you that way. Backbone many seasoned soldiers didn't have.

"I never called you that."

"No?" I stepped closer, looking down on the little woman. "But what did you say when they did? Nothing. I don't know why I expected anything different. That's all you Vishiri women are good for."

Hurt blossomed in Nariko's eyes, and I was dully surprised to find I couldn't rejoice in it. All I felt was bitterness and that scorching anger. I looked to Illya and found him watching me. "We're going to the training yard. I need to hit something."

"No, don't," Nariko pleaded. "It will only make things worse."

I ignored her. "I'm getting changed."

"What will you wear?" Nariko asked with the air of someone grasping for a valid argument.

"The same thing I wore when I arrived."

"No. You can't go walking around half naked. You'll offend everyone who sees you."

"Watch me." I got halfway to the dressing room when a hand closed around my bicep and spun me around. Illya yanked me toward him. I stumbled against his chest before regaining my footing and pulled back. I made it perhaps two inches before he grasped my other arm, holding me tight.

Electricity shocked through my body. Separated from him by a matter of inches, his scent caught in my nose. The smell of cold wind and pine forests instantly quelled my anger. It was the scent of home, the home I was failing.

Illya must have seen it—my shame and my guilt, because when he spoke, his voice was gentle. "Are you determined to do this?"

"Yes," I breathed.

"Then do it right." He looked at me for a moment longer, searching for something, then stepped away. The world seemed to shift when he released me. I braced one hand against the doorway to steady myself. "Wait here."

He left the room, his steps echoing in the silence between Nariko and I.

"Are you all right?" Nariko asked, looking shaken.

The feeling of Illya's hands lingered on my skin. I pushed it away. "Yes. Thank you for asking."

Nariko nodded, turning toward the door. She paused on the threshold, looking back at me. "I really was only trying to help. And I don't approve of how Ozura ambushed you with the letters and about Prince Iskander. But she is my queen." She trailed off with a helpless shrug. "I know our lives seem small to you. Maybe they are, but that doesn't make us foolish. Or powerless."

I thought she might say more. Instead, Nariko gave a small,

regretful smile and walked out of the room. I watched her go, wondering if I'd ever see her again.

Illya returned a half hour later bearing a handful of slightly rumpled clothes. He set them on the parlor table with a meaningful nod and strode from the room. I dubiously took the clothes into the dressing room. Standing in front of the full-length mirror, I held the garments up to my body. The result did not inspire any confidence of sartorial sophistication, but I knew I wasn't getting out of my rooms without putting them on.

With my freedom in mind, I shucked off the beautiful blue gown and stepped into the new clothes. The pants were halfway up my thighs when I realized they weren't made for women. I wriggled them over my hips, sucking in a deep breath before lacing them shut. I pulled on the shirt and long yellow waist sash before looking at the mirror. The sight made me snort.

Turning away from the ridiculous image, I yanked on my boots and grabbed my sword. If looking like an idiot got me out of these cagelike rooms, then so be it.

Illya and my other guards were waiting in the sitting room I'd apparently shamed myself in by having tea with Iskander the day before. Illya, who was giving out a work rotation, paused when I entered. He looked me up and down, his lips twitching with what might have been a smile.

One of the guards guffawed. "You look . . . nice?" Misha was the oldest of my close guard. At six foot six, he was a bear of a man with arms as big as my thighs. His bushy orange beard couldn't hide the grin spreading across his face.

"Oh, shut up, Misha," I said, trying not to smile.

"Don't scowl, my lady, your face might get stuck that way. Who'll marry ya then?"

"A fool, but that was always going to be the case."

A booming laugh burst out of Misha's chest, making something inside me ease. Misha was like a much older brother. He might needle me occasionally, but he always knew how to make me feel better.

"Am I presentable? Can we go?"

Illya shrugged, but it was Misha who responded. "Oh yeah. You look dainty, refined, and deadly as a flowerpot. You'll fit right in with these Vishiri men."

SWORDPLAY ALWAYS ENTRANCED ME. THERE WAS SOMETHING IN the physical exertion, the power of meeting an opponent blow for blow, the graceful sweep of the blade that lulled me into an almost meditative state of hyperawareness. Even though Illya was beating me with embarrassing ease, I felt calmer than I'd been in weeks.

Illya pressed me backward until my feet scraped the edge of the ring. I sidestepped left and parried, but Illya was already moving. With the speed of a trap snapping shut, Illya slid under my guard and batted my arm away. He flicked the tip of his sword to my breast. A perfect kill point.

"Mind your footing. You're tripping yourself up," he said.

I nodded, panting too hard to speak, and grabbed my sword from the dirt-packed floor of the training ring. Wiping the sweat from my brow, I looked around and found that a small crowd had gathered.

The garrison was located to the west of the palace proper. It was a giant complex of barracks, training yards, and armories that housed the emperor's elite army known as the Khazan Guard. Vishiri soldiers, living and dead, milled about on the edges of the ring, watching my men and me work with bemused expressions. I somehow doubted I was living up to their ideas of royal behavior.

I sheathed my sword and walked over to a table at the edge of the ring, acutely aware of the audience. Misha stood guard nearby. He relaxed when I approached and ladled me a cup of water from the bucket on the table.

"You're improving, my lady," he said.

I waved away the compliment. "How can you tell? I didn't even last two minutes."

"No one ever lasts two minutes against the captain."

"I believe it, he's amazing," a voice said from behind Misha.

I craned my neck and spotted Prince Iskander leaning against the rough mud-brick wall of one of the buildings lining the yard.

"I didn't know you spoke Seraveshi," I replied.

"Not well," he said, switching back to Vishiri and pushing off the wall. We watched Illya in silence for a few moments. He'd called two other guards into the ring and was fighting them simultaneously. And winning. "I think he might give my father's swordmaster a run for his money."

"I'd like to see that fight."

"Me too." He paused, giving me the side-eye. "You're pretty good too."

"Thanks," I said, trying not to bridle at the modifier.

A wicked smile tugged at the corner of his lips. He nodded to the ring. "Care for a go?"

I almost said yes until I caught the warning on Misha's face. He gave Iskander a dubious look and shook his head behind the prince's back. Just as well, I thought. Breaking Iskander's arm wasn't going to do me any favors. "Ask me tomorrow," I said. "I'm exhausted."

He nodded, looking slightly put out. "Can I at least walk you back to your rooms?"

My eyes narrowed. "Depends. How much trouble will I get in for daring to walk with you?"

He held up his hands in mock surrender. "It's perfectly proper for me to escort you to your door. I just won't . . . you know, go through it."

I grunted my consent and waited for my guards to gather their things. When everyone was accounted for, Iskander led us out of the ring, through the labyrinthine streets of the garrison, and back into the palace.

The aqua-and-gold corridor we walked down seemed to be one of the palace's main arteries. Men and women passed us in small groups, watching us with bright-eyed curiosity. But there was something knowing in their whispers that made my hackles rise.

Iskander glanced toward me before taking a deep, bracing breath. "My mother told me about your meeting."

I closed my eyes against the gentleness in his voice, the pity. The sound of my guards murmuring to one another made my anger slip. I'd failed them utterly.

"What happened, Askia?"

I could've smacked Iskander for the reproach in his voice. Too bad the hall was full. "Nothing. It was fine at first," I said. "Well, it wasn't fine. Only three of them bothered to show up, but I didn't say anything. I was sitting with your mother, and the other queens were asking me all about how I was and about the men I've been promised to, and why wouldn't I save everyone the trouble and marry Radovan. They went on and on about how, since my mother is gone, they've decided to take me in and look out for me and find me a good husband. And wouldn't it be better for everyone if I would stop sleeping with you?"

Iskander stumbled. "She said what?"

I smiled bitterly. "She said we're shaming the families of your future wives by sleeping together."

"But we're not . . . I mean. You're great but . . ."

I held up my hand to stop him from getting himself into trouble with whatever was coming after the *but*. "I told your mother we only had dinner. She believed me, by the way. Though it's funny that she didn't seem to chastise *you* for coming to my rooms."

He rubbed the back of his neck, no doubt sensing my complete lack of amusement. "I guess I shouldn't have stayed."

"No shit."

"I'm sorry, Askia. I thought . . . I hoped the rules wouldn't be . . ." He blew out a breath. "I'm sorry."

I grimaced. His apology soothed some of my anger. Some. But my story wasn't done yet. "That's not all."

"I'm afraid to ask."

"She confiscated the letters I wrote."

"Why?"

"She said it's improper for an unmarried woman to write to men."

"Day Lord have mercy," he said, weakly. "I had no idea my mother would behave so badly."

"Even so. I shouldn't have let her provoke me, and I definitely shouldn't have yelled at her."

Iskander's lips twitched. "Now, that I'd have liked to see."

I almost smiled, until I saw Ishaq round the corner with a small knot of finely dressed men. His dark gaze glittered as he took us in. "It seems the rumors are true."

My steps faltered. "Just ignore him," Iskander muttered, but I'd taken enough beatings for one day.

"What rumors?"

A smile curled the edges of Ishaq's lips. "That you're not really here for an army— What could a little girl like you do with one of those?"

"Ishaq—"

"If not an army, then what?" I asked, voice filled with so much venom it should have burned Ishaq's skin.

"The same as all young women who come to court," the vizier said, looking down his long nose at me. "A husband."

Iskander put a staying hand on my arm, but I'd had more than enough Vishiri game playing. "I normally don't respond to rumors, Ishaq, but since you've been such a dear companion, I'll set you straight. The only reason I am here is for an army. And as for what I'll do when I get it? Stay out of my way, if you don't want to find out."

I smirked as Ishaq's face went scarlet with outrage. He spun away, flouncing off with his entourage in tow. Good riddance.

"Askia," Iskander said slowly as we started back for my rooms. "I'm not sure that was wise."

"He needed to learn his place," I replied, refusing to let Iskander sour my victory. "You heard what he said."

"I heard him try to provoke you . . . and succeed. In the game of politics, the point goes to Ishaq."

"I don't have time to play politics," I said, struggling to keep my voice down. "You know that, Iskander. You saw that village."

"I know. I do. I did," he said with a heavy sigh. "But you need someone on your side. That's politics. Look, I'm sorry about dinner, and about my mother. I'll speak with her. She'll never apologize, but I think you'll need her help."

I nodded, but didn't say anything. I knew a burned bridge when I saw one. Especially when I had set the fire with my own hands.

"Tomorrow, I'd like to take you to see Lord Marr."

"Really?" I asked, remembering how kind Marr had been in Eshkaroth.

Iskander nodded. "I think he may be willing to help. He's not terribly influential," Iskander warned, like he sensed hope rising in me. "But he's smart, and he has a way of seeing through problems like no one else I know."

I had to swallow down the knot of gratitude in my throat. "Thank you, Iskander."

Iskander's smile was sad, almost regretful. "See you tomorrow, Askia."

10

I woke from a terrible night's sleep with trembling arms and legs and a bright pink sunburn on my face. After a solitary breakfast, I took a warm bath. The water went a long way to ease my muscle strain, but it had no power to quell the strain on my mind.

I hadn't realized how much I was counting on Queen Ozura's support. It never occurred to me I would receive anything but a warm reception from her. It was a stupid assumption to make. My father's magic might have saved Ozura's life, but that hadn't moved her to save his when the time came. Why would it move her to help me?

When the water turned tepid, I stepped out of the tub, shrugged on a robe, and went to the dressing room. My feet paused on the threshold.

"Lady Nariko."

Lady Nariko sat, hands folded, on one of the dressing room couches. She rose. Her face was a mask of polite attentiveness. "Good morning, my lady."

We looked at each other for a full minute, the silence stretching thin. The familiar weight of guilt settled in my stomach. I hadn't always been so quick to anger, but after what happened with the Shazir—the endless days of torture, my parents' murders—there were whole years when I'd have gladly watched the world burn. My anger could be terrible, though I would usually grow to regret my words, like I regretted them now.

"Please sit." I crossed the room but didn't join Nariko on the couch. I clenched my hands together, gathering my thoughts. "I need to apologize, Lady Nariko. I was angry at Queen Ozura, and I took some of that anger out on you. You didn't deserve to be yelled at for her actions. I'm sorry."

Nariko bit the inside of her cheek and nodded. "Thank you, but I should apologize too. I'm sorry I betrayed your trust."

I held up my hand to stop her. "It's not necessary," I said, sinking into the seat beside her. "I understand why you gave Queen Ozura the letters. You owe her your allegiance. You don't owe me anything, but I hope we can be friends."

Nariko smiled. "Me too."

"Good, because Prince Iskander is taking me to see Lord Marr this afternoon. Would you like to join us?"

She smiled, accepting the peace offering with more grace than I could have done.

After I dressed, we spent the rest of the morning chatting, mostly about Nariko's life. She had grown up in Kizuoka Province, an island far to the east. She'd only come to Bet Naqar a year ago with her aunt and uncle, who was the province's lord vizier.

As she spoke, I was struck by how calm Nariko was, a lady born and bred, everything I should have been, but wasn't. Not even the strange and tumultuous court of Bet Naqar could ruffle her. I wanted to envy the trait, but I felt drawn to it instead, like we were two sides of the same coin.

Both Nariko and Illya came to greet Iskander when he came to collect me after lunch. He gave me a questioning look, nodding toward Nariko.

I shook my head before he could ask. "Shall we go?"

"Follow me."

Iskander led us silently through the palace's long corridors to the administration wing. Located behind the onion-domed audience chamber, it was the beating heart of the Vishir Empire. The halls were crowded with advisers and scribes, nobles and even soldiers, all working in concert to ensure the continued prosperity of Vishir. Their industry made the air close and humid enough that sweat ran down my back, a suffocation amplified by the sidelong glances and hurried whispers aimed at me.

I wasn't going to be goaded—not today. But I was glad when we went up to the second floor and down an out-of-the-way corridor to Lord Marr's office.

"Welcome, welcome," Lord Marr said with a warm smile. "Please come in."

Stepping into Lord Marr's office transported me across time and space. My eyes skated over the sitting area to the walls, which were covered in shelves brimming with books and loose papers. My chest tightened looking at them, at the huge cluttered desk on the other side of the room. The office was so like my grandfather's study, I could almost smell the pine wood burning in the hearth. I turned to the window, and for one wild moment thought I would see the red roofs of Solenskaya stretched out before me.

Instead, the squat mud-brick buildings of Bet Naqar looked back at me with the towering spire of a temple looming in the distance. The city was a riot of sunlight and color, vibrant and bursting with life. So unlike what my homeland had become.

I followed Nariko to the sitting area and sank onto the couch as she served what smelled like mint tea. I accepted a cup, but forgot to drink it when Illya sat beside me. He'd never shown any interest in my attempts at diplomacy before. That he was doing so now only meant he didn't trust me to behave.

My gaze dropped to my lap and I sipped my tea.

"I heard you met with the menagerie yesterday." Lord Marr balanced his teacup in the tips of his long dark fingers and surveyed me over the rim.

Nariko sucked in a silent breath and I felt Illya's eyes slide to my face. "I did. It was kind of the queens to invite me." I made myself smile while delivering the bland answer.

"And then you went to spar with your men." There was a knowing twinkle in Lord Marr's eyes.

"You seem very well informed."

He laughed. It was a warm sound that came from deep in his chest. "I think the whole of Bet Naqar knows. Vishir has never played host to any ruler from Seravesh. Curiosity is only natural. Now they know you wield a sword and battle alongside your giants." He gestured to Illya with a smile. "It's a wondrous thing. The bards will already be writing songs about you."

I wasn't sure if *wondrous* was the right word, but I was happy the talk focused on my swordplay rather than the disastrous meeting with the queens.

"It was clever of you to introduce yourself to the Khazan Guard with such flair," Marr continued, expression going grave. "Especially since you won't have the support of the menagerie in your quest for aid."

I almost dropped my teacup. "Have they issued a statement?" I asked, taking in the genuine surprise rippling across Iskander's face.

"Nothing so official," Lord Marr replied. "The menagerie has been known to keep visitors for hours on end. You left after twenty minutes. The obvious conclusion was drawn."

"I don't believe the decision is final," Iskander said. Lord Marr didn't argue, but his expression was eloquent with doubt. "What of the administrative corps?"

Lord Marr shook his head. "I'm afraid the best you can hope for is indifference from that quarter."

"How can you say that?" I asked, utterly aghast. "You saw what Roven is doing to my people."

"I did, but I'm only one man," he said with infuriating gentleness. "I believe you when you said Radovan won't be content with Seravesh. Lord Ishaq doesn't, though, and says there's no proof that even the village we saw was burned at Radovan's hands. Because of him, Prince Vizier Enver doesn't believe you either."

"Prince Enver isn't the emperor," I countered.

"No, but the Council of Viziers runs the entire administrative corps. Their decisions affect every aspect of life in Vishir. Prince Enver sits on the council. His opinion is respected."

"Then he is blind." I snapped my mouth shut, biting my tongue so hard I tasted blood.

"Perhaps," Lord Marr allowed. "He certainly trusts Count Dobor more than he ought."

Illya leaned forward, resting his forearms on his knees. "How does Count Dobor justify his country's actions?"

"Count Dobor says Radovan's wars of conquest are simply to bring peace to the north. He intends to unite the separate kingdoms and bring stability to lands that share a uniform culture and history."

"How uniform can that culture be when we don't even speak the same language?"

Lord Marr acknowledged my point with a bow of his head. "It may sound hollow, but at the risk of offending Prince Iskander, it's the same justification Emperor Kalek used when he unified Vishir."

"No offense taken," Iskander said. "No matter how right or wrong my ancestor was, we never forced the provinces to comply to our customs, or our culture, at the expense of their own."

"Says the conqueror," I muttered before I could stop myself. I set down my tea, pushing back my temper. It wasn't getting me anywhere, better to shut up and listen.

"Nevertheless, it's the excuse Roven is using," Lord Marr said with a face so carefully bland it belied the bloody history his province had with the empire. "For better or worse, the Council of Viziers is disinclined to get involved."

"What about the emperor?" I asked.

"I am not privy to the emperor's inner thoughts. I'm aware he monitors the situation closely and holds Radovan to the pact."

I blinked. "Pact?"

"There is an informal agreement between Vishir and Roven, negotiated by Prince Enver and Count Dobor. Roven may take all lands north of Idun, as Vishir has taken all lands south. Idun must remain free."

His words smacked into the side of my face. All this way. I've come all this way for nothing.

Lord Marr's gaze flicked from me to Iskander. "You didn't know?"

"I thought you knew," the prince mumbled through white lips.

"How could I know if you didn't tell me? I've been in the wilderness for months, fighting Roven and watching my people die. I didn't have time to catch up on court gossip." I forced my muscles to lock into place so I wouldn't strike Iskander. How could he have known and said nothing?

"My lady," Illya said in low Seraveshi. "It's in the past now." His eyes held a warning: *Do not alienate your only ally.*

Iskander mumbled an apology. For Illya, for Seravesh, I exhaled my anger and accepted it.

"It's not a formal agreement," Lord Marr said bracingly.

It was formal enough, though. Formal enough to stay Armaan's hand while Radovan murdered his way across the north. I looked past Lord Marr and saw Vitaly standing by the window, nearly invisible in the sunlight. What had he died for? He turned to me, something ineffable on his face.

To get you to Vishir.

Goose bumps prickled my flesh as magic washed over me. I shoved it away and shook my head, trying to clear my mind. There had to be something I could say to save myself, save my people. Some hope I could cling to.

"Princess Eliska of Raskis also had a pact with Radovan." Illya's voice was soft, but filled with a kind of depthless intensity that drew every eye in the room. "She gave herself to him in exchange for her kingdom's freedom. Did it stop him from killing her? Did it stop him from enslaving her people?"

"No," Lord Marr replied. "And for what little it's worth, I doubt this pact will stop Radovan either. It's only a matter of time before he crosses the Peshkalor Mountains into Idun. It's just not a popular view among the lords of the administrative corps."

My eyes narrowed, sensing an opportunity. "What about the Khazan Guard?"

Marr opened his hands. "The guard believes war is inevitable. Though they won't move without the emperor's permission, the generals want to station the guard in Elon Province so they're ready to cross into Idun. So far the viziers have resisted the idea."

"Is the Khazan Guard strong enough to convince the emperor?" I asked.

"Not alone, but with the princess of Seravesh beside them?" Lord Marr shrugged. "There is a chance. I've taken the liberty of setting up a meeting for you with General Ochan tomorrow afternoon. I expressed your interest in Vishiri fighting styles, and he agreed to train you and your men. I hope I haven't overstepped."

I could have kissed him. Lord Marr had thought of everything, even an adequate cover story to explain why I was meeting with a Vishiri general. "I'm in your debt, Lord Marr."

"You may not want to thank me yet. The Khazan Guard only trains fellow Khazan guardsmen."

My brow creased. "So I'm expected to join the guard?"

"Not officially, but all supplicants who wish to join are tested."

I exchanged an uneasy glance with Illya. "What kind of test?"

"A spar. Single combat against one of their swordmasters."

My first impulse was to swear. Loudly. I bit it back. "And if I lose?"

Lord Marr shrugged, his expression solemn. "Then you will be judged."

I forced a smile at the ominous words. "Thank you, Lord Marr."

From somewhere above us, a bell tolled the four o'clock hour. Both Nariko and Iskander rose at the sound, so I followed suit, taking my cue to leave. The last gong of the bell was still ringing when Lord Marr paused at the door.

"It occurs to me, with how busy you were yesterday, you might not have heard the news?"

"What news?"

"Lord Khaljaq of Shazir Province arrived in the city yesterday afternoon for the funeral of a Shazir priest, a Brother Jalnieth. He asked after your health." He spoke softly, like he was telling me someone I loved had died.

In a way, he was. The scars on my neck and back began to itch in phantom pain and remembered terror. The scar Khaljaq gave me. "He's staying here?"

"No. The Shazir do not reside in the palace when visiting Bet Naqar. They stay in the Shrine of the Day Lord in the Temple of the Two-Faced God."

Without my consent, my eyes rose. I looked past Lord Marr, out the windows where a column of white granite marked the temple. First Count Dobor and Queen Ozura. Now the Shazir.

My enemies were circling, waiting for me to fail.

11

Nariko breezed into the parlor the next day bearing a pair of letters and a package. She set them on the table and slid into an empty chair, perfectly oblivious to the anxiety that electrified the air around me. I winced a smile, leaning over my uneaten lunch to pick up the letters.

I tore open the message from Arkady the moment I spotted his writing on the envelope. His normally harsh hand was made all the more gashlike by his obvious frustration. He and the Wolves were still in Eshkaroth, watching helplessly while the leaders of the Idunese army—such as it was—argued vainly for more resources from the Eshkaroth city maester. The endless infighting meant that it was my Black Wolves—not the Idunese defense forces—patrolling the vast mountain boarder. It simply wasn't tenable. I didn't have enough men to secure the whole range. Not against the entire Roven army. Not alone.

We needed Vishir.

I picked up the second letter without conscious thought, so preoccupied by the needs of my people, people all depending on me, I barely registered the silklike surface of the parchment beneath my fingers. Only when the seal broke with a soft crack did I look down and see who the letter was from.

"It's from Count Dobor."

Nariko looked up from her plate and frowned. "What does it say?"

"It's an invitation," I said, the words sour on my tongue. "He wants to meet with me to 'discuss my future endeavors.'"

"Ignore it."

"Are you sure?" I was relieved to hear Nariko's advice, but it was a weak, cowardly kind of relief that made me wary.

"Definitely," Nariko replied. "It is rude to say no outright in Vishir, or at least it is at court. Ignoring the invitation will imply you're not interested without either party losing face."

I nodded at the package. "Is that from Dobor too?"

"No. The package is from the royal clothier."

I tossed Count Dobor's letter onto my plate and stood, my legs wobbly from the exercises Illya had been running me through all morning. He'd given me the lunch hour to rest before we were scheduled to meet the Khazan Guard. *Rest.* With so much riding on the meeting, even the word sounded imaginary.

The package was wrapped in unremarkable brown paper, tied with rough hemp string. I pulled it free with one long tug, letting the paper fall open. Inside was a neatly folded pile of clothing. I lifted the first item, a navy-blue jacket, and underneath it, trousers. Nariko grinned and hustled me into the dressing room.

I pulled on the new clothes and stood in front of the mirror, speechless. The trousers were simple enough, dark brown linen with square leather patches sewn to the knees for added protection. But the jacket . . .

Down the entire left panel of the jacket, the wolf of Seravesh was embroidered in black thread. It stood on its hind legs, a ferocious snarl on its face. On the right panel stood the golden lion of Vishir, its body a mirror image of the wolf's. The front paws of both animals joined over my heart, not in combat, but friendship.

I let out a low whistle. The jacket perfectly symbolized my goal in coming to Vishir. It symbolized me too. I might have been the rightful queen of Seravesh, but I was also a daughter of Vishir.

"It's not terribly subtle," Nariko said.

"Soldiers don't go for subtle," I replied, steeling myself for the testing I was about to face. "I don't have time for subtlety anyway."

PRINCE ISKANDER WAS WAITING IN THE COURTYARD WHEN I AR-rived, with two men I didn't recognize.

"Princess Askia," Iskander said, taking in my outfit in one sweeping glance. "May I introduce you to General Ochan of the Khazan Guard?"

The older of the two strangers, a small graying man, bowed. His silver breastplate squeaked when he moved. "It's an honor, my lady."

"The honor is mine, General. My men and I hope to learn much from you and yours."

"We hope the same," was the neutral reply. He half turned to beckon the other stranger. This man was in his middle thirties, with a nasty scar that ran down his right cheek and neck, marring an otherwise friendly face. "This is Captain Nazir of the Order of the Lion Throne, the emperor's close guard. He will be overseeing your testing."

The captain smiled, giving me the quick once-over of one opponent studying another. "It's an honor to meet you," he said with the easy tone of a man who had nothing to worry about.

"Likewise," I replied, trying to keep the annoyance out of my voice. Tried and failed, given his growing smile.

"Come," he said.

Nazir and General Ochan led us through the courtyard. I

made it four steps before I spotted a circular brand on the back of Ochan's neck. I stumbled.

Iskander immediately reached out to steady me. "Are you all right?"

I shrugged him off but managed a nod. The circular sun of the Day Lord—the sigil of the Shazir—seared into my vision. It matched the brand on my back in every way, only writ small. Mine was the brand of a suspected witch. Ochan's was that of a devout believer. My eyes latched onto Nazir. He walked beside the general, but his hair was too long for me to see his neck clearly. Was he Shazir too?

Adrenaline burned through my veins, filling me with the childish urge to flee. Lord Marr told me only yesterday that Khaljaq, the Shazir's leader, was in Bet Naqar. Had Marr been trying to warn me?

Illya murmured something in Seraveshi that I didn't catch, but his voice blunted the edges of my panic. I found his gaze on mine. If there was a hint of worry in his eyes, his expression said something else entirely: *Get it the hell together.*

I lifted my chin. Focused on breathing, on posture and stride. When Captain Nazir glanced over his shoulder, I nodded.

"The general wasn't lying. My men are excited to spar against your guards," Nazir said. "Especially your man there," he said, gesturing to Illya.

"Men always want to test themselves against Illya. He's probably the best swordsman in the north," I said, struggling to sound normal. I wasn't sure if I succeeded, but as I walked down a short alley and into the training yard, I was sure it didn't matter.

The yard was surrounded by tall buildings, with two levels of connected balconies and a staircase that snaked from the upper balcony down to the ground. The entire yard, both the dirt-packed ground and the surrounding stands, was filled with soldiers.

My heart sank. I'd fought in many rings. Fought many soldiers and swordmasters, fought before nobles and kings. But never had any match been as important as this. And for some stupid reason, I hadn't expected witnesses.

I felt my men array themselves at my back, felt their eyes take in the waiting crowd and return to me. Their leader. Their rightful queen. The weight of their gazes . . . I couldn't fail them again.

Iskander's smile was somewhat strained from the tension in the air. "You can do this."

I didn't have a choice.

I followed Nazir to the middle of the yard. No one made a sound.

Nazir stopped in the center of the ring. "These," he said, motioning to the dozen or so men in the yard behind him, "are the Order of the Lion Throne. And these," he said, gesturing to the stands, "are the Khazan Guard. They are here to judge your worthiness to join our ranks. Know that this test is about more than strength. It is about skill and accuracy and speed. It is about honor.

"You and I will spar to the first kill point. If you step out of the ring, you lose. If you become injured, or if you are disarmed, you may surrender." His voice was mild, but something in his face made me sure surrender equaled failure.

I turned away, unclasping my sword belt and handing it off to Illya before shrugging out of my jacket. Beautiful though it was, the sleeves were tight, and I would need all the mobility I could get. And then some.

Illya's face gave nothing away. It never did, but rather than worrying me, it felt like a safe port in stormy waters. He held out my sword in both hands. "Mind your feet when you move left."

I drew the sword from the scabbard. Turned back to the ring. Nazir was waiting; the slight curve of his blade shone in the midday sun. He saluted with a flourish. I copied the gesture and had just enough time to bring up my guard before Nazir lunged.

In three steps, I knew I was outmatched. In six, I knew I would lose. Nazir was that good. His every move was a whirl of fluid precision, the sweep of his blade a dance. In under a minute I was on my heels, courting the edge of the ring. He could push me over it with laughable ease, but he didn't. I felt him check his strength, letting me fight.

And then, with sweat already pouring down my face, I knew. The point of the test wasn't to win. Because even though all soldiers knew winning a battle meant living to the end, winning and living weren't always a choice. Death would come to us all, and for soldiers that death was usually hard and painful and bitter. But what you did when you met that inevitable end mattered.

So I dug in, thigh muscles screaming, and pushed away from the edge of the ring. Because even though I was going to lose, damn it, I would lose well.

The clash of our blades was its own kind of music, as I maneuvered to the center of the ring. I feinted right, spun left, and narrowly avoided Nazir's whip-fast thrust. He slashed high and I met it, but the blazing speed with which his curved blade slid down mine made me stumble. My grip faltered. Nazir drew a small circle in the air—the smallest flick of his wrist, but that's all it took. My sword fell, landing in a puff of dirt only three feet away.

I froze. The entire crowd sucked in a breath. Magic, pulled by instinct and fear, raced through my joints like ice crackling over a pond.

"Let me help you."

Vitaly's voice filled my ears a second before I spotted him on the edge of the ring. But he wasn't alone. Other ghosts, Vishiri solders, were with him. Watching, waiting, judging.

Even if I was strong enough to accept the offer, I couldn't. Wouldn't. I'd already failed one test, the one that ended with me shouting at Ozura. If I accepted Vitaly's help, whatever it was, I'd fail them again. Because even if Nazir never guessed I cheated, I'd know. And this was a test of honor as much as anything else.

Nazir hadn't moved. He cocked one eyebrow. A question. A challenge. But I wasn't done yet. I lunged, somersaulting hard on my left shoulder. Grabbing my sword, I rolled back to my feet. I saw Nazir flash a grin, and he was on me again. Impossibly fast. Impossibly strong.

I didn't even see Nazir move when the flat of his blade connected with my right arm. Pain jangled up my bones and into my elbow. My hand went instantly numb, and my blade fell for the second time in as many minutes.

I blinked and Nazir's blade was at my neck.

"Point."

The bastard wasn't even out of breath.

I bowed and clasped my hands together behind my back. Waiting his judgment. My heart raced even faster, as Nazir looked me up and down. He turned to his brothers-in-arms and walked a slow circle. What he saw in their stoic faces, I couldn't say.

I locked my legs together to keep them from shaking as he turned back to me. And grinned. "Welcome to the Khazan Guard."

12

I walked through the garrison gates, a cool north wind picking at my clothes. The sky overhead was heavy and gray
green with the promise of a storm. I shivered from the
unexpected chill. Figures. I'd spent a week getting used
to the heat, and the weather changed. At least I wouldn't get
sunburned.

The weather might keep all the spectators away, I thought, smiling to myself. Within two days of my testing, nobles had started
dropping in on our training sessions. They filled the balconies
around the yard until the Khazan Guard had to start sending
people away.

Even the ghosts came to watch. Many of them were fallen
soldiers. One of them, a sergeant by the look of his uniform,
came every day with a cadre of spectral brothers. I got the feeling
the ghost-sergeant was taking my measure, but what he thought,
I couldn't say.

Vitaly and Tarek also came. Vitaly would brood in the darkness beneath the balconies, watching me intently. Tarek liked
to run across the ring, sliding between the legs of the soldiers
as they sparred. The soldiers never noticed, but Tarek seemed to
consider it great fun.

My guards and I wound through the now familiar streets

of the garrison and entered the training yard through a shaded alley between two buildings. The yard was already filled with Khazan guardsmen going through their warm-ups. Iskander and Nazir were in the center of the ring, too deep in conversation to notice our arrival.

I wondered if they would be coming with us for lunch, where we'd been joining the guards in their mess hall. More often than not, one of the emperor's generals would also appear. While they never openly discussed the possibility of a war with Roven, they always paid close attention when my men told stories about our many battles.

As expected, the balconies were empty—almost. The solitary spectator walked down the stairs, watching me with an expression I couldn't name. The wind scratched at his dark hair and robes like it wanted to toss him to the ground, but to no avail. It couldn't even shift the odd green pendant he wore around his thick neck, as if the necklace were an anchor weighing him down. I frowned, studying his narrow, weak-chinned face, so at odds with the hard chips of coal he had for eyes. He smiled, his lips peeling back like the baring of teeth, and bowed.

"Hello, Your Highness," he said in perfect Seraveshi. "We have not had the opportunity to meet. I am Count Dobor of Roven."

As one, my guards reached for their swords. Only a sharp word from Illya kept them from drawing their blades. A hint of laughter gleamed in Count Dobor's eyes. "I wonder if I could have a moment of your time? Will you walk with me around the balcony? I promise I won't keep you long."

For a second, I was gripped by the unbearable urge to grab my sword, to release all the unending rage I had for Radovan and his cursed kingdom in one vicious thrust. The moment passed. I felt a smile cross my face, though I had no idea from whence it came.

"Illya, take the men. I will join you momentarily."

Illya gave me a flat look, spine stiffening, and I thought he might refuse. The moment passed. He bowed and, with a sharp gesture, commanded the men forward. I moved past Dobor, walking sedately up the stairs to the first balcony without waiting to see if he followed.

I spared a glance to the training yard. The Vishiri soldiers, Iskander and Nazir among them, were oblivious to what was occurring above. Iskander tilted his head back, his laughter filling the air like he hadn't a care in the world. Perhaps he didn't.

My whole body hummed, preparing me for attack. But this wasn't a fight I would win with weapons, but words. All the adrenaline in the world wouldn't help me here.

"I'm honored to speak with you," Dobor said, breaking the silence with an obvious lie. "I've sent several invitations since your arrival in Bet Naqar. Perhaps you haven't received them?"

I weighed all my possible replies in the half second after he spoke and decided the most diplomatic response would be to lie. "I'm certain I would have responded if I'd received such an invitation."

"Well, that is troubling," he said mildly, as though discussing a bit of rain. "Though not entirely surprising. The emperor's court often goes out of its way to ensure certain forms of decorum are followed, no matter how restrictive they seem to us northerners."

Did he know about my meeting with the queens? Did he know about the letters Ozura confiscated, as he parroted my own ideas back at me? I gave him a flat look. Of course, he knew. He probably had many allies in the menagerie.

"Vishir is an ancient empire, and while we are lucky enough to live among them, it's only natural that we abide by their ways," I replied, pushing all emotion out of my voice.

"An admirable sentiment, my lady. Though I understand you

lived among your father's people for many years. This must be like coming home for you."

"I am fond of Vishir. But Seravesh is my home," I said, willing him to see how serious I was even though I knew he'd never understand. Seravesh might not be the land of my birth or the home that raised me. But it was the place that succored me after my parents' murder. It was the land of my heart. The land I claimed.

He smiled, though it was the smile of a cat eyeing a mouse. "I'm glad to hear you say so," he said, stopping in the spot we'd started. He reached into his robes and withdrew a scroll. "This is from Emperor Radovan. He wished I deliver it to you personally, so it wouldn't get . . . lost in delivery."

I took the scroll, relieved that my hands didn't shake.

"Take some time to think on my master's proposal, but don't take too long," he said, with almost jovial admonishment. "You know how harsh winter is in the north, but spring will come soon enough, and even the mountain ice will melt." He gave me another little bow and left the yard.

His words lingered. *Even the mountain ice will melt.* What did he mean? Did he know where the Black Wolves were stationed? Did Radovan intend to move on them? The last time I heard from General Arkady, the legion was still in Eshkaroth. Was Radovan ready to invade Idun? Day Lord help me, I had to warn him.

Something snapped beneath my fingers and I looked down. I'd accidentally crumpled the scroll, crushing the seal that held it closed. That north wind blew at my back, like the downswing of an executioner's blade. I opened the letter.

"My dearest Askia," it began.

My lip curled at the intimacy it implied. It took all my will to resist tearing it up, but there was an edge of fear in my anger. Fear and a morbid curiosity.

"May I call you Askia? It's presumptuous of me, I know, but I feel a kinship with you I cannot quite explain. Perhaps it's because you were not meant to be queen of Seravesh, as I was not meant to be emperor of Roven. You may not know it, but in the days of my youth, Roven was a minor power in the frozen wastes of the north. It was a kingdom at war with itself. A leader was needed, desperately needed, lest it crumble to chaos. It was in those days of darkness that I came to power and restored the peace.

"You see, I am a peacemaker at heart. You can see it, Askia, can't you? I don't conquer out of greed. It's for the good of all that I seek to bring our separate kingdoms together. For the stability of all our peoples, I seek an end to the violent struggles born out of our ancestors' pride."

I wanted to sneer at his supposed innocence but couldn't. I felt the letter building to something. Something terrible.

"Pride is the greatest of all evils. Even I am not immune to it. But I strip myself bare before you, Askia. I lay my pride at your feet. I was wrong. I believed your cousin when he came to me begging for aid. I believed Goran when he said all he wanted was to ensure Seravesh's future, its prosperity and safety. I thought he would be a good king.

"I was wrong, Askia. I was so, so wrong. Your cousin has proven himself false. It's not Seravesh's safety that concerns Goran, but its total submission. But your people are proud, Askia. They do not submit to tyranny."

Dread settled like lead in my gut. I didn't want to read on, but my eyes wouldn't look away.

"Words cannot express the depths of my sorrow for the news I must give you, but it's best you hear it from me. For I am your friend, though you may not see it yet. Despite the peaceful transition of power, the city of Kavondy refused to pay tribute to their new king. They were given a month to rectify the slight.

They refused. Rather than meet with the city's nobles, and come to a reasonable solution, Goran sent an army. He barred the city's gates and burned it to the ground. There were no survivors.

"Oh, Askia. Won't you come to me? With you at my side, we can remove Goran. We can save Seravesh. I yearn to hear your reply, for I see in you all the markings of a peacemaker, a spirit akin to my own. Come to me, Askia. Join me, and save your people.

"Yours in friendship,

"Radovan Kirkoskovich, Emperor of Roven"

I gripped the railing, sure I was going to throw up, or pass out, or both. My skin went numb as invisible icicles stabbed into my side, but from shock or magic I didn't know.

Then Vitaly appeared beside me, his gray face awash with panic. *"What is it?"* He didn't wait for my answer, peering over my shoulder, eyes racing across the page.

"No. No, no, no," the words fell from Vitaly's lips with the shattered hope of unanswered prayers. *"He said if I killed you, Kavondy would be safe."*

"You failed," I replied, my heart crumbling into a hundred cutting pieces. The home he'd betrayed me to protect was gone.

Vitaly fell like a puppet without strings. A scream filled my ears, but I didn't know if it was his or mine.

Kavondy was gone. The words circled round and round in my head. Like Nadym before it. All those people. My people and— Misha. Misha was from Kavondy. His family still lived there, his parents and his wife, and Lady Night have mercy, his daughters.

My vision cleared with ruthless precision, narrowing on Misha's smiling face. He was watching some of the other men spar, laughing, because he was always laughing. Always at the center of the fun.

Ice flooded my body in a great wave, leaving a terrible emptiness in its wake. A ringing sound started in my ears. My legs carried me into the yard, even as my mind screamed at me to run.

"Askia. Hello." Iskander appeared in front of me.

"Oh, there she is." Nazir's voice came from somewhere on my left, but I couldn't quite find him. The world was a blur of color and movement I couldn't comprehend, but Day Lord it was moving fast. So fast. "I'm surprised to see you today. I thought you'd be getting ready for tonight's ball."

Nazir's words rattled around inside my hollow mind, taking a long moment to find their mark. Comprehension didn't bring comfort. One more wound, one more betrayal atop all the others. My mind wasn't up to the task of conveying this.

Guilt flashed across Iskander's face. "I'm sorry, Askia. I tried to get my mother to invite you, I really did, but . . ."

He tried? What did his effort matter if it always failed? The letter was still crumpled in my hand, but it was heavy now, so heavy.

"Get out of my way." I meant to spit the words. To shout them, but my voice broke, shattering into a thousand shards of unexpressed grief.

"Askia, what's wrong?" Iskander asked.

"My lady?" Illya's voice cut through the confusion. He shouldered past Iskander, taking my elbow. I thrust the letter into his hands. Illya's face twisted into a snarl, then froze. He looked up, his gray eyes shining with a depthless sorrow that no words could express. It was a visceral understanding that poured from his very soul, reaching for mine in shared horror.

But the grief wasn't ours alone . . .

I pushed past Illya, past Iskander's confusion, past the men crowding the yard. Toward Misha, who didn't yet know his world had fallen apart.

"Misha." Something in my voice made the men fall silent. Misha turned to me, a smile frozen on his face. His pale eyes widened slowly, like he knew something terrible was about to happen.

"I've had word from the north. The Lord of Kavondy refused to pay the yearly tithe to my cousin. So he sent an army to the city. Branko was with them."

Misha shook his head, all the blood drained from his face. He knew what was coming next; everyone in the yard knew. There was only one reason Radovan released Branko the fire witch into the world.

"They barred the city's gates and burned it," I said, not recognizing my voice. Misha was still shaking his head in denial, but I had to continue. He had to understand. "I'm sorry, Misha. There were no survivors."

The light left Misha's eyes. His face crumpled. His legs gave out. A terrible wail tore from his throat as his knees hit the earth. The force of his agony rocked me back on my heels, hitting me in the gut. My men converged on Misha. They lifted him up and bore him out of the yard. All the air seemed to leave with them.

"Askia, I am so sorry." Iskander was next to me now, his voice in my ear.

I turned to Iskander and saw Vitaly tearing his hair in unseen heartbreak. What had he died for? What had they all died for?

"You're sorry?" My voice cracked. "Two thousand people just died, and their blood is on my hands because I wasn't strong enough to save them. And you're sorry?

"Enjoy your party, Iskander."

13

Nariko wasn't there when I returned to my rooms. No one was. The only thing waiting for me was my half-finished letter to Arkady. The pages glared at me, demanding an ending. But I hadn't the strength to pick up the quill to tell him what Radovan had done.

I stalked from the parlor through the dressing room and into the bedroom, only to turn around and pace back again. The excitement of the ball, the unbearable frivolity of it, electrified the air and grated against my flesh. The walls closed in. I was sure I would scream if I didn't get out of this place. And yet there was nowhere for me to go.

Or maybe there was . . .

I never used the formal dining room, so that was where my men congregated in their off hours. It was deserted now, except for Illya. He sat at the head of the table, his face angled to the bank of windows running down the far wall. He was utterly still, his gaze lost to the gathering darkness outside.

"Illya?" My voice clawed out of my throat, barely louder than a whisper. He turned, looking at me as if from a great distance, not quite sure what he was seeing. "Is it possible for me to leave?"

"Where do you wish to go, my lady?"

I wanted to say "home." I nearly said "Roven," but my lips, moving of their own accord, said, "The Shrine of Lady Night."

Understanding softened the edges of his face. "I will need an hour, my lady."

I drifted out of the study, carried into the dressing room without conscious thought. I looked around, my mind reasserting itself, and caught my reflection in the mirror. My face was deathly pale, but there were bright red patches of flushed skin on my cheeks. The embroidered bodice of my sparring coat glimmered in the low light, taunting me with the image of Seravesh and Vishir standing united. Hands trembling, I fumbled with the clasps, letting the lie fall to the floor.

My eyes slid along the rows, searching. Sure enough, a black gown hung hidden between all the bright colors. A gown for mourning and for loss. Queen Ozura certainly had thought of everything. Or perhaps she simply had the foresight to consider all the sorrow that lay ahead.

The fabric sighed against my skin like it struggled to contain the weight of my unvoiced grief. It wasn't the only one. I pulled my hair free from its braid and my eyes scoured the room for a mourning veil.

Vitaly's ghost appeared on the edges of the room. His night-filled eyes were ravaged by grief. He held my gaze and slowly looked down. At his feet was the small cedar chest I'd brought with me from Eshkaroth. From Seravesh.

I crossed the room and, kneeling, opened it. Its contents were exactly like I remembered, but the veil drew my eye. I'd wrapped the gossamer fabric—still flecked in Vitaly's blood— tightly around my father's grimoire: mementos from two men I'd loved and lost.

I unwound the veil, and the scent of sage and rosemary filled my nose. It was my father's smell, the scent of his magic. It still clung to the grimoire after so many years. Normally it brought me comfort, but at this moment, all I felt was shame.

Illya came to collect me some time later. We walked silently into the hall outside the apartment, where the Khazan Guard waited. I recognized the men, living and dead, from training as they escorted me through the palace to a waiting carriage. These men owed me nothing, but still came when I needed them, to protect me while my people mourned. My heart swelled with gratitude. On its heels was hope. The emotion was almost too strong to bear.

The heavens above Bet Naqar roiled with swirling gray clouds. The city's streets were nearly empty, its residents shuttered in for the night. Our trek was a short one, and soon enough, I saw the Temple of the Two-Faced God spreading out in front of me.

It was a massive structure built from huge white granite blocks. The circular base soared into the air before breaking into two short domes in the east and west. A taller third dome rose in the middle. At the center of each was a pillar capped with one of the deities' three signs. The western pillar bore the full moon; the eastern one, the sun; and the center pillar joined the two aspects with the sigil of the half sun-moon.

My carriage drove past the temple's eastern entrance, which led to the shrine of the Day Lord. The courtyard was packed with the too-thin bodies of starving men and women. They crowded around the shrine's open doors, while red-robed Shazir priests handed out bread. *How magnanimous*, I thought, my eyes filling with enraged tears as my carriage rolled past. The Shazir were so good, so godly. Until they met a witch. Then all they cared about was death.

I tried to shake the anger loose as I stepped into the western courtyard, a space surrounded by trees and giant urns overflowing

with flowers. A large fountain bubbled in the center, with lil-
ies floating in the water. The door to the Shrine of Lady Night
was covered in climbing vines of night-blooming roses whose
white petals were beginning to open. It was idyllic, I thought as
I washed my face and hands in the cool clear water, but empty.

The shrine's circular walls were dotted with arched windows
that dimly illuminated the space in gray twilight. Lanterns hung
from the ceiling, and I imagined when night fully fell, they
would look like stars twinkling in a cavernous sky. The altar sat
against the far wall, dripping in silver and gold and glittering
with gems. White candles blanketed the floor, leaving a narrow
candlelit path to a locked box at its base where believers could
leave prayer requests. Prayers for miracles. Prayers for magic.

I wondered if the box was filled. Or, with the Shazir a courtyard away, if people were too afraid to seek help from witches.

I settled onto one of the kneelers, and the momentary release
I'd felt in the courtyard evaporated in the stillness of the shrine.
Here, I was laid bare before Lady Night, and here I must face
the cost of my failure.

When Radovan ordered Nadym burned, he did it to make
a point. I barely escaped Solenskaya with my life and hadn't
even gathered all the Black Wolves to my camp in the Peshkalor
Mountains when the emperor's fire witch came. Sure, I had harried my cousin's allies, cut his supply lines, cost Roven a few
small losses, but they were truly minor, with minimal casualties.
When Radovan burned Nadym, he did it because he could. He
did it to send a message. To tell me how futile it was to fight him.

Burning Kavondy was personal. It was done to woo me—a
courtship drenched in blood and betrayal and the misery of the
people I was trying to protect. I'd failed. In every way, I'd failed.

I'd come to Vishir for an army, but I couldn't even get invited to a ball, let alone get a meeting with the emperor. Sure, I'd
gained the friendship of the Khazan Guard and by extension the

sympathy of the Vishiri army. It wasn't nothing, but sympathy in soldiers only went so far. Sympathy wouldn't line their pockets or feed their families. Sympathy wouldn't get them across the sea.

My heart beat too loud in my ears, reverberating with the sound of drums. *You failed. Go home. Surrender to Radovan. It's the only way to save your people. Seravesh may die, but they will live. Give up.* The litany went on and on, bearing down on me with each iteration. I thought it would crush me, shatter me completely.

The quality of the air changed. The cool scent of snow blowing through an evergreen forest made me blink, and my eyes, which had fogged with despair, focused.

Illya knelt beside me, back straight, hands fisted on his thighs. His gray gaze seared my face. "Don't give up, Askia," he whispered, reaching across the darkness to clasp my hand.

I felt my eyes widen, both at the heat of his touch and at the sound of my name on his lips. The storm within me stilled.

"He wants you to crumble, to break from guilt and grief. Don't," Illya said, his words wrapping around me in an embrace far tighter than any I'd ever known. "Fight him, Askia. You must fight."

Tears prickled my eyes, but I nodded all the same. I looked up as he released my hand, and I beseeched the Two-Faced God for strength. But all I saw at the top of the domed shrine was a painting of creation. Five panels of faded artwork covered in soot, hardly the divine answer I was looking for.

The first panel showed nothing but darkness and potential, the void from which the Two-Faced God emerged. The second showed It creating the sun and stars and moon and Kinvara. At the planet's core, It laid the molten elements of creation: earth, air, water, fire, and magic. On Kinvara It brought plants and animals, all the creatures that thrive on land and sea. But the Two-Faced God wanted more.

So It divided Itself in two and stepped onto the soil of

Kinvara as the Day Lord and Lady Night. Together they created man. Day Lord gave man order and logic and learning. Lady Night gave choice, intuition, and creativity.

Exhausted by their toils, the Day Lord went to the nearest hill and, pulling it high into the heavens, created Khan-e-Fet, the highest mountain in the world. There he slept, forever bathed in sunlight, and dreamed of his creation . . . and where his followers allowed time and piety to reduce them into hate-filled zealots. Into the Shazir.

Lady Night craved darkness. She journeyed across the world in search of a place to rest her head, but as she traveled, she came across a young girl, cold and alone. Taking pity on the child, Lady Night gave the girl one more gift; a single drop of the goddess's blood. Magic awakened inside her. This last blessing given, Lady Night lay down in her bower, deep in the bones of the world, and slept.

Slept while her night-blooded descendants roamed, sharing their gift through generations of witches. Witches who were being persecuted in the south and kidnapped in the north. Witches who stood to lose everything if Radovan was allowed to conquer the world.

An idea swirled in my mind, but was it wisdom or desperation? A longing for General Arkady reared up inside me. Arkady would have known what to do, would have told me his thoughts and offered advice. Lady Night save me, I needed that.

Then again, I hadn't exactly given Illya a chance to offer an opinion. I turned and found him watching me with a worried frown. "I'm going to request a meeting with the Shadow Guild."

"What is that?"

"It's Vishir's magic guild."

His eyes widened. "They have guilds for magic?"

I nodded, understanding his disbelief. Radovan's unquenchable search for magic meant that northern witches needed to keep their powers secret. That Vishiri witches could have any-thing so normal as a guild must have been alien to Illya.

"It's a good idea," he said after a moment. "The Vishiri witches will certainly have as much to lose as the witches in the north."

"That was my thinking too. It feels like we would be natural allies."

Illya studied my face and though the silence stretched and went taut, I forced myself to wait, to let him decide if he was going to speak. He leaned toward me. Swallowed. "Be careful how much of yourself you give to them. How much you expose."

My eyebrows rose. Whatever I had expected him to say, this wasn't it. Did Illya know I was a witch? Arkady certainly did . . . Had he told Illya before we left? My heart beat slowly in my ears as I weighed a decision I had never considered before. Did Illya need to know? Did he deserve to know?

"Illya, I—"

"Don't." His hand flew out, pressing my lips with the tips of his fingers, like he could catch my words. "I don't need to know," he breathed and though his hand fell away from my mouth, his gaze lingered, kindling something deep within me. "I don't *want* to know because what I don't know, I can't expose later."

My thoughts flashed to Vitaly hanging by his wrists in Esh-karoth's dungeon.

"Not that I plan to betray you," Illya said, his expression shuttering like clouds passing over the moon, "but we both know how much Radovan's men savor torturing their enemies." He leaned away—only a matter of inches—but even that distance slapped between us, a chasm I couldn't bridge. "We should go."

We left the shrine side by side, but I wasn't ready to return to the palace. Not yet. I sat on the edge of the fountain. Closing my eyes for a moment, I let the cool air caress my cheeks and shut out the night-darkened city beyond.

"Askia?"

I looked up at the sound of Iskander's voice to find him looking down at me, with wide, sad eyes. Illya stood in the darkness behind the prince. He gave me a slight bow and stepped back.

"Are you all right? I mean—" His throat bobbed as his eyes raked the ground like he was looking for the right words to say.

"Thank you for coming," I said, patting the edge of the fountain, "though I'm sorry to take you away from your party."

Iskander sat, his smile edged in sadness. "It wasn't much of a party. All anyone wanted to talk about was the destruction of Kavondy. All eight generals of the Khazan Guard wore black in your honor, by the way."

"Truly?"

He nodded. "It raised some uncomfortable questions for Count Dobor. He said it was your cousin's doing, but no one believed him. There isn't another fire witch in the world as powerful as Branko, and he has only one master."

"Radovan."

"Indeed." A sour expression marred the smooth planes of Iskander's face, like hearing Radovan's name was enough to cause him pain. "The talk has caused some veiled criticism of the menagerie's treatment of you."

"Oh?" I was too exhausted to feel smug about it.

"The general feeling at court is the queens are being petty where you're concerned. That their harsh treatment of you is killing your people."

The sentiment was neither true nor entirely false, so I said nothing. Loudly.

"My mother hates nothing so much as looking foolish. You'll probably receive another invitation from her in a few days."

I nodded, considering his words. "I don't think I should wait," I said after a moment. "I think I should go see her. Tomorrow. Try to speak with her privately."

Iskander breathed a relieved sigh. "I was afraid to suggest it, but I agree. You'll never get to my father without her support, and she has far more say in the running of this empire than it seems from the outside. You need her."

"Would you be willing to set up the meeting for me? I'd do it myself, but it's not like I can walk into the menagerie any time I like."

"Actually, I'm betting you can."

I frowned. "What?"

"The gardens inside the menagerie include the cemetery of the royal family and their favored subjects. Your parents are there."

My body stilled while I absorbed this information. In the seven years since my parents' deaths, I'd never given much thought to where they were buried. I assumed the Shazir had done something unspeakable to them and locked away any thought of their burial deep in the back of my mind.

"There was a ceremony shortly after you returned to Bet Naqar," he said, his words halting. "You weren't quite yourself, so I'm not surprised you don't remember it, but you have every right to visit your family's burial site. No one could turn you away."

I tucked the thought of my parents' graves away where I could examine it in private and nodded. "I'll go tomorrow morning."

Iskander bit his lip, looking furtively around the courtyard, at the guards stationed around us. "It would be better if you waited until nighttime. Before sunset, I mean."

My eyebrows rose. "Before sunset? Why?"

Iskander shook his head. "I can't say, and I don't really know much of anything about it, but . . . Every evening she walks in the gardens and through the graveyard of emperors. If you're quick, and quiet, you could follow her."

"Is that really a good idea? If she's mourning, I'm the last person she'll want to see."

"She's not mourning. Like I said, I can't talk about it. No, don't give me that look." He smiled, shaking his head. "Just get to the emperor's graveyard before the sun sets. Use the shadows and follow my mother."

"Why?"

"You'll see." He swallowed hard. "It's a risk, but my mother always admires a bold move. Promise me you'll go."

His eyes shone with excitement and hope—a hope I couldn't feel but desperately needed, for myself and my people. So no matter the mystery, no matter my questions, I knew I'd go. I'd grab my second chance to see Queen Ozura, to prove myself. There wouldn't be a third.

14

skia?"

I blinked. "Sorry?"

"I was telling you about the ball," Nariko said, furrowing her brow at my apparent lack of interest.

I tried for a smile but was sure I lost the expression along the way. The afternoon sun was sinking over Nariko's shoulder, dragging my optimism with it. Seeking out Ozura had seemed like a good idea last night, but I was far from sure now. Still, if it was a chance to change Queen Ozura's opinion of me, it was a chance I had to take.

I cleared my throat when I saw the expectant expression on Nariko's face "How was it?"

"As I was saying, the generals all wore black in your honor," Nariko replied. "It caused quite a stir. Of course, Prince Iskander wore black too. And he left early."

"Yes, he came to see me," I said, replying to the question she hadn't asked. "Don't worry. He didn't come here," I continued when she frowned. "I was at the Shrine of Lady Night."

Nariko's look of reproach turned to one of pity. I looked away. "Of course, you were. It was kind of you to go and pray for your people, and while the rest of us were at a ball of all things.

It doesn't seem right to me. They should have canceled it when the news came in."

I let Nariko talk. My mind was too busy digesting the first thing she said: *It was kind of you to go and pray for your people.* Kind. Right. I was shocked, to be sure. Devastated by the loss of life and heartbroken for Misha. Yet when I knelt before the altar of Lady Night, had I prayed for them? Had I asked Lady Night to shepherd them across the Marchlands to the Lands of Dawn?

No.

I swallowed hard, pushing guilt off to one side—a place getting more and more crowded as my guilt mounted—as Iskander's advice rose in my mind.

"I suppose Queen Ozura is angry with me for stealing Iskander away."

"No," Nariko replied, too quickly. "No, how can she be? It wasn't your doing. I mean, people were talking, but . . . but that wasn't your fault."

"Great." I felt anything but.

I waited until Nariko left for the evening before rushing into the dressing room. I grabbed a dark blue cloak and pulled it over my shoulders. Once I reached the menagerie, I could draw up the hood to hide my face. It might be easier to follow Ozura if she thought I was another of the emperor's wives going for a stroll.

Illya and two of my guards walked with me to the menagerie. I prayed they couldn't see my knees shaking under the folds of my dress and silently rehearsed my excuse for being there. *I've come to visit the tomb of my parents.* I'd practiced it over and over. Perfectly plausible. Right. The guards would probably turn me away, and I would once again be the object of derision because of the menagerie.

Still, better to try and fail than not try at all.

The menagerie doors loomed, and the men guarding them

watched me with expressions carved from stone. I stuttered to a stop and licked my lips. The guards bowed and, not waiting for an explanation, pushed the doors open.

I stepped inside, bracing myself to see the queens of Vishir lounging about the sitting room. However, when the doors closed at my back, the sound echoed across a wide, empty space. No one, not even a servant, wandered among the couches and chairs.

I gritted my teeth. I'd been lucky so far, and I hated counting on luck. It always deserted me when I needed it most. I pulled the hood over my head, pushing my distinctive red hair back into the fabric, and hurried to the garden doors.

Darting right, I pressed myself against the sun-warmed brick wall so I wouldn't be seen by anyone looking out the window. My eyes flew across the garden's open and stone-paved walking paths to my right before slamming into a huge wall of hedges on my left.

How big was this place? I wondered, stretching onto my tiptoes to get a glimpse of the garden beyond the hedge maze. It had to be massive if there was a cemetery back there somewhere.

I rocked back on my heels. It would take forever to search the garden, and I didn't have forever. Surely Ozura would be returning to the palace soon for her dinner.

My gaze peppered the darkness before I forced my eyes shut, focusing on the seed of power at the core of my body. I reached for it, hating the slippery feeling of cold water sliding across my flesh. Hating the deep frigid cold that bloomed in my fingers and toes, sliding up my arms and legs as magic filled me.

"Tarek?"

Tarek's diaphanous form materialized beside me. *"Boo!"*

I flinched in spite of myself, making Tarek crow with laughter.

Thanks. Very helpful, I thought.

Tarek stopped laughing long enough to stick his tongue out at me. Then, smiling, he started walking toward the hedge maze.

"Wait," I whispered, calling him back. *"Do you know where your mother is?"*

"This way," he called waving me onward, running one hand along the evergreen hedge wall as he skirted around the giant maze. I hurried after Tarek, but he soon tired of walking. He began skipping, hopping, and running up and down the path, doing circles around me. Against my will, I smiled. Meandering though his path was, he led me true: right into the graveyard of Vishir's emperors.

I started up the hill, eyes scouring the path for Ozura, but could see nothing in the growing dark. I was alone. Almost. Tarek walked beside me. His spectral face was so innocent, so filled with happiness.

"Where is she?"

A mischievous glimmer lit up his gray eyes, and he pointed up the hill.

Up ahead, on a slight incline, was the largest mausoleum yet. It was set a little way back from the path, away from all the other tombs. Winged angels stood sentinel at its corners, their alabaster features all but lost to time. It was undoubtedly the tomb of Kalek, the first emperor of Vishir.

Tarek took off, but instead of running to the mausoleum of Emperor Kalek, he darted into a smaller tomb beside it, this one built out of dusky black stone, with two pillars that held up the triangular overhang of the roof. The golden sun of the Day Lord was inlaid on the lintel. I peered inside but couldn't see anything aside from the gray, glowing form of the little boy.

I shook my head, trying to shake away the nervousness itching down my back. I wasn't sure what I'd expected when I entered the mausoleum. Cobwebs? Moldering skeletons? If so, I'd have been disappointed.

The room was narrow and unadorned. In the center stood a

huge rectangular sarcophagus with a woman carved on the alabaster lid. She lay as if sleeping, her hands folded over her stomach, her toes peeking out of the hem of the dress. The sculptor had even carved a veil, laid it over the lines of the woman's face, softening her features with the folds of stone fabric. She was breathtaking.

Tarek watched me, his cheeks dimpled with a smile, like he was waiting for me to figure out the trick. I pursed my lips and turned in a circle. Aside from the sarcophagus, the tomb wasn't particularly striking. There were no windows, no doors. The only thing of note was the full silver moon of Lady Night set into the wall opposite the door. The moon sat at the center of an archway of vines. No. Not vines. Night-blooming roses, like the entrance to the Shrine of Lady Night.

On silent heavy feet, I approached the arch. The rose's leaves were lush and green, and its white flowers were still closed. But then, how could they open? The roses only bloomed in moonlight. Moonlight that couldn't possibly reach the back of this tomb. How were they even alive?

Magic.

The answer rang through my bones like the tinkling of tiny bells.

I stretched out my fingers . . .

The wall rippled beneath my skin, rolling in waves of gelatinous stone all the way to the tangled stems of the night-blooming roses.

I snatched my hand away from the portal, for that was what it was. Lady Night save me. Had I stumbled into the Shadow Guild? And if it was, then it could only mean that Ozura was a witch. It would explain why Iskander was so unwilling to go into detail.

I shifted from one foot to the other. In or out? Go or stay?

The options seemed equally unacceptable. I'd wanted to meet with the guild, but turning up on their doorstep uninvited couldn't be a good idea. And I somehow doubted Iskander's hint about "following the shadows" counted as an invitation.

But my father had been a guildmaster. Maybe the witches would welcome me. I snorted at the thought. If Ozura was there, I doubted I'd be ushered in with open arms. But if my father's reputation didn't get me in, then certainly my own powers would, meager as they were.

I shied away from that thought. My parents taught me long ago never to tell anyone about my magic. No one would understand. No one would want to understand. Magic was a liability, a threat that could come back to kill you. The Shazir proved that.

But Radovan was a threat too. A threat I'd never overcome if I didn't find allies here.

No. Going back wasn't an option. I wasn't there for myself, but for my people. If Queen Ozura was there, then I could prove myself to both the guild and the queen.

I took a deep breath and stepped into the wall.

The stone parted around me, thicker and denser than water. It pressed down, covering my nose, mouth, and eyes. My heart galloped in my chest, pounding so hard I thought my ribs would break. My mind screamed for air. Panic burned through the oxygen in my lungs. I propelled forward, fighting against the portal's syrupy substance.

My right foot broke free first, then my arms, and finally my face. I breached the surface of the portal, gasping for air. My arms shook as I braced them on my knees, willing my heartbeat to slow.

"What in the name of Lady Night are *you* doing here?"

Ozura's voice was so cold, it should have given me frostbite. I shoved myself upright, biting back the urge to swear when I realized we weren't alone. There was a man and a woman with her. The woman—no, it wasn't just a woman. It was Soma, and she glared at me from beneath her familiar bushy eyebrows. I blinked away my confusion over her presence and forced my attention back to Ozura.

"I think it should be obvious," I replied with a calm I couldn't feel. "I'm looking for the Shadow Guild. Is this it?"

The room around me was a perfect circle of unremarkable gray brick. High above, the domed ceiling was capped with a metal grate. The last light of the sun shone through, dimly illuminating the eight portals that were set into the wall. Or seven, rather. The archway next to mine opened into a staircase that disappeared into the darkness below.

"This is its entrance, yes," Ozura replied, her words so clipped it was like the admission cost her.

We surveyed each other in silence until the air hummed, daring someone to break it. "So. You're a witch."

"Evidently," was her dry reply. "I'm a truth witch, in fact."

It was a real struggle not to flinch. A truth witch was a lower class of mind witch, one whose only power was the ability to tell the truth from a lie.

No wonder Ozura had taken such an instant dislike to me. She probably thought I was a coward for denying my magic. She crossed her arms, watching me through heavily lidded eyes. Maybe she was right.

"How did you come to be here? It can't be a mistake that took you through the portal and into a meeting of the three guildmasters."

I lifted my chin and tossed the answer at her feet, "Iskander."

Ozura's anger was so palpable, it seemed to steam off her flesh in waves. Behind her, Soma exchanged an uneasy look with the other guildmaster, like they were looking for the quickest way out.

"What did Iskander tell you?" Ozura demanded, her composure fraying. "Did he give you the portal's location?"

"No. All he told me was to go to the graveyard. I found my way from there."

Though I knew she must be tasting my every word for truth, Ozura still looked like she wanted nothing more than to call me a liar. "And why have you come?"

Wasn't it obvious? The thought snarled across my mind, but I contained it. Of course she knew why I was here—and of course she'd make me spell it out. Make me bend and beg. But . . .

But my inability to rein in my anger was why Ozura disliked me. And if I lashed out now, I'd leave the Shadow Guild as alone as I'd entered it. I swallowed hard. "I'm here to ask for your help."

Ozura smiled—not a vindictive baring of teeth, but a genuine expression of surprise and, perhaps, approval.

The man cleared his throat uncertainly, squinting at me through his glasses. "You are Askia Poritskaya e-Nimri? Sevilen's daughter?"

"Yes."

"You have the look of your mother," he said. "But your father clearly gave you his talents."

"Yes, tell us, Askia," Ozura said, her words a challenge. "What kind of a witch are you?"

I almost said nothing. Almost denied my magic entirely despite the near certain fact that only a witch could pass through that portal.

Then I saw Vitaly shimmering in the shadows. His hands were clenched at his side, face pinched with worry. He shook his head, warning me to be silent, but all I could think about was Kavondy. The home Vitaly sacrificed himself to protect. The home Radovan had razed.

I swallowed. My parents made me promise to keep my powers

secret, so I would be safe. But how could I hide behind my secret, knowing the truth could help secure me allies? My people sacrificed their safety, their lives, supporting me. How could I do any less for them?

Tarek skipped around me, bounding past Soma and the man whose name I still didn't know before tumbling to a seat on the ground at Ozura's feet. He looked up at me, smiling beneath his slightly upturned nose. Ozura's nose.

I looked to Ozura, my heart pounding out a staccato beat against my rib cage. "You asked me how I got here, and I told you it was Iskander's doing. But the truth is, Iskander only told me I might find you in the menagerie garden. It was Tarek who showed me the way here."

My words reverberated off the circular walls. Ozura blanched. "Lady Night save us," she whispered. "You're a death witch."

15

Ozura looked to the other guildmasters, but what their silent communication meant, I didn't know. When she turned back to me, I saw something sparkle in her eyes. Something I couldn't identify and knew I wasn't ready for.

"Come with me."

Queen Ozura strode past me, past the still-shocked guildmasters and down the staircase. I followed her after a moment's hesitation and found that the stairs bottomed out into an enormous chamber, whose vaulted ceiling rose at least eighty feet into the air. Six giant columns ran down the length of the room, and between them floated a few dozen melon-sized orbs of fire.

I didn't have time to see any more, for Ozura was already heading through an open archway at the back of the hall. I followed her into a long corridor where she unlocked the nearest door with a heavy iron key.

A round white witchlight flickered to life when we entered the room. The office was sparsely furnished for such a generous space. Most of the room was occupied by a large desk, complete with a few uncomfortable-looking chairs. Bookshelves encircled the study with each book lined up one precise inch from the edge of the shelf. Their gold-and-silver embossing gleamed in the low light. I bit the inside of my cheek to keep from smirking. It was an impressive collection to be sure, but the studied perfection of their arrangement told me they were rarely, if ever, used.

The desk was a different matter. It was covered in boxes and quills and forms and, interestingly, maps. I wouldn't have thought Ozura was capable of clutter, but here was the proof. The queen might not have been a reader, but by the look of things, she didn't have time for it.

Ozura took her place behind her desk. "Please sit."

The chair's unyielding frame carved new ridges in my back when I sat, and I shifted almost immediately. Trying to disguise my discomfort with curiosity, I craned my neck to look at the maps.

There were six in all, each one slightly overlapping the next. The curled parchment edges were held down by various ornamental paperweights. The maps detailed the massive stretch of land that comprised the northern continent. Each one depicted the steadily creeping boundary of the Roven Empire.

I looked up and found the queen's eyes upon me, her dark gaze unreadable. "You've been watching Radovan?"

Ozura inclined her head. "His actions are of grave concern for the guild."

"And the court?" There was too much anger in my voice, too much emotion, and it was clear neither would do me any good. Not with Ozura.

And yet the shadow of a smile flickered over Ozura's face. "Indeed, but it's the Shadow Guild who will help you now."

"How?"

"Among other things: insight," Ozura replied, folding her hands in her lap. "We've been watching Emperor Radovan and we know much he would rather keep hidden. If you're not a fool, you'll listen to what I can teach you. If you're clever, you'll find a way to use it." She paused, leaned slightly forward in her seat. "We can teach you to use your powers."

"I know how to use my powers," I cut in. "My parents might have insisted I keep my magic a secret, but my father still trained me."

Ozura's eyebrows rose into sculpted points. "And you've explored the depths of your magic? Nurtured it? Allowed it to flourish with the same studied practice with which you learned to wield a sword?"

Her words hung heavy in the air between us. We both knew the truth. While I might be able to see ghosts, might know enough to dip my toe in the Marchlands and communicate with spirits, I hadn't nurtured my talents by any stretch.

The queen smiled. "In the Shadow Guild, you'll be free to test your limits. Strengthen your magic. You don't have to be powerless when Radovan comes for you."

"You think he'll abduct me?" I asked, hating the sound of fear in my voice.

"I think he'll try. In a sense, it's a good thing you've made no progress at court. It has kept you safe. The more successful you are here, the more danger you pose to Radovan."

"So you were doing me a favor by keeping me out of court?"

Ozura sat back, crossing her arms. "You're the one who lied to me, Askia. Your lies have wasted time."

"My lies have saved my life." I felt my voice rise again and forced it down.

"Yes, they have." Ozura's voice was mild, like my anger was entirely beneath her notice. "But they won't keep you safe for much longer. Radovan surely knows you're a death witch."

I blinked slowly, refusing to let the words sink too deep to settle in that dark place of fear where they might sour into panic. Not many people knew I was a witch. My parents, my grandfather, but aside from them?

"Is that why he tried to kill me? Because he knows I will never serve him?" My mind flashed to the ghastly memory of Vitaly's face as he lay dying in my arms.

"I'm not entirely convinced he did try to kill you," Ozura replied, her face so grim it belied her matter-of-fact tone.

"What do you mean?"

"I mean that if Radovan Kirkoskovich wanted you dead, you'd be dead."

I swallowed. "So what does he want?"

"The world."

"And my being here helps him? How?"

Ozura breathed a mirthless chuckle. "Your presence has the potential to create a certain . . . instability." She shrugged. "Radovan has always played a long game."

I shook my head. Whatever impression I'd made on the Vishiri court was negligible. Radovan couldn't want me here, where I could make allies.

"What do you know about Radovan?" Ozura asked, clearly reading the doubt on my face.

The question threw me. Radovan was a conqueror, a killer, a warmonger. What else was he? I didn't know. I knew nothing of the man behind the armies, and I hadn't wanted to. I didn't need to know him to defeat him. Humanizing Radovan would only take the fun out of killing him. "Not much," I admitted. "I know he's old, and without heirs. I know he's ruthless, and a powerful healer, that he's perverted his powers to extend his life."

Ozura smiled. "Would you be shocked to learn you're only entirely correct about one of those statements?"

My brow furrowed. "What do you mean?"

"Oh, Radovan is ruthless. There's no doubt about that, but the rest? He's old, though he doesn't look it. He has children, though he's disavowed them. And for all his power, Radovan Kirkoskovich was born without a single drop of magical blood."

I jerked back in my chair. "That's not possible. He's been in power for eighty years—alive for at least a hundred. How could he not be a witch?"

"I don't know." Ozura opened her hands, motioning to the papers on her desk. "All I can tell you is what happened. After that, it's up to you."

I paused. "Up to me to do what?"

"To decide how far you're willing to go to defeat him."

The metallic taste of hate soured my tongue. After my grandfather's murder, after my country's fall, after the destruction of Nadym and Kavondy, there was nothing I wouldn't do. "Tell me."

Ozura rifled through the maps on her desk until she unearthed a very old, very wrinkled map of the northern continent. In the far northwestern reaches, surrounded by mountains and glacial ice, was a land marked *Kingdom of Roven*.

"In Radovan's youth, Roven was a turbulent, dangerous place," Ozura said. "The politics of the day made it next to impossible to gain, let alone keep, power. It may come as a surprise to learn that Radovan, oldest child of a middling noble family, would someday become king.

"In the eight years prior to his ascension, four different kings reigned from the palace in Tolograd. Not one of them managed to keep power or their lives. Roven was at the end of almost a hundred years of strife, famine, and ill-advised foreign wars." Ozura's eyes cut to mine as she spoke with an ironic bent to her brows. "The nobles of the day managed to come together under a flag of truce and form a council. They knew it was only a matter of time before a neighboring kingdom invaded, and should that be allowed to happen, they would lose everything. So this council decided to elect a king."

"They chose Radovan," I said.

Ozura inclined her head. "He was eighteen at the time. I've often wondered why Radovan, of all the noblemen in Roven, was chosen, but I have yet to find any transcripts of the meeting. If I had to guess, it was because of his youth and his family's mediocre standing. I suppose the council thought these traits would make him pliable. If so, they were fools.

"From the beginning, Radovan established himself as a man with an iron will. All activity in foreign wars ceased, even when it meant ceding territory to neighboring kingdoms. Provincial militias were disbanded in favor of one centralized army that answered only to him. And perhaps, most significantly, he forced the redistribution of his people."

"What do you mean?"

"He gave land grants to the peasantry, tied them to their land through contract labor. He funded great building projects—universities, palaces, even the Tower of Roshkot was built during this time. Famine ended, and with it much of the petty lawlessness of desperate men. He was known as the great peacemaker, and it lasted for forty years."

Ozura's words dropped off, her face twisted with bitterness. I knew why. Everyone in the north knew the tale. "All things end. Even peace. Over the border, Polzi and Nivlaand went to war. Refugees swarmed into southern Roven, forcing Radovan to act. For the first time in nearly half a century, Roven went to war.

"The armies of both Polzi and Nivlaand were demolished. Radovan dismantled their monarchies and installed his own leadership. In a matter of months, Roven grew by half, and Radovan found himself a wife. Her name was Katarzhina; she was a Nivlaandi princess and a healer."

"She was the healer? Not Radovan?" Every warrior instinct I had went on alert as Ozura nodded.

She pushed a strand of ebony hair out of her eyes. Her warm complexion looked ashen, like telling Radovan's history was draining. "He was married to Katarzhina for eighteen years, but the union only produced one child: a son with an incurable mental deficiency. By this time Radovan was seventy, and the stress of rule had aged him. He knew his time was running short, and as Radovan's health began to fail, he started to look for ways to prolong his life. I don't know what he found," Ozura said, admitting her ignorance grudgingly. "What I do know is this: Radovan woke up one morning, a seventy-eight-year-old man, murdered his wife, and found his body transformed to what it was in his prime.

"It's a process he's completed again and again, but with each new marriage, each conquered nation, his wives live in shorter increments. Katarzhina survived eighteen years. Ragata, an earth witch from Polzi, lived seven years before he killed her. Asyl, a mind witch from Khezhar, lived only six months. Freyda, a fire witch from Graznia lived only a month. Siv, a water witch from Switzkia; and Eliska—"

"I know their names," I cut in, bracing a hand on her desk. From the day a Roven emissary sauntered into my grandfather's castle with a marriage proposal, I'd known their names. One beloved woman from each conquered kingdom taken and murdered all to snuff out every last inch of hope their people might have for peace.

Except that wasn't why they were taken—not according to Ozura.

"You didn't know they were witches?" Ozura asked, watching me with clinical curiosity.

"I think you fail to understand how dangerous it is to be known as a witch in the north. No. I didn't know. I thought Radovan took them to terrorize, to show the utter futility of resisting him. But you're saying they were taken *because* they were witches."

"Yes, and with each new sacrifice, Radovan gains not only more land, but more magic. Something about the nature of their marriage, and the way he sacrifices them . . . they surrender their magic, and he is there waiting to absorb it.

"All that's left now, Askia, is you."

I gave her a hard look, my mind battle-clear. "What do I do?"

"Exactly what you've been doing. You train. You fight."

"I train?"

"Here at the guild," Ozura replied with a nod. "You'll come here every night, and I will oversee your training myself."

"*You* will train me?"

"Yes. I cannot promise that it will be easy, but I can promise to teach you everything I know." Her voice was heavy, grave, even. Desperate.

I leaned away from the desk as unease skittered across my skin. It was like walking into a dark room and knowing I wasn't alone. "Why are you helping me?"

One of Ozura's dark eyebrows rose into a perfect arch. "Is war not enough? You and I both know it's only a matter of time before Roven provokes Vishir into conflict, before Radovan tries to take you. If you're not prepared to fight, the world will be at war."

I nodded. It rang of truth, but it wasn't the whole truth. Because she could have offered me help for this reason before, but she had not. I waited.

After another minute, Ozura sighed. "Iskander considers you a friend. I think you feel the same for him." She clasped her hands together, studying me through hooded eyes. "It will come as no surprise that I wish for Iskander to succeed Armaan one day. My son is smart. He's ambitious, too, but he lacks the wisdom to properly channel that ambition. You've provided him a certain . . . focus." She spoke the word with such gravity I wondered how Ozura could turn something good into something bad with such ease.

"Your manners are lax, Askia. And because of it, the entire

court knows you're close. Until your arrival, my son, while loved by the army, was not a power in the political sphere. If you succeed, it will be a major victory for Iskander. If you fail, Askia, he fails."

I smirked. How changed Ozura was from our first meeting. Then, Ozura wanted me as far away from Iskander as possible. "So you're counting on our friendship, hoping we'd rise together. Yet you're still afraid he'll want to marry me?"

Ozura's shrug was filled with ennui. "Iskander is too young to know what he wants, but that's all right. He has me to guide him in these matters."

"That sounds an awful lot like a yes."

Ozura deigned to smile. "Speaking of prospects, if you want an army, you'll need to marry. I can make the proper introductions, if you like."

I was shaking my head before she finished speaking. "I don't need to marry to get an army. Not when helping me is the right thing to do."

Ozura's face was so eloquent with condescension no further words were necessary.

I shifted in my seat and rubbed my neck, anxious to get away from Ozura, away from this tomblike magic guild when a thought made me freeze in place. My eyes flew to Ozura.

"Radovan's men take witches. His army scours the countryside for them," I began, struggling to form words. "If Radovan has found a way to steal magic from his wives, what's stopping him from doing it to other witches?"

"Radovan isn't the sort of man who shares power," Ozura said with a dismissive wave. "Those willing to work for him, like Branko, live. He kills the rest. You know that."

Did I? I thought I did. But Ozura's shuttered expression told a different story. Suspicion tiptoed up my spine, but our truce was too fresh for me to push her. Still I didn't need to be a truth witch to know she was lying.

"Now," Ozura said, rising to her feet. "We should begin."

I frowned. "Begin what?"

"Your lessons, of course."

"Now?"

Ozura's laugh was as dark and velvety as a night moth's wings. "Do you have somewhere better to be?"

16

Ozura and I set off across the deserted guild hall and through a nondescript door. The corridor beyond was nearly identical to the one in which Ozura's office sat. Our steps echoed down the length, too loud in a silence that didn't feel natural. Even the air was heady and warm with the scent of people who were nowhere to be found.

"Where is everyone?"

"At home," she replied shortly. "Soma and Cyrus meet in the evening as a courtesy to my busy schedule, but our witches do have their own lives to lead."

I nodded, processing. "And Soma is one of the guildmasters?"

"And Cyrus, too, yes." Ozura angled her chin my way, assessing. "Our stations outside may be different," she said, guessing my thoughts with this vast understatement, "but inside the guild the three of us are equals."

And yet it was Ozura who whisked me away to discuss the great threat of our time. Equals. Right. "What are all these rooms for?" I asked, opting for a safer question.

"Oh, studies, laboratories, bathing facilities, and bedrooms for visiting witches," Ozura replied, without looking at me. "We are going to one of the training rooms in the infirmary."

"Why do you need an infirmary?" I asked, and then shook my head as a second question hit. "Wait, why do you have training rooms inside an infirmary?"

Ozura's lips twitched. "Common illnesses and injuries we can easily treat within a patient's home. But when people require more intensive care, we bring them here," she said, pointing to a set of double doors at the end of the hall. "As to why the training rooms are inside the infirmary, well, you can imagine how much trouble a fire witch can cause when first learning to control their powers." Ozura hauled one of the doors open. "After you."

The first thing I noticed about the infirmary was its scent, or lack thereof. Like many very clean places, it was almost odorless but for the faint notes of sickness lingering in the air. Those vaguely sweet smells were impossible to eradicate despite the determined cleanliness of the chamber.

The long, rectangular room was covered in snow-white tiles from the floor to the vaulted ceilings. Three window-shaped indents were set in each of the long walls. Instead of glass, the alcoves were tiled in a brilliant silver-and-gold mosaic depicting two interlocking crescent moons with a small sunburst at their heart.

The two long walls were lined with a dozen beds, though only seven of them were occupied. The patients were a mixture of young and old, male and female. Some of them were nursing broken bones, others were clearly sick, and one or two looked perfectly healthy as they slept beneath the diffuse white light emanating from a single sunlike orb in the ceiling.

I spotted Nariko, the lone witch in the room, as Ozura and I crossed the threshold. Nariko was perched on the edge of a little girl's bed and didn't even look up as we entered. The girl, who couldn't be more than eight years old, didn't move as Nariko checked her temperature or flinch when Nariko touched her wrist. I pressed my lips together, suppressing a feeling of dread.

I'd seen that kind of too-still sleep in people before. It never boded well.

"Are you free, Nariko?" Ozura asked.

Nariko scribbled a note in the little book on the girl's bedside table, before standing. And freezing. "Askia? What are you—" She looked cautiously between Ozura and me. "Yes, I'm free."

"Good. We're off for training room three."

"Training room—" Nariko started to say, but Ozura had already hurried out the infirmary's far door. "But that means— Are you a—"

I nodded, replying to her unasked question with a weary smile. Ever since I stepped into the menagerie, time had slipped away from me in great heaps, warping the world at an alarming pace. Whether the change would be in my favor remained to be seen. *No going back now*, I thought, following Ozura.

If the infirmary was all but devoid of color, the training room more than compensated. It was almost like entering the Shrine of Lady Night. Indigo carpet blanketed the floor with fat crimson pillows set out for seating. Three of its walls were tiled like a swirling night sky.

On the fourth wall, the stars and auroras coalesced into the breathtaking form of a woman. Her face was veiled, but her right hand was raised in crescent-shaped benediction. It was Lady Night incarnate: unknowable and eternal as the distant starlight.

Her gifts were arrayed before her on a long benchlike altar, seven bowls for the seven types of magic. The first four were filled with the elemental magics: a night-blooming rose frozen in the flush of youth, a bowl of water shimmering with depth that should have been impossible, delicate silver chimes dancing in a wind I couldn't feel, a small crackling fire. Then were the three spirit magics: a bowl of blood representing healers, a white crystal that glowed like a living human soul represented mind witches, and finally a grinning human skull, the province of a death witch.

"Which bowl is yours?" Nariko asked, her voice bright with curiosity.

"The last one," Ozura replied as if she knew my lips weren't up to the task.

I looked down at the skull, the bleached bone too pale in the low gloom of the witchlight burning overhead. I shuddered. Turned away. "What now?" I asked, trying not to see the wonder in Nariko's face or the way she mouthed a silent *Wow*.

"What are your powers like?" Nariko asked, as she and Ozura settled onto a pair of pillows.

"That's what I was just about to ask." Ozura motioned to the empty pillow between them. "Tell us about your magic. You say your father gave you some training?"

"Yes," I replied, smoothing imaginary wrinkles from my skirt as I sat. "But there's not much to tell. He taught me to summon my magic as well as suppress it. Even suppressed, I can see ghosts. It takes only a little effort to speak with them."

"Can you control them?"

I frowned. "I've never tried. The ghosts who are interested approach and will help me. I leave the others alone."

Ozura tilted her head. "What do you mean, 'help'?"

I thought of Tarek leading me through the maze but was hesitant to bring him up to Ozura. "Well, let's say I wanted Vitaly to keep track of someone. If I ask him, I'd bet he'd be willing to do it." Now that I thought about it, this was an excellent idea. I should have sicced him on Dobor the moment we landed.

"Vitaly? The soldier who betrayed you?" Ozura stilled for a heartbeat, then two. "You still see him?"

"Yes. He followed me from Eshkaroth."

"I wasn't aware that was possible."

I shifted, remembering Vitaly's dying oath. "What do you mean?"

"The last record I could find of a death witch was a man

called Alessio Danastio from Serrala Province. It was said he could speak with spirits, compel them to serve him, even bring them out of the Marchlands. What he could not do was move them from where they died. He certainly couldn't make them cross a sea."

I swallowed, caught between fear and pride. "What does this make me?"

"It makes you your father's daughter." Ozura smiled, her expression lambent with a pride neither one of us deserved. "It also means there is no reason you won't be able to master the three things you'll need to defeat Radovan."

"What three things?" I asked, feeling my eyes narrow at Ozura.

"First, you need to be proficient in summoning a specific ghost from the Marchlands. And that's what we will be starting with today," Ozura said. "Then you will need to learn to command them. Finally, you'll need to work on giving them form."

The idea of giving a soldier like Vitaly form was certainly enticing, but the preparation Ozura had already put into what my training would entail made me pause. "How do you have everything ready and waiting already?"

One of Ozura's ebony brows rose. "Well, I wasn't prepared for *you* specifically, Askia," she replied, her tone making it clear she thought I was self-centered for assuming as much. "I've been looking for a death witch for many years, hoping I could find them before Radovan did. The fact that it's you is . . . serendipitous."

I huffed a laugh. "Sure it is."

She gave me a wry smile. "Are you ready to begin?"

I gave a halfhearted nod.

"Good. Now I want you to summon a specific ghost—not your Vitaly, mind you, that would be too easy. Choose one that you've seen around the palace. Nariko will be here to gauge your tether response and ensure it doesn't cause you undue harm."

And you're here to make sure I don't lie about my progress, I thought, managing to keep the sour words behind my lips.

I pushed my hair back. Straightened my shoulders. Closed my eyes.

And dove.

I'd always sensed the power within me, like how I could sense my arm even while lying still. The difference was that throwing a punch took almost no thought. Drawing on my magic to wield, though—that took all the concentration I had.

The magic lay deep in my chest, nestled in the hollow space beneath my heart. It was an ember that couldn't be banked. As I focused, the ember sparked. Burned. But not with heat. With ice.

A sharp prickling sensation overtook my body. I knew without looking that I was going red, as my blood scrambled to protect organs more vital than skin. My breath went cold. It felt like I was wandering through a blizzard with no coat. Frozen air pressed against my face, and I knew if I opened my eyes I'd see not the bright altar of Lady Night but the vast gray sea of the Marchlands.

I grit my teeth, refusing to give in to the shiver that begged to be released. This reaction was my tether, the price I paid for using magic. I knew it was different for each witch. A healer like my father or Nariko would suffer exhaustion. Fire witches from fevers, water witches from pneumonia. It wasn't free, our magic. It wasn't limitless either.

I sniffed, made my breathing stay even and focused on the magic, forcing it to grow inside me. Lady Night, I was out of practice. But I'd be damned if I let the magic defeat me when the task should be so simple.

Call a ghost. Any ghost save Vitaly. It wasn't like there was a dearth of restless spirits in the city. There were probably a hundred in the palace alone. Lady Night, I was below a cemetery! I just needed to pick one, focus, and call. But who?

The sergeant. He seemed friendly enough. And though we'd never spoken, I'd seen him talking with Vitaly during my last few training sessions. I held his memory in my imagination, but it wasn't enough to see a shade of a man. I needed to see him as flesh and blood and bone.

My mind filled in his face; it was angular as a block of wood, his beard bushy and full like General Ochan's, but the ghost was fitter, more like Captain Nazir that way. I recalled the red of Nazir's uniform, the metallic chink of Ochan's armor as he moved. The image filled my mind, and I let it grow, grow until it was too large to contain, and when it was, I would fling it out to the Marchlands, a silent calling.

I circled the image, checking it against what I felt was true, and what I knew from Nazir and Ochan. And I remembered the brand on his neck.

Fear sliced through my control and rippled across the empty sea before me. I shuddered and the brand grew large in my mind's eye. What if the ghost-sergeant was Shazir? What would he do when he found out I was a witch—for I was sure that not even the gray purgatory of the Marchlands could shake that zealotry. Lady Night save me, I already had the living Shazir on my back, I didn't need dead ones haunting me too.

I struggled to breathe, to focus past the sudden panic. The fear. My power flickered.

What was I doing? My parents died to protect me, died at the Shazir's hands, and here I was—

"Well, well. Look at what we have here."

My eyes shot open as the sandpapery voice licked up my spine.

"Three little witches sitting in a room, waiting so patiently for their coming doom." The voice crooned the words, filling them with malicious glee.

"Askia? Are you all right?"

Nariko's voice reached me as if from a great distance. I didn't reply. Couldn't. My head was filled with the sound of shuffling footsteps, with the burn of hate-filled eyes on my back and the peppery stench of madness and rage.

I bit the inside of my cheek. Let blood fill my mouth. I counted silently to three. Turned.

The ghost floated along the edge of the far wall. His eyes were wide and dark as the burning hearts of spent embers. He muttered to himself. I couldn't hear his words, but the growing animal panic in my chest didn't need to hear them to sense the danger. And I was definitely in danger from this man, who even in the gray void of the Marchlands wore robes as red as fresh blood.

A small, childlike whimper wiggled into my ears, and I realized with a start that it was my own.

"Askia!" My name flew from Ozura's lips like the crack of a whip. My chin angled toward her voice. My eyes stayed on the ghost. The ghost who had frozen midglide. Turned.

"Askia, what do you see?" Ozura asked in a voice heavy with command.

"A . . . a man in Shazir robes. A priest, or—"

"A Shazir priest?" Ozura asked. "Are you sure?"

"Can you see me, little witch?" the ghost breathed, his face splitting in a slow grin.

"Yes," I said, inadvertently answering both of them.

"No Shazir priests have died in the city." Nariko's whisper crossed my face, aimed at Ozura.

But that wasn't true, I thought, as Lord Marr's voice echoed in my memory. One had died. Recently. It was why Khaljaq came to Bet Naqar. My hands curled around the embroidered edge of my pillow.

"Brother Jalnieth," Ozura supplied, coming to the same realization as me. "Is that who you're seeing?"

"The witches know my name," the ghost muttered more to himself than to me. *"But am I flattered or furious?"*

"Y-yes. It's him, but . . . But there's something wrong with him."

"What's wrong, Askia?" Ozura asked, clasping one of my hands. Her skin was so warm it almost burned. She squeezed, demanding an answer.

"He seems . . . mad."

"Oh, I'm not mad," he whispered, floating back and forth, back and forth. Inching closer. Closer. *"I'm enraged. Despite a lifetime of good works, witches still pollute my home."*

"I've read about this happening," Ozura said, her voice calm. "Sometimes spirits get stuck in the Marchlands, because of unfinished business, or because they can't accept death . . . can't accept that death is different from what they expected."

"Unfinished business?" he whispered, tasting the words. *"Yes. Yes, that must be it. The Day Lord is calling on me to continue his work. With you."*

His gaze speared through me. I skittered backward. Felt my shoulders slam into the altar. But there was nowhere to escape. Nowhere to flee. Nowhere to hide that this hate-filled shade couldn't follow me. It was every nightmare I'd ever had given form.

"You can see me, little witch. Hear me too. Can you feel me, I wonder? Let's find out. Let me purify you through pain. I'll scour the magic from your polluted bones and deliver you to the Day Lord myself. Earn my place by his side."

"Askia." Ozura snapped her fingers in front of my face. "Askia, you are in control."

"Are you, Askia? Do you feel in control?" he sneered, then paused. Something clicked behind his midnight eyes. *"Aaaaas-ssskiaaa. I know that name. I know you."*

My eyes blurred as the ghost lunged. I loosed a cry. Flung my hands out as if they could protect me. He towered over me, hand stretched out in bony claws. His shadelike body hummed with violence. It coalesced before me. Became firmer and more real by the second.

I felt tears run down my face, conscious of them only by their heat. My arms screamed with the sting of a thousand bees. I couldn't feel my hands.

"Askia," Ozura barked, "*focus*."

She and Nariko knelt before me, oblivious to the ghost standing between them.

"Should I put her to sleep?" Nariko asked, her voice tight with fear. But not enough fear. Because now the ghost was looking at her. "That would sever the magic, wouldn't it?"

"*No!*"

The ghost twisted. His clawed hand flew. Connected with Nariko's pale cheek. Ripped right through it.

Nariko screamed and fell back. She clapped a hand over her cheek, blood bright against her pale skin. She looked around, frantic now, but her eyes couldn't find the looming ghost. The ghost that beheld his bloody hand like a thing of wonder.

"*The witch could feel me,*" he purred, and then with a long cat-like tongue, licked her blood off his fingers. He closed his eyes, shivering with unmistakable pleasure. "*Deelicious.*"

"Askia, focus," Ozura shouted, shaking my arms. "He only has the power you give him, but the power is still yours."

Was it, though?

The ghost's face didn't bear looking at. His gaze devoured Nariko. Nariko, whose entire body shook. Whose eyes overflowed with tears. Nariko, who'd likely never been struck in her whole life. Who would never even dream of striking back. Nariko, who never discounted kindness and decency in a court that saw such things as weaknesses. Who quietly refused to back down when she stood in the right, but never hesitated to forgive. Who saw enough in me, to count me as a friend, scars and all.

And that *fucking* ghost hit her.

"*No.*"

The blizzard in my mind screamed. Numbness raced up my arms. Sweat froze on my skin. I didn't care about any of it. Fury roared in my chest. I used it. Seized the magic inside me. And rose.

"*Why, whatever is this? Does the littlest witch intend to fight me?*"

"*Silence,*" I hissed the word, flinging my hand out like a sword, stabbing straight through his chest. He gasped, doubling over. His mouth worked, utterly helpless as I took his coal-like heart in my fist.

Squeezed. My own heart sang with vicious pride as his whole body went limp in my hand. "*I banish you, Brother Jalnieth. Leave the Marchlands and surrender yourself to the judgment of Lady Night.*"

"*No,*" he squealed, but I refused to be deterred. I let his screams wash over me and clenched my fist.

The shade exploded. Tiny smokelike fragments of ghost rained through the air, disappearing into nothingness before hitting the floor.

Magic whooshed out of me. My knees buckled. I managed to catch myself on the lip of the altar and ease myself to the floor with some semblance of grace. "Nariko? Are you all right?" I asked, crawling over to her.

"I . . . is he gone?"

"Yes," I said, pulling her hand away from her face to look at the gash, but the wound was already half healed through her magic.

"Are you sure?" she asked in a tiny voice that broke my heart.

"Yeah," I said. "I'm not sure if it's possible to kill a ghost, but if it is, I did."

"What happened to him after you banished him?" Ozura asked, kneeling beside Nariko.

"He kind of . . . exploded."

A laugh chuffed out from between Ozura's teeth. "Typical."

She shook her head and rubbed Nariko's back in a motherly sort of way.

"Well, I think we can all agree that this was an absolute disaster," Ozura said, her voice going clipped and business-like. "And since I have no desire to repeat this experience, you will tell me what you learned."

I blinked. My mind raced through the chain of events, struggling to process through what went wrong.

"Who were you trying to summon?" Ozura prodded.

"A sergeant I've seen in the training yard."

"And what happened when you tried to summon him?"

"I was trying to build a better image of him in my mind," I said, painfully aware of the way my voice was rising in defense. "I was using Captain Nazir and General Ochan sort of like templates. Only then I remembered that Ochan has a Shazir brand on his neck, and—"

"Yes, I see," Ozura said, shaking her head with obvious disappointment. "I am sure you will refrain from thinking about the Shazir when you summon from now on, but I think your problem goes deeper."

"Oh?"

"Nariko, did you notice that Askia's tether reaction activated sooner than expected?"

Nariko nodded apologetically. "It did seem to affect you sooner and with greater intensity than it should have. You were feeling cold."

I nodded. It was a massive understatement, but what could Vishiri women know of cold?

"And let me guess, you were fighting the cold while you were trying to summon this sergeant?" Ozura asked, looking at me like she already knew the answer and was not amused.

"Of course I was." I crossed my arms over my chest. "You can die of cold, you know."

"Not with a healer sitting next to you, which is the entire reason she was here," Ozura replied.

"So what am I supposed to do?" I asked, feeling a sudden and terrible longing for bed. "She's not always going to be near me."

"No. So stop thinking of the tether as an enemy."

"What?"

"The tether is part of your magic, Askia. If you fight the tether, you end up fighting the magic.

"*Embrace* the cold."

"Even though it could kill me?"

"So could your sword, but that doesn't stop you from practicing with it."

My words dried up at that, not only because I knew she was right, but also because it made a kind of sense.

Ozura pushed herself to her feet with an arch smile. "If you treat your magic like an enemy, your magic will only attract your enemies. Do you understand?"

I bowed my head. "I think so."

"Good. We'll start again tomorrow. Sleep if you can," she said over her shoulder as she headed for the door. "Lady Night knows I won't."

17

A letter was waiting for me when I stumbled bleary-eyed into the parlor the next morning. I unfolded the message over the dregs of my tea and squinted at the florid handwriting scrawled across the heavy parchment.

"Illya," I called, my eyes glued to the page. "Get ready. Queen Ozura has invited us to court."

"I know, my lady."

"What?" I looked up. Illya stood in the threshold, Nariko behind him.

"Lady Nariko has arrived to help you prepare." Illya didn't smile. His face would probably shatter if he ever tried, but there was a certain softening around his eyes I thought conveyed the expression. He bowed and retreated through the door, leaving me with a grinning Nariko.

"Are you ready for this?" she asked.

"No."

Nariko laughed, no trace of last night's attack marring her face. "That's why I've come to assist you. Come on, let's go pick out a dress," she said, but instead of tugging me into the dressing room, Nariko craned her head out the door like she was trying to make sure we were alone. When she spun around again, her face was creased with concern. "How are you feeling? Did you sleep?"

I breathed a mirthless ha. "Not a wink."

"Because of the ghost?" she asked, her voice so soft I knew that she hadn't slept either.

"Yes. And no." The memory of Brother Jalnieth would no doubt haunt my dreams for years to come, but my mind had been too agitated for rest, and in the wee evil hours of the night it turned to worry. And worry became . . . "Nariko, who else would Ozura tell about me?"

Nariko's expression softened and she took one of my hands, squeezing it bracingly. "The other guildmasters know, of course. And she'll have to inform the emperor. She's telling the rest of the guild that she's helping you work on cementing allies in court as a favor to your father even though you're a magicless half blood. Her words," Nariko said apologetically.

I rolled my eyes. "Well, I suppose it would look strange if she suddenly started being nice to me."

"And it gives you an excuse to come back to the guild tonight."

"You did it," a booming voice exclaimed from the door.

I jumped just as Iskander seized my waist and spun me around with a laugh that made my rib cage hum. He released me, sending me careening into Illya who had planted himself in the door, expression hard.

"Prince Iskander!" Nariko's voice rose two octaves in shock. "You can't be here."

He waved her words away. "You did it. You got on my mother's good side."

Nariko threw herself in front of me, arms out like she was trying to cover me up. "But Her Highness isn't decent."

Iskander cocked his head, looking at my robed body with a wolfish grin. "I know."

Nariko whirled on me, so scandalized her face looked green. "My lady, please."

"How is this my fault?" The urge to laugh bubbled up in my throat. "You know I don't actually control him, right?"

Iskander laughed unrepentantly. "We have to celebrate," he cried, throwing himself into one of the chairs. "Dinner. Tonight."

I raised an eyebrow at the stupidity of the suggestion. "I do learn from my mistakes, Iskander. Anyway, your mother asked me to come to the menagerie." *Not a total lie*, I thought. Ozura had me on a nightly schedule for magic-training. And I was going through the menagerie, after all.

"Wow, you really changed her opinion. How in the Day Lord's light did you do it?" he asked, popping a strawberry into his mouth.

"I did what you suggested—I followed her," I began, eyes narrowing. "I didn't know I was following her to the Shadow Guild. Or that she's a witch, so thanks for that."

"You went *where*?" The words hissed out of Illya's clenched jaw, making the hairs on my arms rise.

"You said you didn't want to know," I whispered back.

"So you're a witch?" Iskander asked, plainly oblivious to the heat coursing between Illya and I.

"I still need to know where you are. Always." For the first time I saw worry creep into the edges of Illya's expression. The mask of anger cracked, and I saw something else. Something more than duty. Something I wanted to reach for.

I blinked, and it was gone. Illya straightened a little, and I felt the distance suddenly whoosh between us.

"Askia?"

"What?" I asked, turning at the confusion in Iskander's voice.

"You crossed the portal—so you must be a witch, right?"

I opened my mouth, but the words got stuck when Vitaly

appeared at Iskander's side. His face was creased into a guarded frown, a warning in his spectral gaze.

"No," I said finally. "I found your mother just as she was leaving the guild. I guess it's like you said; she just admired a bold move."

Iskander's face quirked into a half frown, and he shook his head. "She never ceases to amaze me." He huffed a laugh. "And now you're invited to court."

"Yes," I said, seizing onto an idea to get him to leave. "And I'm going to be late if you don't get out of here."

"All right, all right," Iskander said, pulling himself up. "Good luck today, my lady." He proffered a ridiculous bow, clasping my hand before I could pull away. He pressed his lips to my knuckles with a heat that made me squirm. "We're getting close, Askia," he said, smiling that honest smile.

I smiled back as he left, but felt my face stiffen. Why was I lying? For all the help he'd given me, didn't he deserve the truth? I glanced around the room, but there were no ghosts to be found. No answers either.

"I'll be with you the whole time," Nariko said, fixing the train of my crimson gown as we walked out of my apartment. "Don't expect too much. The emperor might not even be there. If he is, he'll likely be occupied. You should approach to be officially welcomed by Queen Ozura, after which you'll be at liberty to do as you please. I'll introduce you to anyone you wish, but I encourage you to mingle."

I nodded, dry mouthed. Small talk was my personal hell. Not that I was bad at it, but I found the effort exhausting. Arkady and I had even worked out a system of subtle gestures, so he knew when to step in and whisk me away. And though his weekly messages were filled with advice, his words couldn't make up for his absence. Day Lord, how I missed him, but he was in the north perched on the border of Idun and Seravesh. If I failed, he and the rest of the Black Wolves would likely be killed once the mountain passes melted. I could not let that happen. So I squared my shoulders and followed Nariko into the Rose Hall.

The first thing my slightly overexcited mind noticed about the hall was its near absence of color. The white-tile roof was supported by three pairs of alabaster columns that descended evenly down the hall. Couch-lined alcoves sat between the pillars. I assumed, based on the decadent jewelry worn by the men sitting there, the alcoves were reserved for the powerful.

On the other side of the room, directly opposite me, was a dais raised up on two pristine white steps. Emperor Armaan and Queen Ozura sat at the head table with several men, including Prince Enver. Even sitting, I could tell Enver was shorter than his brother. Slighter too. He had a weak chin and a too-sharp nose that gave him a pinched expression.

I forced my eyes away, looking at the two white hexagonal pools standing waist-high on either end of the room. A channel ran between them, though the water was almost entirely obscured by ruby-red roses in the perfect flush of bloom. Surrounded by so much white, the channel looked like an open vein.

Nariko was studying the tables abutting either side of the channel. More noblemen and women sat there, talking and eating and laughing, although none of them had noticed my arrival.

"What now?" I asked.

"We're waiting for the lord chamberlain. Oh," Nariko said, her face brightening. "There he is."

The lord chamberlain, who until now had been leaning over in avid discussion with a man in the alcove to the right of the throne, straightened. His eyes widened when they met mine. The expression was so pronounced, the whole group turned to look at me. I pretended not to notice, but I thought I recognized one of the men. He and his companions wore bright azure-colored robes. I thought they might be from Serrala—the remote Vishiri province home to the finest blue dyes in the world.

I hazarded another look and saw the lord chamberlain cross the room with long, purposeful strides, looking competent if not a little harried. "Princess," he said with a smooth bow that caught the attention of everyone in the room. "Welcome to the Rose Hall."

"Hello, Lord Chamberlain."

"I apologize if you were forced to wait. There has been some excitement at court." He spoke in a conspiratorial way that would have made me suspicious were it not for his merry expression.

"Oh?" I asked, taking the Lord Chamberlain's proffered arm and allowing him to escort me down the suddenly great length of the Rose Hall.

"The delegation from Serrala Province arrived yesterday with a grievance against the crown."

"What kind of grievance?" I asked, careful to look anywhere but at the Serralans.

"The crown has commissioned a garrison to be built outside the main town. The old one is apparently derelict and far too small to support Serrala's needs. The Serralan people, however, are not having it. The Council of Viziers has been closeted with them for the past twenty-four hours, but the Serralans are intractable. It's a vexing situation."

I made a sympathetic sound, the gears of my mind turning.

"Your family spent time in Serrala Province, did they not, Your Highness?" the lord chamberlain asked, a cunning glint in his eye.

"We did."

"I thought so. Lord Marr thought you mentioned you spoke Serralan."

I smiled, sure I mentioned no such thing to Lord Marr. "Indeed, I do. Would the council like me to speak to the delegation?" I asked, innocently. It would be a daring move, meddling in Vishiri affairs, but it could prove I had more power than just my sword arm.

"Oh, no. Nothing so official," the lord chamberlain said in the hurried way that practically begged me to step in. "This is an informal gathering. Eat, drink, and introduce yourself to the court. There are many young people here who are excited to meet you."

My gaze darted to Queen Ozura at his words and I recalled how our conversation had veered toward marriage. I'd told her I wasn't interested. But considering the disproportionate number of young noblemen in the room, and the notable lack of Prince Iskander, Ozura had other ideas.

I hid a smile at the thought of Queen Ozura trying to marry me off. I wasn't a fool. Though marriage was far from my first choice, I knew it wasn't off the table. I'd do it in a heartbeat if it got me an army, but did Ozura really think I'd settle for some young upstart lord of Vishir?

Probably.

I was passing the last set of alcoves nearest the throne when I spotted Count Dobor. He sat in the corner, like a crouched spider waiting for its prey. Ishaq was next to him, whispering in his ear. Dobor saw me looking and raised his glass with a jovial smile.

The urge to crawl over the table and strangle Dobor was almost overwhelming. I forced my neck to bend with the slightest of nods and looked away. This was my introduction to the court. Queen Ozura had cracked open the door. It was up to me to step through, and by my behavior alone would Seravesh be saved. Or perish.

I repeated this to myself, walking the last three feet to the edge of the dais. The emperor was watching. His gaze danced over me like the dusting of snow, and the beginnings of a smile tugged at his lips. The steady hum of conversation stilled, and everyone in the hall turned to watch. Except one.

Prince Enver ate his luncheon in silence, looking at the wall like nothing in the room held any interest for him.

I refused to let anger ripple my expression. Instead, I looked at Ozura and the emperor and managed a smile.

Ozura smiled back, her eyes lighting up with a warmth that was entirely alien to me. The queen might be a truth witch, but she sure as hell knew how to put on an act with the best of them. "Welcome, Princess Askia," Ozura said, leaning forward, her hand resting on the emperor's arm. "We are honored by your presence."

"The honor is mine, Queen Ozura. Thank you for your hospitality, and for allowing me the space to recuperate these past few days." I matched Ozura's warmth with a syrupy reply.

"But of course," Ozura said, laughter glinting in her eyes. "The court of the Empire of Vishir welcomes you. Please join us."

I nodded to both Ozura and the emperor with as much grace as I could muster, knowing I wouldn't be invited to sit at the high table. Not that I really wanted to, with Enver still so pointedly ignoring me. He didn't even know me and already he was set against me. With that realization, cold, vindictive pleasure filled my veins.

Fine. Perhaps the young prince vizier would like to watch me succeed where his efforts failed.

I turned and, ignoring all the fine young men who were trying to catch my eye, approached the oldest man in the room. "Buenviano pancciti alazar," I said, greeting the Serralan delegation with the lilting dance of their native tongue. "May I join you, eldest?"

The old man perked up when I spoke—and he was truly old. When I was a child, I thought Gianno Trantini, Lord of Serrala, had come into the world ancient. Now I knew better and prayed he remembered me, that he would recall the sound of my voice.

His clouded, sightless eyes homed in on my position. The wrinkled skin of his face folded into a smile. "Princess Askia, is that you?"

"Yes, eldest," I replied, smiling my relief.

"Come. You must join us."

The men of the Serralan delegation hurried to make room for me. I shuffled past them and sat beside Lord Trantini. Nariko perched on the edge of the cushion next to me. I felt nervous energy bubbling off her and wondered if Nariko had ever been alone among the lords of the Vishiri court without a chaperone. Illya chose to stand at the foot of the step that led up to the alcove. He watched the assembled nobles, his expression hard. I doubted he would relax, not with Count Dobor present. Not that I wanted him at ease. His every forbidding exhalation only increased my stature in the court.

"May I look at you?" Lord Trantini asked, holding up one wrinkled hand.

"Of course." I guided the tips of his fingers to my forehead, ignoring the scandalized gasps of the court ladies looking on. They could go to hell as far as I was concerned. My family had stayed in Serrala Province for almost a year. Lord Trantini had welcomed us to his home—an oasis in the wilds of southern Vishir. And even if I wasn't playing politics, I would have welcomed his touch. As his fingers brushed lightly against my face, I was momentarily transported back in time, to the salty sea air of many-canaled Serrala.

"My, you have grown," Lord Trantini said, with a wistful smile. "Tell me, are you well?"

"Yes, eldest."

His caterpillar eyebrows rose to his white, well-oiled hairline. "Are you?"

Lord Trantini's voice was low, hardly more than a whisper, excluding the rest of the hall and most of the alcove. I matched it. "No, eldest. Of course not. But I am working. I am fighting, and I have not yet lost hope."

"I thought that might be the case. Yours is the longest of roads, the hardest. But my dear, you were born to it. You were raised a traveler and your journey is not yet done." He frowned, his milky white eyes sliding across the planes of my face as though he saw something in the darkness behind his eyes. "I have heard Count Dobor boast you are to marry Emperor Radovan. Is this true?"

Radovan's letter flashed into my mind, followed by the names of all his dead wives. "No."

He laughed, clearly hearing the rage pressed into that simple word. "Good. He is not the man for you, I think."

His laughter was like a hot cup of tea on a cold winter night, and I found myself smiling. "Oh? I don't suppose you have a man waiting for me in Serrala?" I asked, drawing the eyes of the entire Serralan delegation. I was glad I was speaking their language rather than Vishiri. Serralans were not so prudish as their Vishiri overlords.

"My dear, Serrala would be honored if that were so, but I think you are destined for greater things." He clasped my hand, his face turning serious. "I think there is darkness ahead of you, but you are never alone. Your father and mother were loved the world over, and so it will be with you. Remember, death is not the end of life."

"I remember, eldest, and I look forward to seeing them again." My smile was a tremulous one. I squeezed his hand, knowing the gesture could never fully convey how full my heart felt at that moment. The Serralans believed life didn't end when the heart stopped beating. To them, life continued, albeit on a different plane—one tied to the location where the person died. I wondered what the Serralans would say if they knew I'd brought Vitaly with me from Eshkaroth.

"But that is down the road, Day Lord willing. What of you, though? What brings you to Bet Naqar?"

Lord Trantini's features rearranged themselves into a frown that added years to his already vast age. "We come with our annual tithe to reaffirm our allegiance to the emperor, and to beg favor." He sighed, dropping about two inches in height. "We ask so little, but what we do ask for is met with derision and scorn."

"From the emperor?" I asked, feeling my forehead crinkle.

"No. From his Council of Viziers." Lord Trantini waved his hand like he was trying to rid the air of the sound of the council's name. "They wish to build a new garrison."

"And this is a problem?"

"It shouldn't be, but they wish to build on the Field of Arcatium."

The name rang a bell deep in the recesses of my memory. I paused to let my brain catch up with the conversation. Wherever my family went in my youth, my mother always organized a tutor to school me on all those things a young lady needed to know. I had been only ten when my family lived in Serrala, and at the time history was not something I was terribly interested in, but even my studious disinterest couldn't keep me from absorbing the most important bits of Serrala's history.

"The Field of Arcatium . . . where the Blue Battalion died?"

Lord Trantini's smile was filled with relief. "You understand. They were our greatest warriors. They fell in glorious battle on the Field of Arcatium and rose again on that same field to continue their everlasting life."

I nodded, looking around the small alcove at the proud Serralan men around me. The battalion was the last force the Serralans ever fielded against Vishir. The casualties were massive on both sides, and the result was the dismantling of the Serralan military and the total absorption of the onetime kingdom into the vast apparatus of the Empire of Vishir.

No wonder the Council of Viziers didn't want to change their plans. They wouldn't want to be seen memorializing what they considered to be a rebel group. Why should they care four hundred Serralan men died there for freedom? Some of them, I thought, glancing at the haughty-looking prince at the high table—who was still ignoring me—probably thought putting a garrison on the Field of Arcatium was an appropriate expression of Vishiri dominance.

I struggled not to sigh, wishing I could help. The empire wasn't known for flexibility, and while it embraced cultural differences across its many provinces, there were limits. Those limits almost certainly included changing their plans to honor men who died fighting against the empire.

Not that it was what Lord Trantini was trying to do, but the truth probably sounded so strange to the council. I wouldn't be surprised if they decided it was no more than a flimsy lie. As Lord Trantini said, death was not the end of life, not in Serrala. The four hundred men who died on the Field of Arcatium were not lost to the world. They still lived there, but their continued existence depended entirely on the battlefield remaining intact. If that place was destroyed, they were lost. Their discontented souls would haunt Serrala for eternity. There was no greater curse.

As I thought the words, Prince Enver rose. He folded his napkin with dainty hands and circled the high table, walking to the alcove directly across from mine. With a languid smile and deep, throaty laugh, he sat beside Count Dobor and Ishaq. They bent their heads together. Scheming.

My vision flashed red. What fresh hell was Dobor planning now? Magic, still restless from last night's training, sparked to life. Goose bumps cascaded down my limbs, but with Ozura's words fresh in my mind, I didn't try to fight it.

The ghost of a Khazan Guard sergeant appeared at the edge of the table—the very one I'd tried and failed to summon last night. *"Send me,"* he said, gray eyes glimmering. *"My men and I know Roven will eventually come for Vishir. We are with you, my lady. We will watch him."*

The room stilled for a moment before erupting in a torrent of whispers. Prince Enver's blatant disregard of me seemed to set a kind of precedent that many others were now following. Even though I felt the regard of everyone in the room, it was furtive, as if they didn't want to be caught looking at me or listening to my words. Only the Serralans welcomed me; only they thought me worthwhile.

Well, damn them all, I thought. I wasn't without power, not completely. If they wanted to ignore me because of this petty prince, fine. I could make my mark without them. I sent the ghost-sergeant on his way and returned my attention to Lord Trantini.

"I don't have much sway here," I began, a self-deprecating smile tugging at my lips. "The emperor hasn't agreed to meet with me, nor has the Council of Viziers. But I have friends. Among them is Prince Iskander. I will speak to him, and to General Ochan of the Khazan Guard, and to Queen Ozura. I will ask them to intercede on your behalf."

"Princess, why would you do this?" Lord Trantini asked, his eyes bright.

I gave a dry chuckle. "I'm an outsider here, and you have given me a place, if only for an afternoon." I clasped his hand so he would feel me shrug. "If the council is against me, then I can only gain by succeeding where they failed."

The entire alcove laughed, drawing the attention of the court for one sparkling moment. Not even Prince Enver could keep from looking, though his face was pinched and sour.

"To Princess Askia," one of the men cried, holding his glass in the air.

I ducked my head, feigning modesty while I peeked through my eyelashes at the high table. I looked past the feline satisfaction of Queen Ozura and saw a smile playing about the emperor's full lips. His smile widened when our gazes met, and he nodded to me.

I'd clearly made an impression.

It was a start.

18

A h, Askia, good. You're right on time," Ozura said when I presented myself in the training room with the midnight bell echoing at my back.

"Good evening, Ozura. Nariko." I hitched my father's grimoire closer to my chest and closed the door behind me, stifling a yawn. Meeting in the middle of the night was going to take some getting used to, but it ensured we had the guild to ourselves. Neither Nariko nor Ozura looked any worse for wear after the long day. Then again, neither one of them had gone sparring after lunch.

"What do you have there?" Ozura asked, settling on her cushion.

"It's my father's grimoire," I replied, kneeling beside her.

Nariko's gasp was filled with wonder, and she leaned forward like she could absorb its contents from proximity alone. My fingers tightened and I forced them to ease. This was why I brought it, I reminded myself.

"I thought I would . . . lend it to the infirmary. It has all his spells and medicines, therapies that both do and don't require magic, as well as case studies on his more difficult patients. I thought you might want to copy it."

Nariko's whole body trembled when I set the book in her

hands. She breathed it in, looking more reverent than most templegoers at worship. "Oh, I do. Thank you."

Ozura clasped my hand, squeezing it tightly. "That is very kind of you, Askia."

One of my shoulders twitched and I tried to ignore the growing warmth I felt at Ozura's approval. "It wasn't doing any good sitting in my trunk. And when I saw that little girl in the infirmary . . ."

Ozura nodded as my words wandered off. "Jaida Elon. She's Lord Vizier Elon's granddaughter." The queen shook her head, exhaustion and worry redolent on her dark face. "A difficult case. Owassa sleeping sickness. The healers were able to cure her body of the disease, but still she won't wake."

I winced in pity. Sleeping sickness seemed to break out every decade or so in the central Vishir province. "Hopefully something in my father's notes can help."

"Indeed," Ozura said before rubbing her hands together, transitioning back to business. "Well. Shall we begin?"

It was the very last thing I wanted to do, but I nodded anyway. "You want me to send out a summons again?"

"Yes, but this time, I don't want you to call someone in particular. Try to locate the spirit closest to us and bring them to you."

"All right." It made sense. The guild had an infirmary after all, and even with magical healers, people were bound to die occasionally. And by focusing on proximity, I was less likely to call anything as malevolent as Jalnieth.

I hoped.

"Remember what I said yesterday?" Ozura asked.

"Don't fight the tether."

"Embrace it," Ozura said, her voice firm. "The more you do, the more you practice, the further you will be able to push yourself next time."

I nodded, rolling my shoulders like I was about to go into a fight. Wrong mentality, as I'd learned last night, but—but maybe it wasn't so unlike learning to spar. Train, train, and train some more until my body performed the way I needed it to.

Keeping that comparison in mind, I sank.

I visualized myself diving into a wide frozen lake. Dark blue water parted around me as I dove, deeper and deeper still. I let the tether freeze my skin, let it sink into my bones and compress my lungs. And when I finally hit the floor, I pivoted, and pushed off. Magic filled me as I surfaced, but I didn't have the relief of gasping for breath. Only that slow killing cold.

I opened my eyes, neither fighting the pain nor acknowledging it. The Marchlands surrounded me. A gray veil shrouded Ozura and Nariko, making them look strangely wraithlike, as if they were the ghosts in this gray space.

"Hello?" I called silently. *"Is anyone there?"*

I paused, stretching every sense I had and a few I hadn't felt until then. There was something. Someone. I knew it. Felt it as keenly as the monsters that lived only in the corner of the eye. I could almost hear it, a sound somewhere between a breath and a cry.

"I can hear you," I called, trying to sound kind, though even the voice in my mind was out of practice at such a tone. *"Will you come out? Maybe I can help."*

"No one can help me," the voice answered, pitiful and teary. The body appeared a second later, a little girl whose hands were balled up against her eyes.

"What's wrong, little one?"

"I'm lost." She cried her anguish to the sky in childlike frustration, her hands falling away from her face.

A gasp tore out of my throat, cold air searing through my lungs. "Jaida?"

I'd spoken the name aloud, making Ozura, Nariko, and the little ghost all stiffen with surprise.

"What did you say?" Ozura demanded, but Jaida spoke too. *"You know my name?"*

"Yes," I replied quickly, trying to keep her young mind from despair. *"And you aren't lost. You're in the Shadow Guild. The healers here are treating you."*

"Are you a witch?" she asked, filled with the same kind of wonder I'd seen in Nariko's face when presenting the grimoire. She grinned when I nodded. *"But what kind of witch? And how can you see me? No one else can."*

"I'm a— My powers let me see into the Marchlands," I said, turning a verbal corner before the words *death witch* spilled out. Even I had to admit the title sounded sinister, and I didn't want to frighten the girl any more than she already was. When her face fell, I knew I'd failed.

Her eyes silvered with tears. *"Am I . . . am I dead?"*

"No," I hurried to say. *"No, your body is completely healed. You just haven't woken up yet."*

"I don't know how," she whined, her face cracking open with growing distress.

"It's all right. It's all right. I'm here. You're not alone," I said, biting my cheek. Lady Night save me, weren't women supposed to be nurturing? *"Let me just talk to my friends. I'm sure we can think of something."*

I glanced away from her and found both Nariko and Ozura crouched before me. I licked my lips, felt my saliva freeze, and met Nariko's eyes. "Jaida is here. She says she doesn't know how to get back into her body."

"Lady Night," Ozura breathed.

Nariko's face paled, dark eyes darting from me to Ozura and back again. "What do we do?" she whispered, like she was afraid the ghost-girl might hear.

"I don't know," I replied. "You're the healer, don't you have any ideas?" Nariko shook her head in panicked little jerks. But panic wouldn't help anyone right now. "Well, we'll figure nothing out by sitting around in here. Let's all go to the infirmary."

I turned back to Jaida as the two women rushed from the room and found her watching me with a pinched, suspicious expression. *"Do you know how to help me?"*

I was sliding on very thin ice here. If I told the little girl we had no idea what we were doing, she might lose all hope and run away. But the same thing could happen if I lied and we failed to unite her body and spirit.

I approached her with slow, deliberate steps and crouched so we were on eye level. *"Jaida, I don't want to lie to you. We aren't sure how to help you. Yet,"* I added as firmly as possible. *"But I promise you, we will do everything we can to save you. I won't give up on you. But please, just let me try."*

I held out my hand, let her consider. And when she slid her palm into mine, I smiled and walked with her back into the infirmary.

Ozura and Nariko were already there. Nariko was dancing frantically around Jaida doing checks. Ozura sat on the bed beside Jaida's flipping through pages of my father's grimoire. Her face was so intent, it was almost like she was interrogating the book and believed it was lying to her.

Jaida looked up at me, her lips pursed in an unimpressed frown. *"What do I do now?"*

I repeated the question to Nariko, who turned a full circle, nervous sweat actually beading on her brow. "Um. Well. Has she tried to . . . I don't know, lie down? On herself?"

"Of course I did. I'm not stupid," Jaida said, glaring at the oblivious healer.

"Will you try again?" I said aloud. "And when you do, could you describe what you feel? It might give us an important clue."

Jaida nodded doubtfully and headed toward her cot, walking straight through Nariko as she went. Watching her climb onto her flesh body created a jigsaw of jumbled arms and legs in my mind. She flipped herself over, sank into her skin. Except not.

"What do you see, Askia?" Ozura asked, her eyes hot on my face.

"Jaida's spirit is lying down where her body is, only . . . only it doesn't seem to quite fit." I felt my brows draw together as I studied the image. Jaida's spirit body had mostly sunk through her flesh, but I could clearly see a hair-thin, mist-colored over-lay where her spirit hovered freely, untethered from its corporeal home. *What do you feel, Jaida?*

"Nothing."

"She says she feels nothing," I relayed. *"It doesn't feel any different to you at all?"* I bit the inside of my cheek when she shook her head. "There has to be something we're missing. How do you usually treat sleeping sicknesses?"

"There are spells and potions that we usually use," Nariko replied, but now she looked worried, and guilty. "They only have about fifty percent efficacy."

"What's that mean?" Jaida asked.

"It means they don't always work," I replied.

"There's another treatment here," Ozura said, holding up my father's grimoire, her voice tight with restrained hope.

Nariko raced over like she'd been shocked, peering over the queen's shoulder, eyes blazing across the page.

Letting them work, I went to Jaida. Lady Night above, she looked so small, all lain out like this. Small, and terribly young. Sitting on the edge of the cot, I took her hand, or hands, really, though touching her was like simultaneously holding ice and fire. I smiled, trying not to wonder how much longer my body would be able to withstand the frigid core of my magic. Trying. But my fingers were turning blue.

"I've never seen a treatment like this. Is that music?" Nariko asked, her voice tinged with incredulity.

"Askia, did Sevilen ever sing to his patients?" Ozura asked.

"Um, yes," I said, combing my memories. "Not very often, but I do remember a few occasions when things seemed . . . on the edge. He'd hold their hands and sing. It was almost like a lullaby. My mother used to say he was trying to make the passage easier."

"You mean they . . . ?"

"Not always," I said, saving Nariko from the rest of her question. "Some chose to stay, others chose to go."

"Well, this must be it," Ozura said, shoving the book into Nariko's hands. "Quickly now, Nariko. You must try."

Jaida sat up quickly, popping out of her body as Nariko sat on the other edge of the bed. *What is she doing?*

"She's just going to sing you a song, right, Nariko?"

I nodded for Nariko to continue, willing her to treat Jaida's spirit as she would any other patient. "Uh, yes. That's right. I'm just going to sit here and sing you a song from this book."

"That's it?"

I winced. "She needs a little more convincing."

"I know it sounds odd, but some of our oldest healing spells are cast in song. The way sound moves through the air is very powerful. Have you ever heard a cat purr?"

"Yes," I replied, echoing the little girl.

"Well, their purrs actually help them heal. And that's not so very different from what I'm going to try. And with magic and luck, we might be able to join you to your body again." Nariko smiled hopefully, and though she wasn't quite looking at spirit-Jaida's face, it was warm enough to make the little girl smile. "Are you ready?"

"I've been ready."

Children.

"All right, Jaida. Why don't you lie back down? Let me know if you feel anything with Nariko's song." I shifted back, readying to

stand so I wasn't in the way, when the touch of a child's hand grabbed my fingers.

"Please don't go."

If words had the power to break a heart, mine nearly cracked. *"I'm not going anywhere. I'll be right next to you the whole time."*

Nariko propped the book open on her lap. Pushed her long black hair over her shoulder, clasped Jaida's hands. Exhaled hard. Sang.

Nariko's voice was a thing of beauty, high and clear as a blue sky on a summer's day. Snow-cold tears pricked my eyes. I could almost hear my father singing with her, a four-chord melody, quiet and peaceful and yet inexplicably ancient. My body hummed with it, this song that had been with me since the beginning. Since all beginnings.

The music poured out of Nariko, easy and fluid. But her brow was furrowed. The muscles in her neck and shoulders were tense as she focused on the words, and I knew without knowing that she was summoning every ounce of magic she possessed.

"Do you feel anything?" I asked, watching Jaida's ghost eyes close as the lullaby washed over her.

"I feel . . . I feel warmth in my chest."

"Just in your chest? Nowhere else?"

"No," she said, her voice becoming pinched by my question.

"Try to focus on the warmth. Concentrate on it with all your might. Can you make it grow?"

"I'm trying," she whined. *"But it's not working. It's like there's something in the way."*

"Shhhh, it's all right. Just keep trying," I said, forcing my voice calm as I met Nariko's worried eyes over the girl's body. "Keep going," I said, before the song could falter.

"What is it?" Ozura asked, leaning forward.

"Jaida says that she can feel a warmth in her chest, but it's like something is blocking it from growing."

"You think it needs to grow?"

"Heat is life," I replied to Ozura as a shiver worked its way through my core.

Ozura nodded. "Maybe we need to get another healer. Maybe together they can force open a door to life."

"Open a door to life," I repeated the words slowly, my mind racing with possibilities. I craned my neck, straining to see the words of the song. My eyes raked across the page, reading it once. Nariko was still holding Jaida's hands, so I placed my hands over Nariko's, ignoring her agonized gasp as my icy skin met her fevered flesh, and wrapped my fingers tight.

"What are you doing?" Ozura demanded.

"You said Nariko was opening a door into life," I replied quickly as I could. "What if Jaida needs me to open a door *out* of death."

Ozura paled. But Nariko nodded emphatically. I wet my frozen lips and joined the song.

My voice was weak and reedy to my own ears, made even more pathetic by comparison, but I forced myself to continue. Prayed to Lady Night that intention mattered more than execution. And spiraled down into myself.

Magic filled me, spooling and churning out of me. I sensed it questing over Jaida, crawling forward on legs made of hope and arms made of dreams. And I found it, that seed of warmth, of life at her heart. The ember was bright and filled with promise, but veiled. If I could just shift it . . .

I stretched forward, and even though the action was only in my mind, my body shuddered, racked with shivers that wouldn't warm me. Yet I still didn't fight the cold, but rather let it envelop me, let it lock my joints, let the numbness creep up my arms and legs, into my core. I reached. Further. Further.

Distantly, I realized I'd stopped shivering. Knew this was bad, but not why. All there was, was the song, and the rhythm and that veil that I could almost touch. I reached. Let the edges of my mind go gray, let my eyes fall closed and the promise of sleep surround me.

I felt the silken fall of the veil caress my fingertips.

In the dreamy recess of my mind, my fist closed around it.

I pulled.

19

Well, good morning," Nariko called out brightly as I shuffled into the parlor. "Or, afternoon," she amended.

"Yeah, great," I mumbled, wincing as I lowered myself into the chair.

"Sore?"

I'd have snorted, but it felt like a pair of hot pokers were being skewered into my knees. I moaned when I finally made it down. "What happened last night?"

"You passed out," Nariko said, looking less than amused. "Hypothermia, which could have killed you, by the way. Why didn't you stop?"

"If you could've seen how hopeless Jaida looked, you wouldn't have stopped either." I swallowed hard. "Did it work?"

Nariko beamed. "It worked."

I sighed my thanks to Lady Night. "How is she?"

"Perfect," Nariko said, reaching across the table to squeeze my hand. "You did well. And as I absolutely forbid you from guard training today, we can go visit her later."

I wanted to argue about training but knew better. No way my body could take another beating, and my current state would only cause questions. "I'd like that."

"Good. Let's get some food in you. We can go to the guild after we go to the Great Hall—the walk will be good for your joints."

"The Great Hall? Why? What's going on?"

Nariko's smile was all cat. "You'll just have to go there and find out."

THE SHEER NUMBER OF PEOPLE PACKED INTO THE HALL WAS STAGgering. Of course, it was always crowded on audience days, but this was something else. Women of all ages congealed in great packs bubbling with high-pitched excitement, oblivious to the business of court, except where it dealt with one very crucial topic: the ball. Apparently Queen Ozura had been quietly preparing to hold a masquerade ball in my honor, and the invitations had been sent this morning.

Not bad, considering when I first arrived, I couldn't even get an *invitation* to a ball. Still, this excitement was a bit cloying. Even the ghosts were beside themselves, listening in with shimmering excitement.

"What's the big deal? Didn't she just throw a ball?"

"Not like this." Nariko, like every other young person, was glowing with happiness. "It's the first time in years the queens have held a masque ball." She sighed in perfect ecstasy. "What will you go as?"

"I don't know," I replied, looking around at the packed audience chamber with hooded eyes.

"Well, Queen Ozura has probably arranged something for you to wear. You're lucky. She has excellent taste. Unlike my aunt." Nariko wrung her hands together in quiet agony. "She's possibly the least fashionable person in the entire empire. No doubt she'll bundle me up in a burlap sack that covers me from ankle to chin and call it a traditional dress of Kizuoka Province."

I smiled at the mental image, but something in Nariko's sincere desperation softened my heart. "Don't worry. If your aunt tries to put you in something terrible, sneak into my rooms and take one of my gowns. You can dress up as a beggar princess and win over half the court."

Nariko tutted. "They'll think I don't like you. Not that I'm saying no, mind you. I'm desperate."

I laughed. "If I didn't know any better, I'd think you were trying to catch someone's eye."

A delicate blush crept into her cheeks as her gaze darted forward. Ahead of us, the crowd parted, and I saw Iskander standing beside the throne. As he listened to a man petitioning the emperor, his expression was unusually serious.

My gaze slid to Nariko, whose lip was caught between her teeth. I felt my eyebrows rise in perfect unison. All the time the three of us spent together, Nariko and Iskander had barely exchanged more than a few words—most of which involved Nariko scolding him. I opened my mouth without knowing what to say.

"Ah, Princess Askia. There you are."

The sound of Dobor's voice made me stiffen. "Count Dobor."

"May I have a moment of your time?"

The last time he'd asked to speak privately with me, it was to tell me Radovan had butchered a city full of people. And he wanted to speak to me? He didn't deserve my words. He deserved a knife to the gut. Only the fear of what other news he might have stayed my hand.

I gestured for Nariko and Illya to step back. "Walk with me."

I angled away from the main body of the crowd, where the noblemen and -women were gathered in the center of the Great Hall. There was an empty pocket of space to the left of the throne. It was a dark corner, free of everyone but a pair of servants standing sentinel by a set of doors. It was far enough away from the throne that we wouldn't be overheard, but directly in

Iskander's line of sight. Perhaps with the royal family so close, Dobor would watch his words carefully.

Count Dobor gave me an unctuous smile. "My offices aren't far from here. Would you care to retire and take some tea with me?"

I crossed my arms by way of reply. Privacy in a crowd was one thing, but I didn't think I could be held accountable for my actions if we were ever truly alone. The Khazan Guard had been very thorough in their training.

Count Dobor seemed to take my silence for the refusal it was. His lips twitched into the shadow of a sneer before the well-oiled smile reasserted itself. "Very well," he said. "I merely wondered if you had given any thought to my lord's letter. He is anxious for a reply."

I balked, barely managing to keep it from showing on my face. Had I thought about it? How could I not think about it, the proposal delivered not with a ring but with the deaths of thousands of people? My people. Day Lord curse him, I thought about it every day—every time I saw the utter emptiness in Misha's face.

"I know you're alone in the world, my lady. I'm sure it's not easy to have no one to guide you. So allow me to give you some advice. Marriage arrangements of this kind are negotiations. My lord wants you as his wife." Dobor clasped his hands together and shrugged, smiling as if this was a dream coming true. "I believe it's in the best interest of Seravesh you accept. But if you wish for something more, ask."

Vitaly materialized in the space behind Count Dobor. The ghost's gray eyes were wide and filled with a warning I could no longer heed.

"What I want, Count Dobor, is to be left alone. I want Roven to withdraw their support of my cousin's puppet regime. I want your army off my land. And I *demand* justice for the burning of Nadym and Kavondy."

Count Dobor laughed. "I will not say anything of the sort,

my lady. Consider it a favor, from me to you. A sign of goodwill. I will tell my lord you need more time. You are so young, after all. My lord is a patient man, but how much longer do you think you can afford to wait? Your people suffer every day your cousin wears the Frozen Crown. How much more can they take?"

I grabbed his hand without conscious thought, crushing it so hard his knuckles popped in my fist. "Don't you dare threaten me, you fucking bastard."

Dobor's genial mask evaporated as he wrenched his hand away, face purple. "How dare you lay hands on me? Are you mad?" His dark eyes glittered with anger and spite, and . . .

Victory?

"No wonder the Council of Viziers wishes to expel you from Vishir."

My head snapped back as if I'd been struck. "What?" The temperature in the room dropped, and like sharks scenting blood, the lords of the Great Hall grew still. Excited whispers filled the huge space like the buzzing of bees.

"You heard me. And after what happened here, I'll be forced to lodge my own complaint."

"Is that a threat, Count Dobor?"

My heart stilled, caught between one beat and the next at the sibilant sound of the voice behind me. I turned and saw three men standing in the doorway. They prowled forward, dressed in long red robes, the color of the sun rising over the desert. The color of blood. The Shazir.

"Is the snake troubling you, lady?" The man who first spoke turned to me. His pupils were so true a black I didn't think any light could escape those depths. Short and completely bald, his skin was lined with deep wrinkles like cracks in stone. And I would have recognized him anywhere. The man who killed my parents.

Khaljaq.

Dobor laughed, a jackal-like sound utterly devoid of mirth. "With respect, Khaljaq, this is a private conversation."

"An unbeliever is not capable of respect. They are animals and must be treated as such." Khaljaq's voice carried over the din of the Great Hall with the alacrity only hate can produce.

"This is a matter of international diplomacy," Count Dobor hissed. "It doesn't concern the Shazir."

"We are the guardians of the light, Count Dobor. Of course it concerns us. Anything your lord of darkness does, we will oppose. Princess Askia alone in this court of sin and heresy has passed through the fire of the Day Lord's judgment. She has felt the burning lick of the Aellium Sigil and proven herself a true day-blooded sister of the Shazir. Are you willing to submit to the same?"

Khaljaq stepped forward, forcing Dobor back. "Tell this to your emperor: We know what he is doing in the north. We know about his experiments. How he is spreading the taint of magic to honest, day-blooded men. He is the great corruptor. Bringer of darkness. Witch king. Princess Askia stands against him. She is not alone."

I was drowning. Dark, icy water suffocated me. I couldn't move, couldn't speak. There were enemies on all sides, one to steal my future, three who stole my past.

The only thing sustaining me was seeing Count Dobor's face go scarlet with rage. His lips moved, but I couldn't hear his words. I didn't want to hear them.

Dobor turned on his heel and stormed away. The space in front of me opened. The spell broke. I wasn't free, not yet, but I wasn't trapped, either. There was a way to escape. Illya came to my side. His eyes were wide, face grave. But he was with me. I wasn't alone.

Khaljaq watched Count Dobor's retreating back, but I didn't sense anything like satisfaction in him. Nothing of life, either.

I tried not to flinch when he looked at me but wasn't sure if I succeeded.

"It is our honor to protect you," Khaljaq said in response to a thanks I never gave. "But I must warn you that your nightly visits to the menagerie have not gone unnoticed. Such things could give men like Dobor the wrong idea."

My face hardened. "And men like you?"

The slightest of smiles cracked Khaljaq's lips as he stepped forward, sending the cloying scent of incense up my nose. "Be careful of Queen Ozura, dear girl. She is not a child of the Day Lord." His gaze scoured my face a moment longer before finally stepping back, releasing me from his snake-eyed spell.

"The Shazir reside in the Shrine of the Day Lord in the Temple of the Two-Faced God. Seek us out if you need protection." All three men bowed before melting into the shadows from whence they came.

"Askia?" Illya whispered my name, shifting to block me from the ever-watching court. "Are you all right?"

"Yes," I replied, though I could tell from his expression that he didn't believe me. I balled my hands, only now realizing that Vitaly and all the other ghosts had vanished when Khaljaq appeared.

Khaljaq.

No. Not here, I thought, forcing my gaze back to Illya's worried face. "Did you hear what Dobor said?"

He nodded, his hand twitching as if to reach for mine, only to think better of it. "I did. With your leave, I'll go to Captain Nazir," he said. "Perhaps he knows something."

"Thank you, Illya."

"Go back to the rooms, my lady. And perhaps wait until tonight to go to the menagerie, when Queen Ozura will be available. I know you want to visit the girl, but—"

"But I need to speak with Ozura more," I agreed.

Indeed, the queen had a lot to answer for.

20

I'd remained in my rooms for as long as I could stand it, but I found no comfort there, no sense of safety. Seeing the Shazir, being surrounded by them, had taken that. Again. A suffocation that only increased when Illya came back empty-handed from his meeting with Nazir. Troubles on top of troubles, but Dobor I could deal with. I *would* deal with, I vowed. No council edict would force me from Vishir. Not without an army behind me.

But the Shazir?

I paced through the dressing room, but the feeling of Khaljaq's attention made me want to wilt. To hide.

Khaljaq be damned.

As soon as the sun set, I made my way to the guild to find Ozura. I knocked on her study door, barely waiting to hear a muffled "enter" before pushing it open. The queen sat behind her desk, bent over paperwork. She looked tired, and there were dark circles under her eyes that weren't there before.

Ozura's brow crinkled in apparent confusion. "Askia, I thought I gave you tonight off." She had, so that I'd be well rested for the ball. Yet here I was. "Can I help you?"

Could she? I wasn't sure. My mind buzzed with Khaljaq's

words. His voice had chased me through the palace, ripping open wounds I thought had healed long ago.

And then there was that sense, when Ozura and I first met in this office, like a tingling between my shoulders. Telling me she lied.

But I needed answers. Answers only Ozura would have. "I had an interesting encounter with Khaljaq today."

Ozura leaned back, and a closed, almost wary expression crossed her face. "I noticed he approached you and Count Dobor in the Great Hall. What did he say?"

"Aside from suspecting you of being a witch?" I asked, expecting to see the fear that lived within me ripple across her face. Instead Ozura smiled a satisfied smile and motioned for me to continue. "He said Radovan is corrupting day-blooded men. Spreading magic." I shook my head, half of my mind still in the hall. "Given what you've already said . . . Ozura, is Radovan creating witches?"

Ozura set down her quill and pinched the bridge of her nose. "I was unaware Khaljaq had heard that particular rumor. It explains why he's become so insistent on creating a national registry of witches."

"So it's true? Why did you lie?"

"I didn't lie," she replied tartly. "I have no proof that it's true. It's just a theory. Something one of our sources in the northern continent heard."

My eyes narrowed. "What source?"

"There are pockets of resistance in all the conquered northern kingdoms. Some of them reach out to the Shadow Guild."

I gritted my teeth, determined to find out more about this resistance, but unwilling to get sidetracked. "And they believe Radovan is able to do this?"

"They believe Radovan is abducting witches because he's

found a way to strip them of their magic and share it with normal humans. Sorcerers, they call them."

"How?" I demanded, crossing my arms when she didn't reply. "You can't keep this from me. How is he doing it, Ozura? I need to know."

Ozura closed her eyes and took a deep, labored breath. When she opened her eyes, her gaze was edged with sadness and something else I couldn't name. "What do you know of Aellium stones?"

A pregnant pause filled the space between us as I chose my words. "That is the second time someone has mentioned Aellium to me today."

"Oh? Who was the first?"

"Khaljaq."

Ozura's head tilted to the side. "And what did he say?"

"He was pledging his allegiance to me, actually," I replied, my upper lip twitching. "He boasted to Dobor that aside from the Shazir, I am the only one at court who has been burned by the Aellium Sigil and proven myself pure."

Ozura said nothing for a long moment "Do you know why the Shazir use Aellium stone to make their brand?"

Numbness spread through my limbs the way it always did when anything related to my parents' trial and subsequent execution was mentioned. And Aellium was more than tangentially related. It was at the heart of everything. "Aellium was only found in the caves at the base of Kahn-e-Fet. The Shazir consider it sacred to the Day Lord."

Was found, I thought. For the earthquake my parents and their friends were accused of causing brought down part of the holy mountain, covering the caves in rubble.

"Yes," Ozura replied. "Oddly enough, they do consider Aellium sacred. But they also use it because it is a natural amplifier of magic. The application of the brand, combined with their barbaric methods of interrogation, are enough to make even the most experienced witch lose control of their magic."

"Magic that is then used to condemn them," I said, hating the weakness in my voice.

"Oh, the Shazir are too clever to admit that magic is the reason they execute witches. They're quite creative with conjuring up crimes where none exist."

I slumped in my chair. "I wasn't any stronger than those other witches." The admission slid out of me. "The Shazir simply couldn't see the ghosts I summoned."

"It saved your life, Askia," Ozura said, leaning forward. "Don't be ashamed that you survived."

I nodded, willing myself past the pain. "What do Aellium stones have to do with Radovan creating these sorcerers?"

Ozura drew away, crossing her hands in her lap. "Given enough time and the right spells, an Aellium stone can be bound to a specific witch. According to my source, Radovan knows how to exploit the bond. He can fracture the stone into many pieces and give them to his faithful servants, giving a nonmagical person powers with a simple bit of jewelry."

The words washed over me, ringing with the truth. "You think this is what Radovan did to his wives? What he will do to me?"

"To you and to any witch he can't convince or coerce into serving him. But only Radovan has the power to use multiple types of magic—the very magic he stole from his wives. He's too cautious to let any of his minions become powerful enough to oppose him."

"What happens to the witches?"

Ozura shook her head. "I don't know, but given the fate of Radovan's wives, I doubt they survive."

Natural-born witches made up only a tiny fraction of the population, but if their powers could be stripped and given away through shards of stone . . . Radovan could create an army of sorcerers. One too powerful to oppose.

Dread dragged long fingers up my back as my mind worked to put two and two together. "Where does he get the Aellium?"

"There is a mine in the north, heavily guarded. The rebels have attempted to destroy it over the years, but none were successful."

I closed my eyes against the words, against the truth threatening to be exposed. I'd survived the last seven years believing my parents had been falsely accused, savoring my rage and planning my vengeance against the Shazir. My hate had given me purpose. But what if the Shazir had been right?

My heart hammered in my chest, begging me to run, pleading me not to ask. Because if I asked, I would know, and if I knew . . .

"Were my parents responsible for the earthquake in Shazir Province?"

Ozura didn't answer for a long time. Her dark eyes were trained on my face, searching for something. "It was your father's idea. He theorized Radovan was using Aellium to steal magic. Sevilen thought it was only a matter of time before Radovan extrapolated the process to steal magic from all witches for . . . redistribution."

Ozura's voice was filled with quiet pity and well-aged grief.

"Sevilen warned the northern rebels, told them to destroy the Aellium mine on their continent while he did the same to ours." She shook her head, eyes trained on her hands. "I begged your mother to stay in Bet Naqar, but she didn't want to leave Sevilen."

Ozura's mouth twisted. "Your parents, along with four earth witches, traveled to Khan-e-Fet. They planned to strike at night, when no one was in the cave shrines. No one was supposed to die."

But two people did die. And when my parents tried to save them, they were caught. Tried. Killed.

I bowed my head.

"What Sevilen did was necessary. It saved Vishir from committing the same terrible crime as Radovan. And believe me, eventually, someone would have tried. After all, many people want to be witches. Few actually are. Sevilen didn't anticipate that his actions would start a war between the Shadow Guild and the Shazir."

But war was coming all the same. And if Vishir killed all their witches, then there would truly be no one strong enough to oppose Radovan.

Assuming I could convince Vishir to stand with me. And given Dobor's words this afternoon, his threat . . .

"Ozura," I began, slowly. "Dobor said that the Council of Viziers might have me expelled from Vishir."

"That decision is not ultimately up to the council."

The ground yawned open beneath me. "But they've petitioned the emperor?"

"Not yet."

"Not yet—" I glared across the desk, scrambling for what to say, for a way out. "But why?"

Ozura gave me a flat look. "Your actions at court have made you enemies, Askia. I don't know why you're surprised."

"Enemies?" I thought back on my paltry interactions at court. What had I done but sit with the Serralan delegation? Sit while Dobor and Ishaq and Enver schemed. "I've done nothing wrong. What, are they angry I haven't been following them around and fawning? I don't have time for that—for any of it."

"You had time to speak with Trantini. Time you've yet to take with any other lord vizier save Ishaq, and I think even you must admit your interactions haven't been—"

"Trantini is an old friend, and unless I'm mistaken you took the letters I wanted to send to the rest of the council."

"Because letters are inappropriate. But you've had days to ask Iskander to set up a meeting, as you did with Marr. Yet you haven't."

"Like any of them would agree to meet," I said, voice rising with the urge to tear out my hair. "I don't have time to waste playing political games, Ozura."

"And that is certainly a choice," Ozura replied. "But let me ask you this: In what world can you win a game by refusing to play?" She leaned toward me, like proximity could drive her point home. "Not this one, Askia. And certainly not in the court of Vishir."

I SAT ON THE MOONLIT TERRACE OUTSIDE MY PARLOR, MY ARMS wrapped around my knees. A slight breeze blew from the north, making the silk sleeves of my dressing gown ripple across my skin.

The garden was beautiful, bathed in silver light. My eyes skated over the concentric circles of hedges and orderly beds of flowers. Gravel paths, girded by high trellises, meandered the length of the garden. Water burbled in the fountain, the only noise in the otherwise still night.

If the garden sighed in stillness, my mind screamed in chaos. Every small victory here had brought my people closer to destruction. Count Dobor knew it. Radovan knew it. He was counting on it, counting on the pressure to bring me to my knees.

And my parents were guilty.

My anger, my righteous thirst for vengeance, had sustained me for more years than I could count—far longer than my quest to save Seravesh. And it was a lie.

The shuffle of footsteps sounded behind me. I spun, half rising from the steps. Only a few candles were lit in the parlor, hardly enough to illuminate the tall form that emerged from the darkness. I couldn't see his face, and for a moment I thought . . .

"Hey." Iskander moved into the moonlight, halting on the threshold with an uncertain expression.

"Your mother is going to have kittens when she finds out you're here."

Iskander laughed. He sounded tired. He looked tired too. His normally dark skin was drawn and slightly wan. "I saw you in the Great Hall, with the Shazir, and I wanted to make sure you were all right."

"Ah." I eased back onto the steps, looking out at the garden. After a moment, Iskander joined me, his arm brushing mine as he sat.

"So how are you?"

I sighed, but it couldn't express the depth of my exhaustion. "I don't know, Iskander. My parents' killers, the people who . . ." The words suck in my throat with the weight of stale fear. "They ruined my life." I glanced at Iskander and away again, trying to sort through what I could say, what I couldn't.

Eventually, I settled for the most obvious pain, and the smallest one. "That the Shazir are even here at court is bad enough, but that they stood with me today against Count Dobor—against the threat of my expulsion from Vishir . . ."

"What do you mean expulsion?" he asked, voice rising.

"Apparently the council is going to ask the emperor to make me leave."

"The council? You mean Enver," he said with a muttered curse. "Don't worry about that. I'll make sure my father shuts it down."

With your vast political power, I thought, shaking my head bitterly at the moon. "Dobor is one thing, but the Shazir are painting themselves as my allies. What am I supposed to do with that?"

"Use it."

"What?"

Iskander leaned forward, eyes wide and beseeching. "Askia, I know you won't want to hear this, but you need allies. Whatever else the Shazir are, they are against Roven."

"You can't be serious." I sat up straighter, crossing my arms over my chest. "They're zealots, a cult, everyone says so. They have no power. No one wants them here."

"Perhaps not at court, but in the provinces? Believe me, their power is growing. The Council of Viziers won't be able to ignore them much longer. They could be useful allies."

The scar across my throat grew hot. Impossible. They killed my parents. They would kill me, too, if they ever found out the truth. "I can't."

"Askia—"

"No, Iskander." My voice sounded high to my own ears, far sharper than it should have been. I closed my eyes. "Can we change the subject?" I asked, softening my voice. "Please?"

Iskander nodded. His face was in profile, his expression serene as he looked out at the garden. He shifted and his hand grazed mine.

"Are you excited for the masquerade ball?"

I snorted.

Iskander's smile lit up the darkness. "Is that a no?"

"Yes. No?" I cringed. "I don't know. I don't . . . flourish in those situations."

"In what situations?"

"Social ones," I said and smiled when Iskander laughed.

"You'll be fine. Besides, the entire court will be strutting around in ridiculous costumes. Everything will be very relaxed."

I arched an eyebrow. "So you don't think I need to be concerned with any political maneuvering?"

"Political maneuvering is second only to breathing in Vishir,"

Iskander replied. "Don't count on your enemies to take the night off. Though the Shazir probably won't attend. It's too frivolous for them."

"Thank the Day Lord for small mercies," I muttered.

"What are you going as?" he asked, after a small pause.

I shrugged. "Not sure. Your mother arranged it all, so I'll find out tomorrow. What about you?"

"Eh. Probably some kind of bird." I laughed at his lackluster response. He smiled down at me with warm eyes. "I, too, am subject to my mother's whim. For some reason, she always dresses me as birds: eagles, hawks, ravens. Thank Lady Night we don't have a masque every year."

"All right. I'll keep an eye out for random bird number four and come find you tomorrow."

"Well, that's awful forward of you. What will my mother say?"

"This from the man who snuck into my rooms in the middle of the night," I said, poking him in the ribs.

"I won't tell if you don't."

Too late, I thought. Queen Ozura probably already knew he was here. "Whatever you do, don't ask me to dance tomorrow."

"And give my mother a heart attack?"

I shrugged. "And keep me from looking like a fool."

Iskander quirked a look at me. "Can't you dance, Princess Askia?"

I grimaced. I was something of an indifferent dancer, always losing track of the rhythm and taking the lead. I required a firm partner to come out the end of it with anything like grace. "Dancing is not a strength of mine."

"Wow. Princess Askia attempting to be political. You must be awful."

I groaned and buried my face against my knees. It was true, I was awful. "Don't laugh," I begged. "I'm a terrible dancer to begin with, but at least in the north you can actually touch your partner." Iskander was laughing hard by this point, so I rushed on. "If I stepped wrong, my partner could kind of . . . tug me back into place. But Nariko said you don't touch your partner in the Vishiri style. If I make a wrong step, everyone will see it."

My plaintive cries must have struck a chord with Iskander because he stopped laughing. He nudged me with his elbow. "Let me teach you."

I shook my head, a *no thank you* on my lips.

"Trust me. Come on, you picked up Vishiri fighting quickly enough. A dance should be easy for you."

"So you think I should treat the dance like a sword fight?"

Iskander barked out a laugh. "Why not? It's a different kind of battle, different moves, but no less precise or graceful than any other kind of fight. All moves and countermoves."

This was ridiculous. I rolled my eyes and drew away, but Iskander placed a hand on my arm.

"Dance with me." His eyes were full, brimming with an emotion I was afraid to define. It was too vast. Something so depthless it scared me. I didn't think I could give it back.

"Iskander, I—"

"Heh-hem."

I spun as if I was under attack and looked up. Illya stood in the darkness of the parlor, only his toes touching the moonlight. I could only make out the hard line of his jaw; the rest of his face was obscured.

"You should go now, Prince Iskander. My lady needs her rest."

The emphasis Illya put on *my* echoed across the garden.

"Of course." Iskander nodded in my direction, face scarlet, and hurried out the door.

Silence thudded between Illya and I. His gaze burned my skin, but I couldn't read his expression. "May I speak freely, my lady?"

I swallowed, not sure I wanted to hear what he was going to say. "You may."

"What you're doing, it isn't wise. Prince Iskander is your ally, but Queen Ozura has made it clear that a marriage alliance with him is off the table. Encouraging Prince Iskander's affections will not gain you anything. All it can do is alienate him."

I wrapped my arms protectively about my chest. "Illya, I think you're reading something that isn't here."

"Am I? Or are you just refusing to see?" Illya rolled his eyes, showing more expression in one exasperated gesture than he had in the entire time I'd known him. "My lady, you are obviously unaware of how unusual you are. Even by northern standards you're unique, but here in Vishir, there are no others like you."

"That's not exactly an asset, Illya."

"But it is. For all his worldliness, Prince Iskander's experience with noble ladies will have been restricted to heavily supervised encounters with young women who are taught to be silent and pliant and fragile. Nothing could have prepared him for you," he said, gesturing helplessly in my direction. "Believe me, you've made an impact. Or did you think he took up your cause for morality's sake?"

"Illya, he's a decent person. I'm sure he . . ." My words petered out as I struggled to deny something that deep down I knew to be true. But I was never good at lying, least of all to myself.

Iskander always watched me; he had ever since I stalked into the castle of Eshkaroth. Lady Night save me. Didn't I have enough on my plate without having to worry about Iskander's feelings?

"I do like Iskander, but I never meant to lead him on."

Illya ran a hand over his hair and came to my side. "Just . . . tread carefully. Prince Iskander is a good man, and not unintelligent. He must know the folly of becoming attached to you. He can't marry until his father dies anyway. You need to remain free, my lady. An unmarried princess has more to offer than a married one."

"So I should remain unattached in case my only hope in getting an army is to tie myself to an influential family?"

Illya opened his mouth to reply and I held up my hand to stop him. I turned a slow circle, glaring at the garden around me. It was so damn perfect, orderly, everything so suffocatingly arranged. How I longed for my unkempt, unwalled gardens. Where I could ride in any direction and no one would think twice about propriety.

But I wasn't in Seravesh. I was in Vishir facing the possibility of a perfectly ordinary arranged marriage. My hands curled at the thought. I didn't want to be shunted off to the highest bidder. I wanted to choose and be chosen in turn for, well, love.

Even thinking it sounded childish, and naïve. Especially with Ozura's advice echoing in my head. "I know I may have to marry," I said, turning back to Illya. "But I don't think now is the time to consider it."

"Askia," he began, only to swallow whatever words he was going to say. He shook his head, the moonlight gilding his face like a shroud of mourning. "You're thinking of marriage as the option of last resort," he said at long last. "You shouldn't. It is your greatest bargaining chip. And every day we spend here is another day Radovan has to entrench his army farther into Seravesh."

Illya reached across the night-filled distance, clasping my shoulder. "You've made progress. You've found allies, good allies, but finding friends among the Council of Viziers is going to take all the tools you have."

I took a careful breath and thought back to my wild overgrown garden. To the home I'd left behind. For Seravesh, I could do this. I could do anything.

I looked up at him as the breeze tossed a lock of hair into my face. "I don't suppose you know any men I should woo?"

Illya caught the loose tendril and tucked it gently behind my ear. "None who deserve you." He whispered the words like a prayer, drawing me in.

I felt the ground beneath me shift at his touch, his smell. His presence cracked open a chasm of longing deep within my core. His gaze was all wolf, hunger edged with desire prowling the edges of my face. It was suddenly impossible to speak, to breathe, or think.

"Askia, what are you doing?"

I sensed Vitaly appear behind me but didn't have it in me to respond. What was I doing? I was standing, alone in the garden with a man I wanted nothing more than to—

I stopped myself before I could even finish the thought.

"How will this help Seravesh?" Vitaly's voice was low, sad even. He disappeared without waiting for my reply. He didn't need to wait. He knew he had me.

"Illya," I murmured, my voice husky to my own ears. "I'll take your advice but—"

"But?"

"But I need you to stop looking at me this way."

His mouth twitched in an almost smile, but he didn't step away. Neither did I. "What way is that?"

"Like I'm something you want to spend a long time devouring."

Illya chuckled at that, but it was short-lived. His lips parted for a moment before he pressed them closed again. His throat bobbed as he stepped away. "If that's what you wish. Sleep, my lady. I'll wake you when it's time."

21

When sleep finally came, it was tinged with troubled dreams of being chased, of cold so intense it burned my skin. They jolted me awake near dawn. The pink beginnings of daylight shimmered through windows, but I didn't rise to meet it. Sleep still beckoned, and I obeyed. The dreams that came then were a jumble, a dizzying twirling Vishiri dance, but my partner never stayed the same. First came Iskander, his brown-black gaze filled with unmet desire. I looked away, not recognizing this man and missing my friend.

I turned in the dream, but when I turned back it was Armaan's face that met mine. His golden eyes and sensuous lips hinted at laughter. I blushed, longing to be let in on the joke, but the dance moved on. I spun, and it was Illya who caught me next. His gray-eyed gaze caught mine, and I felt as if I were being seen, truly seen, for the first time.

The last face was a blur. I got only the faintest impression of pale skin and dark hair and features I couldn't place. But the eyes—those eyes I would never forget. Pale, clear green, cold and hard as glacial ice. They beckoned.

A hand clamped down on my shoulder and my eyes shot

open. I gasped for breath and was confronted with the stern, wrinkled face of Soma in her white servant's dress.

"It's about time," Soma grunted, surveying me with crossed arms. "It's nearly three. High time to be getting up, don't you think?"

I sat up with a wince, feeling sore, and slightly winded, as if I'd been fighting rather than sleeping. "What are you doing here?"

"Helping you prepare for the ball, of course." She shook her head and turned toward the bathroom. "There's some food in the dressing room. Go eat while I fill the tub."

I groaned, swinging my feet to the floor, and stood. My pretty white dressing gown was a mess of crisscrossing wrinkles because I hadn't bothered to take it off before falling into bed. The memory of why I'd rushed to sleep flooded my mind.

Iskander. Illya, too, but . . .

Iskander came to my rooms last night. Alone. In my rooms after dark. I clenched my eyes closed as though I could will the past to change. Ozura was going to be livid.

And Nariko. What would Nariko think when she heard Iskander had visited in the middle of the night?

No. I'd tell her it wasn't my fault. I didn't invite Iskander, he just showed up. Nariko would understand.

I hoped.

"I'm ready for you, my lady," Soma called from the bathroom.

I very nearly enjoyed the next three hours I spent under Soma's care. By the time she was done beating my body into something like beauty, I almost felt like I'd done a complete and thorough penance for last night's indiscretion.

As the sixth bell rang, two more middle-aged servants whisked into my room. At Soma's direction, they pulled me from the bathroom and marched me to the vanity table. As they plied my skin with countless creams and serums, Vitaly appeared at my side, a question in his mist-colored eyes.

"Nothing happened," I said before he could ask. *"I know nothing can happen. Do you think Illya will accept that?"* I willed the regret out of my words.

Vitaly nodded. *"Don't misunderstand, I think Illya has loved you from the moment he saw you, but he'd never cross the line of duty. Not unless you did first."* Vitaly's voice petered out under the weight of things left unsaid.

"That long?" A year ago, perhaps more, when Seravesh had stood proud and free, my men and I had ridden west up the mountain passes to meet a delegation from Raskis: the same delegation that would have taken my cousin Goran into Raskis to marry their young princess, while I would remain in Seravesh promised to a prince I'd never met.

Only when we arrived, Raskis had already fallen. The delegation had been butchered, and the town around them set to flame. Of the four hundred people, all but eleven had died. Illya was one of the eleven. General Arkady and I had pulled him from the still-smoldering remains of his family's smithy.

He'd never spoken to me of his life before. Never really spoke to me at all, until we came to Vishir.

"We all protect ourselves in different ways, from the things we cannot have." Vitaly's words reached me, gentle as the caress of a moth's wings against my cheeks. He disappeared, leaving me with thoughts too heavy for the eve of a party.

The sun was hovering above the horizon when I was pulled out of my chair and told to stand, back to the mirror, on the pedestal. With almost religious reverence, Soma unwrapped my gown, beginning with a black under-dress of fabric so light, it seemed to float.

I smiled as the women fitted the corset around my abdomen.

My fingers slid down the cool surface of pounded metal, a corset literally made from shining silver. Scrolling vines and flowers were etched into the metal. It was utter perfection. I'd have worn it into battle if I could. Then I remembered how Iskander related Vishiri dances to sword fights, and I thought wearing a corset of silver plate could not be more appropriate.

The overlaying dress wasn't so much a cohesive garment as a series of twelve-foot strips of thin, gauzy fabric. The women danced around me, laying and weaving the translucent fabric over my shoulders, hips, and abdomen.

"Ready?" Soma asked, her eyes dancing with a rare appreciative smile.

I turned to the mirror, freezing at the sight of the woman looking back at me. My skin was luminous, glittering silver like starlight. Even the scar at my neck, normally a line of puckered flesh, was muted. Across my eyes, temple to temple, was a shimmering band of gray-black powder, almost like a delicate fabric mask, but made of makeup rather than cloth.

My hair fell in a wild cascade of crimson curls to my waist, the only splash of color against my black-and-white body. And the dress . . . The sheer bands of material hugged my upper body in an hourglass of cloth. Where my thighs began to narrow, it loosened into a full skirt of airy fabric that seemed to be made of night itself. It danced in the slight eddies of air that twirled around the room.

"It's beautiful," I said, my voice tight. *I* was beautiful—and it had only taken three women and six hours. I nearly laughed at the thought, as I took in my reflection, barely recognizing this formidable, wild-looking woman. Perhaps that was the point of all the primping. Perhaps beauty was the weapon you forged of yourself. A weapon I had never dared to wield. A fact I hadn't lamented until then.

"The costume was Queen Ozura's idea," Soma said fondly. "She thought it might serve as a useful rebuttal to the zealotry of some of your so-called allies."

I chuckled. It was perfect. The Shazir reviled Lady Night, and this costume was the personification of the Two-Faced God's dark aspect. The court would get the very clear message that I didn't share their views. That I was a daughter of Lady Night.

"Your men are waiting in the outer sitting room." She turned to walk away, but I caught her hand.

"Thank you, Soma."

Soma nodded, the shadow of a smile glancing across her mouth. "Try to stay out of trouble."

Smiling, I wound through my apartment and pushed open the sitting room door. It took me two steps to register the stunned silence that met me. It didn't last. My men hooted and whistled and clapped their approval, so boisterous I had to laugh.

I found Illya in the crowd. His gray eyes were wide, his lips slightly parted. He walked toward me, almost like he was in a daze, and took my hand. Bowing, he brushed my skin with his lips. His gray eyes never left mine. Suddenly the longing I'd felt in my dream—and in the garden—rushed back and that line of duty between us felt like fragile protection.

The men started catcalling, which only made Illya look slightly smug. He tucked my hand into his elbow and escorted me from the room.

We walked through the halls, the two guards I was permitted to bring following close behind. Illya's arm felt surprisingly warm beneath my hand. I looked at him from the corner of my eye, studying the details of his black-and-blue short coat. The fine silk fabric stretched tightly over his broad chest. The silver clasps hardly seemed up to the challenge of containing Illya's strength.

His chin angled down; our eyes met. I looked over my shoulder at Misha and Ivin, trying to ignore the trill moving through my core. "You three look very smart."

"Aye," Misha replied. "The maid brought them with your own clothes. Though how she knew our measurements has given some of the men pause," he added with a smile.

Something in me eased, seeing Misha's humor return after the death of his family. "Soma must have a keen eye for the male form." I grinned, wiggling my eyebrows up and down.

Misha barked a laugh that echoed off the staid and empty halls of the palace. "You'll make me blush, my lady. It almost makes me wish for the ridiculous mask the captain has to wear."

I cocked an eyebrow at Illya. "What's your mask?"

Illya sighed. His hand went to his right hip, where a papier-mâché mask bounced from his belt. He handed it to me. I turned it over and saw the ears, forehead, and upper snout of a wolf, complete with fur and a too-realistic-looking nose.

"The black wolf of Seravesh." I ran my fingers through the silky fur. "You're going to cut quite the dashing figure, Captain. Prepare yourself for a promotion, Misha. I fear we're in danger of losing Illya to the ladies of Vishir."

Misha and Ivin guffawed, but Illya tugged the mask out of my hands. "The ladies of Vishir have nothing I want."

We turned the corner before I could formulate a response and found nearly twenty people waiting outside a set of massive doors. They all seemed caught in orbit around the still figure of Emperor Armaan. The lion of Vishir. Literally. The golden lion mask covered the top half of his face. His long, red jacket was resplendent with golden embroidery, and a crimson sash was tied about his trim waist. He turned, Queen Ozura on his arm, Lord Trantini on his other side. All the assorted attendants and guards turned with him.

I stopped a few feet in front of the emperor, offering a slight bow. "Good evening, Emperor," I said. "Hello, Queen Ozura. Lord Trantini."

His amber eyes swept over my bare shoulders, following the lines of my collarbone. "You look stunning, Princess Askia." The emperor's voice was gravelly and quieter than I remembered. His entourage had to bend forward to hear him, which they tried to do while maintaining a respectful distance.

"Thank you."

"What are you dressed as?" Lord Trantini asked, his rather plain white robes setting off his spectacular speckled owl mask perfectly. His head tilted to one side as if in preparation for a reply, his clouded white eyes pointed in my general direction.

"She is the huntress. The wild and untamed beauty that is Lady Night," Queen Ozura purred. Her wide, leonine eyes glittered from behind her leopard mask, and I detected a slightly brittle point to the way she said "untamed."

"I owe it all to Queen Ozura, of course," I said, trying to make my thanks obvious. "Without her assistance, I'd likely be here in my sparring clothes." Appreciative laughter sounded around me, but I kept my eyes on Queen Ozura. She smiled, giving no indication whatsoever if she knew about Iskander's nighttime visit to my apartment.

"But it was a pleasure, my dear. Come, we must go through. Lord Chamberlain, are we ready?"

The lord chamberlain slid through the crowd of milling nobles, ushering them through the door as he went. He'd have had more luck herding cats, but as soon as Queen Ozura spoke, the men and women jumped to attention and started heading through the double doors, into the hall.

I saw Illya get caught up with a group of Serralan noblemen. His gray eyes pressed against my skin, almost in warning. This was my chance to cement my access to the emperor. There might not be another opportunity. I gave Illya the slightest of nods, before turning away.

As the last of the latecomers filed into the hall, the lord chamberlain cleared his throat. "Lord Trantini will escort Queen Ozura through first, then the emperor will lead in Princess Askia. His Majesty will present the princess to Lord Trantini and take his wife's hand. Together the four of you will share the first dance and officially open the ball."

Silence. Queen Ozura exchanged a look with the emperor. I bit my tongue wondering what the problem was and then realized the obvious.

Lord Trantini laughed. "It would be my great honor to dance with Princess Askia, but I am an old man, and far too blind to dance."

A pained expression crossed the lord chamberlain's face, staining his skin crimson. "Of course, Lord Trantini. I apologize."

"Not to worry, Lord Chamberlain. We know there was no offense meant," Queen Ozura said, her rich voice pouring smoothly into the corners of an awkward silence. "I would be honored to be escorted in by Lord Trantini. Let Princess Askia and my husband have the first dance."

"A perfect solution," Lord Trantini exclaimed with a toothy smile.

It was all done so smoothly, Ozura must have planned it, right down to the lord chamberlain's embarrassment. I locked gazes with the queen as she took Lord Trantini's arm. Something like a challenge flared in Ozura's catlike eyes. I knew, no words necessary, Ozura was aware of Iskander's visit. That I would take all the blame if the court found out. Again.

"Princess Askia?"

The emperor's voice gave me a reason to look away. I tucked my hand into the crook of his elbow and tried to focus on the feeling of silk beneath my fingers rather than the frustration gnawing away my calm.

But the small anger didn't last, not as nervousness swirled through me. Ahead, Queen Ozura and Lord Trantini were walking through the doors and into the dimly lit hall. The emperor shifted and took a step. My legs locked. For a sickening second, I was sure I wouldn't be able to move.

The feeling passed, but relief didn't come with it. As if in a dream, I passed through the double doors into the Starlit Hall. The emperor stopped us at the top of the stairs, and it was truly by his will I stopped. It was as if he controlled me through the slightest touch of my fingers on his arm. I dreaded letting go, dreaded walking down the stairs to start the dance. Without his touch, would my body remember how to move?

I dimly registered my surroundings. Hundreds, maybe thousands of tiny witchlights floated near the ceiling. The starlit effect suffused the room in a twilight glow. Simple decoration, but perfect for the menagerie of costumed nobles and longing-filled ghosts all watching me from the foot of the stairs. I searched the crowd for a friendly face but saw nothing familiar behind those masks.

The emperor moved, walking down the steps, tugging me in his wake. My limbs felt heavy as we took our places on the dance floor. With enemies on all sides, I faced him. As he bowed, I curtsied. The well-oiled movement was probably the most graceful I'd be all night. Out of the darkness, the sound of a flute whispered in the air.

The emperor moved with the music, each step infused with a kind of prowling elegance I couldn't hope to match. I clung to Iskander's advice, did my best to copy the emperor, to anticipate his next step like I would with any other opponent. I didn't stumble, but there was nothing soft in my movements.

The emperor's expression never changed. The slight smile he

seemed to wield like a shield never wavered, but his golden eyes softened. I stepped forward, my hands rising to almost meet his.

"You dance like you fight."

The words brushed across my cheek, too soft to be overheard by the surrounding crowd. I turned away, bowing to the demands of the dance, wondering when he'd seen me fight. His eyes glimmered with contained laughter, and a flash of longing blew through me, a desire to be let in on the joke.

"I'll have to spend more time in the training ring," I murmured when I came in for the next pass.

The emperor breathed a smile. "You're more graceful than you give yourself credit for."

I was saved the necessity of replying as the dance separated us again, but soon enough I was stepping back in. "Do you fight like you dance?"

"I can't say I've ever danced with any of my sparring partners." One of his brows arched. "Is this a challenge?"

My mind whirled, and I suddenly remembered that first night in Eshkaroth. *Like father like son*, I mused, flashing a wicked smile. "If you think you can keep up."

The emperor chuckled. The soft sound reverberated through the hall and set the court whispering. "I'm going to enjoy having you here, Askia."

How's that for game playing? I thought, filled with so much satisfaction I almost missed the end of the song. I looked up at him and curtsied, my smile returned. The silent laughter in his face was a kind of summoning—one I would have obeyed, if the court had not converged, flowing between us like a wave, as the final note fell.

22

I was tugged away by a small army of courtiers who were suddenly in agony to befriend me. I bit my tongue in an effort to keep unkind words locked safely behind my lips. I smiled, a silent, mocking laughter filling my chest. These people, who had ignored me for weeks, had suddenly and collectively decided to give me the time of day.

My gaze crossed over the wolf-masked face of Illya, and I contained myself. For the men who traveled with me, and for those I left behind, I could do anything, would do anything. So I let the courtiers fawn. I danced with the men who had power and the sons who someday would, and though I seldom spoke, I smiled. I laughed at their arrogance and, as the hours passed, I laughed at their vanity too. Laughed at the many soft young men who wore dashing replicas of my fighting clothes. As if imitation could make soldiers of them.

As the clock chimed twelve, I turned away from my latest suitor and slid through the crowd before I was ensnared again. My feet ached and my stomach was grumbling. I wound toward the back of the hall to the food tables, but when the way was too congested, I angled to the wall. Fewer people stood on the fringes, where row after row of double doors looked out onto a garden. I glanced at the doors. The court of Vishir was reflected in the glass. It was like a dream, these dancing creatures, something out of a storybook.

A flash of white caught my eye, the fall of ebony hair. I stopped, turned away from the doors, and spotted Nariko on the edge of the crowd. Her dress was so white, it glowed. It sat tight on her waist, giving her girlish body a woman's curves. Alabaster feathers were stitched onto the full skirt, and mirrored in the swanlike mask on her face. Nariko was beautiful, utterly and devastatingly so.

I smiled and stepped forward. Nariko frowned. She stepped back but not before I saw anger bloom in her dark eyes. Nariko fled, disappearing into the crowd. Before I could move, before I could call out to stop her, a man took her place in the crowd. His face was partially obscured by a jackal mask, but I would know those cold, cunning eyes anywhere. Count Dobor bowed.

I didn't give him time to speak. I darted through the crowd, feeling Dobor's eyes on my back even as I scoured the room for Nariko. I caught a sliver of white fabric and chased it down until I spotted her. I felt every bit the huntress when I pounced.

"Lady Nariko, there you are." My words were bright, airy enough for a ball but too loud for Nariko to ignore. I hooked my arm through Nariko's before she could slide away again. She didn't reply, but a hard smile curled her lips.

Something like a punch hit my gut. Nariko knew. Of course, she knew; of course Queen Ozura had told her about Iskander's visit. Lady Night have mercy, why was this my fault?

I licked my lips. "You look lovely tonight."

"Thank you, Your Highness."

I smiled blandly, trying not to let my disappointment at Nariko's wooden reply show on my face. I steered her toward the food tables at the end of the hall, where there was a small gap in the crowd occupied only by a pair of oblivious dancing ghosts. "I half expected to see you burst through my doors this morning in need of a dress."

"No, Your Highness. Not everyone in Bet Naqar is obliged to come to your rooms at all hours of the day and night," Nariko said, yanking her arm away.

It was a real struggle to keep up that stupid smile, especially when I saw the accusation in Nariko's eyes. I swallowed, surreptitiously looking around to see if anyone had heard. "Nariko, I don't know what you know, but—"

"I know Iskander was in your rooms last night," she hissed.

"Yes, but I didn't summon him," I replied, willing Nariko to look at me, but she was busy smoothing the downy feathers on her dress. "Nariko, I didn't ask him to come. In fact, I told him to leave."

Nariko's head whipped up. Her dark eyes were wide, anger receding, giving way to sadness. "So . . . you aren't interested in him?"

"No," I said fervently. "We're friends."

Nariko swallowed. Nodded. A tremulous sort of smile quirked her lips, like she was smiling through tears. "It's just . . . the way he looks at you sometimes, like you're the only one in the room. He doesn't even see me."

I squeezed her arm. "Well, you never talk to him. How can he see you if you don't show him who you are?"

Nariko rolled her eyes; an exasperated huff sighed out of her. "An unmarried woman isn't supposed to speak to an unmarried man."

"You talk to Illya and my guards all the time."

"That's different. My aunt would be so upset if she ever saw me sit down and have a chat with Prince Iskander like you do."

It was my turn to roll my eyes. "Screw your aunt." Nariko choked, apparently caught between shock and laughter. "Seriously. It's your life, not hers. What harm is there in speaking to him in the middle of a crowded room?"

"I don't know," Nariko said, like it was the most hopeless thing in the world.

"Go ask him to dance."

Nariko gasped. "I couldn't."

"Do it. Oh, do it in front of your aunt. She'll drop dead of shock, and you can kill two birds with one stone."

Nariko's breathy laugh chased away my misplaced guilt and I silently vowed to put some distance between Iskander and me.

"What are you two grinning about? Do I need to alert the guards?"

I turned at the sound of Iskander's voice and smiled. "Oh, Lady Nariko was letting me in on one of her many schemes."

"Was she?" Iskander's black eyebrows rose above the edges of his raven mask. "Anything I need to worry about?"

Nariko's eyes slid to mine, a hint of panic shining in their inky depths. I fought my laughter and gave Nariko the tiniest of nods.

"Yes?"

"Absolutely wicked, this one. I'd watch out for her if I were you," I said with mock severity.

Iskander shrugged. "I'll take your word for it."

Fair enough. I deserved his doubt for trying to paint the kindest person in Bet Naqar as something dangerous. I switched track. "I see the two of you conspired to wear bird costumes. Should I be jealous?"

Iskander looked at Nariko. Really looked at her. His eyes trailed from the silken crown of Nariko's head down to the downy fall of her feather train. He laughed. "Well, I can't speak for Lady Nariko, but I warned you my mother always dresses me in bird costumes."

"She must know how you like falconry."

"Ah." He waved away Nariko's timid reply. "She dressed me

as a raven this year, so that can't be it. I think she was cramped for ideas after throwing this whole party together."

I couldn't disagree more. In fact, as I took in the blue-black plume of feathers covering his mask and capping the shoulders and cuffs of his ebony jacket, I thought he looked more like a black swan than a raven.

"So are you enjoying your first Vishiri ball?" Iskander asked.

"Eh. My feet hurt, I'm starving, and one of the ministers grabbed my backside." I shrugged. "It's a ball."

"Who grabbed you?" Iskander demanded. At the same time, Nariko said, "Oh. Lord Kammet. I forgot to warn you about him. He can get rather handsy."

I laughed, both at the horrified look on Iskander's face and the casual acceptance in Nariko's voice. "Is there anyone else I need to watch out for?"

"Hmm . . ." Nariko looked around the room, biting her lip as she surveyed the guests. "Lord Haram for sure. Lord Calgo, but only when he drinks too much. Lord Telen, though you're probably too tall for him."

Iskander's eyes rounded. "My court is filled with perverts."

Nariko's shoulders rose and fell in an elegant gesture of ennui. "So is the world. Although . . ." She looked at Iskander, a smile pushing up her cherub cheeks. She nodded toward an older woman with iron-colored hair and a maroon gown that wasn't quite big enough for her girth. "It's not just the men. You should watch out for Lady Ursu. She's been plotting ways to trap you in the garden."

"Oh dear." Iskander looked over his shoulder as Lady Ursu turned. Her eyes widened when she saw him, her lips parting in a predatory smile. Iskander turned away, looking from me to Nariko and back again. "She's spotted me. Quick, dance with me before she comes over."

"Not a chance," I said. "My feet will fall off if I have to dance again."

Like the good boy he was, Iskander turned to Nariko. "Lady Nariko? Will you save me?"

I expected Nariko to glow with happiness. Instead, her eyes narrowed. She heaved a sigh. "Oh, all right, but don't you dare step on my dress." Nariko flounced off toward the dance floor, giving me a sly wink as she passed.

Iskander looked slightly dumbstruck. He watched Nariko walk with a furrowed brow. He shook his head after a moment, like he was realizing he was supposed to follow her. "I'll see you later," he said, and then he, too, was gone.

I watched them for a few moments, the white swan dancing with the black. It fit somehow, Nariko's effortless grace and Iskander's raw power. A small weight settled in my chest. Not jealousy, but loneliness. *We all protect ourselves differently from the things we cannot have.* Vitaly's words echoed in my mind with the half-formed fantasy of Illya leading me across the dance floor.

I crushed the thought, delicate as it was, and found Ozura watching me from across the room. There was something satisfied in the way the queen smiled. She raised her glass, a salute that conveyed both approval and forgiveness. I wasn't sure I wanted either.

A puff of myrrh-scented cologne slithered up my nose as someone stopped beside me. Prince Enver didn't hide the cold glimmer in his gaze as he watched me from the corner of his eyes. I cocked my head, wondering what his game was.

He graced me with a thin-lipped smile. "We haven't been properly introduced yet. I am Prince Enver ibn Vishri."

I bent my neck. "It's good to finally make your acquaintance, Prince Enver."

He nodded by reply and turned his gaze toward his brother. Iskander's eyes widened when he spotted us over Nariko's shoulder, and I gave him a tight smile.

"They're a fine-looking couple, aren't they?"

"Indeed," I replied, smiling blandly in their direction. "They look like a pair of swans."

Enver huffed. "Yes, Ozura always was one for symbolism. Not terribly subtle." When I glanced at him, he was already watching me, a cruel bent to his lips. "Lady Nariko's family has hardly made it a secret that they want her to marry the next emperor. It seems Ozura approves of the idea of Nariko marrying her son."

My eyebrows rose. Nariko never said she was in negotiations to marry Iskander. I wondered if Enver was saying this in hopes it would get under my skin. If so, he missed his mark. "Lady Nariko is a kind woman. Any man would be lucky to call her wife."

"Oh, that's right. You're friends." He sneered the word like it was beneath him. "How does she feel about my brother trailing after you like a puppy?"

My eyebrow rose, a cruel smile of my own emerging. "Why, Enver. Are you concerned for your brother's well-being?"

"Why shouldn't I be? He's family, and you're toying with him, preying on his feelings to bring you to Vishir, where you don't belong."

Anger honed my focus to a knife-sharp edge as I remembered Dobor's threat about the council expelling me from Vishir. So even though I wanted to smack Enver, I repressed it. There were other weapons I could use—this court had taught me that. "I suppose you know all about not belonging," I hissed, thinking of everything Iskander told me about poor unwanted Enver. "Be honest. You don't give a damn about Iskander's feelings."

"But I do care when he brings shame to my family by whoring around with a betrothed woman."

I blinked. Caught between anger and confusion. Betrothed? Then it clicked. I laughed. "You mean Radovan? No, Enver. Of the two of us, only you have crawled into bed with Roven."

"That's not what Count Dobor says. He says it's only a matter of time before you go traipsing back north. And my poor brother will be poorer for having championed your cause."

"And you'd be heartbroken about that, wouldn't you?" I shook my head. I was done with this conversation, and this haughty ass of a prince. "I'm sure Count Dobor spins you many pretty bedtime stories. I hear Radovan tells the same kind of tales, but only a true fool falls asleep to them expecting to see anything but blood when they wake."

I leaned in, plastering a pleasant smile onto my face. "You're not the first person to be taken in by Roven fairy tales, but you'll be the first to lose an empire for believing them. Have a nice night, Prince Enver." I managed to nod before I turned on my heel and walked away, a blind flight to the nearest door.

Muggy air planted wet kisses on my face and neck as I stepped onto a wide terrace overlooking a manicured garden. I was slightly surprised to find the terrace crowded by the bulky forms of middle-aged men. No doubt they found the ball as tedious as I did.

I slid through the gathered men, half searching for a friendly face, half for an empty spot to sit and be alone. A group of men, Serralan by the olive cast of their skin, pushed past me. Their expressions were stony with ill-disguised anger.

At least I wasn't alone in having a rotten time, I thought, as I stepped aside to let them pass. My promise to Trantini—to speak to my allies on his behalf—bore down on my shoulders. I was destined to fail everyone, it seemed.

"Would you care to join us, Princess Askia?"

Lord Marr's voice was like a friendly pat on the back, but between the darkness and the costumes, it took me a moment to locate him. I smiled when I spotted him standing at the back of the crowd.

"Good evening, Lord Marr," I said, when I worked my way back to him.

He and Illya leaned up against the terrace's iron railing. Both men were in high spirits, wineglasses in their hands, their masks discarded on a nearby table. I tried not to feel bitter about being thrown to the jackals of the Vishiri court while these two enjoyed a fine evening in this bastion of masculine peace.

"How are you enjoying your first Vishiri ball?" Lord Marr asked.

I bit back the words I wanted to say before they spilled out of my mouth. It was a close thing. "I'm honored by Queen Ozura's thoughtfulness."

Lord Marr chuckled, sharing a knowing glance with Illya. "I must say you've comported yourself beautifully this evening. You've certainly made a favorable impression on the court. Your detractors will have a harder time painting you as an impulsive young woman, too quick to anger."

I suppressed a grimace. Marr obviously hadn't seen my heated exchange with Enver. He leaned closer, silent laughter lighting up his face. "Though I don't think anyone would have blamed you for taking one of Lord Kammet's fingers when his hands began to wander."

I laughed. "The thought crossed my mind. Unfortunately, none of my swords matched the dress."

"Ah. That is perhaps for the best. However, it does suit you. Captain Illya and I were saying how stunning you look as Lady Night."

I fought back a blush and thanked the darkness as I hazarded a glance at Illya. He was looking over my head, giving no indication of hearing Lord Marr's words. *For the best*, I thought. I had asked him to stop looking at me like . . .

I hitched on a smile. "That's kind of you to say, Lord Marr."

"I didn't mean it as a kindness, my lady, but as truth. You are radiant, and if you're not careful, half the young men at court will be in love with you by morning."

"And if I'm not careful, I'll have to marry one of those pricks." *Shit.*

Lord Marr's eyes widened. Illya's face turned to stone. Stunned silence radiated outward, engulfing the entire terrace.

Someone behind me chuckled, and somehow the sound released the men around me from their silence. Soon, others joined, and I felt their outrage slide into amusement. I should have felt relieved, but I had recognized that initial, gravelly laugh. I didn't need the slight narrowing of Lord Marr's eyes to warn me. The emperor had given me a reprieve, turned my appalling lack of manners into a joke.

I knew the safe thing to do would be to apologize, and I turned, looking up at him through my lashes to do just that. He stood a few feet behind me, his powerful form silhouetted against the light of the ballroom. I couldn't see his face at first, but he positively towered over me when he stepped forward. Armaan smiled, his lion mask tied to the sash on his waist. Laughter shone in his eyes. I thought it was the first actual emotion I'd seen him express. My lips turned upward in a mischievous smile. Safety, I thought, was overrated.

"Surely, you're too hard on our young men, Princess." His voice was pitched low, but somehow it was impossible to miss.

"Perhaps. But I've always found young men to be rather raw for my liking." I shrugged. "I prefer my food well done."

Laughter rumbled in his chest. "What do you have to say for young women, such as yourself?"

"Am I young? I don't feel it." I felt my smile slip and turn bitter. I forced it back into place, shoving the emotion away.

His expression softened. "Perhaps you just need some fresh

air to renew your spirits. Will you walk through the garden with me?"

"I'd be honored," I replied, hope lining my voice.

We walked arm in arm down the length of the terrace, passing a veritable who's who of Vishir's rich and powerful. I almost wished Enver was there, if only to see his face. The lords all bowed carefully to the emperor, watching me with a predatory gleam in their eyes.

The garden was centered around five teardrop-shaped pools. Each pool, like petals of a giant flower, was separated by a narrow path, just wide enough for us to walk together.

I was caught between admiring the garden and wondering if I should say something. Only what could I say? What clever observation or witty comment could I possibly offer this man who had surely heard them all? I glanced up at the smooth line of his jaw, the careful masklike smile, and thought perhaps he wanted a bit of silence.

So I let him lead me through the garden and the flower beds, and eventually up to the edge of one of the tearlike pools. I watched the water as we walked, observing our reflections. We looked like something out of a storybook, the handsome emperor and the woman of darkness.

His gaze felt heavy on my face. He'd paused in the center, where the tips of all five pools met. "Do you like it?"

"It's beautiful."

He cocked his head to one side. "Do you not have gardens like this in Seravesh?"

I smiled at the thought. "No. Nothing so delicate could survive in Seravesh, but . . ." I took a deep breath and for a moment could taste the cold, clean air of home. "We have vast forests, where it's green for miles and miles around. At their heart are ponds and lakes so blue they hurt to look at. We have mountains. Huge ranges that stretch hundreds of miles and peaks so high, the snow never melts. It's hard and forbidding and wild, but beautiful nonetheless."

The corners of his lips tugged upward, like he couldn't quite believe me. I breathed a laugh and thought back on all my travels, trying to find the words to make him understand how a place so harsh could still be beautiful. "It's a bit like southern Vishir, actually," I said, thinking about the far reaches of the empire, past the deserts of Bet Naqar, where the climate was cool. "Like Serrala or Minossos."

"Ah, but I have never been to those places." His voice was grave, like he was admitting to a great failing.

Perhaps he was. He ruled an empire, but had he ever left Bet Naqar? It certainly explained why Lord Trantini was having such a difficult time explaining why the garrison couldn't be built on sacred ground.

My promise to Trantini chimed through me a second time. Dobor and his council pets, Ishaq and Enver, were trying to paint me as a hotheaded warmonger. To twist my impatience into recklessness. But if I spoke for Serrala now, it would prove I could see past my own self-interest. That I wasn't a little girl begging for scraps, but a ruler worthy of support.

"Well, I hope you get the chance someday. Minossos is a striking city, with its whitewashed walls and blue tile roofs. It's beautiful to behold. And in Serrala, they have huge festivals at the turn of the seasons, where they bring food and offerings to the gravesites of their loved ones so their spirits will want for nothing in the afterlife."

I tried to keep my voice light, like I was commenting on an interesting custom, but his expression seemed to close. "That seems wasteful."

I cringed inwardly, but soldiered on. "Oh, I'm sure it seems that way. Most customs must seem silly to those from foreign lands. But I think there's something nice in believing the people we love don't leave us. That so long as we maintain the site of their deaths, so long as the ground is undisturbed, unsullied, they will never really leave us."

The emperor's silence had a weight to it. He gave me a long, hard look that left me with little doubt that Ozura had told him about my powers. Perhaps he thought I was speaking more of Tarek than I was of the Serralan killing fields. Maybe I was. What would happen to Tarek's ghost if this palace were destroyed? I didn't know. Maybe he would be lost.

The emperor sighed and looked away. His mouth twisted into the semblance of a smile. "I see Lord Trantini has gotten to you. A foreign royal advocating for one of my lords, what has the world come to? Rest assured, the Council of Viziers has the matter in hand."

The feeling of ice cracking beneath my feet made me shiver. The emperor's back had slowly straightened, his gaze increasingly cool. The last thing I wanted was to make him think I was attacking him.

And yet . . .

"I know it's unusual, and I'm sure the council has their reasons for denying the request to relocate the new garrison. Perhaps I'm overstepping, but Lord Trantini made me a flower crown for my tenth birthday; we're friends for life." I smiled, trying to draw him in, but neither my expression nor my feeble attempt at a joke softened the mood. "Look, I'm not saying you should approve the request for nothing, but I think if you give them this, there is very little you couldn't ask for in return."

He looked down at me, his golden eyes revealing nothing. I bore his scrutiny in silence, but refused to look away. I'd overstepped, there was no denying it, but I was also right. There were ways to build the new garrison without desecrating a holy site. It was either laziness or spite on the council's part to even suggest building on the fields. Having met Enver, I thought spite was the more likely culprit. The emperor could step in. Should step in.

My self-righteousness was little comfort, not if it convinced the emperor to side with Enver and Ishaq. Without words, he held out his arm. I took it and let him lead me back to the terrace. I kept my face smooth, but disappointment was bitter in my mouth. I prayed I hadn't ruined my chance at arguing my case for troops. I wanted the emperor to think of me as an equal, someone whose opinions were worth hearing. Now he probably thought me a complete fool. At least I'd kept my promise to Lord Trantini, though seeing Enver's face at the top of the stairs made it impossible to be proud of the fact.

Enver's black eyes scoured over the emperor and darted to me. He smirked, clearly reading his father's displeasure. I looked away from Enver, staring over his head, but seeing nothing.

The magnitude of my situation caught me like a kick to the ribs. Lady Night, had I failed my people in speaking for the Serralans? Sealed my exile? Would I have nothing to show for my weeks of effort but a few new dresses? What good would that be against Radovan?

As if the thought summoned him, Dobor slid to the front of the crowd. He stood beside Enver, wineglass in hand. He smiled a broad, catlike smile, and, with a grin, toasted me.

It was a struggle to breathe through the weight of my responsibility, through the threat of Roven literally looming over me from four steps up. I willed the fear away from my face in a screaming command for normalcy.

Too late. The emperor's gaze was on me, trailing across my cheeks and down my neck to the line of my scar. The scar his people gave me.

I forced myself to look up at him when we reached the top

of the stairs. The emperor's golden eyes were hard on mine. His eyes flicked toward Count Dobor and I detected the slightest, worried frown mar the emperor's face.

Whatever the cause, the emperor took my hand in his. His lips brushed my knuckles, sending a wave of goose bumps cascading down my arm. He smiled. "It was a pleasure, Lady Night."

He gave my hand a small squeeze and was gone, back through a set of glass doors and into the ball. The lords of Vishir followed him like the waves of an outgoing tide. In minutes, I was alone.

Though, never truly alone. Illya and my guards were there. So was Vitaly, but only Illya came to my side.

"That was cleverly done, my lady," Illya said, his voice warm with approval and, perhaps, pride.

I breathed a smile. "Let's get out of here before I'm forced to do any other clever things."

23

ood morning."

Nariko's voice echoed brightly through my bedroom, where I'd been lounging for the better part of an hour trying to decide if I was up to the task of rising. Nariko's arrival settled the matter. I lifted myself up from the mountain of pillows and smiled. "Grab the food—we're having breakfast in bed."

Nariko giggled and hurried to the parlor where the servants had left breakfast. I smoothed down the front of my nightgown before rearranging the pillows so Nariko had a place to sit.

"Breakfast is served," Nariko said, sliding a platter of powdered pastries and honeyed rolls onto the bed.

I picked up one of the rolls while Nariko hopped up beside me. She looked impossibly awake, her pale skin bright and glowing, not even a trace of last night's festivities evident in her complexion. I shoved some of the roll in my mouth, trying very hard not to feel bitter about this. I didn't need a mirror to know my hair was a rat's nest.

"So," Nariko said, taking a careful nibble of one of the pastries. "Tell me everything."

I gulped, feeling my brow crinkle. "About what?"

"About the emperor," Nariko said, rolling her eyes. "I heard you walked with him in the garden. What was it like? What did you talk about?"

I smiled. Nariko and I were the same age, but I wasn't lying to Armaan last night—sometimes I felt so much older. Then again young women in Nariko's position weren't exposed to men in the way I was. After months alone surrounded by an entire army of men, I knew there was nothing mysterious about any of them. "There's really not much to tell."

"Well, what did you talk about?"

I shrugged. "We talked about the garden. I told him I thought it was beautiful, and he asked if we had anything like it in Seravesh."

"And?"

"I told him it was too harsh for such ornate gardens, but it has a natural beauty that's hard to describe. I told him the mountains were rather like those in Serrala." I frowned, remembering how the conversation went from there.

"Oh dear, I know that face." Nariko tilted her head to one side, eyes narrowed. "What did you say?"

I tried for a smile but felt myself wince. "I may have argued to approve the Serralans' request to relocate the new garrison."

"You didn't."

"Oh, I did." I tossed the remains of my roll onto the platter. "I had to," I said, forcing myself to face the worry in Nariko's voice. "I promised Lord Trantini I would help if I could."

"Well . . . if you promised him, then I suppose it was the right thing to do," she allowed. "Although I'm surprised you didn't ask him to give you men to fight your cousin and Radovan instead."

"Believe me, I wanted to. It's not like he doesn't know why I'm here. I didn't think a ball was the right time to bring it up. Anyway, he hardly knows me. I wanted him to see me as an equal. Instead I just . . . imposed."

Nariko patted my hand, smiled bracingly. "I'm sure it will be all right."

"I hope so. Enough about me. How was your evening?"

Nariko beamed and launched into a dance-by-dance recap of her entire night. I leaned back against my pillows, happy to listen to Nariko's wonderfully girlish delight. She described each of her suitors in minute detail, from the cut of their costumes to how well they danced.

Nariko's description of the early part of her evening paled in comparison to the in-depth analysis she gave about Iskander. She gushed about his costume and the way his calloused hand scratched hers—a sure sign of his strength. I nodded, going in for a pastry while Nariko went on and on about every single word Iskander said to her on the dance floor, all ten of them.

"And when the song ended, he didn't stop, not even for a moment. He kept dancing right into the next song. Can you imagine?"

I smiled. "It sounds like you had a wonderful time."

"I did." Nariko beamed. "What about your conversation with Prince Enver?"

"You saw that, did you?" I was surprised Nariko had noticed anything beyond Iskander's face while they danced.

"I did, though . . . I mean, Iskander noticed first. He was almost staring."

Pity poured through my veins as Nariko's smile cracked. "You should join us in training with the Khazan Guard." The idea was all impulse, but now that it was out I was sure I was right. What use was propriety if Nariko's happiness was at risk?

"What?" Nariko's voice rose with surprise. "I couldn't possibly learn to sword fight. I'd be terrible."

I grinned at her coy reply—coy because secretly Nariko *wanted* to come. "It'll be fun."

Nariko scoffed. "Why do I feel like you're changing the subject? Spill. What did you talk to Prince Enver about?" She shot me a sultry look. "It looked intense."

I snorted. "That's one word for it. I swear, if I hadn't walked away, I'd have punched him."

"What did he say?"

I considered telling Nariko the whole truth for about a second, but how would she feel about Enver's accusation that I was toying with Iskander's feelings? Best not. "Basically, that I'm wasting everyone's time. That it's only a matter of time before I go crawling north to Radovan."

"He didn't," Nariko gasped. "What did you do?"

I flashed a brittle smile. "I told him, just because he's in bed with Roven, that doesn't mean everyone else needs to be."

Nariko laughed breathlessly, shaking her head in apparent disbelief. I stretched out my arms, heaving a great yawn. I wanted nothing more than to stay in bed and insult Enver for the rest of the day.

Then Illya appeared in the doorway, making my stomach flutter. He stopped in the threshold, taking in the humongous tray of pastries. One of his eyebrows rose when he looked at me, his eyes lingering on the long line of my bare legs. "An imperial courier delivered this," he said, smiling with more heat than was strictly necessary as he glanced at the paper in his hand.

I straightened. "What does it say?"

"You're invited to attend the Council of Viziers."

Nariko jumped out of the bed like she'd been shocked. "*Today?*"

"Yes," Illya replied.

"Lady Night have mercy," Nariko moaned, seizing my arm and practically dragging me off the mattress. "Get up, get up, get up."

I shrugged off Nariko's hands. "All right, I'm up. Relax, please."

"No time. The council convenes at noon. We have to get you ready now."

I hurried into the dressing room, while Nariko shooed Illya out. When it was just Nariko and me again, we stood side by side, staring at the rows of gowns, speechless.

"Just pick out anything," I said.

Nariko turned to me, her eyes wide. "I've never been to the council," she admitted, her voice shaking with barely concealed terror. "Women aren't allowed. I'm not even sure Queen Ozura can attend without the emperor escorting her. And foreigners are forbidden."

"Then why was I invited?" I asked, my mind racing to the worst. What if I'd offended the emperor last night? What if he was calling me before the council to deny my request? What if I really was being expelled from Vishir? Oh, Day Lord, save me. How would I face General Arkady?

Black spots clouded my vision. For a sickening moment, I thought I was going to pass out.

"Strength, my lady."

Vitaly's voice reached me, soft as the kiss of butterfly wings. I turned toward it and found him standing by the glass garden doors, barely visible in the sunlight. I didn't need to see his face to feel the bracing steel imbued in his words. Succeed or fail here, I was needed at home. No weakness. Not while my enemies surrounded me.

I forced my shoulders back. "Bring me the most modest dress you can find. Demure is usually the safe choice."

Still white-lipped, she went to the rack and pulled out a navy-blue gown. With Nariko's help, I dragged it on and threw myself onto the vanity chair to have my hair fixed. It would have taken four more hands and far more time than we had to untangle all the knots, so Nariko settled with pinning it up high on the back of my head. Forgoing makeup entirely, Nariko wiped away the dark circles beneath my eyes with a tear-inducing zap of magic.

The moment I was ready, I hurried out of my apartments, picking up a half-dozen guards on the way. The administrative wing felt too quiet. Something about the space seemed to beat with anticipation, like the very halls were holding their breath. I saw only a handful of scribes as I walked. They scurried past me, their eyes carefully averted and their scrolls pressed to their chests. Each door we passed was shut tight against me, and I felt the corridor stretching out, tunneling inexorably toward the chamber at the end of the hall.

Vitaly appeared on my left; his body was so distinct, I could almost imagine he was alive. Only the gray wash of his skin and the utter silence with which he moved betrayed the truth. I tried to take solace in the show of solidarity his appearance implied.

Two soldiers guarded the council chamber doors. They came to attention when we approached. Their arms extended, the long shaft of their spears crossing against each other with a sharp *thwack*, barring the way.

I licked my lips. "The emperor has invited me to attend this council meeting."

One of the soldiers, a short man with a barrel chest and arms so large they strained the sleeves of his uniform, nodded. "You may enter, Princess, with one of your guards. The rest must remain here with Lady Nariko."

Nariko nodded without comment and stepped dutifully back to the wall. My soldiers fell back as well, until I had only Illya on my right, and the ghostly figure of Vitaly on my left. The Vishiri soldiers straightened and pushed the doors open.

The Council of Viziers chamber was an odd, oblong shape. It had six rows of wide wooden steps built into the walls, almost like a small amphitheater. At least seventy noblemen sat on the steps. They chatted idly with one another, like they were waiting for the meeting to begin.

The floor of the chamber was mostly taken up by a huge rectangular table. I recognized the men sitting there as the Council of Viziers. There was only one empty spot at the table, a lone chair on the far right-hand side. I pitied whoever was to sit in that chair, for Enver sat across from it, almost but not quite at the head of the table. The emperor claimed that spot, reclining in an ornately carved chair. I wondered if Enver would have sat there were it not for the emperor's presence. Day Lord save us from that fate.

The emperor turned to speak to someone sitting behind him, and I saw Ozura's masklike face as she bent toward her husband. The queen sat to the left of her husband, and slightly behind. I wondered if her placement was Enver's doing—a reminder that, while she might be present, she wasn't there to participate. He certainly had a sour look on his ratlike face, watching his father speak to Ozura rather than to him.

Ozura's midnight eyes rose to mine. The older queen gave me a slight nod before she replied to her husband. Her words were lost in the steady murmur of conversation flowing through the hall.

Enver must have spotted the gesture, because he turned instantly. His muddy eyes latched on to me, and his face twisted with a vindictive smile. He rose and the hall fell still, as if the gathered lords were attuned to his every movement.

My stomach contents turned liquid. This was it. They were sending me home.

"Princess Askia, it is lovely to see you awake so early in the day; however, the Council of Viziers is closed to foreigners."

What the hell was that supposed to mean, "early in the day"?

As if I normally lounged in bed all day long. I forced the anger well clear of my face—it had never been of any use to me in this court.

"Although, since you are here," Ishaq said, sharing a smug look with Enver, "perhaps now is the time to discuss your presence in Vishir."

"Specifically, your departure." Enver smiled like a dog baring its teeth. "I'm sure a lady as well-bred as yourself would hate to overstay her welcome." His voice dripped with so much condescension it drew the simpering sounds of muffled laughter from his fawning courtiers.

The men around me craned their necks, drawing closer with barely concealed titillation, waiting to see how I would respond. They wanted me to scream, to shout, I realized. They wanted me to shake my fist or throw a knife, to behave like the soldier I was rather than the queen I needed to become.

"Are you teaching me manners now, Enver?" I asked, letting my head cock to one side. "Interesting, considering how you're stepping on your father's toes with each word."

Enver huffed an outraged breath, but his squirrelly eyes darted to Armaan. "Nonsense."

"Really? Because unless I'm much mistaken, my expulsion from Vishir is your father's decision to make. Or do you already see yourself stronger and wiser?"

The room filled with a collective intake of breath, as Enver went completely rigid. "No, of course I don't."

"Good." Armaan didn't need to raise his voice to be heard. Though his tone was soft, his gaze was sharp with appraisal. "Because if this is how you plan to treat foreign nobles, you are very far indeed from being ready to take my place."

Enver visibly wilted. "No, Father. I was just—"

"I know what you were doing, Enver. But Princess Askia is here at my request." He looked at me for the first time, and a smile softened his face. "Will you join us?" he asked, motioning to the empty chair at his left.

"It would be an honor."

I crossed the room, plastering a smile on my face as if Enver's ploy was entirely beneath me. Still a chorus of whispers chased me to the head of the table. I scanned the crowd, trying to determine if the murmured conversation was angry or merely curious, but I couldn't make out enough to tell.

I spotted Iskander sitting on the lowest step about halfway down the room. He gave me an encouraging smile as I passed, but I didn't return it, keeping my eyes focused on my place at the table.

One of the viziers rose and held out a chair for me. He was an older man, easily in his later seventies, with a patch of white hair that didn't quite cover his whole head. He smiled kindly, his face crinkling in fine wrinkles like it wasn't used to accommodating such an expression.

"Thank you."

"Of course," he murmured. "I am Lord Vizier Timma Elon, the Imperial Exchequer."

I smiled in recognition. "It's a pleasure to meet you. How is Jaida?"

"She's doing beautifully, Your Highness. Thank you for asking." His voice was heavy with gratitude.

"If you are quite finished, Lord Elon, we can begin this meeting," Ishaq groused from across the table.

The smile evaporated from Lord Elon's face, and he surveyed Ishaq with an unimpressed expression. Elon sat without responding, leaving the air around the council table soupy with tension. The silence stretched, only increasing the sensation. With Illya and Vitaly standing at my back, I felt like I was about to be attacked. Maybe I was. Perhaps my altercation with Enver was but the opening volley.

From somewhere high above, a bell began to toll the hour. Enver banged a circular stone against the tabletop, a well-worn gesture judging by the dent in the wood. "The Council of Viziers in now in session, His Imperial Majesty Armaan ibn Vishri the Tenth presiding."

Though I was marshaling my arguments, the council proceeded as if I wasn't there at all. Rather than calling for me to present my case for the use of Vishiri troops, the council called a lord from Minossos to make a report about the state of the province's crops. After that, a lord from Yalbrika reported on the drought there.

I thought about the starving people I'd seen in the streets when we'd first arrived and my heart ached. The council argued round and round over what to do, but no solution was reached. They could only agree to build temporary housing for the refugees. Somehow, building a refugee camp for dying people hardly seemed enough.

The Council of Viziers went province by province, compiling reports from each area to obtain a detailed account of the health of the empire. They offered aid in some cases, denied it in others, but always provided reasoning behind their response. Where disagreements occurred, the lord viziers argued their points to the council in an orderly fashion before bringing the issue to a vote. If there was a draw, they would recess the matter until a consensus could be reached.

I was fascinated. As king, my grandfather—and by extension, I—was expected to know in detail everything of note that happened in Seravesh. It had been a daunting amount of information to learn when I was named heir, since everything from history to prevailing weather conditions was vital.

But Seravesh was tiny compared to Vishir. The monstrous task of ruling an empire that spanned half the world depended on the efforts of many people, not just the emperor. As I watched the council meeting unfold, it occurred to me the emperor didn't usually attend these meetings. It was obvious in the furtive looks the lords kept throwing him . . . and in the way they had to catch themselves before they addressed Enver rather than Armaan.

What could he be doing with his time if not guarding his position among his lord viziers? By the looks of things, this council decided the lion's share of policy for the Vishiri court. If it was up to the emperor to give the final consent, it was the duty of these men to present him a complete picture. Yet how could the emperor trust he was hearing the whole truth? How did he maintain his position on the throne?

Enver certainly wasn't the kind to be content with his power if there was more to be had. Especially with Ishaq by his side, murmuring to him through the meeting. If I were Armaan, I'd be concerned. Not only because the council deferred so easily to Enver, but because many of its members cast flickering glances toward him, seeking his blessing before issuing an opinion. No wonder Ozura wanted my help to increase Iskander's value at court. Iskander might have the loyalty of the Khazan Guard, but Enver clearly held the favor of the council.

The third bell of the afternoon came and went. My back was stiff and my muscles aching for the guard training I was missing. Judging by the tired expressions of those around me, I thought the meeting must soon be over. Enver looked over his notes, creating a slight lull in the meeting. Ishaq shot an amused look my way and whispered something in Enver's ear.

The prince pushed his notes into a neat stack and glanced up at me, a small smile on his lips. He cleared his throat. "Lord Khaljaq. Please come forward for Shazir Province."

Khaljaq pulled himself out of the dark corners of the room and slithered to the end of the table. He bowed to the gathered lords and gave me a little nod.

I forced myself to remain calm even as I choked on anger.

On fear. I lost my grip on magic, and Vitaly blinked out of existence.

"What is there to report?" Enver asked in a bored voice.

"Nothing. Shazir Province flourishes under the eternal benevolence of the Day Lord. I do, however, wish to address the drought in Yalbrika."

"The drought has already been addressed, Lord Khaljaq. You're here to speak for Shazir Province."

"Is it not Shazir Province who feeds these refugees in their time of need?"

Point to Khaljaq. Shaziri lands were so fertile, they provided grain to most of northern Vishir. Including the refugees.

Enver stilled for a moment, as if sensing that Khaljaq was going to cause trouble for more than just me. "It is," he allowed.

Khaljaq's eyes crinkled, implying a smile his mouth didn't deign to give. "So you see the drought does concern Shazir Province. The Shazir demand an answer."

"An answer? For a drought?" One of Enver's brows rose. "It's a natural disaster."

"Not all disasters are natural."

Khaljaq's eyes darted to me, and the rest of the room followed suit. The scars on my back itched. The one on my throat burned.

"Are you suggesting the Shadow Guild is causing the drought?" Lord Elon asked, his rumbling voice filled with doubt.

Khaljaq shrugged. "I simply think it prudent to make sure they aren't."

"You want proof that the Shadow Guild *isn't* using magic?" Elon shook his head. "How do you imagine you'll get that?"

"The same way we prove any other crime. Give us a list of all the witches in the Shadow Guild and let the Shazir question them."

Ozura had mentioned the Shazir were pushing for a registry

of witches. And I was damned sure that if they got it, every witch in the country would be found guilty of starting the drought.

Lord Elon's frown deepened. "This is highly irregular."

"I agree," Enver said, though there was no small amount of satisfaction in his face. "We must give the Shadow Guild time to respond. When they are ready, they will send us a *proper* representative." Enver's eyes cut to Ozura. "In the meantime, Lord Khaljaq, the council will take your recommendations under advisement. You are excused."

Khaljaq bowed and returned to his seat. The sound of uneasy conversations filled the room. I looked around, trying to judge how many people seemed convinced by Khaljaq's request.

It was more than I would have liked.

Enver cleared his throat, but it did nothing to quell the crowd. "I believe that is all we have for today."

The emperor raised a single finger and complete silence fell. "A moment more, Lord Viziers." My eyes widened. As confused as I was about how he kept his power, it was obvious, by this tiny gesture, Armaan was firmly in control. "Lord Gianno Trantini, please come forward."

The ancient lord of Serrala used his cane to pull himself up from the bottom row of benches. With the help of a younger man, he maneuvered to the end of the table and stood blind before the council.

Was Lord Trantini to be punished for my impertinence? Lady Night save me, I was trying to do some good. I was trying to be something more than a painted doll, a figurehead of a lost kingdom. I refused to let my emotions surface, but it was a close thing. Lord Trantini looked so fragile, so vulnerable standing alone at the end of the table.

"Lord Trantini, you came to Bet Naqar to protest the building of a new garrison outside the city of Velenz, correct?"

"Yes, Your Majesty."

"The Council of Viziers has heard your complaint and undertaken to ease the financial burden of the new outpost. However, you reject every offer."

"Yes, Your Majesty. The Field of Arcatium is sacred to us."

"So I am told." The emperor's reply was clipped and grim. His hooded eyes flicked to me before returning to the aged lord. Across the table, Enver smirked. "I've called you before the council to make a final offer. Lord Vizier Elon, please present your ideas."

Enver did a double take. His dark eyebrows disappeared into his hairline. He glared over the table, his face turning steadily scarlet.

Lord Elon cleared his throat. "We will halt plans to build the new garrison on the Field of Arcatium and instead have new ones drawn to expand and renovate the existing structure. Understand this expansion will require the demolition of any structure currently in its place. While the renovation is under way, the people of Serrala will house and feed the soldiers currently stationed there at their own expense. The crown will raise taxes in the province by three percent for the next ten years to finance the project."

I listened to the plan in shocked stillness. The emperor had taken my advice. He was offering the people of Serrala a way to preserve their holy land. Sure, it came at a cost—and it was a steep one for the people—but that was the way it had to be. The Serralans got their way and the emperor wouldn't lose face in the process.

Lord Elon continued. "If this is acceptable, we will begin the process of expanding the garrison. What say you?"

The smile that cracked open Lord Trantini's face was answer enough. "I accept the offer, Your Majesty. Thank you. This is beyond anything we could have hoped for."

"Your gratitude in this matter belongs to Princess Askia,"

Armaan responded. "It was her good counsel that guided us to this resolution." He looked at me as he spoke, his eyes glittering with an emotion I couldn't identify.

Lord Trantini's eyes were also bright with emotion and unshed tears. "Thank you, Princess Askia. May they sing your name on the Field of Arcatium beneath the moon of Lady Night."

The hushed whispers of rapid conversations were almost deafening. Not all of it was happy, I noted, and stunned looks of outrage masked some of the lords' faces. But for every two indignant lords, there was one who looked pleased, or at least thoughtful.

Iskander beamed, and I struggled to give him only a dignified smile in return. Ozura's gaze was warm with approval and something almost like pride. Play the game, she'd said, or lose by default. She was right.

"Majesty, I'm not sure how we will accomplish these things on such short notice," Enver said, his voice so pinched and whiny one of the older viziers rolled his eyes. Perhaps Enver wasn't the favorite of the whole council after all.

"Lord Elon and I will be happy to alleviate whatever concerns you have, but I don't see any reason to make the council remain in session for us to do so," the emperor said, voice dry and amused. "Princess Askia, may I escort you to the door?"

Part of me knew it was ridiculous to escort someone a few hundred feet, but another, smaller part of me was quietly thrilled at the show of support the gesture implied. "Yes, thank you."

I took his arm, and we walked sedately down the length of the room. When I glanced up, I found the emperor watching me out of the corners of his eyes. I smiled. "That was a wonderful thing you did."

"Ah," he said, stopping at the end of the hall, out of earshot of his undoubtedly fascinated court. "It was all you. Your guidance that led me to this decision."

My eyebrows rose, and I couldn't stop my eyes from darting toward Enver's still-livid face. "Guidance?" I asked, looking back up at the emperor. "I think some would call it impertinence."

He chuckled. "Never. There cannot be impertinence between equals. You and I alone know what it's like to hold the lives of men in our hands." He leaned closer, his golden eyes fastened on me. "Perhaps you more than me. Though I confess, I found it extremely galling that a foreign princess knew more about my lands than I did."

I smiled. "It shouldn't be. I've lived among your people most of my life."

He placed his hand on my shoulder and an unexpected shock sizzled through my body. My gaze cut to Iskander, who had paled. Beside him, Ozura watched with a calculating look on her feline face. I wasn't sure which bothered me more.

The emperor squeezed my shoulder, recalling my attention. His gaze danced over my face. He smiled. "*Our* people, Askia. They are our people."

24

I sat on the squishy grass in the garden outside my parlor, the sun shining on my back. I knew it was warm; it was Vishir after all. But I had to remind myself of this because, as I sat with my eyes closed against the unforgiving Vishiri sun, a penetrating, bone-deep cold had settled into my hands. And neither three extra blankets nor a hot morning bath had relieved the feeling.

Last night's training had me practicing my compulsion skills on Vitaly. It had not gone well. Not for me anyway. Vitaly had thrown himself into the challenge, shrugging off my commands with laughable ease.

It didn't help that Soma had stepped in for Ozura, I thought with a pang of unease. Soma said that the queen was too busy to be stuck here holding my hand. And while I was sure Soma was right, her choice in wording felt suspect. So every time I settled into the trance and tried to summon my magic, all I could think about was the emperor's hand on my shoulder.

If Ozura was angry about my friendship with Iskander, how did she feel about her husband touching me in public?

The urge to flee my current reality was overwhelming. My heartbeat quickened. A tingle of magic whispered across my skin, like the answer to a question I hadn't yet asked.

Softly, as if from a very great distance, I heard the delicate strains of a child's laugh. It was Tarek. Though my eyes were closed, I sensed him playing in the garden fountain. If I reached a little deeper, could I bring him out of the Marchlands?

"There you are."

Iskander's voice crashed into my ears. I folded beneath it. Magic fled and I stifled a growl.

Iskander's shadow fell across me. He smiled, his puppy-dog eyes wide and guileless. I took a deep breath. It wasn't Iskander's fault I was struggling to master my magic. He didn't even know I was a witch, after all.

"I came by last night, but you weren't here," he said, a whiny note of accusation creeping into his voice. "What are you doing?"

I opened my mouth, and for the hundredth time, I considered telling him the truth. But then he'd be upset I'd lied in the first place, and the last thing I needed was for Iskander to become more . . . unsettled.

He'd been shadowing me ever since the council meeting. It was as if seeing his father's hand on my shoulder opened a vast well of insecurity within him, and I didn't know what to say or do to make him relax.

"I'm just resting," I replied.

"Well, are you ready to go to training?"

"Yeah."

Iskander held out his hand to help me up. I hesitated, and then, deciding it would do more harm than good to refuse, let him pull me to my feet.

"Lady Night, you're freezing," Iskander exclaimed, grabbing both my hands in his. "Are you well?"

"Fine," I said, yanking my hands away. "I caught a little chill. Nothing exercise can't fix." I smiled brightly, turning away from the surprised, pained look on his face. "Where's Nariko?"

I strode up the stairs and into the shade of the parlor. Nariko was waiting by the table, fingering the edge of her tunic, looking ready to bolt. It had taken some convincing, but she'd finally agreed to come train with us. Though by the panicked look on her face, she was having serious second thoughts.

"I can't go out like this. What will my aunt say? I'm wearing *pants.*" She mouthed the word as if it were an oath.

I repressed a laugh. Nariko wore a fighting outfit similar to mine; however, her jacket fell in pleats almost to the floor. It practically was a dress. Sure, she was wearing trousers, but no one would know it by looking at her. "You look fine, Nariko."

"You look more than fine." Iskander breezed into the room, his shoulder grazing mine as he passed me to approach Nariko—whose face promptly turned scarlet.

She dipped her head and sank into a graceful curtsy. "Thank you, Prince Iskander."

"Please, we're training partners now. Call me Iskander."

"All right," Nariko replied in a breathy giggle.

I rolled my eyes and went to the table. He'd been like this yesterday too. If Iskander wasn't following me around, he was ignoring me, or flirting outrageously with my friend. If he was trying to make me jealous, he was failing horribly. But toying with Nariko's feelings?

I snatched a long knife off the table and shoved it into my sleeve. Illya had given it to me as an early birthday present. He still didn't like that he couldn't go to the Shadow Guild with me and didn't want me unarmed when he wasn't within reach. So he gave me the knife, with the firm instruction I take it everywhere. The blade was beautiful, perfectly weighted for throwing, with a hilt that was inlaid with ornate silver Raskisi knots.

"Don't worry," Iskander said, in response to a complaint of Nariko's that I had completely missed. "I'll be with you the whole time. Swordplay is not so difficult. You simply take it one step at a time."

"Askia said it's like dancing."

"Did she?" Iskander shot me a sneering glare.

I shrugged. "Someone gave me good advice once. Shall we?" I turned away from the confusion rippling across Iskander's face and walked out the door.

Together with Illya and a half dozen of my men, Iskander, Nariko, and I walked quickly to the garrison and into our usual training ring. As usual, nobles crowded the stands. Their robes and dresses were a riot of bright fabric blazing in the sun. I did my best to ignore them. I supposed I should be gratified by their attention, but at the moment it was annoying.

An annoyance compounded by the shock rolling through the Khazan Guard at Nariko's presence in the ring. Ridiculous. They fought with me nearly every day, didn't they? How was Nariko any different?

Captain Nazir clearly didn't share my opinion. He crossed his arms over his chest, shaking his head. "It's inappropriate for a woman to fight."

My eyebrows arched. "So what, I'm not a woman?"

The captain winced a terribly pained smile. "You are a royal, my lady, and may do as you please."

"Nice save," I snorted. "Very smooth." The men milling around us laughed, but I understood the reason for the captain's discomfort. He didn't want a Vishiri woman to fight. I sometimes got the feeling the men of the guard didn't strictly view me as a woman by their standards. Not that it meant I was afforded all the leeway of a man, of course.

"Propriety aside, Lady Nariko hasn't fought to join the guard."

"Don't worry, Captain Nazir. I will handle Lady Nariko's training," Iskander said, stepping forward gallantly.

Captain Nazir didn't seem particularly comforted by this, but all he could do was shrug. "As you wish, my lord."

Iskander gave me a smug smile and led Nariko over to one

of the weapons racks. I swallowed a swear and stalked over to the targets, grabbing a set of throwing knives like the one Illya gave me. Iskander, I noticed, took Nariko to the other side of the yard.

"Back straight," Illya said, coming to my side. "That's it. Now follow through on the release. Good."

After a few silent moments, Illya cleared his throat. I paused. He looked around surreptitiously and rubbed his hand over his whiskers. "Is everything all right with Prince Iskander?" he asked in a careful undertone. "He seems . . . agitated."

I gave him a humorless smile. "I've been trying to put some distance between us like you suggested," I said, resisting the urge to lean closer—Iskander wasn't the only man I needed to be careful around. "I know I can't afford to discount a marriage alliance. In fact, it seems more likely every day, but it's come to my attention that his future lies in a different direction." I nodded meaningfully toward Nariko.

Illya's eyes widened with comprehension. "So that's why you insisted she come."

"I care for them both, and I want them to be happy. If that means I need to step aside, that's fine."

Illya's pale gray eyes scoured my face. "Is it?"

"I'll always be Iskander's friend, but . . ." I bit my lip, thinking about my feelings for Iskander. About my lack of feelings. "I care about Iskander, but I care about Seravesh more. Does that make me heartless?"

"No," he said, his eyes lighting up with what I thought was relief. "It makes you a queen."

I took solace in Illya's words, in the approval I felt behind them. In the lack of jealousy in his tone. As muddled as our relationship was, sometimes it felt like he was the only one on my side.

A hush cascaded through the balconies. I looked up and

saw why: the emperor walked along the second balcony, smiling at the bowing lords. He made his way to the stairs and descended into the ring.

The Khazan Guard dropped everything to stand at attention, while Captain Nazir and Iskander hurried to the emperor's side. Pulling my back straight, I strode toward them. The emperor smiled, stepping past the still-speaking Iskander to greet me.

"Good afternoon, Princess Askia."

"Hello, Your Majesty. How do you do?"

"Well enough," he said. "Though I confess to feeling a little stifled from rather too many meetings. It got me wondering if your challenge was still on the table?"

I blinked. Spar with the emperor? What if I hurt him? Day Lord save me, what if I accidentally killed him?

Captain Nazir cleared his throat. "I'm not sure that's entirely wise, my lord."

"Oh?" The emperor turned his lazy, leonine gaze on Nazir. "Why not? I've seen Princess Askia fight before and know her to be an able warrior. I'm interested to try my hand. Or are you afraid I'd be careless enough to hurt her?"

Captain Nazir's face blanched to a queasy-looking shade of green. Though I agreed it was probably a terrible idea, I wouldn't have taken Nazir's place for the whole world. A kind of reckless bravery filled my veins. The emperor obviously had his heart set on fighting me. Why not play the game?

"You must take pity on Captain Nazir," I said. "I've already bullied him into accepting Lady Nariko."

"Ah, well, if Lady Nariko can be allowed in the ring, certainly I can as well, Captain."

"Of course, Your Majesty."

"Perfect. Princess Askia?"

I smiled. "A moment, while I swap the knives for a sword."

"Choose your blade," he replied, his eyes sweeping appreciatively over me.

I nodded and walked back to the weapons rack, bypassing a long row of Vishiri scimitars. I was better with the falchion, and though I had no idea if the emperor was any good, I didn't want to face him at less than my best.

"I don't think this is a good idea," Iskander said, appearing at my side.

I tutted. "Well, I can't very well say no, can I?"

A frustrated sound scraped out of Iskander's throat. His eyes darted across the yard, an edge of panic in his face. He licked his lips, and when he looked at me it was with an air of desperation. "Win, Askia. You have to win."

I felt my brow furrow. Win? There wasn't a chance in hell I was going to win. Nothing would hurt my chances of keeping myself in the emperor's good graces more than beating him in front of all these people. It might be stupid, but no man liked losing to a woman.

"Trust me, Askia." Iskander grabbed my forearm like he could see my doubt. His grasp dug the edge of the knife into my skin. "*Win.*" Iskander released me, retreating into the crowd of gathering guardsmen.

I turned to the rack, trying not to let Iskander's words get under my skin. By the time I'd selected a sword, Armaan was going through his forms. He'd removed his jacket and wore only a loose tunic over tight leather pants. It was hard not to admire the corded strain of his arm and chest muscles as he worked. It was easy to forget how young Armaan was. He had only been a teenager when he took the throne, only eighteen when Enver and Iskander were born. Now, only a handful of years into his forties, his body was anything but soft.

Armaan grinned when he caught me looking, and I couldn't

help but smile back. He swept the curved edge of his scimitar up to his nose, holding the salute. "Ready?"

"You'll find out," I said, copying the gesture.

We touched blades, and I jumped back, anticipating Armaan's thrust. I kept moving, easily blocking his attack as he swept through the proscribed opening of the e-Ashrah sequence, a standard warm-up combination used by the Khazan Guard. I wasn't sure if he was testing my ability or easing himself into the spar. Either way, I felt my body settle into the rhythm of the fight.

Armaan seemed to be waiting for me to relax. The moment I did, he picked up the pace, moving away from choreographed sequences and into a true, improvised bout. Forcing me on my heels, I managed only a few attacks in the minutes that followed. Blinking sweat out of my eyes, I knew I was completely outmatched.

I could have been fighting Illya or Nazir, the emperor was that good. Day Lord above, someone should have warned me Armaan was a swordmaster. And Iskander wanted me to win? I would have laughed if I had the breath.

I brought up my guard, as he pressed in for the attack. Armaan's blow shuddered up my arm, jarring my shoulder. I stumbled, my right side open for the kill shot. I braced for the impact, but it never came. Armaan backed away, letting me recover. He winked.

Armaan circled. I took a deep breath, willing myself to focus. Without meaning to, magic leapt into my arms, tingling across my skin. I smiled and flung out my powers, calling for aid.

I welcomed the tether's cold as it breezed across my skin. Vitaly appeared at the edge of the ring. I couldn't see him; I was too busy meeting the latest of Armaan's attacks, but I felt his presence in the back of my head. Surprise rippled through me, but I didn't have the space to express it. Day Lord above, Armaan was fast.

"*Spin,*" Vitaly ordered, obeying my wordless call for help. "*Now block, thrust, turn left, swipe, block.*" Vitaly barked out his instructions with the precise rat-a-tat-tat cadence of rain against glass.

My mind receded, focusing the whole of my body on following Vitaly's command. Slowly, I began to gain back ground. Surprise flashed across Armaan's face as I went in for an attack. He parried it, giving me a reckless smile before turning my attack on its head and forcing me back.

Even with Vitaly's help, I knew I couldn't win. Armaan's sheer strength overwhelmed me. My muscles creaked with strain. My breath came in burning gasps.

"*I can fight through you, if you let me in,*" Vitaly said.

I shuddered—and refused the offer. I still had to lose the match. I just didn't want to look like a fool in the process.

A wicked idea filled my head. A way for me to lose without losing. It would take daring, but I had that in spades. What I didn't have was the tactical foresight necessary to pull it off. Vitaly did. I felt him frown at the idea, shaking his head with ghostly exasperation. I gave him a mental prod and sensed his assent.

With Vitaly still calling out orders, I slowed my pace. Incrementally at first, like I was being gradually overcome by Armaan's attacks. It was an easy ploy, mostly because I was indeed tiring. I funneled my energy away from speed and into precision. If my plan was going to work, I needed to look tired without getting sloppy. One careless move, and I could maim the man who ruled half the world.

The thought shook my resolve, and for a terrible moment, I felt Vitaly slip away. I willed my mind to concentrate and let Armaan push me to the edge of the ring. I pounced forward with a sloppy-looking thrust. Armaan parried with ease. I overbalanced. My sword arm flew out wide. My body half turned away from Armaan. Perfect bait.

Armaan took it. He slapped the flat of my blade with his own. My sword went flying, landing harmlessly in the dirt a few yards away. I turned, but Armaan was there. In a blink, he had me pinned to his chest, hugging my arms to my sides with his left hand. His sword came to my throat, and I leaned back instinctively, so far the back of my head thudded onto his shoulder.

I angled my chin up until our eyes met. His golden gaze burned across my skin. A handful of inches separated us, so close we breathed the same air. "Yield."

"Never."

His eyebrows rose. "You've been outmatched, Askia," he said, purring my name. "If I so much as cough, I'd make you a queen in the afterlife."

I gave him my sweetest smile, twisting my left hand up into my sleeve. The knife fell into my hand. I rotated the blade, scraping it up his left inseam. His pupils dilated. "But if I so much as cough, you'll be an empress."

Time stopped. His eyes widened. A slow, wolfish smile spread across his face. I felt him harden against my backside. Heat flooded into my abdomen. His hungry gaze lowered to my lips and, for a wild moment, I thought he was going to spin me around and kiss me.

Armaan tossed his head back, his laugh echoing through the courtyard to the raucous cheers of the crowd—the crowd I had completely forgotten about. He released me and gave me a graceful bow.

"A draw then," he cried to the adoring crowd.

I made myself smile, bowing to hide the confusion that threatened to surface on my face. The feel of him behind me, the desire in his face sent me reeling. But it was my own yearning, which even now made my legs weak, that had me most on edge.

Guardsmen closed in, and I nodded vaguely at the congratulations I received. My mind was still too addled by the fight to comprehend a word anyone said.

Armaan cut through the crowd and took my hand. He brought it to his lips, his golden eyes burning. "Until next time, Askia," he murmured, releasing me once again. The crowd separated us, and I was surrounded once more by unfamiliar, smiling faces.

I felt Illya come to my side, felt his eyes drilling into my face, but I couldn't meet his gaze. Not now. I searched the yard, desperate to find somewhere safe to look. I spotted Nariko first. Her back was turned, and the hem of her new jacket was coated in fine brown dust. I opened my mouth to call out but caught myself when I realized what she was looking at. Just beyond the orbit of the crowd, I saw a glimmer of blue-black hair: Iskander, walking quickly out of the ring.

25

*G*o *into the infirmary.*"

My words echoed through the Marchlands, loud and ringing. And wrong. I narrowed my eyes at Vitaly's unmoving form. Took a bracing breath and shoved myself deeper into my power, falling—no. Falling was the wrong word. Sinking was more like it, like a stone through water. I let the thought slide away, as more power filled me, making frozen sculptures of my bones.

"*Go to the infirmary.*"

Vitaly shifted his weight from one foot to the other, crossing his arms. But he didn't move. Didn't turn to the training room door and disappear through it. No. I could feel his soul scraping against mine, jabbing at me in a quick succession of parried blows, testing me for weakness.

Cold sweat poured down my back as a ragged shiver wormed through my core. I submitted to the pain, even as I brought every inch of my will down on Vitaly, refusing to be defeated. I felt his soul begin to buckle under the weight of compulsion. My magic slid across his skin looping like a leash around his neck. I felt his resolve twitch.

Revulsion whipped through me with the voyeurlike shame of seeing something too private for my eyes. Vitaly must have sensed my hesitation, for his soul lunged against mine, locking me in a tug-of-war that made my muscles ache with exhaustion.

Ozura insisted that this should be easy. That I'd compelled Brother Jalnieth when I banished him, so compelling Vitaly should be child's play. But just because a thing should be easy didn't make it so.

Which was why Ozura and I were sitting alone in the training room, watching me fail time and again. Ozura's obvious disappointment was only making this harder. She had gone from studying my every move, to calling for a lap desk and supplies so she could catch up on her correspondence. The scritch-scratch of her quill on parchment felt like its own kind of punishment.

The sound of writing stopped. It was as if the queen sensed my focus wavering and was now prepared to watch my failure. I tried to let the thought pass, tried to cling to my focus, tried—

Gone.

I slumped, scrubbing my face with my hands, and barely managed to turn a curse into a groan. I crossed my arms, tucking my frozen hands against my rib cage, and looked up at Ozura.

She held the quill over her letter like she'd stopped writing midsentence. Ozura's expression was sharp enough to cut skin. She heaved a deep sigh, and with deliberate slowness, continued her letter.

I resisted the urge to curl up in a ball on the floor, but it was a near thing. The queen had a way of making me feel disappointed without even speaking. It was like her ability to tell the truth from a lie had sprouted passive-aggressive wings and was now drowning me in a sea of my own shame.

That, of course, was the problem. I did feel ashamed, and about a hundred other things that made it impossible for me to be calm enough to reach the void. Doubly so with Ozura watching. Sitting beside her, I could still feel the warmth of Armaan's body pressed against mine, and Iskander's petulant jealousy.

"I really don't understand why your progress has stalled," she said, setting her quill down with a snap that echoed across the room. "You were doing so well when we started. So what is the matter?"

"It's just—" My words faltered as I tried to express how wrong it all felt. "It just feels wrong. Immoral somehow."

Ozura tutted. "Why? What is the difference between summoning a ghost and commanding one?"

"It's the same as knocking on a person's door and breaking it down to slap a collar around their necks."

Ozura huffed out a tired breath, closing her eyes as if the sight of me was exhausting. "Askia, you do not have the luxury of being squeamish. You will never be able to give a spirit form if you can't first will their journey from the Marchlands into life." She leaned toward me, eyes now open, heavy and intense, and filled with concern. "You *must* master this, Askia. Your life may someday depend on it."

"I know! It's just—" I swallowed my words, knowing she was right. I'd commanded Jalnieth's spirit away that first night on instinct, but I knew better than to rely on that. "Shall I try again?"

"Not now, but I'm giving you an assignment; from now on I want you constantly pulling a small but steady stream of magic. Perhaps we need to strengthen you before you can take the next step."

I nodded. "Is that all?"

"No," she said, her expression closing. Hardening. "We have other matters to discuss."

Her dark gaze took me in, traveling the length of my body in a too intimate survey that made me self-consciously relive the memory of Armaan's gaze scraping against my lips.

Ozura pushed the wooden desk onto the floor, curling her legs beneath her. She leaned forward, an amused smile on her lips, and for a second it was almost possible to imagine she was Nariko, lounging beside me to share the latest court gossip.

"About Armaan . . ."

The image shattered.

"It would seem my husband has taken an interest in you."

"No." The word slid out from between my teeth quicker than a knee jerk.

Ozura raised one ebony eyebrow.

I forced my hands down to my lap, feigning an indifference I didn't feel. "I came to Vishir for an army, not a husband."

Ozura huffed an exasperated laugh. "How you ever convinced yourself you could get one without the other is beyond me." She shook her head at the ceiling before returning her feline gaze to me. "Your intentions aside, Armaan is interested. Enough so that he has brought up the matter with me."

"Why?" I could not believe I was having this conversation with anyone, let alone the wife of the man in question. I snatched up the water skein beside me and took a sip, a weak attempt to hide my unease.

"I am his principal wife. He is honor bound to tell me of any potential changes to the menagerie. I assume you're no longer a maiden."

A mouthful of water slammed the back of my throat as air sputtered out of my lungs.

"Yes, that's what I thought," Ozura replied as if my spraying water all over the floor was answer enough. "I suppose things are bound to happen when you're surrounded by so many soldiers. Though I do hope you aren't harboring any secret loves or mooning over that handsome captain of yours."

From the corner of my eye, I spotted Vitaly burying his face in his hands, and thanked Lady Night Ozura couldn't see his embarrassment. But what did I have to be embarrassed about?

Even if something had happened, my relationship with Illya was none of her business.

I met Ozura's gaze with a cold one of my own. "I'm not the mooning type. That is all you need to know."

Ozura only shrugged. "Armaan already has heirs, so he won't care about your past indiscretions. That would not be true of any other Vishiri lord, in case you're harboring hopes elsewhere."

"I'm not looking to marry anyone, let alone your husband. We don't even know each other."

She tossed the argument aside with a lazy flick of her hand. "My husband has always been a creature of passion. So is my son," she added, with a pointed look. "A man can afford passion. A woman cannot."

"No one can afford that kind of passion," I replied with an arch frown. "No one in your court would accept it. Count Dobor has too many allies. Worse, my people would suffer if I agree to the match."

"Your people already suffer," Ozura said, utterly unmoved. "And while you're correct in assuming there would be resistance, it's far less than it would have been a few weeks ago. You've made allies, become stronger for your ties both with the guard and in the court. But you will never be so powerful you receive an army for nothing. I'm telling you now—there is no other course for you here. Marriage is the price you pay."

Ozura leaned forward, and a beam of light lit the edges of her face. I was struck by how waxen her skin looked. "If you continue the way you have, and you *should* continue, Armaan will make an offer in the coming weeks. If your people truly are your only concern, you will accept." A frown pulled down the corners of her mouth. "Didn't your mother explain these things to you?"

"She didn't have the chance. The Shazir murdered her for her ties to *your* guild, remember?" The words tasted like ash in my mouth. "She never wanted this life for me."

Pity darkened Ozura's gaze. "No," she murmured. "She didn't. But you have been engaged before, Askia. Surely this isn't so different."

Thinking of that faceless prince made a small seldom-used corner of my heart ache. "That was an alliance of necessity, a joining of two kingdoms to fight Roven."

"So is this," Ozura said, leaning toward me. "And if I'm not mistaken, you agreed to the match without ever having met that Raskisi prince. At least you've spent time with Armaan."

And some of his wives, too, I thought, biting my tongue to keep the words locked behind my lips. Ozura wouldn't understand my resistance. She was born knowing she would be one wife of many. That she'd be trapped here—yes, with influence, but not a true partner. And that wasn't what I wanted. What Ozura didn't see was that not knowing that Raskisi prince had been part of the allure. Without the interference of reality, he could be anything I wanted him to be: strong and kind, loyal and brave. An equal; and that was something Armaan and I would never be. Lady Night save me, I wouldn't even be equal to his other wives. I'd always be the last. The least.

Ozura pursed her lips when my reply never came. "We needn't discuss it any further now. Barring any unforeseen aggression by Roven, Armaan won't make an offer tomorrow. In the meantime, you must reconcile yourself to the idea. The sooner you're married, the safer you will be. As his wife, Armaan will protect you and yours. And Radovan won't be able to sacrifice you to gain your power. That is the most important thing."

"No. My people matter more than I do."

Ozura shook her head. "Not to the rest of the world."

"The rest of the word?" I snapped. "The rest of the world

is Vishir, and Vishir has grown fat sitting idle while the north burns. No. I'm not going to reconcile myself to your fate, not when it's completely unnecessary. Not when fighting Roven is the right thing to do."

"The right thing to do?" Ozura scoffed. "Armaan is an emperor. Right or wrong is meaningless, there is only what he wants. And if you want his help, you will accept the offer when it comes. Or are you really willing to sacrifice your people to save your pride?"

Vitaly took a step back at the brutality of her words. I would have, too, but my limbs were too heavy to move. Marry Armaan, or let Seravesh fall? Were these really my only options?

"Is everything all right?" Illya asked. He'd been watching me with a vaguely worried expression ever since I all but ran out of the menagerie.

"Yes. Fine," I replied, hurrying onward. "I need to send a message to Arkady."

"What? Why?" Illya's voice was tight with surprise, but I couldn't respond to it. Couldn't even look at him. "Askia, talk to me."

I shook my head, only for Illya to grab my hand, pulling me to a stop. I glared at the darkness gathering in the corners of the hall. With the sun long set and the moon no more than a sliver in the sky, night crept into the palace on spidery fingers. For a moment it was possible to imagine we were alone in the world, Illya and I.

I forced myself to look up, to meet his gaze. "The emperor is considering making me an offer."

Illya's whole body went still. "An offer of what?"
"Marriage."
Pain lanced through Illya's gaze a second before his expres-

sion shuttered. He dropped my hand. "And if you do, he'll send his army to fight for Seravesh."

"I wouldn't accept any other way," I replied, matching his business-like tone even if it was quietly killing me.

"I'll arrange for a messenger to be sent today. But if the offer comes"—he paused, then took a deep breath as if bracing for a blow—"I think you should accept."

I rocked back, unable to guard against his words. "You do?"

"Yes, my lady."

My lady. Not Askia. *My lady*. The words sounded like a door slamming shut. I opened my mouth reaching for something to say. Something to make Illya understand how hard this was. That I didn't want to marry an emperor, I wanted . . . I wanted him. The guard I wasn't supposed to have. Couldn't have. Not if I wanted Seravesh to be free.

Illya knew it though. It was why he had always tried to maintain such a careful distance from me. Why, even when he failed and came too close like that night in the garden, he still advised me to keep my options open. Even though I'd seen the pain it caused him, he wasn't jealous or proprietary like Iskander. Illya was putting Seravesh first. And so must I.

"Illya, I—"

The sound of fabric rustling from the next hall made me stop short. Illya frowned, opening his mouth, but I held a hand up to silence him. Magic leapt into my limbs. I felt command ripple out around me, instinctual and easy as Ozura promised it should be, as I dragged Vitaly to my side.

"Is someone there?"

Vitaly frowned, scouting ahead, only to return a second later. *"Shazir. Hide."*

I seized Illya's arm and dragged him through to the nearest doorway—it was open, leading to a sandy-bottomed courtyard with deserted paths lined in knee-high shrubs. I flattened myself to the wall. Illya followed my lead, hand on the hilt of his sword. He bent low.

"What's wrong?" he whispered, breath hot on the shell of my ear.

"Has she come out yet?"

Khaljaq's voice felt like the unexpected caress of a strange hand. I jammed myself closer to Illya and the wall, praying the night would hide us.

"No, my lord," a second voice replied, then paused. "Shall I keep watching?"

"No, Brother Losh. I don't think that will be necessary. This late, I can only assume Princess Askia is staying in the menagerie for the night." Khaljaq's voice dripped in displeasure.

My face flushed in outrage. The urge to leap out of my hiding spot and demand answers, demand to know who he thought he was to have people follow me, was overwhelming. Prudence won out and I stayed put.

"It is troubling to see the princess associate with a snake like Ozura."

The other man, Brother Losh, made a noise of agreement. "Ozura is a known witch . . ." His voice faltered, like he was gathering nerve. "Can we be certain Princess Askia isn't—"

"I put the girl to the question myself," Khaljaq hissed with such malevolence my knees went weak. "Are you doubting my word, Losh?"

"No, my lord," was the hurried reply. "I just worry that with a creature like Ozura, anything is possible."

"Indeed."

"What should we do?"

"We wait," Khaljaq replied. "We watch. We listen. Prince Iskander may know what Ozura is up to with Princess Askia. I will ask him about it when we meet tomorrow."

"The Day Lord smiles upon us, there."

"He does," Khaljaq agreed, voice brimming with satisfaction. "The prince is becoming disillusioned with his father's avarice and his mother's wicked scheming. Princess Askia is . . . important to him. I sense he worries that she will not survive this court. But he needn't. We are here after all, even if she isn't ready to accept us."

"Will she ever be?"

"The Day Lord wills it, Brother Losh," Khaljaq replied, words cold and severe. "Eventually the witch king will try to take her and when he does, we will be there to protect her. She is exactly what we need: a child born of sin yet fighting evil. The perfect symbol. A symbol I will take for the Shazir and use to finally rid the world of the scourge of witches."

My heart was beating so loudly in my chest, I barely heard them leave. Not only were they watching me, but Iskander—

"My lady?" Illya murmured, his voice pulling me back to the present. I looked up, only to find I'd practically wedged myself under his arm for fear of Khaljaq. "Are you all right?"

I nodded. "Yes," I said, trying for a smile. "Just not sure I want the kind of protection Khaljaq's offering."

Illya's gaze softened and for a moment, I thought he'd draw me closer. Draw me in. The moment passed. He pulled himself straight and stepped away.

I swallowed hard as if it could clear away my rising regret.

"Don't worry, my lady. You'll never need the Shazir. I'll make certain of it. But . . ." Illya's words trailed off like he wasn't sure what to say next. "What Khaljaq said about Prince Iskander— What meeting?"

"I don't know," I admitted, words bitter on my tongue. "But I'm going to find out."

26

I paced through my rooms, my body torn between narrow-eyed exhaustion and anticipation. Between Ozura's—and Lady Night help me, Illya's—words about Armaan, and Khaljaq's about Iskander, I'd barely slept. *The ibn Vishri family had better be worth all this trouble*, I thought, tapping the worn edge of a letter against my thigh.

Nariko should have been back by now. I'd sent her to find out where Iskander was meeting the Shazir almost an hour ago. I was just settling in for an anxious wait when Arkady's letter arrived. The parchment was practically burning in my hand.

Arkady's scouts had seen Roven troops move out of four of my northern cities. Heading south. Arkady cautioned that they might simply be moving toward Solenskaya. There had been unrest in the capital and talk of rebellion in the towns dotting the Peshkalor Mountains. Radovan might simply be trying to strengthen his position.

Or he could be preparing for a spring push into Idun.

Either way, it was news I wanted to share with General Ochan. He had been receptive to my calls for action against Roven. This could be the motivation he needed to formally petition the emperor.

Instead of meeting with Ochan right now, though, I was

hunting down a petulant prince. The thoughts snarled through my mind, all the fiercer for their impotence. If I left to find the general, Nariko might not reach me in time for me to interrupt Iskander's meeting. A smile prickled my lips, imagining his expression when I barged in.

Bells chimed from somewhere above, calling out twelve o'clock.

Where was Nariko?

"I've got it." Nariko's voice filled the room a half second before she entered with Illya on her heels. "Rose Hall. Three o'clock."

"That gives you time to find General Ochan," Illya said, nodding to the letter.

"Ochan?" Nariko asked, thinking for a second. "Well, it's audience day. He'll be in the Great Hall."

"Lead the way."

This was why I'd courted the Khazan Guard, I thought as we hurried through the halls. Together Ochan and I could formulate a plan, maybe even find some support in the Council of Viziers. General Ochan could speak to Armaan on my behalf. No matter what Ozura said, marriage didn't have to be the only option. I could still secure the army without it. And without whatever idiotic scheme Iskander was cooking.

With Khaljaq.

My hands curled into fists. I hadn't seen Iskander since the fight with Armaan and there was no point in pretending he wasn't avoiding me. No. Not just avoiding me, but working with the monsters who murdered my parents. *What a child*, I thought. Hurt feelings weren't an excuse to ally with the Shazir.

And I wasn't the only one he was betraying. What would Ozura say when she found out? Unlike me, Iskander knew *she* was a witch. And all because of a stupid crush I couldn't return.

At the edge of my vision the ghost of the Vishiri sergeant shimmered into existence, pulling me back to the present.

"Report," I silently commanded.

"Count Dobor received instructions from Roven yesterday," he said, falling into step beside me.

"A letter? Did you read it?"

"No. Not a letter. It was some kind of magical communication."

My jaw nearly dropped. *"Is Dobor a witch?"*

"Uncertain, my lady."

My brow furrowed, focusing on the ghost-sergeant and the puzzle of Dobor until the gray space of the Marchlands swirled around me, muting the sound of Illya and my men and drenching me in a cold wind. *"Describe what you saw."*

"Just after noon yesterday, Dobor went to a locked cabinet behind his desk, removed a silver bowl and filled it with water. The water instantly turned to ice and began to glow. Dobor obviously saw someone in the ice, because he began giving a report. I couldn't see to whom he spoke or what that person said."

I nodded. It sounded like the bowl was ensorcelled. *"What was Dobor saying?"*

The sergeant hesitated, and a pregnant pause writhed between us. *"He was speaking of you, my lady."*

"Oh?"

"He was reporting on your growing position at court and the increasing tension it's caused. He said that even though you've caught the eye of Emperor Armaan, your actions at court are causing instability. He boasted that because of you, Prince Enver has become more pliable to Dobor's influence. And Prince Iskander's insecurity is straining his relationship with his father. Dobor sounded quite pleased."

A numbness that had nothing to do with the cold of death tightened my chest. *"It sounds like Dobor is anticipating a war between the two princes."*

The sergeant shrugged. *"There's always more than one potential heir, and they always fight. Don't worry over this. It's the Vishiri way, my lady."*

I nodded and drew away from the Marchlands, letting my magic fade. Wasn't this what Ozura had predicted? That Radovan let me reach Vishir precisely so I could create this kind of instability? I was playing right into his hands: pushing Enver closer to Dobor, and Iskander to the Shazir.

The Shazir.

Their name hissed through my mind like the darkest curse.

Damn Iskander!

The instability brewing here wasn't all my fault, I thought, tossing my hair over my shoulder. Iskander was a fool for befriending them. They were evil. Didn't he know that? Didn't he know what the Shazir did to me?

I stuttered to a stop as my anger ran into a wall of truth. No. He *didn't* know the whole story.

My whole story.

And whatever pretty tale Khaljaq had spun for Iskander— and there must be one to make Iskander turn his back on Ozura—it wouldn't hold up. Not if I told him what really happened, all those years ago. It was time—time to admit I lied to him about being a witch. And, in all probability, I was going to have to tell Iskander there wasn't a future for us.

But would it help? Or would telling him the truth just push him closer to Khaljaq? Still I had to try. Didn't I?

Nariko touched my shoulder with a gentle hand, a question on her lips. Her gaze lifted, taking mine with it. The doors of the Great Hall lay closed before me, and I heard the sound of many conversations humming through them. My muscles felt weak at the thought of all those people, but I knew I had to go in. Go. Find Ochan. Make a plan. Everything was better with a plan. I nodded to the guards and the doors slid open.

"Why, hello, Princess Askia. How are you today?"

I stifled a groan and turned to find Prince Enver walking toward me with a broad smile.

"I'm well, thank you," I replied, my voice wooden with disbelief. Given our last conversation, Enver had no reason to be smiling at me. "You?"

"Very well." He slid past Illya and offered me his arm. "May I escort you in?"

Disbelief blossomed into outright suspicion, but I couldn't very well say no. People were already staring at us. "Thank you."

Enver took a circuitous route through the hall, dragging me along in his wake, grinning at some people, nodding to others. He was acting like he'd won something. Too bad he couldn't see the disgust rippling across the features of the nearest ghosts. Interesting that the dead disliked him as much as I did.

"Are you enjoying your day?" Prince Enver asked quietly.

"I am," I gritted through a bland smile.

"Doing anything interesting later?" he asked, eyes glittering with knowledge. "Meeting with old friends, perhaps?"

"*Oh, do smack him,*" said the ghost of a matronly noblewoman.

I'd have smiled, but Enver's words could only mean he knew about Iskander's meeting. Everyone probably did. I looked down the hall just as Iskander slid into the room from a side door. The fool took his post near Ozura, his eyes meeting mine. There was an intensity in his gaze I'd never seen before, something haunted almost. What I didn't see was guilt. "The Shazir are hardly my friends," I bit out.

"But is Iskander?" he asked with little laugh. "My dear little brother has never been the most dependable. Always flitting from one thing to the next. He doesn't do it on purpose, of course. But he's never been skilled at maintaining alliances."

"Now, now, Prince Enver. I hope you don't intend to monopolize all of Princess Askia's attention on her birthday."

Dobor's voice boomed across the lofty ceiling, immediately capturing the attention of everyone around. Enver slid out of my grip, clipping Nariko's shoulder so hard she fell into Illya.

Count Dobor slithered from the crowd grinning triumphantly at Enver. It was obvious Enver had been steering me toward Dobor, but I'd been too preoccupied by my anger to see it coming. Idiot.

"It's not my birthday."

"Yes, it's tomorrow, I know," Dobor said, smiling at my stiff reply. "But you'll forgive my master his excitement."

Dobor raised both arms with a flourish and bowed almost to the floor. I stilled. This was not the bow a dignitary gave a foreign noble. It was the bow of a subject to his queen. What the hell was Dobor up to?

He rose, producing a wooden jewelry box from inside the pocket of his robes. Silence rippled out from where he stood, like we were the eye of some terrible storm.

"A gift from your dearest friend, his Imperial Majesty, Radovan Kirkoskovich of Roven."

Dobor's hands hovered in the air between us, the little box perched in his open palms. A flash of panic lanced through my mind, and I had the sudden mental image of opening the box to find General Arkady's finger sitting in its depths.

"Steady."

Vitaly's voice sank into my mind on a breath of cold wind. I pushed away the panic, useless as it was, and forced myself to take the box in a two-fingered pinch. Its hinges moaned as I opened it.

Nestled in black silk was an emerald the size of an egg. Nearly identical to the gem Dobor always wore, the emerald glistened in the light of the Great Hall. It was perfectly cut, but not quite flawless. A hint of gray clouded its core. Revulsion rattled through my bones, so fierce it took an act of will not to smash it on the floor.

Count Dobor gave me an unctuous smile. "Emperor Radovan asks me to say that this is but the smallest token of his very great affection for you. Though he is confident he will see you soon to properly celebrate your upcoming birthday."

See me soon? The bastard was making it sound like I had decided to forsake my country. Like I was marrying the monster who'd burned two of my cities to the ground. I snapped the jewelry box shut and shoved it at Nariko.

A hand landed on my shoulder. A hand I'd last seen hurl a stone at my mother's skull. My eyes trailed up the crimson-clad arm to its source and found the shrunken body of Khaljaq standing beside me. His deep-set eyes were a striking sea blue. They would have been beautiful in anyone else, but on Khaljaq they glittered with malice.

Those eyes had haunted me through years and across continents. Now the man they belonged to was beside me. *Touching* me.

"Your words imply Princess Askia will soon be leaving us for the witch king." Khaljaq always spoke in a whisper when he intended the most harm, as if the weight of his hate was too much for his voice to bear.

Dobor's lips twitched into a sneer. "It's certainly not something that needs to be discussed with you, Khaljaq, but Emperor Radovan desires—"

"The witch king will never have Princess Askia. He is an abomination. His existence a sin against the Day Lord."

Dobor's answering grin was more like a baring of teeth. "And you consider yourself pure, Khaljaq? How quaint. You will forgive me if I don't take seriously the opinion of a man whose followers torture and murder anyone who disagrees with them."

Khaljaq's hand tightened on my shoulder. My already rigid body swayed under the pressure. My mind flashed back to other hands on other places. Memories screamed out of the darkest, most hidden parts of my heart. Memories of bruising and slicing and burning echoed through the shocked silence of my mind.

"My lady," Illya whispered, "let me take you back—"

"The Shazir are pure. Each man among us has been tested and proven clean. Princess Askia has endured the testing. She is one of us now, and we will protect her against any witch." Khaljaq turned his depthless attention onto me. I felt myself quail. "Cast that stone into the sea, Princess. I have no doubt it is a tool of corruption meant to poison you with magic."

The gathered crowd gasped; scandalized whispers filled the hall.

Dobor sputtered with impotent rage. "What fresh nonsense is this? Can my master now create witches? Is he a god?"

I looked past Dobor to the dais upon which Queen Ozura stood. Her face was set in a mask of stone, grave and unmoving. She stared at Khaljaq and did nothing.

Beside her, Iskander's face was ashen, his mouth hanging open as he watched the spectacle unfold. But he didn't come. *The Vishiri never come, not for me. Well, damn them all.*

"Enough." I wrenched myself out of Khaljaq's grip. "I don't need your protection, Khaljaq."

"Indeed, you don't," Dobor sputtered. "Emperor Radovan intends no harm to Princess Askia."

I rounded on Dobor. "No harm? So he murdered his wives by accident?"

"I've heard enough from this cockroach," Khaljaq hissed. "Your presence soils this court. Your life offends it."

"You're out of line, Khaljaq," Enver said, standing beside Dobor. "Roven is our ally, and Count Dobor is a great friend of this court."

"This has gone on long enough."

Iskander pushed in, planting himself between Dobor and Khaljaq. His eyes blazed, and the crushing weight of being cornered receded. Despite everything Iskander had come to help me.

"I'm glad you agree with me, brother," Enver said, his brow

furrowing in apparent surprise. "Khaljaq, you owe Count Dobor an apology."

"No, Enver. He doesn't. Khaljaq's words may sound harsh to the soft ears of this court, but he's not wrong about Roven. Our alliance with Radovan is a pleasant fiction. One we can no longer afford."

"What do you mean, Iskander?" I asked in a dry rasp.

"Our alliance has been in place for decades," Enver spit through gritted teeth.

"And it's about to be broken."

"Iskander, what are you talking about?"

Iskander flinched as I spoke his name, but he didn't reply. He drew himself up to his full height, turned his face to the watching crowd. He didn't look at me.

"If Roven is truly our ally," Iskander said, "then why are they amassing an army on Idun's northern border? Clearly they mean to violate the treaty and invade Idun."

Arkady's message said that Roven was on the move—but clearly the spies the Shazir had in the north knew more. Iskander knew more. And he hadn't said a word.

The news was like a slap in my face. Betrayal scoured through me, leaving something hard and burning in the place where our friendship had been. How could he not tell me?

"Enough." Though he didn't shout, Armaan's voice thundered through the hall, echoing off the vaulted ceiling and into the storm raging in my mind.

Armaan surveyed us from his throne, radiating cold anger. I could tell by the way his sons seemed to shrink, the weight of their father's considerable displeasure hit them the hardest.

"Now is not the time to discuss this matter. There is a proper time and place for everything. This is something both of my boys must learn if they ever mean to become men."

Armaan looked away from his sons, away from Iskander's

flinch and Enver's flush. He turned instead to Dobor, his face masked as the count bowed. The emperor's gaze shifted to me and softened with compassion. He was the only one here who cared about what I was feeling.

"On behalf of my subjects, allow me to apologize to you, Count Dobor, and most especially to you, Princess Askia."

"Thank you, Emperor." My voice sounded small to my ears, the slightest of whispers. "If you will excuse me?"

He nodded, his face sorrowful. "Of course."

I pushed through the parting crowd. My shoulder tingled, as the phantom hand of the man who murdered my parents clung to me. I made it into the hallway before I broke into a sprint.

27

I raced down the hall, stumbling on my hem after the first blind turn. I hitched up my skirts and kept going with no concept of destination, only the visceral need to run, to escape. I heard the thudding sound of footsteps behind me, and a small part of me knew it was Illya and Nariko trying to keep up. The larger part of my mind, the terrified, irrational part, was back in the dust-filled streets of Shazir Province, where the mountains leveled off in vast grassy plateaus and men spewed hate into the cold, thin air.

The palace walls shrank around me, caving in, crushing me. My lungs burned. *Out*. I needed out. The walls opened into an archway, and I hurtled into the light.

The severe lines of the courtyard were barely visible in the glare of the midmorning sun. I tilted my head back, letting the sun burn away my tears, as I walked blindly through the sand-filled bottom of the rock garden. I willed myself to return, to lock away memories of the Shazir and death and the unspeakable torment that followed. I clawed my way to the present, pushing back the feeling of rough hands crawling over my skin.

"Askia?"

A hand grasped my arm. I whirled, a half-feral snarl ripping out of my throat. I was done with men just thinking they could take hold of me. I brought both hands up, my fingers curled into claws, and slammed them into his chest.

Iskander stumbled back, his arms wheeling through the air. "What is your problem?"

"My problem?" Rage blazed within me, fiercer for its utter impotence. "How could you ally yourself with the Shazir? You know what they did to my parents."

Iskander shook his head, and I saw the muscles in his jaw tense as he clenched them shut. "I know what happened to your parents was awful," he said with the forced slowness of someone struggling to remain calm. "But it's not as if Khaljaq killed them."

"Yes, he did."

Iskander's body stilled, but his eyes worked in silence as if he were processing. He didn't know. He didn't know what Khaljaq had done. Enough. Ignorance was no longer an excuse.

"Didn't your new friend tell you? Didn't he tell you how he had my parents tied to a pole in the center of town? That he had them stoned to death while I watched? That he himself cast the first rock?

"How do you think I got this scar, Iskander? Khaljaq held a knife to my throat and made me watch my parents die. And I struggled. Oh, I struggled."

The words tumbled out of my mouth in a soft-spoken stream of confessed horror. I was powerless to stop it. I stepped closer, until we were nose to nose. "Until eventually, I stopped struggling. Khaljaq's knife was already at my throat. How hard would it be to end it? All I had to do was fall forward. But I hadn't counted on my father's power. Even as he stood dying, he saved me one last time."

My hand fluttered to my neck, tracing a jagged, shaking line across the scar knotting my skin. Iskander's wide eyes trailed after my fingers. He looked sick.

"The wound didn't close all the way. All my life, every bump, every cut had been healed instantly. Not this one. That's how I knew he was dead."

My words, though whispered, crashed into the utter silence that blanketed the courtyard. I realized we weren't alone. Nariko stood a few yards away. Tears streamed down her face. Illya stood beside her, looking torn between coming to my side and holding himself back in front of witnesses.

But Iskander . . .

Iskander's ring finger tapped against his thumb. His lips moved silently like he was testing his next words. I felt his mind whirling. My mouth twisted. After everything, he was going to try and politic his way out of trouble.

"I understand this must be terrible for you, and I'm sorry I didn't come to you first, but—" He swallowed hard and took a deep breath. "You're the rightful queen of Seravesh, Askia. No matter how great your personal tragedy, your duty is to your people. The Shazir could be your fiercest allies. They would fight for you if you let them. They would help you overthrow Radovan." Iskander stepped forward, his hands held out as if suing for peace. "I know the thought is distasteful, but sometimes you have to sacrifice your principles."

"I've sacrificed enough." My voice scraped out of my throat. "How could you do this? How can you defend them and still call yourself my friend?"

"I am your friend," he cried, jabbing his finger into his chest. "I'm the only one doing anything to help you. What are you doing?" He turned away from me only to come full circle, his own sense of betrayal brimming in his eyes. "What are you doing, Askia? Nothing. Nothing but chasing after my mother and flirting with my father."

I rocked back on my heels. "Like they weren't your ideas to

begin with? You were the first to suggest I marry Armaan. And you're angry at me for considering it? You don't think *that* is a sacrifice? You have no right to judge me for trying to find allies, sane allies, where I can."

"Oh, please. If you could put away your pride for one second, you'd see that even though the Shazir wronged you in the past, they're your friends now."

"Wronged me?" I fell back a few steps, all my fire guttered. "Do you even understand what they did to me?"

"Your parents confessed, Askia. What did you expect the Shazir to do?" Iskander paused, finally registering the hollow cant of my words. "What do you mean, 'did to you'?"

I opened my mouth but couldn't get the words out. My entire body trembled. I wrapped my arms about my middle, as if they could keep me from crumbling.

"What do you think they did to her, Iskander?" Ozura stepped from the shadows beyond the courtyard.

"You aren't wrong," Ozura said. "The Shazir will fight for her, but why should they? They murdered her father for his magic and her mother for loving him. Yet they spared Askia. Did you even think to ask them why?"

Iskander squirmed under the heat of his mother's glare. "Because she's not a witch."

"And how could they possibly know that?"

Iskander's mouth opened, but no reply came. He looked at me, still unable to speak. Dread cemented in my veins, threatening to drag me to the ground. I resisted, just as I had all those years ago. Resisted and survived. Stronger—I was stronger than this moment.

Ozura took a single step forward, her eyebrows arched high. "They're so sure of her purity. Did you honestly believe such surety comes for free? Are you naïve enough to believe it was without cost?" Ozura shook her head, as if she couldn't believe Iskander was so foolish. "They tortured her, Iskander. They tortured her in every way. In every way."

The blood rushed out of his face. He looked at me like he was about to be ill, but I felt nothing. I had no time for his shock or pity. I was a husk.

"And for what?" Ozura asked with a mirthless smile. "All to ensure she's not a witch."

Iskander did a double take. "But you don't . . . you're not—"

"Of course she's a witch," Ozura snapped.

His expression hardened. "You lied to me?"

I heard the pain in Iskander's voice. Refused to flinch away from it. My lie saved my life. Saved my people. His lies could undo all that.

"Yes."

"And why shouldn't she have lied?" Ozura asked. "You've always known that I'm a witch, yet you still allied yourself with the Shazir."

"Yes. And they've never moved against you," Iskander said, seizing on Ozura's words.

"And you think that absolves them?" I hissed. "That because they haven't tried to kill *your* mother, I should forgive them killing mine?"

"They would kill me in a second if they could," Ozura added before Iskander could speak. "Only I have a husband to protect me, an empire. What does Askia have, surrounded as she is by enemies? Who will protect her? Not you, it seems."

"I'm trying to." Iskander's voice was tight but utterly devoid of regret. "Yes, the Shazir have done terrible things, but they're changing. Roven is their real enemy—not the witches of Vishir. Don't you see? They're a means to an end, a weapon to be aimed. I can control them. Set them in the right direction, and they will destroy Roven."

"You think you can control a man like Khaljaq?" Ozura huffed her disbelief. "Can you control wildfire? That's what the Shazir are. They may burn for you, but that doesn't mean the people around you, the people you claim to care for, won't be burned too. Who will stop them then, my son? Will you?

"*Can* you?"

28

Wakefulness came to me in restless degrees. While my mind craved the oblivion of sleep, my body was unwilling to comply. I tossed around on my bed for several minutes before finally surrendering and opening my eyes.

A soft luminescence trickled in through the windows heralding the end of a long day. I sighed into the growing twilight and sat up. My fine court dress was a rumpled mess, tangled between my legs. I gave the full skirt several hard yanks to shake it free and then slumped from the effort.

After a few interminable minutes, I slid off the bed and padded toward the dressing room, pausing on the threshold. From somewhere beyond the boundary of my private rooms came the muffled sound of conversation. I wilted at the slow rumble of Illya's voice. I was too far away to make out any words, but the unmistakable cadence of spoken Vishiri meant I had visitors. I grimaced. No doubt there would be fallout from today's disaster. I should go out and deal with it.

Instead, I crossed to the doors on the other side of my bedchamber. Sweeping aside the chiffon curtains, I slipped outside, crossing the sun-warmed terrace to the garden.

The soggy caress of humid air kissed my cheeks as I walked.

The trellis-lined path filtered the sunlight into a green twilight. All was quiet but for the rustle of leaves, the soft trill of finches fluttering by, and the slight burble of the fountain somewhere ahead.

It was peaceful, idyllic even, but I didn't have it in me to enjoy it. Lady Night above, I was such a fool. I shook my head. I shouldn't have let the Shazir unbalance me so. And Iskander.

I took a deep breath, walking blindly toward the steadily growing babble of the fountain. The look of hurt on Iskander's face when he found out I'd been lying to him about being a witch chafed. But I'd run out of pity the moment I told him what the Shazir had done and I received nothing but excuses in return. And that was something I didn't think our friendship could survive. If I even wanted it to.

The grass transitioned to stone, and the path opened to the center of the garden. I looked up, ready to beseech the fountain's goldfish for advice, and froze. A man sat on the edge of the fountain, his elbows resting on his long legs . . . A man with smooth Vishiri skin stretched over a well-proportioned face. A man with golden eyes.

"Emperor," I said, my voice high with surprise, keenly aware of my bare feet and rumpled dress.

"Hello, Princess Askia." He rose, his smile a kind of beckoning.

My body moved of its own volition, joining him at the edge of the fountain. "I hope you haven't been waiting long."

He waved away my concern. "I told them not to wake you. I hoped we'd have the chance to speak, but not at the cost of your rest."

I nodded and waited for him to continue, but instead of speaking, he looked down at the water. I bit my lip, unsure of what to do or say, and followed his lead. A half-dozen fat-bellied goldfish swam through the clear water. They darted this way and that, wonderfully oblivious to the two royals staring down at them.

"I remember the day they brought you back here."

I looked up at the sound of his voice, at the quiet gravitas with which he spoke. His eyes remained trained on the fishes, but I doubted he was seeing them.

"A Shaziri horse trader dropped you off at the stables with the year's foals. When the guards realized who you were, they rushed you into the palace, interrupting a meeting of the Council of Viziers to bring you to me. Do you remember?"

I shook my head. My supposed liberation from the Shazir and the time afterward was still a blur. I had only the smallest memories, flashes of color and scent.

Armaan nodded slowly. "It doesn't surprise me. The look on your face, the depthless sorrow, it . . . It has never left me. You were so broken. I didn't know what to do with you, so I gave you to Ozura. She cleaned you up, fed you, made sure you were comfortable, but it didn't help, not really. You stayed with us for almost a year, never speaking a word. It was like you were waiting to die."

His eyes skated across my face, like he was searching for something. "When I learned the details of what happened, of what they did to you, I wondered if you could ever heal here. So I wrote to your grandfather. I cursed him for shirking his duty to you. I told him he was no man at all if he left you to fend for yourself. I even offered to pay him to take you back."

My lips twitched into a smile. "I know." Armaan's brows rose in apparent surprise. I shrugged. "My grandfather and I had something of a unique relationship. If it didn't start out with much fondness, it ended with it."

"Well, I'm glad for that. I was relieved when he finally agreed to take you. But then Tarek got sick."

The guilt in his voice was obvious, a shame that had ripened over time. I reached out instinctively and clasped his arm. "Tarek's death wasn't your fault. You couldn't have known the Shazir would kill my father."

"I knew he was on trial. I could have stepped in."

"My parents confessed," I said, unable to keep the bitterness out of my voice, the bitterness that revealed a hard truth I didn't want to confront. "They confessed, and interfering with the judicial system is a tricky business. Even for an emperor." I squeezed, willing Armaan to listen to me. "Tarek's death wasn't a punishment."

Armaan smiled. It was such a sad smile, I thought, so heavy. His gold-flecked eyes gazed at me with a warmth I couldn't quite identify. They drew me in, swallowing me whole.

His eyes trailed down my face, across my lips and down my neck, lingering on my scar. I went still as he raised his hand. The tips of his fingers skimmed across the scar and down the length of my collarbone, lingering at the notch at the base of my throat.

I swallowed hard. "Were they ever punished?"

His hand fell away. "No," he murmured. "The Shazir may be a minority voice, but they're a strong one. They say Shazir Province produces only two things: soldiers and grain."

"And hate."

Armaan nodded tiredly. "Yet most of the Khazan Guard are Shaziri. Including Captain Nazir, though he doesn't share Khaljaq's zealotry," he said, his gratitude for the fact plain. "But with the drought, Shazir Province now feeds almost half the empire. They're too powerful to punish. The Shazir are your most vociferous allies." He shook his head. "It's terrible, the compromises we have to make."

His expression hardened; there was a darkness in his eyes. "I hate them." Armaan whispered the words as if the admission cost him. "I hate them, and someday I will make them pay for what they did to you. But . . . Roven casts a long shadow."

I nodded. A long shadow indeed. Was it long enough? Was his fear of Radovan enough to convince him to send an army?

Now, Askia. The memory of my grandfather's voice rang in my mind and on its heels was Ozura's: *Armaan is a man of passion.* I could use it. Make it personal. Make him see.

"It wasn't just their deaths that destroyed me. My family traveled the world, unanchored, unmoored, tied only to each other. My home wasn't a place, it was them—my mother and father. So when the Shazir murdered them, I wasn't just orphaned, I was made homeless too.

"I returned to Seravesh expecting to die. I longed for it. But going there wasn't the end of me. It was the beginning. It brought me to life—not as the girl I was, for she is well and truly gone, but as someone new.

"Seravesh isn't my duty. It's my home. And I will die before I let it fall." My skin prickled, but not from cold. I pushed it away, the fear, and stepped closer. "I can fight him, Armaan. With your help, I can fight Radovan and win. But I need your army."

"I know."

My heart stuttered. "So?"

Armaan's expression never changed. He still wore that small smile like a shield, but something in his eyes seemed gentle. "Your birthday is tomorrow. Will you dine with me?"

I felt my future, my people were balanced on the tip of a blade. But if I pushed too hard, my people would fall. Armaan knew it. In the great game of power, I only had one more card to play. Me.

"I will."

29

The Rose Hall was filled with courtiers—living and dead—all gathered together for some sort of early luncheon, though the exact purpose of the meeting was yet to be revealed. The moment they spotted me, standing on the edge of the hall in full Khazan Guard regalia, all other business flew out the door.

Captain Nazir had sent the uniform and the duty roster to my rooms before dawn this morning. I knew it was a joke the moment I'd read it, but what the hell. I'd missed Khazan Guard training for the past few days, missed the camaraderie of my fellow soldiers. So I'd put on the uniform and reported for duty to the quiet hilarity of the soldiers standing beside me. Though with Illya guarding my back, my presence wasn't totally up to regulation—as the lieutenant in charge was quick to inform me.

"You've got incoming, my lady," the ghost-sergeant said from somewhere off to my right.

I didn't relax my stance, glued my eyes to the far wall, and waited. The warning could only refer to Ishaq, Enver, or Dobor, and I'd be damned if I let myself look nervous at their approach.

"Well, look at this," Ishaq said, sliding into view, not alone but with Enver by his side. "A woman on guard duty."

"Is this supposed to make us feel safe?" Enver asked with a malicious laugh. "What could she defend us from, I wonder? Our silks getting stained?"

I flicked my gaze lazily over Enver's teal-and-gold robes, cocking an eyebrow. "I'm sure you fret over your clothes enough, Enver. You can hardly expect the rest of us to do the same. But if you're worried about the standards of the guard, I'm sure General Ochan would let you take the test for entry."

"Join the guard?" Enver sputtered, oblivious to the warning hand Ishaq laid on his arm. "Like I would ever sully myself or my title by wading through the dirt with peasants."

The living guards beside me were too well-trained to react, but I felt their anger in the stiffening of their spines, in the way the ghost-sergeant hissed between his teeth and clenched the hilt of his sword. Oh, how I'd have loved to draw my own blade and challenge this fool right here. But I'd learned a thing or two, in this court of vipers.

"Enough, Enver. You may insult me all you like, but you will not insult the honor of these men—men who risk their lives every day protecting not only this kingdom and its people but even sheltered little princes like you."

Enver's face went purple. "You can't speak to me this way."

"And yet, she just did." The quiet laughter in Ozura's voice made Enver whirl like he was under attack, but the queen just watched him, arms crossed, face amused. "Run along, Enver. Let Lord Vizier Ishaq explain why you lost today."

I watched Enver storm out of the hall with Ishaq at his heels, quietly amazed that he went without further protest. But then the dry boredom in Ozura's voice was a thing of beauty. There was no way Enver could respond to it without looking like a petulant child. And he didn't need more help with that today.

Ozura turned to me, eyebrows high. "Interesting choice in activities for your birthday, Princess Askia."

I shrugged. "I am a member of the guard, and Captain Nazir said he needed help."

"I'm sure he did. I can only hope you're as fastidious in honoring your other commitments." She gave me a pointed look, one that asked how I had time to play soldier when I hadn't gone to the guild last night for training.

But my absence wasn't a matter of spare time. After everything that happened yesterday, I'd just . . . I'd needed to be alone. "I am, Queen Ozura," I replied, meeting her gaze, secure in the knowledge that she'd feel the truth in my words. For I'd spent the whole morning pulling up a steady stream of magic. It made the living nobles, in all their finery, look washed out to my eyes.

"Good. Now if Lieutenant Umari can manage without you, Lady Nariko requires your assistance. And it is nearly time for you to begin dressing for the emperor's dinner."

She shot a questioning look to the soldier in question. Umari bobbed a quick bow before flashing me a grin. I nodded to him and Ozura before joining Nariko in the hall. Her jaw dropped as she took in my appearance

"I cannot believe Captain Nazir had you report for duty on today of all days."

"I really don't mind," I said at her outrage. Any day I got to take Enver down a peg was a good one in my book. And anyway, soldiers were bigger gossips than court ladies—I was sure the whole guard would know about the incident before dinner. "Half of being friends with soldiers is laughing at the shit they pull," I said fondly.

"Only half?" Illya asked.

We shared a laugh, one sparkling moment of ease before he cleared his throat, face falling, and stepped back.

I forced my gaze back to Nariko. "Ozura said you needed help?"

"Yes," Nariko said, producing a scroll from her gown's pocket and handing it to me.

"What is all this?" I asked, my eyes skating across the massive list.

"Birthday presents," Nariko replied. "The court knows the emperor is celebrating your birthday tonight, and as he does, so do we all. Happy birthday, by the way. Are you hungry? I thought we could start writing thank-yous after lunch."

I groaned at the idea, beseeching Lady Night for mercy when the most girlish thought I'd ever had nearly knocked me over. "What am I going to wear tonight?"

"Don't worry," Nariko said, with a terribly knowing twinkle in her eye. "Soma is coming this afternoon to help you prepare."

"Good." My relief practically carried me back to my rooms. I'd have been lost without Soma's ministrations. Sure, my mother had taught me to manage my hair, but beauty wasn't a priority in Seravesh the way it was here. Confronted with the legion of serums and cremes and powders that lay on my vanity, I was helpless. Besides, there was something heavenly about being pampered. I shook my head, glad my grandfather couldn't hear the thought. He'd have smashed every mirror in our castle and cut off all my hair if he'd been alive to see how soft I was getting.

I looked over the list of presents as Nariko and I waited for lunch to arrive. The account was staggering. The number of loose-cut gems alone was worth more than it cost to run my castle for a year. There were weapons, too—enough to outfit my entire personal guard, command staff, and anyone else who wanted a shiny new toy.

"This is ridiculous," I said, an idea taking shape in my mind.

Nariko shrugged. "This is Vishir."

"You've been spending too much time with me." I laughed. "May I have your quill?"

She pushed it over to me, watching with a small frown as I scoured the list, adding tick marks every once in a while. "Dare I ask what you're doing?"

"Well . . . that depends."

"On?"

"On if you're going to be scandalized."

Nariko's eyebrows rose. "Why should I be scandalized?"

I cringed. "Because I'm only keeping the items I'm marking. Everything else needs to be sold." Nariko probably thought I was being ungrateful, or tacky, or both. "It's not that I don't appreciate it, but to be completely frank, I have no money. Whatever funds I had were confiscated by my cousin when he seized the throne. The Black Wolves joined my side out of loyalty, but they still need to be paid."

"Hmm."

"Hmm?"

"Well," Nariko said, looking over the scroll with a speculative gaze. "I suppose that is prudent."

"You do?"

"Of course," Nariko said, clearly surprised by my surprise. "Let me pass along a copy of this list to Cyrus."

My brow furrowed. "Cyrus? From the Shadow Guild?"

Nariko nodded. "He also holds a prominent position in the Merchants' Guild. He'll know how to sell those items you wish to have liquidated with the proper discretion. Though if I may offer a spot of advice about what you should keep?"

"Please."

"The emperor will of course give you something tonight, and it should go without saying you ought to keep whatever it is. I think you should also keep anything from the individuals you think you might need. Wearing or displaying those items will send a message to the rest of the court. You should also keep the gifts from the other viziers, the queens, and the princes."

"Prince," I corrected, my voice wooden.

Nariko frowned. "What?"

"Only Enver sent a gift. That ugly lapis pendant. Nothing from Iskander."

Nariko took a deep breath. "Nothing from Iskander *yet*. Perhaps he wishes to give you your present in person."

"Doubt it. I don't think our friendship can survive what happened yesterday." Despite everything, I wanted Iskander to be my friend. Especially if I was going to stay in Vishir.

"Don't worry about Iskander," she said coolly. "His anger is baseless. He'll get over it."

I nodded. "Maybe I shouldn't have lied about being a witch."

"Do you think his knowing would have changed his actions?" Nariko shook her head, her hands curling into small claws. "His own mother is a witch, a fact she has never hidden from him. Yet he still allied himself with the Shazir. He should be ashamed of himself. I know I am."

My eyebrows rose. The girl who blushed every time Iskander looked her way was gone. A new woman had taken her place. A strong one. "Look at you, ready to scold a prince."

Nariko flushed. "I suppose I am rather hungry."

I laughed. "Then let's feed you before I find out what you really think of me."

Nariko and I ate a quick lunch and then spread out on the table to tackle the mountain of cards. After a few hours of utterly insincere sincerity, I was unspeakably relieved when Soma strode into my rooms, arms laden with bags.

"Hello, Your Highness," Soma said with a small smile. "Best wishes on your birthday."

I threw down my quill. "Oh, Lady Night bless you. I don't think I can write another note."

"You'll have time to finish them tomorrow," Ozura said, sweeping through the parlor with a smile. "Come. Come."

I followed the women into the dressing room, forcing back a wave of nervousness. I took my place on the pedestal, shifting my weight from one foot to the other. In the mirror I saw Illya appear in the doorway with a sack that I assumed held my dress.

"I'll take that, thank you," Soma said.

Illya handed off the dress with a nod. He didn't so much as look at me. *Illya is your guard*, I thought, yanking my gaze away. *Nothing more.*

Nariko patted my arm. "Don't look so grim."

"She's just nervous," Ozura said, rounding the pedestal to look up at me. "But you don't need to be, dear."

I didn't recognize the expression on Ozura's face, or the warmth in her words. Kindness wasn't something I had ever associated with her. It certainly wasn't something I thought I could trust, especially tonight.

Ozura slid her hands into mine, squeezed gently. "It's only dinner. You'll eat, you'll talk, and he'll give you a birthday gift. It's nothing to worry about."

I blinked. Something in the way Ozura spoke made it sound as if— But no. The Vishiri would never allow such a breach of propriety. Except . . . I licked my lips. "You'll be there, too, of course. With the other guests?"

"Certainly not." Ozura tilted her head to one side. An amused smiled crossed her face. "It's a private dinner, my dear. Only you and Armaan will be present."

"How is that allowed? When Iskander—"

"That isn't the same," said Ozura tartly. "Armaan is an emperor. The rules are different where he is concerned . . . and you are of a certain age."

My mind went blank, and suddenly the floor felt very far away. Ozura laughed. She shook my hands, causing my whole body to sway back and forth in a boneless way.

"You're worrying again," Ozura said with a knowing smile. "There's no need for this. Why, I'd bet you dine alone with men all the time. How often do you enjoy a quiet meal with Captain Illya?"

"Illya is—" I started only to scramble at the idea of defining what exactly Illya was. "It's not the same thing."

"Of course it is."

Ozura dropped my hands and stepped back. Her catlike eyes narrowed, her lips pursed. This was the Ozura I was familiar with. For some reason, seeing her disappointed and slightly annoyed was exactly the balm I needed.

"Askia, stop panicking. It's only dinner."

It wasn't, though, and she knew it. But I swallowed my retort, knowing it would do me no good, and let the other women take over. While they primped and painted me, undressed and redressed me, tried on and cast off this necklace or that bracelet, I sank into myself. I spiraled down, reaching for my power. Not because I wanted to speak with Vitaly or watch Tarek play, though both ghosts did appear. It was because I needed the cold, the bracing ice at the center of my power. I let it wash over me, taking refuge in my magic, letting it anchor me, reminding me I was not, in the end, powerless.

"Now how about that?" Soma said, stepping back to admire her work. "What do you think, my lady?"

I took a deep breath before confronting the figure in the mirror. The dress was magnificent, a sleeveless gown of solid gold from the tip of the straps to the sweep of the hem. The front dipped almost to my navel, and when I turned, I saw the back also fell low, exposing skin and scar alike.

The gold silk was embellished with small plates of fragile gold leaf that dripped down my shoulders, over my breasts and hips in molten rivulets of armorlike scales. A tiny gold chain hung at my waist, so delicate it was hard to see. I hoped with some trepidation that it wasn't the only thing keeping the gown together.

"This is . . . This is a masterpiece, Soma. You've outdone yourself."

"I certainly have. Believe me, it was murder to attach all those golden flakes. Took weeks."

I nodded almost absently, noting the twinkle of golden pins in my hair. Even my skin was dusted in glimmering powder, hiding the worst of my scars. Then Soma's words sank beneath the cosmetic veneer. *Weeks*. Soma had been working on this dress for weeks—long before Armaan began showing any interest in me.

Soma's casual comment betrayed a truth I doubted Ozura would ever admit. Despite our rocky beginning, Ozura had had plans for me from the moment I arrived in Bet Naqar. Somehow, those plans included me marrying Armaan. I spotted Ozura standing beside the vanity watching me with a wistful expression. What kind of game was she playing?

"It's time," Ozura said stepping forward. "Are you ready?"

No. "Yes." *No.*

"Let's go."

Ozura, Soma, and Nariko accompanied me to the door of my apartments, but they didn't take me to Armaan. That dubious honor belonged to Illya, Misha, and Ivin. Their footsteps echoed heavily on the stone floor, rapping out a steady beat. It was the thrum of marching orders, of war.

I followed Illya through the gilt halls, but the palace passed me in a blur. I was keenly aware of the slither of silk against my skin, of the slight shimmer of gold on my body. Anticipation shivered through me. This was my chance.

My people were dying, and they would continue to die until someone stood up to Radovan. Armaan could be that man, but he had no skin in the game, no reason to fight. If he married me, he would. Through me, Vishir would have a foothold in the northern continent. Seravesh wouldn't be free, not truly; it would become a vassal state, beholden to Vishir, but Roven would be gone. Wasn't that enough? Duty and responsibility bore down on my shoulders. Invisible and inescapable.

Illya's gaze brushed across my skin. He frowned and stopped. He walked to the nearest door and gave the wood a solid rap. No reply.

"Come." Illya placed a hand at the small of my back and guided me through the door, shutting it behind us.

I caught only a glimpse of the cramped office before Illya rounded on me, eyes blazing.

"You're afraid, my lady. You must not be."

I choked out a bitter laugh. "I'm not afraid, I'm just . . ." Just what? What words were there for my situation? If I wanted to help my people, I had no choice but to—

"My lady," he began, only to sigh as if wounded. "Askia. Look at me."

I met Illya's colorless gaze. There was a fire in those eyes, a depth of emotion that made me ache.

"I know I told you to accept the offer if it comes," he said, grinding out the words through clenched teeth. "And when Arkady's reply arrives, I'm sure it will say the same, but . . ."

"But?" I asked, seizing the word.

He exhaled a hard breath, looking at the floor. When he looked back up, he took a step closer, bending toward me until our faces were only inches apart.

"When you step through the emperor's doors, never forget you are the true queen of Seravesh. He cannot force you to do anything, Askia, and if he tries, I am only a shout away. Summon me, and I will come. I will burn this city to the ground for you and return to Seravesh empty-handed if you command it. You are not alone."

Illya's gaze bore into me, leaving no room for uncertainty. Despite everything that lay between us, our stations and duties pulling us apart, Illya was still mine through and through. If I needed him, Illya would come.

"This choice you face, Askia . . . it's not one you need to

make tonight," he said, a plea swimming in his eyes—a plea I knew he'd never speak. No matter how much I wanted him to. No matter how much I wanted him to close the distance and . . .

I closed my eyes, crushing the fantasy. I put away Askia the woman, summoned Askia the queen. And in that blessed darkness, the queen in me knew Illya was wrong.

Perhaps it was better that Armaan and I would be alone. Choices would be made tonight, at this dinner that wasn't simply a dinner. There was a seed of something between us—not the same as what lay between Illya and I, or Ozura and Armaan. But something. And whether it withered or grew would decide the fate of Seravesh. For the queen in me, it was enough, even if my heart didn't bear looking at.

I clung to her—to the idea of the queen I needed to become: the woman who could live her life in moves and countermoves. Victories and sacrifices. I opened my eyes. "I'm ready."

Illya nodded and ushered me back into the hallway. Neither Misha nor Ivin commented on the detour, which was a blessing as the imperial apartments were just around the next bend, guarded by a dozen Khazan guardsmen standing motionless at equal intervals down the length of the corridor. Captain Nazir was among them. He bowed to me and smiled.

"Good evening, my lady," he said. "The emperor awaits within. If Captain Illya and your men would remain here, you may go through."

Misha and Ivin peeled away to stand with the door guards. Illya tarried. I met his steady gaze. A moment passed. Illya's eyes didn't waver. There was no uncertainty in them, only confidence.

I smiled, feeling some of his certainty slide into me. I nodded to him, and then Captain Nazir.

The doors slid open.

30

I stepped into a square sitting room and squinted; the setting sun blazed in through the glass doors studding the walls. The room was large and, in typical Vishiri fashion, had several tables scattered artfully around the space. What it did not have, I noticed, was a table set for dining.

A white-robed servant stepped away from the wall and bowed, motioning for me to follow him out the garden doors. On one end of a long veranda was a wide staircase that led not down into the garden, but up to the roof.

The servant stopped at the foot of the stairs and dipped another bow, motioning for me to continue alone. My eyes narrowed, feeling like I'd ceded the high ground to a clever opponent. *Not the right mind-set*, I thought, forcing my shoulders down. Armaan wasn't some battlefield enemy, he was the man who could save my people. If I gave him the chance. If we gave each other the chance, I thought, taking the first step. Then the next.

The stairs leveled off onto a gleaming floor of white granite covered in a sea of tiny white candles. A path snaked to the center of the roof, where a square-columned palisade stood. White gossamer curtains hung between the columns, glowing softly in the fading sunlight.

The emperor sat in one corner of a three-sided couch. He

stood when I approached, his golden eyes growing wide with unguarded attention that made me smile.

He slid between the edge of the couch and a food-laden table and crossed to me in a few quick steps. "Askia," he said, taking one of my hands. "You put the setting sun to shame." He brought my hand to his lips and kissed it.

"Thank you, my lord."

"Please, you must call me Armaan," he replied. "Sit with me?"

I sank on the couch and found the garden sprawled out below me. My eyes raced across the open space where the image of the Vishiri lion was writ large. It stood in profile on its hind legs, its front paws up for a fight. Its mane was made from flowering bushes, its eye an almond-shaped pool of water. Tarek appeared in one of the pools, jumping up and down like he was trying to see how big of a splash he could make.

"What do you think of my garden?"

I shook my head. What could I say? "It's beautiful," I replied, tearing my eyes away to look at Armaan. "Even by Vishiri standards, it's beautiful."

His answering smile was easy, and something in it made me think he was genuinely pleased by the compliment. He leaned forward and began serving food on two gold plates. "I've always loved it up here," he said. "It's one of the few places I can come when I wish to be alone."

I watched, silently humbled, as the man who ruled half the world served me dinner with his own hands. I thought he would have a whole phalanx of servants ready to carry out such a menial task. Though why I held such an assumption, I couldn't say.

"I'm sure as a ruler, you understand the need for occasional solitude."

"I do." His bright gaze darted to me, his curiosity so open, so sincere I made myself continue. "I haven't had the luxury of solitude in some time, but when I have the chance, I relish it."

Armaan nodded solemnly and handed me a plate before leaning back into the corner of the couch. "Did you have a place like this in Seravesh?"

"Like this? No," I replied, more firmly than I'd intended to. I set my plate aside and leaned back, trying to mimic his nonchalance. "I always found the castle . . . restricting. I had too many distant relations with too many expectations," I explained, seeing the quizzical bend to his eyebrows. "When I became heir to the Frozen Crown, I struggled to live up to those expectations. I still do, I suppose. When I needed it, though, I'd go for a long ride. My close guard accompanied me, of course, so it wasn't quite solitude. But on the back of a horse with the wind in my face, it was close."

"You remind me very much of myself at twenty-two."

His smile was so wistful, it was impossible for me to feel like I was being condescended to. "Oh? Was it a good year for you?"

Armaan chuckled. "Let's see." He rubbed his hands together, his gaze lost to the past. "Enver and Iskander would have been four that year. That was the summer they wandered out of the palace, and the entire Khazan Guard was called out to search for them."

My eyebrows rose. "How did they manage that?"

"To this day I have no idea," he said, laughing. "Enver liked to explore during the summers he spent here in Bet Naqar. And Iskander liked to follow him." Armaan shook his head, a nostalgic smile playing on his lips. "Other than that?" He shrugged. "I'd been emperor for six years by that point. I had heirs. My rule had finally begun to feel . . . secure. Overall, I'd say it was a very good year."

Twenty-two and already ruling for six years. I shook my head, studying his face. It was still smooth, his caramel skin unlined but for the slight crinkles around his eyes. The memory of his body, slick with sweat from our bout in the ring, rose to mind. Heat crept low into my stomach.

He tilted his head to the side, eyes searching my face. "What are you thinking?"

"I'm thinking you were very far ahead of where I am now," I lied, pushing the memory away.

Armaan shook his head. "You've faced more adversity in twenty-two years than I have in twice that time. Despite your cousin's ambition and Radovan's design at domination, you still fight. More than that, you have men loyal to you, a country behind you. This is not something to discount. And you've done all of this without once wearing the Frozen Crown.

"Which reminds me," he said, "I have a present for you."

"You shouldn't have."

He ignored my protest, reaching across the dishes to retrieve a slim black box. He presented it to me, his expression unguarded and filled with light.

I took it gingerly, carefully ignoring the brush of his fingers against mine. I set the box on my lap. The lid creaked open. My breath caught in my throat.

On a bed of dark blue silk lay a circlet. It was wrought from intertwining silver and gold strands with tiny silver and gold flowers blooming off the bands. Small diamonds winked at me from the center of the petals.

"It originally belonged to my grandmother," Armaan murmured, "but when you told me about the flower crown Lord Trantini gave you, I knew it was meant for you."

He watched me carefully. There was something apprehensive in his expression, vulnerable almost. I smiled. "It's beautiful, Armaan. Thank you."

Armaan breathed a smile. "May I?"

I nodded, not trusting myself with words. He shifted closer. The circlet drooped like molten metal in his hands. I held myself very still as he placed it on my head.

A lock of hair sprang loose from the chignon at the base

of my neck. It bounced into my face, swaying in the breeze of our shared breath. His fingertips glided up my cheekbone, then tucked the hair behind my ear. I didn't breathe, didn't move. His eyes glittered. His lips looked soft.

I flinched as an icy hand clamped down on my forearm, deadening my skin. Tarek stared up at me, his face impatient with childlike curiosity. He looked so solid in the half-light, like the setting sun had lent him form.

Rising to his tiptoes, Tarek reached for the circlet. I smiled and leaned closer. Lady Night only knew what would happen if Tarek snatched the thing off my head, but I suspected he only wanted a look. He inspected the circlet, his cold fingers sending a chill down my spine.

He went still for a moment and then pulled my hair. I hissed as the lock of hair sprang free once again. Tarek poked out his tongue and, with a wicked smile, ran down the stairs.

I shook my head and then saw Armaan. My smile froze. The color had drained from his skin. His mouth hung open. His eyes were wide. "That was Tarek, wasn't it?"

I nodded, gutted by the sorrow on Armaan's face. "How did you know?"

Armaan's answering laugh was low and quaked with loss. "He could never resist a present, my Tarek. He always thought they were for him." Armaan's eyes misted with unshed tears. He looked away, bracing his elbows atop his knees.

"Becoming a parent changes everything about you, and it changes you instantly. When you hold that tiny life in your hands for the first time, there is this . . . this all-consuming rush of love, and no small amount of terror you won't be able to live up to the task. But fear is the cost of living."

He looked at his hands as if he could still see Tarek there. "It's worth it. It's worth the moments of wonder, the indescribable joy of seeing that first smile, the pride of seeing those first steps. The potential of childhood is endless." His eyes were bright, willing me to understand. "I love my sons without reservation, but they're grown now. They're already men. Already formed and shaped and limited by the lives they've lived. But Tarek . . ."

His words trailed off like he couldn't express the emotion welling up in his voice. "Tarek will always be unfinished. Unlimited. Tarek will always be my boy. My boy who time cannot touch."

My eyes watered. I understood loss. I understood the ways it ravaged, the ways it maimed, but this . . . The grief Armaan felt wasn't something that could ever heal. No amount of time would ever salve the wound of losing Tarek. I wished there was something I could do—

But there was.

Armaan knew I was a death witch. That dark writhing truth I'd kept hidden from the world wasn't a secret to Armaan. It should have scared me, that risk of exposure, but it didn't. For the first time in a long time, I felt seen.

"He's not unhappy. Tarek. He's not sad." Armaan's eyes flew to mine. "He likes to play, likes to run." My lips quirked as I remembered him laughing at me in the menagerie. "He's a bit of a troublemaker to be honest."

Armaan breathed a husky laugh. "He always was." His smile slowly faded, leaving something indescribable in its stead. "Askia, why do you think you can see him? Hundreds of people must have died in this palace over the years, thousands even. Why Tarek?"

I bit the inside of my cheek. "That might be a question for a priest, but . . . There are layers to the world, layers that separate this plane from the next. Some people don't pass cleanly through. They linger in the Marchlands. Waiting."

I paused, gathering strength to say what I needed to say next. "Tarek is waiting, I think. For you. For both of you."

Armaan closed his eyes, fielding my words like a blow, but

I knew I had to continue. "As to why I can see Tarek specifically, and see him so clearly, well . . . I think it's because we're connected in a way."

"Because of your father?" Armaan whispered, his eyes still closed.

I flinched at the guilt in his voice, at the implied blame he clearly felt for not saving my parents. "My father helped bring Tarek into the world, yes, but that wasn't my only connection to him."

Armaan's eyes shot open. "What do you mean?"

"After I returned to Bet Naqar, I struggled," I said, choosing my words with agonizing care. "I couldn't make myself get out of bed most days, let alone speak. I don't remember a lot of that time, but I remember Tarek. He used to come and visit me."

"He did?"

I nodded. "He wanted to play, but I couldn't make myself get up. I didn't even open my eyes most the time, but he still came, almost every day. He would slide into my bed and tell me stories."

"What stories?"

"All sorts of things. Fairy tales sometimes, or he'd tell me about his dreams. Mostly, he told me about you and about Ozura and his siblings." My eyes burned with the threat of tears but I forced myself to speak past them. "I think I see Tarek because he reached me when no one else could. He told me about his world and his life.

"He made me want to live, Armaan. Live until I was *alive*."

I didn't fight the tears that slid down my cheeks. I didn't wipe them away either. Armaan's eyes were bright. He clasped my hand. Squeezed. I sniffed and looked away, not sure where to go from there.

Tarek was in the garden. He was doing log rolls across the

lawn, only to flop himself to a stop beside a trellis of overgrown wisteria. I wanted to laugh, to cry. Weep for the boy whose loss was so keenly felt.

Armaan's hand was warm against my skin. I looked at him, truly seeing how deeply Tarek's death affected him. The wound was so profound that, despite all his wives and almost a decade to grieve, Armaan had not had any children since Tarek.

"I could show him to you if you'd like." The words slid out of my mouth before I had the chance to consider them. "I mean, I've been training with the guild. I haven't been successful yet, but I could try. For you."

Armaan's body went still. He didn't breathe, didn't blink. He looked at me, but it felt somehow that he was looking through me as well.

"Yes." Armaan's voice was almost too low to hear, like it was whispered from the deepest part of his heart.

I rose, and still holding his hand, walked to the edge of the palisade. My arm brushed the smooth stone skin of the corner column right above where Tarek played. I pointed to where he was lying, making angels in the grass with his arms and legs. "He's right there, under that weeping wisteria. Just give me a few minutes of quiet, and keep looking there."

Armaan nodded. I turned to the ghost. Sank. My delving was a deep dive, a free fall down to the heart of my power. The magic within me leapt in response to my desire. It was easy, so easy. This was how calling magic was meant to be. My wish to help Armaan, to give him some sense of closure, had unshackled something within me.

The cold came, as it inevitably did, biting my fingers and toes. I embraced it as it crawled into my hands and feet and slowly up my arms and legs. It was the price incurred for meddling with death. A price I was willing to pay for Armaan.

I forced my mind to work past the cold and flung my powers out to the Marchlands. Pulled. Tarek sat up. His eyes went straight to me, as if he sensed the movement.

I called more power. More. Ice colder than any winter snow bit my limbs with a thousand tiny teeth. I let it wash over me, submitted to the pain. I felt the veil thin, saw Tarek's insubstantial form growing sharper.

"Come." The command came from my mind in a voice that wasn't entirely my own. It was lined with power and edged in iron, an order that not even the boundary of life and death could bar.

Armaan gasped. His legs buckled, and his knees hit the ground. Tarek's gaze moved silently from me to Armaan. His eyes rounded. A grin spread over his face. He jumped to his feet, bouncing on his toes, waved wildly.

Tremors shuddered through my body while I struggled to keep the connection open. My muscles twisted with cramps before going dead altogether. I didn't fight it, but even my submission was an act of will. The cold worked into my core and into my chest. My lungs burned with frozen air. My chest ached with the ice that crept into my heart.

I kept my eyes on Tarek. I made myself see the pure joy on his face. I made myself hear the chime of his childlike laugh. My heart writhed against my rib cage. One thud. Another.

My vision went dark.

CONSCIOUSNESS CAME WITH THE SCENT OF CITRUS AND THE SILKEN feel of fur against my skin. I burrowed into the fur, felt the muscles of strong arms tighten around me. I heard the faint thrum of a heartbeat next to my ear and felt the prickle of a man's whiskered cheek against my forehead.

I opened my eyes. The sky above the palisade was black and peppered with stars. I could tell by the cast of the shadows in the garden below that the moon was high overhead. Several hours had clearly passed.

Armaan drew back, and the edge of the fur blanket he'd wrapped around me slipped down my shoulder. He held me to his chest, reclining against a mountain of pillows in one corner of the couch.

"How do you feel?"

I took a moment to assess my condition. There was a soreness in my left hip I thought might have been caused during my faint, but otherwise, I was fine. "I'm all right. A little sore. Did I fall?"

"You passed out." Armaan frowned down at me, eyebrows drawing together. He pulled the blanket back to where my hands rested on my stomach. He squeezed my hand gently in his fist. "Hmm. You're not as cold as you were." Still frowning, he set my hand down and shifted so his right elbow was braced on the top of the pillow pile. His gaze was serious. "You scared me, Askia."

"Well, I'm sorry for that." I shrugged, unsure of what else to say. "Magic comes with a price, and the price I pay is the leeching cold."

"Doesn't it strike you as reckless? Is your health worth the risk?"

I felt anger rise off his skin in waves. My brow furrowed. I was only trying to help him. Why was he angry? Armaan looked past me to the garden spread out below. A muscle in his jaw twitched. He wasn't upset.

He was worried.

I tried to wet my lips, but my mouth was suddenly very dry. I pulled my left hand from the blanket and pressed it to his chest. His eyes fell to me, his expression softening.

"Did you see him?"

Wordless, he nodded. Beneath my palm, I felt his heart beat faster.

"Then it was worth it."

He opened his mouth, but no words came out. Time shuddered to a standstill as his eyes caressed my face. The small hairs on my body came to attention; I realized how close we were. The length of his body pressed against mine. A warm ache bloomed in my core.

"Oh, Askia," he whispered. "You reckless miracle."

His left hand slid behind my head and pulled me toward him. Our lips met softly at first, then harder, deeper. Fire engulfed my body, igniting me. His hands traveled over me, pulled me closer, close enough I felt the length of him against my hips. I shuddered as pleasure rushed up my spine. Something inside me loosened. I felt unleashed. Free.

I moaned and ground my pelvis against his. My skin strained against the confines of my dress. More. I wanted more of him. All of him.

"Askia," he gasped, pulling his mouth free. "Askia, wait."

I stilled, my mind foggy with desire. "What is it?"

"Wait," he said again, nuzzling my nose with his. "You have to go."

I froze. Lady Night, what was I doing?

"No, no," he said quickly, dipping down to give me a quick kiss. "Not that, my love." He kissed me again. "Never that." His fingers brushed across my bruised lips, trailing down my neck to my breast, stroking the tip of one hard nipple as if to emphasize his point. "If you don't go now, I'll keep you here all night." He smiled a wicked smile, kissing my lips. "And all tomorrow," he said, his voice a whisper as his lips traveled to my neck, "and all the next day too." His hand dipped down, away from my breast. He slid it beneath the v of my dress to the base of my waiting sex. "I'll keep you here until you scream my name and forget about the world outside." His hand dipped lower, delving into the wetness between my legs. A low growl escaped his lips as he took my nipple between his teeth.

My body shuddered. Desire made mush of my thoughts. A slight moan whined out of me the moment his hand slid free. My body was taut, caught in the middle of pleasure and pain.

And he wanted me to *leave*?

"Oh, Askia." His voice was husky in my ear. He kissed my lips once more and rose, pulling me up with him. His eyelids were low, his gaze ravenous. I smiled a wicked smiled of my own. He dipped his head and kissed me again, deep enough to make my legs quake.

He pulled back. "Go." He smiled against my lips, a feral, animal thing. "Go now, before I change my mind."

I laughed, letting him give me a little push toward the stairs. I took a deep breath before beginning my descent. Fresh air cleared my thoughts. I looked over my shoulder at him, found his gaze hard upon me. I smiled.

A servant was waiting when I entered the sitting room. This time it was a woman in her middle years with a blank expression and a gaze that didn't meet my eyes. She escorted me to the doors but didn't open them.

She turned to me instead. "If I may, my lady?"

My brow furrowed, but I nodded all the same. The servant worked quickly, straightening my circlet and fixing the drape of my dress before brushing my skin with a fresh layer of golden dust. It was a quick but thorough adjustment, the kind that spoke of practice.

My cheeks flamed as reality hit me. I wasn't the first woman to receive such treatment. I wasn't the first. And with Armaan, I wouldn't be the last.

I drifted into the hall, picking up Misha and Ivin as I headed to my rooms. We were two corridors away by the time I realized Illya wasn't there.

He hadn't waited.

31

Illya's absence washed over me, leaving me numb and reeling. He promised to be there. Promised he'd stand by me. So where was he? Was he called away? I half turned to Misha but stopped myself before I could ask.

What if Illya hadn't been called away? What if he'd stood outside waiting, only to have hours pass? What did he imagine happening between me and Armaan? My hands shook. I clenched them closed.

Probably exactly what did happen.

The thought sent a snarl echoing through my head. It wasn't fair. Illya knew there couldn't be a future for us, knew I needed to accept a proposal when it came. Was it so awful that I was attracted to Armaan? So terrible that we'd . . . I was unable to complete the thought.

I hadn't gone to dinner planning to seduce Armaan. I hadn't gone intending to use my body as collateral, to sell myself for my country, but that was exactly how it looked. That was exactly what Illya, what Ozura and Iskander and the whole of Lady Night–damned Vishir, would think come morning.

And for what? Armaan never promised me his army. Sure, Ozura had dangled the prospect of a marriage before me, but no offer had been made. Even if there was, could I be happy in a shared marriage?

And would it get me what I needed?

I shook my head at the floor. I was a fool. A fool who'd gotten in too deep. I liked Armaan. Someday, given the chance, I thought I could grow to love him. But my affection for him and our obvious chemistry wasn't enough. It wasn't enough of a reason to marry him. I needed the army. I could sell my freedom for nothing less.

The sound of footsteps bounced off the walls from one of the adjoining corridors. I grimaced. The last thing I needed was a witness, someone to see me scuttling back to my rooms in the middle of the night.

The footsteps were getting closer. They sounded like they were coming from outside my apartments. I made myself stand tall, let my face grow hard, let my eyelids fall, hooding my gaze. My skin stretched with the effort of holding the mask, but I clung to it, willing myself to look too haughty, too imposing to question.

I turned the corner to my apartments and stuttered to a stop. My eyes widened. The mask hit the floor. Iskander paced the width of the corridor with a pale face, and a cloth-wrapped cylinder clutched in one white-knuckled fist.

His eyes latched onto me. I watched him in silence, watched him watch me. His gaze traveled the length of me, but I couldn't say what he saw.

"I brought you a birthday present." His voice was raw, like a man who'd gone too long without water.

How long had he been waiting? Had he come so late to make sure I didn't spend the night with Armaan? And what if I had? What business of it was his?

He took a tentative step closer. "Can we talk?"

We sure as hell needed to, but I couldn't let him in my rooms. Not at this hour. Not after what had happened with Armaan. I turned to Misha. "Will you give us a moment?"

Misha nodded and gestured to the two men on door duty. The door guards slid silently into my apartments, while Misha and Ivin walked down the hall and disappeared around the corner. Out of sight but not out of earshot. It was a frail illusion of privacy, but it was the best I could do.

Iskander's eyes narrowed. His shoulders were high, muscles tense. He stalked forward, closing the distance between us. "What happened?" His words were pitched low so they didn't carry up the hall, but the anger in them was plain.

Anger—and for what? I hadn't done anything wrong. Yes, I knew Iskander liked me—or thought he did, but he'd never courted me. And even if he had, he had no right to assume, demand that I return his feelings. "We had dinner, Iskander. We talked. Eventually our conversation turned to his family, to you and Enver and Tarek."

Iskander blinked. Some of the anger in his face ebbed away, replaced by a surprise that made his shoulders drop. "Tarek? Why? He never speaks about Tarek."

I wasn't surprised, but it was strange Armaan had been so open with me about Tarek. I pushed the thought away. I couldn't think about Armaan with Iskander standing three feet away. "He blames himself for Tarek's death. He thinks it was his punishment for letting the Shazir kill my parents."

"That's ridiculous."

"That's humanity." I shrugged. "I told him he shouldn't feel guilty, and that despite everything, Tarek seems happy."

"You can see my brother?" he asked through bloodless lips.

"I can," I whispered. "I have ever since I arrived in Bet Naqar."

"And my father knew? The whole time?"

I frowned at the self-pitying way Iskander's voice rose. "No. Ozura told him."

Iskander's hand twitched like he was throwing that piece of information aside, but his face grew hard. "You expect me to believe you were talking about Tarek? This whole time?"

"Why do you think you deserve an answer?" I asked, bridling at the judgmental edge to his words.

"We're friends, I—"

My eyebrows flew high. "*Friends?* Fine. Then in the interest of our friendship, I'll tell you that I thought I could help Armaan find some closure. I offered to try and bring Tarek through to this plane."

Iskander blinked. "You brought Tarek back to life?"

"No." I gestured sharply, trying not to hear the strained hope in Iskander's voice. "Tarek is dead, and there's nothing I can do to change that. I thought if Armaan could see Tarek's spirit, though, see him happy, he could stop feeling so guilty."

Iskander's eyes moved rapidly back and forth like he was struggling to process this information. "Did you do it?"

"Barely." I sighed. "I was able to bring Tarek out of the Marchlands and give him form, but I passed out when I tried to hold him here. That's why I'm so late. I only just woke up." It wasn't the whole truth, but it was as much as I was willing to give. Again— not that this was any of his business, I thought, crossing my arms.

He didn't move for a long time, just stared at me. His eyes gleamed with a kind of manic desperation, a flailing, vain need to believe me. It was a need seeded in doubt. I saw it in the downturn of his lips, in the way he shook his head. Part of him knew it wasn't the whole truth.

The part of him that knew exactly who his father was.

"Here," he said, thrusting the present into my hands.

I looked at it, wishing there was more to inspect than cloth, because Iskander's anxious eyes were waiting for me. I forced myself to look at him. Forced a smile. "Thank you, Iskander. Should I open—"

"Promise me you won't marry him." The words seemed to bubble out of Iskander, out of a dark, terrified corner of his heart.

Oh, Iskander. My chest ached. "I can't—"

He seized me, cupping the sides of my face, and pushed me backward. My head smacked stone as he pressed me to the wall. Our lips collided in a mash of skin and teeth.

My hand fisted on his collar, nails raking against his skin as I pushed him away. "Stop, Iskander."

He pulled back, pain twisting his face. His breath came out in ragged gasps, almost sobs. "Please don't marry my father."

His words sounded like a whisper, a prayer. I closed my eyes against them. When I opened them again, he was gone.

My throat was too thick to call him back. But what would I have said? Nothing, because that was all I had to give. What lay between Iskander and I—it wasn't the melody of two souls singing the same song, or even the bright flash of two bodies burning as one. He wasn't what—who—I wanted. And I prayed that someday soon, he'd realize that I wasn't what he was searching for either.

I turned to my rooms and pushed my way through the door. I nodded to the guards waiting for me in the sitting room but didn't tarry to speak with them. Iskander's gift was still in my hands. Its weight was almost too much to bear.

I padded through the empty dining room and spotted a lamp burning in the study. I knew who it belonged to and pushed myself forward before my joints locked into place. I'd already faced Iskander's despair. What was Illya's disappointment compared to that? At least he wouldn't kiss me, though the thought made my already fragile heart twist.

Illya sat behind the desk with a quill in his hand. Its tip

scratched too loud in the oppressive quiet of the room. I paused on the threshold. The green whorls of his tattooed scalp shone dully in the lamplight. He didn't look up.

Fine. Ignore me like a child. I glowered at the wall, refusing to lower my head or slump my shoulders. I stalked across the room toward the parlor. Illya was my subject, I thought. I didn't have to answer to him.

"Your new crown is very pretty."

Illya's words hit me square in the back. He spoke them softly, but the accusation in them was sharper than any knife. I stiffened. My eyes stung. I couldn't turn around, couldn't knock him down for his impertinence. I couldn't let him see me cry.

"My lady," he called before I could flee. "I'm sorry I didn't wait for you, I . . ."

His voice faltered and in its absence his words grew large in my mind. *Didn't* wait. Not couldn't.

"I needed to send a request to the general. If there is anything you need to tell him—any news you wish to share—"

"What request?" My voice scraped out of my throat, almost too soft to hear. I made myself face him, wondering if I looked as hollow as I felt.

The sadness in his eyes was its own kind of answer. "Tomorrow, my lady. We can discuss it tomorrow."

I could only nod before drifting into the quiet sanctuary of the dressing room. Two lamps were lit for me on top of my vanity, but their light wasn't strong enough to illuminate the room. Darkness crowded in the corners, reaching out with crooked fingers to snuff out the light. A north wind wailed a sad song outside my windows.

I kicked off my shoes and slumped on the chair in front of the vanity, letting Iskander's present rest on my knees. My reflection stared back at me from the table's oval mirror. I grimaced at what I saw: a lost little girl with too-hard eyes and a crooked crown.

I ripped off the circlet and set it on the table with shaking hands. My eyes drew downward. Iskander's present was wrapped in burgundy velvet. It wasn't quite cylindrical; one of its edges curved outward at an odd angle. I bit my lip and pulled the fabric free.

A harsh laugh ripped out of my throat. A sword. Iskander had given me a sword. A Vishiri scimitar, in fact. I didn't draw it, didn't test its balance or its weight in my hands. Instead, I shoved it on the vanity and turned away.

I stood and peeled the golden dress off my skin. It was too beautiful to leave on the floor, so I crossed to the closet and hung it with care. Shrugging on a nightgown, I pulled the pins out of my hair, walking back to the vanity.

I couldn't help but look at the table while I worked a brush through my hair. A crown and a sword. I came to Vishir for swords, but I couldn't get them without the crown. I was an idiot for ever thinking I could.

The swords are what matter, I thought with a snarl. *Armaan can give you an army, the army that will save your kingdom. Nothing else matters. Marry him and be done with it.*

Giving up, I tossed the brush onto the vanity and carried a lamp into the bedroom. I didn't even flinch at the sight of Vitaly standing at the foot of my bed.

I smothered my magic before Vitaly could speak. All the men in my life seemed to want something from me tonight. Why not Vitaly too? I wouldn't even be that surprised if Enver came traipsing through the doors. Or Count Dobor.

I set the lamp on my nightstand beside Radovan's emerald, nestled in its open box. Nariko had probably brought it, I thought. The last time I'd seen it was when I pushed it into her hands in the Great Hall. I glowered at the gem and shoved the box into my nightstand before turning down the covers on the bed. I slid in, ignoring the insistent look on Vitaly's face, the way he mouthed my name. I didn't want to talk to him right now. I rolled over on my side and pressed the pillow around my ears, as if doing so would block out the voice I couldn't hear.

A cold hand clamped on my arm. *"What the hell is wrong with everyone tonight?"* I rolled over, anger pouring heat into my veins. *"What?"*

Vitaly's lips moved, but I couldn't hear what he said. He kept pointing toward the dressing room, a frantic look on his face.

I rolled my eyes. He wasn't going to quit until I spoke with him, but Lady Night help me if he had something to say about my love life. I closed my eyes, dipped into my power. The magic responded at once, flooding into my chest.

I opened my eyes as my skin prickled with goose bumps. *"What?"* I snapped.

"Get your sword."

32

A second of silence followed Vitaly's words.

Adrenaline poured into my veins. My heart ricocheted off my ribs as my gaze flew toward the garden. I heard the howl of gale-strength wind a second before it hit the garden doors. The wood moaned. The windows cracked. I launched out of bed and ran.

Shattered glass rained down on me, ripping though my feet and arms. The wind yanked through my hair. It screeched in my ears. My left foot slid out from under me. Splintered wood tore into my thigh. And then:

Silence.

I watched in mute terror as shards of glass hung suspended in midair. None of this was natural. This was magic. I screamed.

Something grabbed me. Someone. They pinned my arms to my sides. There was a hush and then a push. I felt my feet leave the floor. I screamed again, but no sound came out of my mouth. I couldn't see anything. Couldn't hear anything.

Pressure mounted behind my eyes. My ears rang. Something crushed down on me, suffocating and flattening me all at once. My mind whirled in uncomprehending panic, and I felt death marching toward me.

A terrible rushing sound reached me, reached *for* me. It

shuddered through my bones, plucking my muscles like harp strings. Light seared my eyes and then was gone.

I gasped. Opened my eyes. All I saw was gray space. Ghostly impressions of walls and furniture. I saw people, my people, Illya and Misha. Their bodies were washed out, no more than a pale phosphorescence from a different plane.

My mind rebelled against the sight. This was the spirit world, the Marchlands, but I wasn't dead. I couldn't be. And if I was alive, I could fight.

Fight, Askia!

I bucked. I twisted and kicked. My feet connected with an unseen something. I dug my heel into meaty flesh and heard someone groan. I fought harder. I screamed for help. No—not screamed. Compelled. My will cracked through the Marchlands, rippled across the emptiness, trapping every soul it touched along the way.

Voices responded to my call. Men came. No. Soldiers. Khazan guardsmen led by my ghost-sergeant rushed forward, swords drawn. The sergeant was quickest. His now solid form shot across the empty space. He struck, faster than any snake. His sword sliced into my attacker.

I heard a stifled cry. Saw blood. The invisible hands vanished.

I hung in the air for a second that stretched to eternity. My stomach lurched and every hair on my body rose in the moment gravity reasserted itself.

I fell.

I heard myself hit the floor with a sickening thud. White hot pain stabbed through my left wrist. I breathed a sob and clutched my arm to my chest.

More sound. The clanking of armor. I was sitting on the floor of a huge, dark room. Guards, living guards, ran toward me, their swords drawn, faces tight.

"Sound the alarm," Lieutenant Umari said, taking control of his men as he knelt before me. "Are you all right, my lady?"

"I . . . yes. I think so." My voice croaked out of my sore throat. "Where am I?"

His face wrinkled with confusion. "The Great Hall, my lady."

The Great Hall? How? Somewhere overhead, a bell began to clang.

Umari whirled around to his fellow guards. "Get help," he yelled, and three of his men tore out of the room. He turned back to me, his face gray with shock. "Just . . . just lie there, my lady," he said. "Help is on the way."

I managed a nod. With a clenched jaw, I cradled my arm against my chest, willing the pain away.

"Her men are here," another voice shouted.

"Bring them up," Umari called.

Illya slid between the arrayed ranks of the Khazan Guard. He sank to his knees in front of me. His face was white with terror, his eyes were wide with rage. Illya clasped my shoulders, fingers digging into my skin as he looked me up and down. "You're hurt. How?"

"I . . ." I paused, swallowing down bile rising in my throat. "I fell."

"I'll say," Umari said, shaking his head.

Illya turned to him, a silent command in his face.

"She fell out of the damn sky," the lieutenant said, pointing to the empty space above us with an open hand. "I saw it with my own eyes. One second nothing. The next, I hear a scream and see her appear ten feet above the ground and falling fast. She hit the floor right where you are now." Umari shook his head like he couldn't quite believe his own words. "I have to ask, my lady . . . what happened?"

As I opened my mouth, the guards came to attention. Boots snapped together and swords were quickly sheathed. Through the wall of armor-clad legs, I saw Armaan stalk down the length of the hall, Ozura hurrying behind him. His face was ashen, lips pressed together in a furious frown.

"Step aside," he commanded, and the guards instantly fell away. Illya was slower to stand. Armaan glared in his direction, but it didn't have the effect Armaan clearly expected. Illya stood but he did not move back.

Armaan crouched in the spot Illya had vacated. He stared me up and down, all trace of his usual smile gone. I watched him, marking the tightness of his jaw and the tension in his neck. His gaze fell to my leg, where the skin was raw and shining from my skid across the bedroom floor. He looked at the small cuts scarring my feet and hands. Very slowly, he took my arm, frowning at the pale skin around my wrist, which was already mottled with bruises.

Armaan shook his head, blowing out a long breath. "Are you all right?"

I nodded.

His hands fell away. "Tell me what happened."

I glanced around, keenly aware of how many people surrounded me now. The shadows at the edges of the hall were thick and churning with indistinct forms. Shaziri forms. I gave Armaan a serious look, willing him to understand what I was about to say would only be part of the story.

"I was in bed when it happened. I was still awake, and I heard this . . . this massive gust of wind from the garden. So strong, it made the glass doors groan." I shook my head, reaching to find a plausible reason for why I got out of bed. Vitaly's terrified face flashed into my mind. I wondered where he was, where the ghosts of the Khazan guardsmen were.

"Askia?"

"I was scared. It didn't seem natural. I got out of bed to go to the dressing room."

"Why?" Armaan asked.

"There was a sword on my vanity. I went to get it in case something was wrong."

Armaan nodded. "And then?"

"The glass broke. The wind blew so hard it shattered the door right on top of me. It tossed me across the room. And—"

"And?"

I licked my lips. "Something grabbed me. I don't know what, or who, it was. They pinned my arms down and lifted me up. I don't really know what happened next, I couldn't see or hear anything, but my legs were still free so I fought."

Armaan breathed a weak-looking smile. "Of course you did. That's how you got away?"

I nodded, glancing from Armaan to Ozura. Her eyes were narrow, silently vowing to get the whole story later. Good. I looked back at Armaan, but he had turned to Lieutenant Umari.

"You were the one to find Princess Askia?"

"Yes, sir."

"And?"

Umari's face flushed. He stared at a point over Armaan's shoulder. "We were on duty, my men and I, patrolling the hall, when we heard a scream. I looked up and saw Princess Askia appear out of thin air. She fell about ten feet to the floor."

"And you saw no one else with her?"

"No, sir."

Armaan turned away from the lieutenant. He looked at my various injuries, almost like he was memorizing them. I sensed a great well of anger boiling within him. "Are you able to stand?"

I nodded, and let him help me up, wincing as my weight settled on my feet.

"Armaan, give her your jacket," Ozura said, her face pinched with unfeigned worry.

Armaan nodded, pulling off the rumpled blue jacket he'd

worn during dinner. It was still warm from his body as he draped it over my shoulders.

"Excuse me, Your Majesty."

General Ochan slid between the guards, a scroll clenched in his hand. Annoyance flickered across Armaan's face. "Not now, General."

"I'm sorry, my lord. You asked me to bring this to you the moment it arrived."

Armaan sighed but took the scroll, breaking the seal at once. I looked from Armaan to the general. Ochan gave me a tight smile.

"All right, my lady?"

"Yes, General. Thank you."

A strangled snarl grumbled out of Armaan. I started at the sound. The emperor's expression was closed, his gaze stony. He looked at Ochan, the letter crumpled in his fist. "Call the Council of Viziers. We meet immediately. Princess Askia, you will join us."

A chill ran down my spine. "Of course."

"Armaan, please. You must let her dress," Ozura said quickly. "You can't expect her to stand before the council in nothing but her nightgown."

Armaan nodded distractedly. "Yes. Of course, you're right, Ozura. Please go with her. Lieutenant."

"Yes, sir?"

"Take your men and accompany Princess Askia. Make sure her rooms are clear and remain there until she is ready. Bring her directly to the council chamber."

"And you." Armaan turned to Illya. The men looked at each other, their gazes hard. "No one gets to her."

Illya nodded.

"Come on, dear." Ozura hooked an arm around my waist and guided me toward the door. "Quickly now."

I hobbled along, my feet aching, but regardless of the pain, or the bloody footprints I left on the floor, I couldn't let myself slow down. The look on Armaan's face as he read the letter gnawed at me. Judging by the tension in Ozura's body, I wasn't alone in my worry.

Khazan guardsmen surrounded us, creating a human shield between me and the rest of the hallway. I could make out a half-dozen soldiers rushing past the guards. No doubt they were en route to my apartments, to ensure it was clear of intruders.

The doors to my rooms were open when I arrived and crawling with guards. Ostensibly, they were searching for intruders, but the result was a whirlwind of overturned furniture that left the remains of my few possessions toppled across the floor.

It was the same in the dressing room when we arrived. Garments were strewn across the floor in careless piles of painstaking embroidery. A very rumpled-looking Nariko and Soma stood on one side of the room. Soma's arms were crossed over her chest. She glared murderously at the three men who rifled through the room while Nariko clutched a dark-colored dress to her chest like she was afraid someone was going to take it from her.

"All of you, out," Ozura said, snapping her fingers at the soldiers.

The guards leapt to attention and hurried from the room. She released me and strode into the bedroom, chivvying four more men out. "Make sure no one disturbs us," Ozura ordered, her expression forbidding. "All right. We don't have much time. Askia, sit. Nariko, put that dress down and come tend to Askia's feet. Soma, fix her hair."

Before I could speak, I was rushed to the vanity, and Nariko and Soma got to work. Ozura stepped forward. Her face was drawn, her lips white. "Tell me exactly what happened."

"Vitaly was waiting for me when I went into the bedroom,"

I said, praying Ozura wouldn't ask why I was so late to bed, for no half-truths would be allowed. Not now. "He was agitated, like he wanted to speak with me, but I was tired. I ignored him at first," I confessed, accepting Ozura's look of incredulity with a bowed head. "It became clear Vitaly wasn't going to go away until we spoke, so I summoned the power to speak with him."

"What did he say?" Ozura asked.

I took a deep breath. "'Get your sword.'" I reached out, placing a single finger on the sheathed blade that still rested on the table. "All he said was, 'Get your sword.'"

"And the wind?"

"I heard it coming. I was halfway to the dressing room when the glass shattered. The wind literally tossed me across the room. The intruder was on me before I could do anything but scream. He pinned down my arms and lifted me up and . . . out."

"Out? Explain."

I shook my head, grasping for words. "There was this . . . this enormous pressure and then this flash of light, and somehow we crossed over." I looked up at Ozura, confusion leaving me hollow. "We were in the Marchlands. How is that possible, Ozura? I'm supposed to be the only living death witch, and I can't even manage to bring a spirit over here for more than a few moments."

Ozura sighed and shook her head at the wall behind my shoulder. "Yours are not the only powers that interact with the Marchlands, the threshold of life and death. Healers and mind witches also court that space."

I shook my head. "Why?"

Ozura shrugged. "Every act of living is an act of dying. Healers and mind witches by necessity can access the Marchlands. Elemental witches don't need to."

My brow furrowed, and I wondered why this information hadn't been brought up during my lessons. I'd have asked, but a more pressing concern shouldered past my annoyance. "Wait a minute. I only sensed one presence. If a wind witch couldn't access the Marchlands, that means the intruder could wield both elemental *and* spirit magic." The blood rushed out of my face as I made the connection. "That means . . ."

"Yes," Ozura replied, her face gray and laden with worry. "It was Radovan."

"But . . . If Radovan had this power, why did he wait? Why didn't he take me months ago?"

"I don't know." Ozura reached out to me like she wanted to hold my hand but brought herself up short. "I don't know why he waited, but it doesn't matter. I'm sorry, Askia. You're out of time."

Numbness crept from my brain into my neck and chest. Radovan? No. It wasn't possible. But it was. He had done this. He was finished with waiting, and he was willing to pit his empire against Vishir to get to me.

"We need to hurry," Ozura said, her voice business-like. "Nariko, are you done?"

"Um . . . well, her feet are, but I haven't gotten to her arm."

"Bandage it." Ozura gave me a pitying glance. "Too many people saw it injured. We can't let you come under suspicion from the Shazir."

In a matter of minutes, I was walking out of my apartments with Ozura at my side and Illya at my back. Crimson-clad shapes melted out of the shadows, prowling along the edges of the hall. An honor guard, or at least that's how I knew the Shazir saw it. To my mind, they looked like prison wardens.

The doors to the council chamber were open when we arrived, and the guards on duty let us through without comment. The room was hot. The press of so many bodies and hurried conversations created invisible plumes of humidity that clung to my skin as I crossed the room. Ghosts both familiar and new darted through the crowds, their indistinct forms making the whole room blur.

I followed Ozura to the head of the table, where Armaan sat speaking with General Ochan. Both Enver and Iskander stood near their father, listening to the discussion. Whatever was being said, Enver looked nervous. His eyes were slightly wide, and his gaze kept darting around the room.

Two empty chairs stood to Armaan's left. Ozura took the one closest to Armaan. She immediately leaned toward her husband and began to whisper in his ear. I slid into the remaining chair and caught Armaan throwing a grave look in my direction.

I wasn't sure what to do. What to feel. This was what I wanted, after all, for Vishir to commit their troops, to help me fight Roven. My desire was closer than ever. Then why was there a pit in my stomach?

Iskander stepped closer. I'd never seen him look so serious before. All traces of the manic desperation I had seen in him only a few hours ago was gone. All that remained was grave determination. "Are you all right?"

Before I could find an answer to that, Ozura leaned between us, beckoning Illya closer as well. "I must meet with the three of you this evening," she said, her voice low enough to be lost in the chaos around us. "I will be in my study at sundown. I expect all of you to be there as well. I will send someone to show you two the way," she said, gesturing to the two men.

"Yes, Mother."

Iskander didn't look at me as he stepped away. Illya did. There was a shadow of something on his face I'd never seen before.

Fear.

"Thank you all for coming on such short notice." Armaan's gravelly voice echoed off the chamber's wooden walls. A hush blanketed the hall; men leaned forward in their seats. "This meeting was called for several reasons, but I would be remiss if I did not first address the attempted abduction of Princess Askia. A witch broke into her bedroom and spirited her away. It was only through the princess's quick thinking and fortitude she was able to break free."

Armaan shifted in his seat. His golden eyes swept across the room, resting for a moment on Enver before glancing past Khaljaq and his phalanx of Shazir warriors. "We must consider this attempt a personal insult to our honor. Never has a foreign royal been harmed while on Vishiri soil. We need to determine the proper measures to take to ensure her safety in our halls."

"The measures that must be taken are quite clear, my lord." Khaljaq lifted himself to his feet. His voice was like the rustle of dead leaves. "We must gather the witches of Bet Naqar. It's time for a reckoning. A purge. You can no longer suffer these demons to defile your city. Only when the empire is free of the taint of magic will she be safe."

"Enough, Khaljaq," Armaan said. "There's no reason to believe the witches of Bet Naqar would hurt Princess Askia. It is unlikely any Vishiri was behind the attempt, and more than likely the true culprit has already fled. All we can do now is make sure it doesn't happen again."

"The Shazir are more than ready to step in. We will protect Princess Askia at all costs."

"I don't need to be protected," I said, hating the tremble of fear in my voice as the memory of Khaljaq's words came back to me. Lady Night curse him, there was no way I was becoming a symbol for the Shazir. I looked around at the gathered lords. This was it. My chance.

I stood. "We all know Radovan is responsible. And if he was bold enough to try and take me from under your nose, what's to stop him from trying to take more? From moving on Idun? On Vishir?"

My eyes met Armaan, drawing him in, willing him to act. "I'm ready to fight him. But I need your army."

Silence met my words. The air between us shivered, like the hum of electricity before a storm.

A sharp, almost childish laugh burst out of Enver's mouth, breaking the spell. "Surely you don't expect us to answer you now? It's three in the morning. We need time to discuss."

"And in the meantime, you can stay in the menagerie." More than one man sucked in a breath at Armaan's words. He tilted his hands toward the ceiling in an elegant shrug. "There is no place the Khazan Guard protect more fiercely. And the Shazir would not need to trouble themselves with your safety."

I took a careful breath. Armaan was correct. The Shazir wouldn't be able to reach me in the menagerie, but that blessing would come with a cost. Illya and my men wouldn't be able to reach me either. No one would. If I entered the menagerie, I might never leave it again. It was an implicit proposal of marriage, and judging by the shocked expressions on the faces of the men around me, I wasn't the only person to think so.

The real question was, did I have any choice? *Moves and countermoves, Askia. Victories and sacrifices.* No. Entering the menagerie didn't mean I could never leave it again. I didn't have to be just one more Vishiri queen. *Play the game.*

I smiled. "Your guardsmen have been like brothers to me; I trust them with my life." My gaze went to Ochan and Nazir, who both straightened with a quiet pride echoed by every other soldier present. "However, I would still need to have access to my men. Is that possible to arrange?"

Armaan nodded. "Of course. All your needs will be seen to. Ozura, please ensure Princess Askia's possessions are moved into one of the spare rooms."

"I'm afraid I must interject on Her Highness's behalf." Count Dobor's voice echoed across the room.

He stood, framed by the doorway, hands clasped in front of

his billowing ebony robe. His over-oiled goatee glinted in the low light.

Armaan's brows drew together on his forehead. "The Council of Viziers is closed to foreign dignitaries, Count Dobor. Enver, is this your doing?"

"No, Father," Enver hurried to reply. "Ishaq must have told him."

More than one of the watching ghosts laughed, laughed at how quickly Enver threw his ally to the wolves in a gray-faced attempt at distancing himself from the slightest whiff of Roven sympathies. But nothing, not even Ishaq's hiss of betrayed surprise, could make me smile. Not with Dobor looking on with mocking laughter.

"My presence may be unorthodox," Dobor began, "but I felt it was my duty to come, lest there be any misunderstanding between our two empires. It would be unseemly for Princess Askia to take up residence in the menagerie while she is engaged in marriage negotiations with Emperor Radovan."

"I never agreed to marry Radovan," I snapped. "I never once even entertained the thought. Just because Radovan invaded my kingdom does not mean he is entitled to my body."

"You misunderstand the situation, my girl," Dobor said, his smile slipping into a disdainful sneer. "Seravesh belongs to Emperor Radovan. You are *his* subject. Your consent is not required."

My words failed as my hand went to a sword that wasn't there. "Your master invaded my country, murdered my grandfather, butchered my people, and now he thinks he can sneak into my bedroom and claim me?

"Never."

Dobor raised himself up to his full height, his face purpled with apparent outrage. "How dare you speak to me in this manner? What proof do you have Roven was behind this?"

"There is no evidence, as you very well know." Armaan leaned back in his seat. I'd never seen him look so forbidding.

"But since you took it upon yourself to intrude in Vishiri matters of state, perhaps you can also take a moment to answer for your master?"

"I would never presume to answer for Emperor Radovan, but I would be honored to convey any concerns you have."

"Two days ago, the Shazir claimed Radovan was amassing an army on the northern border of Idun. You denied that claim. Yet I have just received word from Governor Erol of Idun that confirms this information. Roven is coming perilously close to violating the pact between our nations. Tell me. What does Radovan intend?"

Count Dobor coughed a little embarrassed laugh. "I assure you, my lord, there's no need to alarm yourself. The army was sent to ensure peace in war-torn Seravesh. I tell you this as a gesture of friendship. However, duty dictates I not say any more. These are, after all, internal matters of state."

Armaan seemed to muse for a moment, but there was nothing soft in his eyes, nothing thoughtful. He stood. Placed his hand over mine. "Well, then. In the spirit of friendship, I will tell you this: you may consider the safety and future of Princess Askia a Vishiri state matter. No further overtures of either alliance or marriage will be welcome. Or tolerated."

Count Dobor's face darkened. His small black eyes glittered with malice as his gaze flicked to me for a moment before returning to Armaan. A smirk twitched on Dobor's lips. "You would put the peace of our two empires at risk for a woman?"

"Would Radovan?" A growling laugh rumbled out of Armaan's chest. "Your master started this game, Dobor. I'm ending it. Princess Askia will not be forced out of Vishir by either magic or might. Remove your army from Idun's borders, or we will be at war."

Dobor's bow was the slightest spasm. He turned on his heel and marched out of the council room. The chamber erupted in excited whispers, hushed voices emphasizing the worry sizzling through the space.

"You should go rest, my dear," Armaan said, gaze heavy on my face. "I'll send news as it comes."

I nodded, accepting the dismissal, not because I wanted to leave, but because I knew Armaan needed a moment to get his court in order—in order and behind the decision to help me.

I stood, trying to ignore the rising tide of panicked voices reverberating through the chamber. Before I could even step away from the table, Ochan, Nazir, and every other guard present pushed through the crowd. They arrayed themselves before me, a wall that could not be ignored.

"Princess Askia, sister-in-arms," Ochan said, deep voice echoing in the sudden silence. "We salute you." As one, they drew their swords and knelt before me.

My eyes flew wide and I read the sincerity in each of their faces, the subtle shift in power that this display surely showed. I had the guard behind me. And with Enver and Ishaq now toothless, and Lords Marr, Elon, and Trantini even now in conversation with the emperor, I just might have the court too.

I smiled, offering Ochan and Nazir a hand, drawing them up. "Thank you, my brothers. I look forward to fighting beside you in the days to come."

33

Ozura, Iskander, and Illya were already waiting by the time I slid through the office door and into the middle of the three chairs arranged before Ozura's desk. The air in the room was thick, oppressive almost.

I could feel time slipping through my fingers, transforming my day into a blurred haze of troubled thoughts and half-written letters to General Arkady. I'd sent word to him when Ozura first warned me of Armaan's interest, but his reply hadn't yet arrived. And now I was somehow supposed to conjure the words to tell Arkady that I'd moved into the menagerie? That an offer was imminent? An offer I thought I had to accept.

Ozura didn't even look up from her letter writing while I settled myself. It looked official, judging by the great seal weighing down the bottom half of the parchment.

I glanced at Illya but he didn't return my look. He sat rigidly in his chair, body coiled, like he knew what this meeting was for and struggled to contain himself. He probably did know. We all did, I thought looking to Iskander.

He stood on the right side of the room, facing one of the bookshelves. He held his shoulders in a rigid line, and there was a tension in his back that instantly put me on guard.

"How is your arm, Askia?" Ozura asked, finally setting her quill to the side.

"Her arm is fine, Mother," Iskander said through gritted teeth, flopping down in the remaining chair. "No doubt, one of your witches saw to that. Why did you summon us?"

I felt one of my eyebrows rise at the belligerence in his voice. There was too much at stake to waste time on Iskander's rudeness. "I can't have my wrist healed. Too many people saw it injured. The Shazir saw it injured. I can't take the risk." I turned away from Iskander's flushed face. "My wrist is fine. A little sore, perhaps, but the pain will pass. Thank you for asking."

"Good." Ozura glanced at her son, her dark gaze lingering for a few long moments. "I called you here not simply out of duty as Armaan's principal wife, but out of fondness as well. I don't want the two of you to be taken off guard," she said, motioning to me and Iskander. "And Captain, it's clear Princess Askia values your advice. She's going to need your good counsel."

Ozura's eyes cut to me, and the weight of that gaze settled on my shoulders, bearing down. Attention locked on my face, she pushed the parchment across the table. "Your marriage contract to Armaan. You know you have to sign."

"No."

Iskander snarled the word, his chair crashing to the floor as he leapt to his feet. He towered over his mother's desk, hands balled into fists, face twisted. "She can't," he spat. "You can't make her."

"Iskander, no one is forcing me to do anything," I said. "I came to Vishir for an army. If this is the only way . . . I have to consider it."

"I know this wounds you," Ozura said, "but this is the best choice we have of a bad lot."

Iskander shook his head. "She can't. Radovan won't stand for it. It will mean war."

"War was certain the moment you brought her here," Ozura's voice rose half an octave in obvious frustration. "You made your father responsible for Askia's safety. What was he supposed to do, let Radovan take her?"

"No, of course not," Iskander replied. "But why is marriage the only option? We can still reach an agreement diplomatically. He doesn't have to marry her."

Bitterness filled my chest. "Iskander, the only diplomatic choice the emperor has left is to turn me over to Radovan." Lady Night above, hadn't Ozura told Iskander anything? Hadn't she bothered to explain? No wonder he sought out the Shazir's help. He knew nothing.

"He wouldn't do that."

"You're wrong," Ozura replied, rubbing her eyes. "He wouldn't want to, but if it averted a world war? He would do it, Iskander. Any good emperor would. He simply doesn't have that option."

"What do you mean?"

"It all comes down to Radovan's wives," Ozura said, folding her hands together. "Did you know they were all witches?"

Iskander threw a worried glance at me before looking back to his mother. "No. Does it matter?"

"It's the only thing that matters."

Ozura's attention shifted to me. There was something pitying in her expression. Something I immediately wished to reject. I didn't need pity, and if I was smart, I wouldn't ever need it.

"Radovan chooses only the most powerful female witches," she said. "He marries them, and he kills them. Can you imagine why?"

Iskander shook his head, but his expression made it clear he had a good guess.

"It's so he can absorb their power. He's married six witches in the past century, six witches with the six most common types of magic. Only one alludes him. Only Askia."

"You're a death witch," Illya said, a tremor running through his voice with the promise of violence.

I met Illya's gaze, though my breath hitched at what I saw there. The longing and the loss. "Yes."

"And Radovan knows it too," Ozura added, oblivious as Vitaly appeared at her side. "Who knows when he will get another opportunity like this. So, no. There will be no diplomacy. Radovan will stop at nothing to attain her, and when he does . . . He believes he will be a living god. He may be right."

Ozura's words crashed into a silence so complete I couldn't even hear my own breathing. Illya's hand clamped down on my arm, like he could keep me safe by sheer will. Vitaly watched me, ghostly eyes wide as if I was mere moments from joining him in the Marchlands.

Iskander's eyes cast about the room, searching for something, for anything, that could countermand his mother's words. I recognized this growing despair. It was the same blind panic he'd had when he kissed me last night. I opened my mouth, reaching for something to say, but all words fled.

"If Askia must be married, then I will marry her."

Illya shifted in his chair while Vitaly shook his head, starlit face alight with pity. Even Ozura closed her eyes for a moment. It was the first time I had seen her give into anything like exhaustion, anything like defeat. "Any possibility of a marriage between the two of you died the moment you allied yourself with the Shazir."

A strangled noise worked its way out of Iskander's throat. His hands hit the desk with a thud, like he was too weak to stand without support. "What?"

"Think about it, son. Askia's enemies are powerful, but her allies are not without strength, not now that you have legitimized the Shazir. They could tip the balance in this country, perhaps even topple an empire. By marrying Askia, Armaan can appease them. It will give him time to send them to war, where, Lady Night willing, they will all die."

"That's not a reason I can't—"

"Isn't it?" Ozura looked at Iskander, her eyes widening. "Your father has two grown sons, one a favorite of the court, the other a favorite of the guard. Despite Enver's recent missteps, showing either one of you overt favor is still too dangerous. Yet you want your father to give you a princess for a wife. One who has the Shazir and the Khazan Guard behind her? What will he have to give Enver to keep the balance? Your father won't live forever, Iskander. Someday soon he will have to name an heir, and the war between you and your brother will begin in earnest. Vishir will not survive Roven if you two boys begin your battle now."

Iskander shook his head. His face was drawn and gray. A vein leapt in his temple. He rose to his full height and pointed a shaking finger at his mother. "This isn't going to happen. Do you hear me? It isn't." He rounded on me so quickly, Illya rose and slid between us. "I forbid it," Iskander snarled.

A soundless snarl rippled across Vitaly's face, but I had my own anger to deal with. "Forbid what?" I asked, my words echoing with the crack of a whip. "An alliance that could not only save my life, but the lives of my people? You do not own me, Iskander."

Iskander's face slackened. The anger seemed to leech out of him. His muscles loosened, drooping toward the floor like a puppet whose strings had been cut. He walked out of the room.

The door swung shut on Iskander, leaving behind a void of dull acceptance. This was what I wanted, wasn't it? Anything to get an army—that's why I was there. This was the price.

But it didn't have to be the end of me. *Be the queen, Askia.*

I turned away from the door—away from Illya who stood

by silently while I bartered myself away—and focused on Ozura. Her eyes were closed. She looked exhausted, older somehow. Dark circles bruised her eyes. Her lips were slightly blue. There were fresh lines on her face, like years had passed while we sat in this study.

I swallowed back my pity. Ozura wouldn't appreciate my sympathy just as I didn't want hers, and anyway I had questions that required answers. "What will happen to Seravesh?"

Ozura opened her eyes, gazing at me with a closed expression. "That's up to you now, isn't it?"

"If Vishir defeats Roven, Seravesh is to be free."

Ozura snorted. "The most I can offer is to make Seravesh a vassal kingdom, led by a monarch of our choosing."

"No," I said, making my voice as firm as possible. "I will marry Armaan, but I will rule Seravesh in his name as an allied nation. Nothing more."

Ozura drew back in her chair, disbelief written on the lines of her face. "Impossible."

"Our marriage seals our nations as allies. It's the best I can do. And, anyway, what other choice do you have?" I pressed, when Ozura remained silent. "You as good as told Iskander that Armaan's only options were to marry me or send me to Radovan for slaughter. If it's to be marriage, then—"

"You mistake me, Askia," she said, voice frigid. "The only way to save your life, and keep your magic safe from Radovan, is to marry. We are fond of you, but keeping your magic away from Radovan is the primary goal, which makes the third option rather obvious, don't you think?"

Ozura tilted her head to the side. "A vassal kingdom would be cherished. Protected. An allied nation?" She shrugged her shoulders in feigned nonchalance. "Well, anything could happen to an ally . . . or their queen."

Illya stepped forward as if proximity could save me from her threat, but Ozura ignored him. She only had eyes for me. Good.

I met her gaze, and summoning every ounce of steel I had, I smiled. "I know Armaan well enough by now to know he doesn't have the stomach for that. But you? You and I are the same. So you'll believe me when I tell you that if I should suffer any . . . mishaps before you and I come to terms, I'll make sure the Shazir know every detail about this guild and the witches who run it.

"So," I said, leaning back in my chair, hands folded. "Allied nations?"

Ozura studied me for a long, heavy moment, but there wasn't any anger in her appraisal. No, if anything it felt like I'd finally earned her respect. "Agreed."

She picked up her quill, striking out part of the document before quickly amending it. "Now as for your accommodations. You'll have to reside in the menagerie; however, your men will be posted in adjacent rooms with free access to the main sitting room."

"I'm not spending the rest of my life in the menagerie," I said flatly.

"You will if you want the court to accept Seravesh's favored status. Vishiri queens must remain under the emperor's eye as surety of their province's loyalty."

"But I'm not a province! I don't care what your court will accept," I cried. "My people need me."

"Your people are about to be wiped off the map."

"Which is why I must return to Seravesh. I'm useless here, but I can fight. I have an army to lead."

"You would risk your unborn child in battle?"

Illya made an incoherent noise—the grunt of a wounded animal, but I pushed past it. Past the sight of Vitaly's body flickering with shock. "What are you talking about?"

"You want allied nation status, then marriage simply isn't enough for the alliance to last. We must be tied together by blood too. So. You and Armaan must have a child."

I sat momentarily stunned, Illya's eyes drilling into the side of my face. Vitaly paced behind Ozura's chair, shaking his head in frantic thought. There had to be another way.

"What about Iskander? You'd really muddy the line of succession further by allowing another child?"

"Of course not," she replied, tossing the argument aside. "The contract will stipulate that your child will be heir to Seravesh alone. But a child there will be."

"After the war, surely."

Ozura huffed a mirthless laugh. "After the war." She rubbed her temple, taking a deep breath like she was exhausted by this whole mess of a meeting. "The two largest armies this world has ever seen are about to go to war, Askia. Armaan will have to ride out with the army to lead. You know the risks better than anyone. He may never return. So if you are to continue your line, you must conceive immediately. My healers will make sure you are successful."

So this was it? The sum of my life? From future heir and exiled princess, to Vishiri queen and expectant mother all in the space of a year? I clutched the arms of my chair like they could somehow keep the world from spinning out of control.

I swallowed. I could do this. I was already getting married. Wasn't this just the next step? If my country was going to become a battlefield for the world's two greatest armies, then the least I could do was have a child. A child who would one day lead them.

"Agreed. But I want to choose the steward who leads in the interim," I pressed, feeling like I was begging for scraps.

"Yes, I assumed as much."

All my demands dried up in my throat at Ozura's easy acquiescence.

She flashed a bitter smile. "Perhaps you do not completely understand what is on offer here. You will be a principal wife someday—*the* principal wife. Armaan cannot promise you fidelity, but you already have his respect. You will eventually have his ear and his last child. The great queens of Vishir have done much more with much, much less. Indeed, you have many advantages, including your intimate knowledge of our enemy's tactics and the terrain in which we're about to fight. Armaan will grow to rely on you, and as he does, your influence will grow."

I felt myself being drawn in like a fish on a line. Ozura was practically handing her position away to me. Why? Why would Ozura do all this?

Illya rubbed his eyes, dropping into the chair beside me. "How long do you have to live?"

A sad sort of smile stretched across Ozura's face. "Not long now. The healers are reaching their limits. I have a few months, perhaps."

"You're *dying*?" My mouth clicked open. "Does Iskander know?"

"No, and you won't tell him." Ozura grimaced. "Iskander has a good heart, but he is too prone to acts of passion. He will learn. You will teach him, shape him into the man he needs to be, the emperor he needs to become."

"You would trust me to do this?" My voice was high with disbelief. "You would trust me with Iskander's future, with the future of Vishir?"

Ozura barked out a bitter laugh. "What's the alternative? Would you let Enver take the throne?" She shook her head. "I should hope not. He'd kill both of you in the first week."

Ozura gestured to the marriage contract, with one scrolling

signature already in place. "Armaan has already signed the contract. If you sign your name, you will legally become a queen
of Vishir guaranteeing Seravesh's protection. The ceremony is
tomorrow."

"*Tomorrow?*" I asked, my voice cracking at the speed of all this.

"There's no time to lose," she said with a regret-filled nod.
"Not when Radovan could come for you at any moment."

"And you're so sure I'm going to sign?"

"I am," Ozura replied, her voice a strange mix of softness and
unyielding resolution. "Go and take a moment. Collect yourself.
Then come back here and sign the contract. Become the queen
your people need you to be."

34

Silence did not lay easily between Illya and me. It had a texture, a vibration that could not, *would* not, be ignored. Still, I clung to it as we made our way through the guild's gloomy halls and into the vaulted portal room.

"The menagerie is through this archway," I said, holding out my hand. I wasn't entirely sure how he and Iskander had made it into the guild, but that wasn't important now. Not with the weight of my responsibility crushing down on my shoulders and Illya looking at my hand like it was something too fragile to touch. "You'll need to hold my hand to pass through it."

He stared at me for a moment longer before sliding his calloused palm into mine. His touch was the only point of heat in my body, one I lost the moment we stepped into the mausoleum. I pushed myself across the tomb, but couldn't escape the feeling of loss.

Bracing myself against the doorway, I took a breath. The cemetery sprawled down the hillside. It was so quiet. So desolate. Nothing living moved here, only the indistinct shades of spirits waiting to move on. And it was going to be my new home?

"Are you all right?" Illya asked, leaning against the door's other edge.

"Why wouldn't I be? I'm about to get everything I ever wanted."

Illya nodded, his gray eyes dancing over my face. "If not quite in the way you hoped."

A bitter laugh scraped out of my mouth. "Hope. My grandfather used to say that only fools think they can change the world with hope."

"What would he tell you to do now?"

"He'd tell me to quit blubbering and do my damned duty." I smiled. Everything had been so black and white with my grandfather that it was oddly comforting to think of him. "He'd be right. I really don't have a choice."

"You always have a choice, Askia."

"Do I? You think Vishir will still send their army north if I don't marry Armaan?"

"I think it's likely too late to stop Vishir and Roven from going to war," he replied, his voice so damned reasonable. "Regardless of what you do."

I wasn't as sure. "Radovan is nothing if not cunning. If I leave Vishir now, he might halt his plans to invade Idun just long enough to steal my magic. Then Vishir would be at war against a madman with the might of all seven magics."

"Emperor Armaan knows that. He won't risk you returning to Seravesh alone, even if you do reject him."

"True, but . . ."

"But?"

"If I refuse Armaan, if Vishir and Roven go to war and Radovan is defeated, if by some miracle Vishir doesn't simply take Seravesh, we'll still need them."

"For what?"

"For money. Two of our cities have already burned. We missed the last harvest and with so many people displaced, the fields won't be planted this spring. Even if the war is won by summer, we'll still be facing famine come winter. We won't have the money to rebuild without Vishir."

"Ah."

I could've laughed at Illya's tired excuse for a reply. We were all so focused on the war, on defeating the great evil of our time, it was almost impossible to see past it. But the fact was that we could fight insurmountable odds and win our freedom, only to be felled by the utter banality of an empty treasury.

"So you're going to marry Armaan."

"You think I should?"

Illya scrubbed his face with his hands. "I can't answer that for you," he said with a rough voice. "But I think you think you should."

A lump rose in my throat as I met Illya's eyes, and the fragile queenly mask I clutched shattered. A question rose within me, delicate and hopeless and achingly precious, for it was filled with all the things that might have been. "Ask me not to."

Illya's expression softened, and pain flashed through his eyes. But he faced it. Faced me. "I can't," he whispered. "Lady Night save me, I wish I could. But I can't. You don't belong to me, Askia. You belong to no one."

"Except Seravesh," I said, my voice catching on the words he hadn't spoken.

"The north needs you. So I have to let you go." He paused, and I felt my heart break in that brief silence. "But I can't stay here."

My eyes instantly filmed. "What?"

"I thought I could. I thought I could stand aside and let you go, but . . . Necessity means I must watch you marry him. But I can't stand by and watch you *become* his wife. Bear his child, I—" His voice faltered. "I will go to war for you. I will lead the Black Wolves to victory, but I can't stay. I've already written to Arkady."

"No, Illya, please," I whispered, seizing his hands.

He drew me close, pulled our joined hands to his lips. Kissed each one. "Please let me go."

I bit down hard on my tongue, letting blood fill my mouth as my damned eyes shed a stream of tears. And let him go. "So that's it then. I will marry Armaan."

"You'll marry Armaan," he murmured on a long exhale. "You'll stay here while the rest of us go to war. You'll learn from Ozura and guide Iskander. You'll raise a child and . . ." His words petered out like he hadn't the heart to say the rest. He didn't have to. I already knew what was next.

"There will be no more training with the guard. No more wild horse rides or raucous hunts. Everything that I love, everything that I am, will be curbed, stifled. Until it vanishes. I'll live out my days in this garden and my nights in the guild. I'll be a true queen of Vishir, a caged bird in the emperor's menagerie."

Illya's eyes shone with an emotion I was too afraid to identify. "It's a lot to give up for a man you don't love."

"It is. But is it enough to give up for the country I love? If it frees Seravesh, isn't it worth it? What is my freedom versus that of all our people?"

Illya's eyes never wavered from mine, as he reached across the few inches and chasm that separated us and drew me to his chest, held on tight. But he didn't reply.

I choked out a laugh that sounded like a sob. Illya knew what I had to do. So did I. If I was honest, I'd known it all along.

"He was wrong," Illya murmured long after night fell over the menagerie. "Your grandfather. It takes courage to hope for a better world. Even more to reach for change."

35

I stood unmoving while servants flitted around me, sliding bracelets on my wrists and adjusting the fit of my gown. I did my best to ignore them. My body was heavy from lack of sleep. It was an exhaustion I felt in my bones.

My dreams had taken me home. Seravesh. I longed to feel its cold wind on my face. To see its snow-capped mountains and the way the sun fell in dappled prisms through the leaves of its ancient forests. These were wishes, hopes, and dreams. And they all must be put aside.

Right?

There would be no going home. Not for me. My only choice was to forge ahead.

Wasn't it?

I blinked and looked around, taking the room in for the first time. The dawn sky was still a velvet crush of pink and gold when Soma dragged me from my new bed in the menagerie. She and a half-dozen servants had scrubbed me clean and wrapped me in a plain dress before rushing me off to the front of the palace where a royal carriage waited to whisk me off to the Temple of the Two-Faced God. Soma led me up a side staircase I hadn't known existed, pushing aside sleepy-eyed priests and priestesses.

The office space she'd dragooned for my use was small, its

walls covered in tiny tiles of yellow, orange, and gold. Each shade ran in rivulets down the wall like an elegant finger painting. The lush blue carpet still bore the indentations of where a desk usually sat, the same desk now pushed against the wall and covered with cosmetics. A full-length mirror stood before me, but I had yet to look at it. My eyes were trained on the open window, on the pale curtains dancing in the breeze and the steadily growing roar of the many people gathered outside, hungry for a glimpse of their new queen.

I forced the thought away, clinging to each moment as it slid through my fingers too fast, far, far too fast. Soma stepped onto the wide pedestal beside me, the delicate strands of a familiar circlet in her hands. She smiled, my anchor in all this strangeness. I tried to smile back, but my face wouldn't obey. I nodded instead and steeled myself to look in the mirror.

The gown they'd dressed me in was simple but regal. The dark evergreen fabric—the color of luck and fidelity in Vishir, was cut straight across my breasts, nipping in at my waist and falling in a column to the floor. Rather than sleeves, it had a cape. It clasped to the top of my bodice on either side of my arms, leaving my shoulders bare as it draped down my back, the train pooling on the floor.

They'd left my hair down, too, taming my curls with serums and irons until it fell in gentle waves to the small of my spine. I felt Soma slide a few pins into my hair, securing the circlet before stepping away.

"One last touch," she said, bending over the desk. She turned back to me, holding a heavy chain between her meaty fists. A familiar emerald pendant winked at me in the low light.

My eyebrows rose. "Are you sure that's a good idea?"

Soma chuckled. "What better way to mock Roven than by wearing their gift while you marry our emperor?"

There was something savage in Soma's tone that made me

smile for the first time all day. I lifted my hair, letting her clasp the chain about my neck. The pendant felt heavy between my breasts and for a second my magic leapt up into my skin. Vitaly materialized across the room, eyes wide with fear, then disappeared, my magic fading with him.

I heaved a measured breath to calm my nerves and took a long look at myself in the mirror. The scar above the pendant looked particularly red against my pale skin. Two wide metal cuffs encircled both wrists. *Shackles*, I thought. *Two shackles to chain me here.* I looked away before a frown could pull at my lips.

"Queen Ozura and the emperor should be arriving momentarily," Soma said. "She'll look in on you before the ceremony. Is there anything you need? Water or . . ." The older woman's words petered out knowingly, and I wondered how many times she'd helped nervous brides prepare for their weddings. Probably quite a few if she knew to do the preparations on the second floor of the temple with no easy escape route.

"Perhaps just a moment alone."

Soma smiled and squeezed my hand before ushering the other servants from the room. The sound of the door closing was lost as an excited cry erupted from the crowd outside. Ignoring the noise for a moment, I lifted my skirts and went to my pile of discarded clothes. The knife Illya gave me was there. And even though I knew I wouldn't need it, the simple act of strapping the blade to my ankle centered me. That small weight made me something more than a pretty woman in a beautiful dress. It made me, well, me.

The noise outside rose to a fever pitch and I couldn't ignore it any longer. Like a moth to a flame, I crossed to the window, careful to keep the curtain between me and the onlookers below.

Hundreds of people—thousands probably—crowded the square outside. They cried out and waved in joy as Armaan and Ozura walked up the temple steps, the other wives and the invited nobles congealing behind them. Armaan turned, his face glowing with triumph, and held up his hands for silence.

The crowd only grew louder, coating the plaza with adoration for their emperor. I couldn't blame them. Armaan cut a dashing figure in his crimson jacket, laughing and smiling for his people like he was the happiest man in all the world. Beside him Ozura looked radiant in blue—the picture of a happy wife. The gathered nobles looked less sure. Oh, they smiled and waved to the masses, but there was no laughter, no ease, and that fact was more telling.

"Friends. Brothers and sisters," Armaan called, his voice echoing through the clear morning air. "For five hundred years this empire has thrived, endured, prospered in the face of time. Our nation spans from Talria in the west to Shazir in the east, to faraway Kizuoka and Calormaña across the sea. For five hundred years, our lands have remained unchanged, our borders untested. No more. Today, Princess Askia of Seravesh and I will swear our loyalty and fidelity before the Two-Faced God, and Vishir will gain a sister kingdom, a true ally in the north. A new era will begin. This era won't be without opposition. But we will face it together, stronger for our alliance."

The mob outside screamed anew, feeding on the excitement in Armaan's voice, heedless of the warning in his words. "Witness the birth of a new Vishir."

The door banged open behind me, and I flinched into the wall. Iskander flung himself into the room, seizing my hand.

"Iskander, what—"

"Hurry," he breathed, pulling me forward.

I dug in my heels, dragging him to a stop. "What are you doing?" I demanded, even as I saw the glassy light of desperation filming his eyes.

"I'm getting you out of this. I have horses waiting outside, but we have to go now."

"Oh, Iskander."

It was his turn to wince, like the pity in my voice caused him pain. "Please," he said, his voice breaking. "Please come with me. It's not too late, you don't have to marry him."

"I've already signed the contract."

Iskander dropped my hand. He knew what my signature meant. His face crumpled, and I saw something within him break. "Don't do this."

"It's already done."

He scrunched his face with his hands. "No. No," he cried. "Contracts can be broken. You don't have to do this."

"I do, Iskander." I stepped up to him, eyes wide, willing him to look at me, to see it from my side. "This is the only way to save Seravesh."

"It's not. I can save Seravesh," he said with a manic gleam in his gaze. "You and me. We can do it."

"With the Shazir by my side?" I asked, my voice colder than I'd intended. "With them watching my every step, waiting for me to slip up, to reveal myself?"

Iskander started pacing back and forth in tight circles. He shook his head at the ground, his hands curling in impotent claws. "You don't have to do this. You're the rightful queen. You don't have to do anything you don't want to."

A laugh barked out of me before I could stop it, coating the air between us in pity and bitterness. "Someday you'll learn that ruling has nothing to do with your own desires. If you ever find it does, you're doing something wrong."

Pain shone in Iskander's eyes. "So that's it? You're giving up on us?"

Pity made my chest ache, but I couldn't let him see it. I had to be strong now, for Iskander. "There is no us."

The last of Iskander's denial seemed to gush out of him. His shoulders drooped, but his face hardened into an indolent, uncaring mask. He turned on his heel and left the room.

I closed my eyes. The sound of his retreat made me flinch, like each step away from me severed our friendship that much more.

"I think you handled that quite well."

The clipped, business-like tone in Ozura's voice was like a slap. My eyes flew open, an insult poised on my tongue, but Ozura wasn't alone. Nariko stood in the doorway behind the queen. Her face was gray, but a blotchy flush stained her cheeks. My words shriveled.

Ozura's eyes darted from my face to Nariko's and back again. She arched an ebony eyebrow at me as if to say, *I told you so*, as if any of this was my fault. "It's for the best," Ozura said.

Bullshit, I thought, refusing to let my anger show even though Ozura's self-righteousness and Nariko's blame made me want to scream.

"Iskander is hurt now, but eventually he will see you were only trying to do right by your people. Hopefully he'll realize it's time for him to do the same." Ozura shrugged, brushing an invisible wrinkle from her gown. "He will understand better when the war begins," Ozura said. "Are you ready?"

I was too angry for words, too anxious. So I shouldered past Nariko and her precious hurt feelings and followed Ozura out the door. The temple entrance was empty, and though the doors were closed against the city, I could still hear the people's cries like the roar of the ocean in a conch shell.

We stopped behind a golden screen whose wide mesh did nothing to hide the crowd of people waiting, hungry for the sight of me. Goose bumps prickled across my skin, a weight pulling my heart low. Ozura gestured to a temple attendant, face masked. But when the queen looked back at me, her eyes softened.

"Everything is going to be all right," she murmured, her words too low for Nariko or the guards to hear. "You're doing the right thing for yourself, and your people." She smiled, cupping my cheek, and a warmth, like the ghost memory of my mother's touch, filled my bones. "Your parents would be proud."

Her eyes assessed my face. She nodded at whatever she saw and then she was gone, continuing forward into the temple as the tenth bell rang. I peeked through the mesh, watching Ozura walk sedately down the center isle toward the altar where Armaan waited with an ancient-looking priestess.

The joined Temple of the Two-Faced God was bigger than the Shrine of Lady Night by half. The ceiling vaulted in a huge fanned dome painted in alternating gold and silver, like the scales of some enormous fish. Sunlight burned through the many stained-glass windows, painting the air with rainbows of purple and blue and green.

Soldiers ringed the circular temple, ceremonial spears held proudly tall against the gilt walls. Like any of the gathered nobles would give them trouble, I thought, scanning the crowd of nervous-looking men and women. What did they have to be nervous for? For the new day Armaan had proclaimed from the temple steps? Or for the wedding that would declare a war?

I felt the edge of my cape lift and glanced back at Nariko, but her gaze was fixed on my hem. Her eyes were wet. Her lower lip trembled.

Bitterness writhed in my gut, bitterness and an aching loneliness, a bone-deep sense of abandonment. I'd already lost Illya. Lost Iskander to hurt feelings. Now Nariko too? And why? What had I done but fought for my people?

I scanned the crowd, hoping to see Vitaly or Tarek or even the ghost-sergeant. None of them came, and with the Shazir congealing at the southern edge of the temple, I was too scared to summon them. Loneliness chimed a dirge on my rib cage. My legs begged me to run, but it was far, far too late for that.

The tenth bell fell silent. The priestess gestured. Everyone rose. Turned.

I forced my chin high and rounded the screen. The lords and ladies of Vishir bared their teeth at me in a grim pantomime of pleasure as I passed. Though some of them, like Lord Marr and General Ochan, looked at me with happiness, even pride, many more looked worried and outright disappointed.

I tried not to see it. Tried not to hear the cacophony of falsely bright oohs and ahhs. Tried not to feel my heart hammering out a staccato beat on my ribs, tried to ignore the way panic itched down my legs.

I locked my gaze forward and saw Ozura waiting to the left of the stairs leading up to the altar. Illya waited on the right. Her smile was serene. Satisfied even. Illya just looked sad.

"Come, my dear," Ozura murmured as I reached her.

She took my hand, cold and corpselike though it felt to me, and escorted me up the three short steps to the altar. To Armaan.

He smiled, taking my hand from Ozura and drawing me close. The scent of him, of cinnamon and saffron, filled my nose as he leaned down and kissed my cheek. "I know we do this for duty," he whispered, his lips brushing the shell of my ear. "But I think there will be some joy as well."

"I'm certain of it," I replied, with a smile that seemed to crack the porcelain edges of my face.

Armaan squeezed my hand as he straightened and turned to the priestess. I probably should have known her name, that old, bent woman who was marrying me. I should have heard her prayers, should have spoken vows.

Instead, my mind seemed to detach, watching from afar while my body went through the motions, numb and graceless.

The priestess circled the altar, offering the golden dagger of the Day Lord to Armaan, and the silver dagger of Lady Night to me. She held an ancient-looking chalice between us, wrought with the sun-in-moon sigil of the Two-Faced God.

With barely a second's hesitation, Armaan swiped the dagger across his left palm. Blood poured down his skin, dripping into the cup as he held his hand out to mine.

I looked at the chalice, at the tiny pool of blood staining its depths. Panic echoed in my chest. It reverberated outward, reaching my skin with a twinge of biting cold.

Beside me, Armaan shifted. I licked my lips. Raised the dagger. Pressed the blade to my palm. All I had to do was move.

Move, Askia.

Move.

Run.

I glanced up. Saw Iskander, his eyes wide, beseeching. Illya was beside him. He nodded, but was he urging me on, or telling me to stop?

I will burn this city to the ground for you.

But he wouldn't need to. If I didn't act, I'd be burning all our hopes. Seravesh's hopes. My people's futures.

The thought of their suffering, the inescapable weight of my duty dragged my eyes to the knife. The fate of my people crushed down on me.

I pulled the blade across my skin.

The doors flew open, hitting the wall with a bang. Frigid wind hit my face, and I stumbled into the altar.

"I'm afraid I must object."

Count Dobor's icy voice filled the temple from the open doorway. The crowd outside sounded strangely distant, and the sky roiled electric and green. Dobor watched Armaan with a sardonic smile, a smile that widened when he looked at me—at the necklace. It was a perfect match to the one that hung from his neck. He twirled the pendant, his gaze filled with malice.

The Shazir leapt to action, surging through the gathered nobles. They crowded the space between Dobor and the altar.

"What is the meaning of this?" Armaan growled.

"Why, I'm here to stop you, of course, though it pains me to puncture a man's dreams."

Dobor's smile was a baring of teeth that made my hackles rise. He hadn't moved, not even a step. Just stood there, toying with his necklace.

Dread shuddered through me. Dread and a nameless worry. "Where are the guards?" I asked as a warning screamed in my mind. I looked past Dobor. No one was there.

"This little spectacle of a marriage will not be allowed. It's in direct contravention of the peace accord between our nations."

Armaan smirked. "This is none of your concern. *Queen* Askia is none of your concern."

Dobor sighed. "Yes. I thought you might say that."

I watched, transfixed, as Dobor shifted. He ripped his necklace off, holding the green stone in his outstretched hand.

My heart stopped.

The stone burned with a sickly green light. Dobor smiled.

Air sucked past my shoulders, racing toward Dobor. I could almost see it hit the pendant. Ricochet. Ice erupted from the stone, like an arrow. It hurtled across the room. I screamed and, in the same moment, lunged for Armaan. Unable to look away. Unable to stop it. I wasn't fast enough.

Ozura was.

Her body folded around the ice arrow. She tipped into my outstretched hands. Her weight dragged me to the ground. My knees folded beneath Ozura, her head cradled in my arms. Ozura's mouth worked, but no words came out. No sound. Blood bubbled in the corners of her lips. Her eyes were wide, searching, scared.

Armaan's knees hit the floor. "Ozura. Ozura, no, stay with me," he begged, his voice small—so small.

My heart cracked and I looked up in horror. The lords howled with naked panic. Enver bellowed for help. Iskander drew his sword. Nariko screamed. Ozura . . .

Her eyes brimmed with tears.

My mind whirled and was blank. I opened my mouth, utterly speechless as her blood slowly soaked my dress. A chorus of screams echoed through the room. A winter wind barreled through the door. It smelled like snow.

Ozura's eyes snapped to mine. There was fear there. And that fear, Ozura's fear, sent me tumbling over the edge of panic. All I could do was watch, watch as terror ran wild across her face. Terror and resolve. "I will serve you better when I see you again."

"No!" I screamed the word, but it was too late. Ozura sagged in my arms and was still.

"Ozura!" Armaan ripped Ozura from my arms and pressed her body to his chest. His grief was so visceral it brought Iskander crumbling to his knees, face white with horror. His body shook with sobs, but I couldn't hear it. Not over the screams.

Fury tore apart my soul and churned down my spine. It raged through my limbs, burning away both grief and reason. I wrenched the knife from my ankle sheath and rounded on Dobor.

His face glowed with madness. Ice shot out of his pendant. Bolt after bolt speared through men and women regardless of whether they were trying to fight or flee. Blood and bodies pooled on the floor—an indiscriminate carnage that only Roven could bring.

I stood. Dobor's eyes met mine. He smiled.

Ice erupted from the stone's dark heart.

I threw the knife.

Time slowed, as we stood frozen in the midst of this dance of death. The ice hurtled toward my chest. I could almost feel it coming, feel the cold air ripple past my face. I couldn't make myself move, couldn't force my legs to lunge. The arrow's flight was unstoppable. And if it was going to kill me, then damn it, Dobor would die too.

Illya cried out, a sound scraped from the depths of his soul. Muscles in his arms rippled as his blade arced high. Metal flashed in the sunlight . . .

And cleaved through the arrow.

It shattered, sending a shower of ice into my face. I barely felt it slice through my cheek. All my attention was on Dobor and the knife that hit him square in the chest. He crashed to the floor with a thud that echoed across the hall.

Shazir forms descended upon him, and I almost hoped—for his sake—that he was dead.

Almost. But there was a shadow in the temple where Ozura should have been.

Everyone in the room, from the still-crying children to the powerful men of the council, turned to me. I took in their ashen faces, the way their eyes tightened on the sharp edge of terror. Fear coated the room. I could feel its gelatinous fingers on my skin, taste its sweaty tang on my lips. Panic was brewing. And I didn't have time for it.

I looked down, saw Armaan and Iskander still crouched over Ozura's body, lost in the oblivion of sorrow. Nariko knelt near Ozura's foot, a hand hovering over her lips as tears left tracks on her face. A line of guards stood between them, between the emperor and his court, but Armaan and Iskander needed more privacy than a wall of armored men.

"Captain Nazir," I said, drawing a sharp look from the gray-faced soldier. "Have your men take them into the Shrine of Lady Night. High Priestess, please go with them." The old woman nodded, letting one of Nazir's men draw her to her feet. She didn't look scared, I noticed when she looked up at me, just terribly frail. "There are rites that Queen Ozura would want spoken."

The priestess nodded. "Of course, Your Majesty. I will take care of it all."

The ragged edges of my heart trembled as Armaan refused to let anyone touch Ozura. He lifted her in his arms, tears streaking down his face, and stumbled out of the temple. The high priestess took Iskander's limp hand and led him away. He looked so young. Like a child lost in a storm. I wanted to go with him, to help my friend. For I knew what it was to lose a mother.

Instead, I turned away. Looked to the Shazir at the end of the isle. "Khaljaq." My voice was all edges as it filled the room. The old man looked up at me, face glimmering with violence. "Is he alive?"

"Yes, my queen."

I nodded once. Swallowed down bile. "Patch him up and take him to the dungeons. I need answers."

"It will be done."

I looked away, trying not to dwell on this first, dark order of my reign as a queen of Vishir. Khaljaq and his men dragged Dobor out the door. Two enemies gone. But now I needed allies. As if summoned, Illya took up a post on my right, while Captain Nazir took my left. Both men held the hilts of their swords.

My gaze scoured the crowd, searching out the faces of those I could trust. Enver was cowering on the floor, squirrelly eyed and shaking. Behind him stood Lord Marr, still shielding his family with his body.

"Lord Marr, I need you to take command of the city guard and lock down the Roven embassy. Captain Nazir, have your men close the port—blockade any Roven vessel."

"Yes, Your Majesty," both men answered. Marr rushed from the room, but I held up a hand to stop Nazir before he could move.

"Close the city gates as well. No one leaves until we find out if Dobor was acting alone." I waited long enough to see Nazir nod, before scanning the crowd for General Ochan. He stepped forward when my gaze landed on him.

"My lady?"

"Send the order to the provinces. Call in the army. Lord Vizier Elon, summon the Council of Viziers. I want to meet with them now."

"You have no authority to call the council," Enver sputtered from the base of the stairs.

I looked down on him slowly. His face was ashen, blurry with naked fear. As if he felt my disdain, he sprang to his feet, but his legs were so weak he nearly fell all over again. "You don't have the authority to do any of this. You aren't a queen of Vishir and even if you were—"

"Enough." My bloodstained hand slashed through the air in a cutting motion that made Enver blanch. "We don't have time for you to play at emperor, little prince. Not with blood still wet across the temple floor. Your great ally and friend, Count Dobor, has just murdered one of your queens, along with countless other lords and ladies. He nearly killed your father."

I squared my shoulders. "Roven has come, and you, Enver, are unqualified to meet that threat." My voice echoed through the temple, touching on the gathered lords, drawing them in.

"You ask what authority I have?" I hissed through gritted teeth. "I have the authority of experience. And if that's not enough, then remember that the second I signed the marriage contract, I became your queen. And you *will* obey, because as of this moment, we are at war.

"And make no mistake . . ." I paused, letting my words soak through the fear, watched that fear become anger. Resolve. "I do *not* intend to lose."

36

Sunlight filtered in through the mausoleum's high windows, but it didn't survive the passage through the cold room. Gray walls, gray floors, gray twilight, and the body of a woman in a white gown, that was all the room contained.

Ozura lay on a bier atop a thick gray preparation slab. Her face was done up with rouge painted lips and eyes lined with kohl. Her long black hair was set in tiny braids laying over her chest. She looked like a sleeping bride from a children's book, but for the terrible stillness shrouding her, and the way her cheeks and eyes had sunken inward already beginning the slow descent into ash.

I knelt before her, my legs long since numb, seeing all this. Seeing the motes of dust dance through the air like the soft caress of ghostly fingers. Seeing Ozura's face cleaned of blood and terror. Seeing this mighty woman struck down and silent and somehow no more remote than she had been in life.

But it was what I could not see that was breaking my heart.

"Ozura, please. Please come to me." My voice was thin and pitiful even to my own ears, but I could not bring myself to care.

The last twenty-four hours had been filled with questions and meetings, with supply lists and troop movements, and through it all, I had remained as strong and immovable as the preparation stone beneath Ozura's back. In the urgency of the coming war, I hadn't even paused to change. My wedding gown pooled around me, almost black in the low light, but not even the semidarkness could hide the stains of Ozura's dying blood or quench the malevolent glimmer of the stone about my neck.

And while my preparations for war were under way, a different preparation had been undertaken here. Ozura would be buried within the hour. The menagerie gardens would open for the first time since little Prince Tarek had died. The emperor and his sons and his court would file through the door behind me. They'd lift Ozura one last time and carry her through the portal in front of me.

Portal, I thought, *not door.* The tunnel-like entrance to the menagerie's Garden of Emperors was like a maw, yawning open with a silent scream.

I tried to shake the thought away as I looked down. A servant I didn't recognize had disappeared down that tunnel twenty minutes ago, promising to bring fresh clothes. She'd no doubt be back soon, and my solitude would be gone. But I'd still be alone.

Because Ozura was not there.

I will serve you better when I see you again.

The words haunted me across oceans, across continents—a responsibility I didn't know how to satisfy. Accepting that burden from Vitaly was one thing. I knew what he needed, what he craved most; the redemption and forgiveness he desired was palpable. He forsook the last sleep of Lady Night to clear the debt of his betrayal. But Ozura?

The sight of her face as she spoke, of the blood bubbling on her lips and the terrible resolve that glittered in her eyes even as her face grayed with fear. She'd spoken the words, but it was I who owed the debt. I was the one who needed forgiveness. And redemption.

"Please, Ozura. Please tell me what I'm supposed to do now. Please." My words filled the mausoleum. And still Ozura did not appear. Her absence felt like an indictment. I was unworthy of her sacrifice. She was dead. And for what?

Tears slid down my face. I didn't try to hide them, for I was alone.

"I'm so sorry, Ozura. I never meant for any of this to happen. I—"

I'd gotten everything I ever wanted. Vishir was at war. Roven might finally fall. And all it had taken was my grandfather's death, the burning of both Nadym and Kavondy, Misha's hollow-eyed heartache, Vitaly's execution, and Ozura's murder.

Who was I to cause all this? And in the end, was I any better than Radovan?

"Please, Ozura. Please, please forgive me."

A warm hand clasped my shoulder. I looked up through blurry eyes to find Armaan looking down at me. His face was etched with sorrow. Open, vulnerable, but aged. He pulled me to my feet, cupping my face in his hands. "This isn't your fault, Askia. You didn't cause this." The quiet conviction in his voice nearly drove me to my knees. I let him draw me to his chest, envelop me in his arms. "None of this is your fault."

His lips brushed my temple as he spoke, but as I looked over his shoulder, past Iskander and Enver waiting frozen behind us, I saw Illya standing in the doorway. Something behind his eyes broke when our gazes met. He turned away, closed the door, and the truth was revealed: Yes. This really was all my fault.

I stepped carefully away from Armaan. Turned my back and wiped my tears. There would be time enough to mourn for Ozura, but now wasn't it. Not when my grief paled in comparison to Armaan's and Iskander's.

"I've been conferring with the high priestess," I began, clasping my hands together to keep them from trembling. "She has confirmed that everything has been prepared to Queen Ozura's wishes. The ceremony will begin at the twelfth bell."

Armaan only nodded, sad eyes gazing past Ozura's still form, across my bloodstained knees and bodice. "Will that be enough time for you to . . ."

"Yes. A servant should be returning momentarily with a clean . . . with a change of clothes." The words curdled on my tongue. No matter how many times I washed my skin, I doubted I'd ever feel clean again.

My eyes snagged on Iskander, who was staring at my bodice. His face was waxen, unreadable. He inhaled, though the effort seemed to cost him, and pulled his gaze away. With heavy steps, he approached his mother and braced his arms on the edge of the bier.

Armaan's throat bobbed, and I knew he was struggling to contain his emotions. He clasped Iskander's shoulder, knuckles white, like he was afraid he might lose Iskander too. I pressed my lips together, feeling like an interloper, a voyeur spying on this too-private moment of mourning. My gaze flicked to the door, to where the other outsider stood.

Enver's face, normally so guarded, was an open wound of emotion. Jealousy, sadness, hate, and regret vied for place, and—for the first time since I'd heard his story—I almost felt sorry for him. How must it feel to know that his life was created by Ozura's command only to be swept aside when something better came along? It was a terrible feeling, I knew, knowing you didn't belong.

I made myself move toward the menagerie's tunnel-like entrance. Forced myself to approach the black wall of darkness that shrouded the way. It was foolish to be afraid—foolish for me to be afraid. "I'll leave you to say good-bye," I murmured, stepping into the dark.

"Askia, wait." I turned and met Armaan's grave gaze. "There are things I need to say to the three of you."

If Iskander didn't react to Armaan's words, Enver did. He slid forward, not quite approaching Ozura's body. "What is it, Father?"

Armaan opened his mouth, but it seemed to take an act of will to make him continue. "Ozura and I spoke at length about what war with Roven would mean. While I must go with the army, it has become clearer each day that I cannot leave Vishir without a leader."

"Of course, you can't," Enver said, licking his lips like a dog at supper.

But if Armaan left, who would stay to rule in his place? Surely he wouldn't—couldn't—leave his eldest son in charge, not with how close Enver was to Dobor. Ozura would never have allowed it.

"Ozura, tell me what to say." I stretched for my powers, sensed the seed of magic deep within, but the all-too-familiar cold did not come.

I stepped forward, struggling to find a way to argue with a man who'd lost the love of his life. "Armaan, perhaps now is not the time to make any large announcements."

"Nonsense," Enver said with a harsh laugh. "He is the emperor of Vishir, it is his purpose to announce changes."

Armaan's expression didn't even flicker at the scathing heat in Enver's words; his face seemed carved of stone. My legs carried me forward to the very lip of the bier, as if sheer proximity to Ozura could help me reach her.

"I have come to a decision, though it is an unorthodox one, the last few days have only confirmed my choice. And both of my sons *will* support it."

It was impossible to miss the emphasis Armaan laid on that last sentence, or the hard look of command he cast at both his sons. Enver took a hesitant, hungry step forward. Iskander was still staring at Ozura, lost to the world.

I shoved the bonds of my spirit, but the Marchlands slipped through my fingers like smoke.

"I cannot leave Vishir unprotected. So when I ride to war, Askia will rule from the Lion Throne in my name and as my empress."

For the second time in as many days, time stopped in its tracks. I heard Enver's strangled cry of rage. I saw Iskander's face dart to mine, stained with betrayal.

The room went cold.

"What?"

Enver and I spoke the word in unison, a discordant melody of incredulity and disgust.

"You cannot be serious."

"I assure you, Enver, I am very serious," Armaan replied, his voice so carefully even it betrayed a deep chasm of emotion.

"But she's . . . she's—"

"Be careful of your next words, son. You stand before your empress, and you've gone very far out of your way to ensure she has little fondness for you."

I would have laughed had I not been standing in a mausoleum, had my skin not been prickling with goose bumps, had I not been covered in blood, had Iskander not been staring at me, eyes brimming with angry tears.

"Are you happy now?" He breathed the question, like rage made his voice too heavy for volume.

"Iskander—"

"Don't" he snarled, as if hearing his name on my lips caused him pain. "My mother is dead because of you, because of your blind need for revenge. Well, you've gotten everything you wanted. You got your army, and your war. And now you have my mother's place and my father's title."

"You know I never meant for any of this to happen."

"And yet here you stand," Iskander spat. "First empress of Vishir."

I resisted the urge to close my eyes against the rage in his voice. Instead, I reached within, scrambling for my magic, for the help it promised. And Lady Night save me, I needed that help.

"That's not fair, Iskander," Armaan said, coming to my side. "You brought Askia to Vishir because you knew fighting Roven was the right thing to do. And it was your mother's idea to elevate Askia from queen to empress. Ozura knew the empire needed a sign of surety and strength. Askia is that sign."

Oh, Ozura. Why didn't you tell me? Why didn't you trust me? Prepare me?

"No." Enver's voice cracked as he cried the word. "No, Iskander is right. This is all her fault. She had this all planned from the moment she landed on our shores. Don't you see? She's probably been working with Roven all along."

"Enough," I growled. "Iskander has a right to his anger and grief. But you? You have no right to speak to me of Roven sympathies, not when you willingly aligned yourself with Dobor and Radovan knowing all the horrors they're responsible for."

"Oh, please—"

"No, Enver. Askia's right. Your thirst for power blinded you. And it is something you will have to answer for." Cracks appeared in Armaan's cool composure. A muscle in his jaw ticked with brimming anger as he surveyed his eldest son. "You will prove your loyalty to me . . . to Vishir, when you ride to war."

Enver blanched. He'd clearly never considered the possibility he'd have to join the fight. He swallowed, eyes glassy with fear. "But Iskander—"

"Iskander has already volunteered," Armaan replied, then shook his head slowly. "Battle will be the making of you. Or the unmaking."

"But . . . but I could die," Enver said through bloodless lips.

Armaan's gaze went flinty. "I'd say our deaths were the exact outcome your friend Dobor desired."

"No. No, Father, please."

Enver's whines filled the small space, bouncing off the walls and echoing back on us like frozen rain, almost obscuring the distant sound of footsteps.

"Wait," I said, holding up a hand.

Enver's face twisted in animal rage. "I do not take orders from you, you—"

"Someone is coming," I said, gesturing toward the menagerie portal. "Or do you want more witnesses to your cowardice?"

Enver's jaw snapped shut with an audible click. He stormed to the far corner of the room. I exchanged a heavy look with Armaan, saw the exhaustion washing over him anew. I patted his arm. He smiled sadly. Side by side, we waited for whoever was coming.

Air hissed out between my teeth when I saw the flutter of a red robe emerge from the darkness. I turned away. What could the Shazir possibly want now?

"What is it?" Armaan asked, his voice forbidding.

I focused on the ice in my veins, on the magic that lay sleeping. I could feel it waiting just out of reach. If only I could grab it. My gaze skated across Ozura's ashen face, unease niggling across my spine.

"I have a gift for Queen Askia," the Shaziri man replied.

"A gift?" Armaan asked.

I lifted my eyes from Ozura. Instead of tunneling my magic toward her, perhaps I should aim it at the Marchlands itself.

Tunnel.

"Of a sort," the stranger replied, approaching with soft even steps. "I just want to return something that belongs to her."

A mote of dust caught the sunlight. Sparkled in a way that dust *doesn't* sparkle. Because it wasn't dust.

It was snow.

"Wait." I spun toward the stranger, but Armaan had shifted, blocking me with his shoulder. Over it I saw the stranger freeze a foot from Armaan. In his outstretched hand, I saw my own knife. The blade I'd last seen buried in Dobor's chest.

Blood drained from my face as my mind whirled. "Wait. The portal leads to the menagerie? How are you here?"

Armaan stiffened. The stranger smiled. Light slashed across his face illuminating a pair of pale-green eyes I'd last seen in a dream.

"Very good, Askia," the stranger murmured.

"Answer the question," Armaan commanded, his hand reaching for a sword that wasn't there.

"Well, it's simple really," the stranger replied, one dark eyebrow cocking in amusement. "When you can fly."

His left hand twisted. Something green flashed.

Frigid wind screeched out of the tunnel. It threw me into the stone so hard my back cracked. Iskander and Enver both lunged, but the wind lifted them off their feet and threw them into the wall. Armaan shouted in fury, but the stranger's right hand was already moving.

Faster than an adder could strike, he swiped the knife—my knife.

And slit Armaan's throat.

I screamed. Blood showered across my face and mouth. Armaan slumped to the ground. And did not move.

Wind howled in my ears. It tore my hair and ripped my clothes. Something hit my head. My sight fractured. Pain flickered my vision.

The world went black.

37

I felt the bite of cold air nibbling at my bare arms. Eyes still closed, I grimaced and nuzzled deeper into the fur blankets. I shifted my head against the pillow and felt a deep aching pain run down the base of my skull into my neck and shoulders. Carefully, I forced my muscles to relax. I took a deep breath. My nostrils filled with the scent of cold air, evergreen needles, and a masculine, cinnamon musk.

My eyes shot open. The unfamiliar crimson canopy of a strange bed was stretched out above me. It was dark in the room, though as my eyes adjusted, I became aware of a soft orange glow coming from somewhere beyond my feet. The last embers of a dying fire, I thought, still staring at the sagging velvet cloth overhead.

I blinked rapidly, trying to clear my fuzzy mind. A stab of horror lanced through my chest as I recalled the blank look in Armaan's dead face and the searing heat of his blood on my lips. I brought my hands to my face to rub away the tears stinging my eyes. Froze.

I looked at my hands. At my wrists, free of bracelets. At my arms, no longer shrouded in green fabric or stained with blood. My mouth went dry as I looked down and found myself wearing a white shift that was so thin, even in firelight I could see through it. Someone had changed me. Washed me. I shuddered.

Only the green emerald remained, still hanging from my throat, but the delicate chain was gone—replaced by heavy silver links more suited to a dog's collar.

What the hell was happening?

"Askia."

I tore my eyes away from the emerald. The ghost of a young woman stood beside the bed. Fear pinched her gray face, but her eyes danced ferociously. *"Don't be afraid,"* she said. *"I'll find a way to get you out of here."*

Here? Where was I? I sat up and looked around the darkened room. There was a fireplace at the far end of the chamber with two winged armchairs arranged before it. The fire cast grotesque shadows on the gray walls. Four windows were set in pairs on either side of the hearth. The glass in the arrow-slits was slightly warped and revealed nothing but the unforgiving blackness of the night beyond. They barely muffled the wailing, baleful sound of the winter wind.

Winter.

I blinked. Winter. Not the winter of Bet Naqar. True winter.

My mouth dropped open, but as I scrambled to make sense of it all, something moved in the corner of my eyes.

I spun toward the fire and saw a man watching me. He was tall and powerfully built. His skin was a too pale white gray that stretched over sharp jutting cheekbones. His hair was red, almost burgundy, the same color as mine. But where my eyes were a deep rich green, the man's eyes were pale, like an artist had poured too much water in a vial of green paint.

My mind put two and two together. Ozura's death. Armaan's murder. The unnatural wind in the mausoleum. The blow to my head and the darkness that followed.

The cold winter wind screamed against the glass, making it rattle a warning in its casing.

Radovan smiled. "Hello, my love."

ACKNOWLEDGMENTS

This book started off as nothing more than a dream of a woman on a hill riding to war. It's almost impossible to believe that that dream has become my reality, not only because of an image that wouldn't fade but the many wonderful people I've met along the way.

Thank you, first and foremost, to my agent, Jennifer Udden. Your guidance, knowledge, and ready humor have made this (often lonely) process feel like a journey with an old friend. Thank you also to David Pomerico and the entire Harper Voyager team who not only believed in this story but in this newbie author. Askia wouldn't exist without your insight.

To Rebecca Heyman for suffering through the early drafts of this book. You not only taught me to think critically about plot and character, you believed in me enough to invite me to your amazing Work Conference. You opened the door. Thank you doesn't seem like enough.

A huge and heartfelt thanks to all of my beta readers and critique partners: Alyssa Eatherly, Dan Scott, and Claudia Berry. To my brother, Karl Stonger, who read this book more times than I can count and still manages to look excited by it. To my dear friend, Rachael Butterfield, who believes I can do anything. To Steve Berry and the whole of my Seventh Sea crew, for showing me that stories can live and breathe in crazy and unexpected ways. And a special thanks to Summer Hanford of All Writers Workplace & Workshop for teaching me the fundamentals I would one day need to bring this story to life.

Love and gratitude to my parents and siblings, family and friends who supported me through this strange and winding process, and who didn't laugh me out of the room when I finally admitted I wanted to be a writer. To my daughter, Lorelei. You may only be a few days old, but loving you has changed me forever.

Finally, to my husband, EJ, to whom this book is dedicated. Your support, love, and depthless belief did more than make it possible for this book to exist. You make me exist too. *(See! I told you I love you more.)*

Be sure to check with your favorite bookstore

for the thrilling conclusion to Askia's tale in

Fall 2021.

IN THE MEANTIME, ENJOY THIS

EXCERPT FROM BOOK TWO!

"Hello, my love."

All the room's meager heat died at those three words. Even the fire in the hearth dimmed. But I didn't need light to recognize the man responsible for so much death. "Hello, Radovan."

He smiled though the expression strained his waxen face, as if he were more magic and clay than flesh and blood. Radovan raised both hands, long fingers splayed as if to show the many riches of his stolen empire. "Welcome to Tolograd."

For all the long years of conquest, the decades of Roven pillaging and theft, the room around us told a drab tale of privation and strife. Not at all what I'd expected. It was a simple grey-walled bedroom with narrow, arrow-slat windows and a few dusty bookshelves. The only glimmer of finery in sight was the bed upon which I sat. Its crimson canopy was made of plush Graznian velvet and the sheets were soft and warm against my skin.

Sheets which I was clutching to my throat like some woolybrained damsel. I forced my hands down, pushing past the revolting realization that I had been changed and bathed while unconscious. So despite the fact that I only wore a thin white shift, I stared at Radovan as if I wore every jewel in my kingdom.

No—empire.

A metal chain—links as thick as a dog's collar—shifted when I moved. I didn't need to look down to know that an emerald the size of a man's fist hung between my breasts. It was Radovan's birthday present to me, this damned necklace. And the fact that I just happened to be wearing it on the very day I was abducted was too suspicious to be coincidence.

Those final moments in Vishir flooded my mind: Armaan's confused, pained face as he died in my arms; the screams, the wind, the blood soaking my face and souring my tongue; the searing pain in my skull as I was knocked out. . . .

No. Not now.

"I was beginning to worry," Radovan said, clasping his hands behind his back when I didn't speak. "I thought you might have been damaged when you didn't wake up this morning."

This morning? My gaze tripped to the night-darkened windows. How long had I been out?

"I'm sure that would have been terrible for you," I replied, searching the room. I needed something—a knife, a club—anything I could use to get the better of him. But there was nothing. Even the ghost-girl who'd promised to help me had vanished.

"It really would have. I've been looking forward to speaking with you for some time now." Radovan's head tilted to one side, studying me like I was something strange, something wild.

But I was strange and wild. I was *more* than that. I was dangerous: a witch, a warrior, a queen. And I didn't need a blade to fight this man.

I shoved the covers back. Rose. And though the floor was cold beneath my feet, it was nothing compared to the glacial ice surging through me, filling my veins with power and might and the promise of violence. This was going to end. Now.

"Vitaly."

I dove deeper, stretching for the silent storm in my heart where chaos reigned and witchcraft raged. Magic filled my ears with the howl of frigid wind, and the room grayed around me.

Power leapt deep in my chest. . . .

And hit a wall. My magic crumpled against an internal barrier that shouldn't exist. Because the power that conjured that barrier wasn't my own. It was Radovan's.

The chain about my neck slithered in warning, and pain lanced through my skull. It thundered with the sound of bells that burned my vision. My knees buckled. I gasped, lurching for the edge of the bed to keep myself from falling.

Radovan's laughter filled my ears. I stared up at him through watery eyes, barely keeping a curse behind my lips.

"Oh dear," he said, closing the distance between us with a few long steps. "You didn't try to use your magic, did you? I'm afraid that won't be allowed."

"What did you do to me?" I gasped.

"I didn't do anything to you, Askia," he replied. "You must know that I don't mean to harm you."

"Then why am I here? Why did you kill Armaan and Ozura to get to me?"

Radovan's face rippled with shock, as if the accusation was insulting. "I didn't kill Queen Ozura."

The image of Count Dobor's dagger plunging into Ozura's chest writhed in my mind. "She died because of you."

His mouth folded into an understanding frown, "That dagger wasn't meant for her—you know that."

I'd have screamed at his words were it not for the memory of Ozura's ashen face, of her eyes tight with fear as she bled out on the temple floor.

I will serve you better when I see you again.

Radovan reached toward my face, but he brought himself up short when I stiffened. "You must feel her loss very keenly." He sighed. "It was a regrettable end for a truly remarkable woman. And Armaan as well. He was a good man. It's a shame he had to die."

"He didn't *have* to die."

"Of course he did. He married you, Askia. I told him not to, but he did it anyway. The poor fool just couldn't stop himself, I suppose," he said with an almost rueful chuckle as if my skin wasn't still slick with the phantom stain of Armaan's blood and Ozura's dying oath. "Not that I blame him. You are quite lovely."

An animal snarl tore from my throat. My hand moved without my consent, and my balled fist hurtled toward Radovan's jaw.

And collided with nothing. My arm locked, caught by a hand that I couldn't see and couldn't fight. I pulled back on instinct, but the hand only tightened, refusing to release me. It clenched down harder. Harder. Until I felt my tendons snap against muscle and my bones begin to bend. I grit my teeth to contain a scream of pain. Of rage. But my fury was no match for his power.

Radovan's eyes glittered as they flickered to my fist, frozen a hairsbreadth away from his face. All his stolen magic slithered through me with a knife-sharp pain that stabbed into my arm. Without moving a muscle, he shoved my hand down and locked my body into statue-like stillness. My mind railed against it—against the helplessness. Lady Night save me, a stiff breeze would topple me over.

"That's better," Radovan said, as I came to an involuntary attention. "I had hoped our first meeting wouldn't be so . . . fraught, but I suppose it is to be expected. You've no doubt heard horror stories about me your whole life. Though I confess it is tiresome to always be seen as the villain." He shook his head with a put-upon sigh.

"I am not a bad man, Askia. I'm not a monster. And I'll prove it to you," he vowed. "Roven is your home. Tolograd is your home. And if you can't see that yet?" He shrugged. "You will soon enough. Now, I know you must be exhausted, but before I allow you to retire, I do have some guidelines for your new life here.

"As you have discovered, you won't be able to use your magic. The enchanted chain about your neck is preventing that."

I blinked. The muscles of my neck strained to look down, but even that much movement was beyond me.

"Surely you can guess what that necklace truly is?" Radovan's fingers slid across my shoulder, and the thin fabric of my nightgown was no protection against the revulsion I felt at his touch. Slowly, like he was relishing my reaction, Radovan lifted the chain, holding the necklace high enough for me to see. "My Aellium stone—glamoured, of course. Not that it needs to be anymore."

One of his long thumbs wiped across the gem, and a film of slimy magic shuddered across my face. The brand on my back burned in recognition, as the stone's heart turned black, its edges shimmering evergreen in the firelight.

An Aellium stone. The magical amplifiers that were used by Shazir zealots to force a witch into exposing themselves. And used by Radovan to steal magic from his wives. And he'd given it to me. But—

But if the chain was suppressing my magic, then how had I seen that ghost-girl? The one who promised to help me escape. My gaze strained toward the edges of the room, but I couldn't sense the ghost anywhere. Couldn't sense *any* ghosts.

"The chain's enchantment is quite thorough," Radovan continued. "You won't be able to remove it—only I can do that. It will burn you if you try," he said slowly, gravely as if I were a child playing with fire.

He placed the stone gently back on my chest, a smile playing on his lips as he studied my face. "So many questions. I can see them swimming in your eyes. Even now, alone and terrified, you're soaking up information. Trying to find a way to gain an upper hand. But you can't, my dear. And to ensure you take this lesson to heart; a demonstration."

The stone warmed on my chest a half-second before his magic seized my left hand. Each tiny muscle tensed so fast my joints cracked as my hand twitched and rose. My eyes flew wide, but I was powerless against his silent command. Powerless to move, to stop. My fingers closed about the stone . . . and pulled.

Heat seared through skin and bone, through muscle and tendon. I couldn't even scream as the fire kissed my bones with forked tongues of invisible pain. More than pain.

Agony danced through me, pillaging and burning for a second that stretched to eternity. Until, after an age, my fingers opened and the stone fell from my blistered, bleeding palm.

Radovan cupped my hand in his. Magic licked across the wound, and in a blink the pain was gone. The wound now looked days old but was still red and livid. A reminder, I thought, as if the meaty scent of my own burning flesh wasn't enough of one.

Radovan searched my face a moment longer, then chuckled at whatever he saw. "Oh, we are going to have fun, my dear."

He angled his face toward the door behind him. "Enter."

The door opened at his command, revealing four armed guards waiting in the hall outside. A strange circular tattoo marred each of their left cheeks. One of them, a captain by the cut of her uniform, stepped forward. She had a round face, with high, flat Khezhari cheekbones and smooth terra-cotta skin. She looked me up and down, her dark gaze carefully blank.

All at once his magic evaporated. My muscles went slack, and I stumbled, barely catching myself before I hit the floor.

Radovan just smirked. "Captain Qadenzizeg."

The woman in the doorway snapped the gleaming heels of

her black boots together with a click that echoed through the room. "Yes, Your Majesty?"

"Please escort Princess Askia—"

"Queen," I snapped, drawing an amused look from Radovan and an outraged one from the captain.

"Really, my dear. I know you consider yourself the Queen of Seravesh, but is now really the time to argue semantics?"

"I don't *consider* myself the Queen of Seravesh. I *am* the queen of both Seravesh and Vishir. And if I wanted to argue semantics, I'd insist upon you calling me Empress, for that is the title Armaan was going to grant me before you murdered him."

Radovan's damned smile didn't even flicker. "Very well. Captain, please escort Her Majesty Queen Askia up to her room."

"Red protocol?" the captain asked. I wasn't sure what that was supposed to mean, but the disgusted way she was staring at me made my hackles rise.

"Oh no," Radovan crooned. "That won't be necessary. If there is one thing I trust about my dearest queen, it is her will to live."

I felt confusion chase across my face, but pressed my lips shut. I needed to get to the room he promised. Get some space to regroup. Plan.

His watery green eyes danced as he lifted my still-throbbing hand to his lips, daring me to react, to strike. But I wouldn't give him the satisfaction. I locked my body woodenly in place as he kissed my hand, and endured, like I would always endure. "I shall see you soon, my love," Radovan whispered.

I yanked my hand away. "Fuck you, Radovan."

ABOUT THE AUTHOR

Greta Kelly is (probably) not a witch, death or otherwise, but she can still be summoned with offerings of too-beautiful-to-use journals and Butterfinger candy. She currently lives in Wisconsin with her husband, EJ, daughter, Lorelei, and a cat who may, or may not, control the weather.